I0689689

GRAVITY MASTERS
ORDER OF SCION
BOOK 2

TOBY NEIGHBORS

MYTHIC
adventure
PUBLISHING

Gravity Masters: Order of Scion book 2

Copyright © 2024 by Toby Neighbors

ISBN: 978-1-952260-75-9 print

978-1-952260-74-2 ebook

Mythic Adventure Publishing, LLC

Idaho, USA

All rights reserved.

No part of this book may be reproduced in any form or by any electronic or mechanical means, including information storage and retrieval systems, without written permission from the author, except for the use of brief quotations in a book review.

CHAPTER 1

HE COULD NEVER SAY why he did it. Sometimes events happen in a person's life and they report feeling like spectators watching from the outside and seeing themselves do things they would never have imagined. That was not what Mitch Murphy, Second Lieutenant, Colonial Marine Corps, experienced. He was fully aware, and fully in control, but what motivated him to follow the three strange aliens was a complete and utter mystery. It wasn't until several minutes later, after watching the ship rise up and into space through the dust clouds caused by the Space Force bombardment, that he contemplated his decision.

"You are tired," the alien called Arq said.

Mitch still didn't know how they knew his language, or how their strange mouths could even form the words. All three of the aliens looked like animals. They stood on two legs and had two arms, but all four limbs seemed identical to Mitch. They all had split hooves on the ends instead of hands. They were all covered in short, white fur. They had heads shaped somewhat like bulls, with thick, white horns that curled around the back of their skulls. Their appearance was shocking to his mind and simultaneously calming. Mitch thought of them, especially Arq, as wise old men, sages, or counselors of some type. Perhaps it was the clothing they wore, which consisted of long strips of loosely woven fabric that were wrapped around them and hung loose from their shoulders and upper arms, forming what Mitch thought of as a robe.

"I'm fine," Mitch replied. He was exhausted, hungry, and tense, but he didn't want that to show. He was a guest on their very fine spaceship and the last thing he wanted to do was insult his hosts.

"Our vessel has many services available," Qwii said. "We have everything you will need to be very comfortable."

"He's eager," Juj said. "Who can blame him?"

"Maybe we can satisfy your curiosity enough that you will feel comfortable resting," Arq said. "Food is being prepared for you. Soon you can bathe, then sleep. Our journey will last several Earth days."

"Where are we going?" Mitch asked.

He was standing in what felt like a throne room, even though there were no thrones. It was a large space with a transparent wall that was so clear it almost looked like there was no wall or glass there at all. He could see so much, and it wasn't like looking at a display screen showing live video, or a hologram. It was more like he was standing outside the ship rather than inside.

Nothing about the alien vessel was anything like human star-ships, which were small and cramped spaces. Mitch was seven and a half feet tall, and in most spaces on the *S.F. Wellington,* he had been forced to duck a little to keep from banging his head. In many of the corridors, he had to turn his shoulders to avoid banging into the narrow walls. But the alien ship was open and airy. Mitch admitted he had only seen two parts. They had entered via a ramp that led into what looked like a garage or staging area. There had been several platform vessels parked inside. But it had a tall ceiling and plenty of light, even at night. The light came from glowing orbs that hung suspended in mid-air. Mitch couldn't see how they hung, or what they were exactly. There was no sight of a bulb or diode, just light.

From the garage, they passed into the observation deck. As far as Mitch could tell it was a huge room with no purpose. He knew the very existence on a spaceship was a grand extravagance. Through the huge window, Mitch saw the trio of battleships. They were spread out in a line hundreds of kilometers apart, but from a distance, they appeared close together. They were stubby, ugly vessels in comparison to the crescent-shaped alien starship. The battleships bristled with guns but didn't seem like much of a threat as the alien vessel began to accelerate out of orbit. Mitch was no aerospace engineer, but he had seen a few documentaries on space travel and found it odd that the alien ship didn't seem to be held back by the planet's gravity at all.

"We will start on Vodex," Arq said. "The Order of Scion has a spacious facility there that will meet our needs."

"And what are those?" Mitch asked.

"Eager," Juj said, with what Mitch learned later was considered a smile by the Nagani.

"A proper introduction to the Power & Knowledge," Arq said. "It is not our intention to hold anything back from you, but we must pace ourselves. Too much of a good thing, too quickly, can still be bad."

Mitch had a thousand questions, but at the top of his mind was the fight between the three members of the Order of Scion, and the other alien. Mitch had seen the aliens move in ways that didn't seem possible. Juj had even floated in mid-air for a time. It didn't seem real.

"How are you doing the things you do?" Mitch asked. "How did you fly?"

"We are Gravity Masters," Arq said. "It isn't magic. We don't fly. But we can manipulate the gravitational forces all around us."

"This entire ship is an example," Qwii said.

"Propulsion is one of the easiest ways to understand," Arq said.

"You are aware of how your human vessels move through space. We manipulate gravity to move our vessels."

"That's impossible," Mitch said.

"And yet, you are experiencing it now," Arq said, waving an arm toward the opening.

Mitch could see the ship racing through the system. Things were moving too fast for any spaceship. New Terra and the Space Force battleships were lost to sight behind the alien vessel. Ahead of them were the system gas giants. It was like watching a movie. He could see their movement, but he couldn't feel it. And so, his mind told him it wasn't real.

"Gravity is the sinew that holds the entire universe together," Arq said. "From the smallest hydrogen atom with its lone electron in constant motion, to the largest celestial bodies, they are all joined and fixed in space by gravity."

"Even your human scientists have known this for hundreds of years," Qwii said.

"It is the gift of the Creator, given through the Scion to the people of every system," Arq said. "We are committed to helping restore the universe to the glorious state it was created in before the fall corrupted everything."

Mitch suddenly felt weak. It was a novel sensation. His body was stronger than it had ever been. Despite being physically tired, he was still more capable than he had been on his best day before the LE Protocols had transformed him into a super soldier. But his mind was overwhelmed. The alien ship was still accelerating. It raced by one gas giant in a flash, as if he were watching a simulated flight through the Terra system on fast speed.

"Maybe some rest would be good," he admitted.

"Yes," Arq said. "Rest, nourishment, refreshment, those should be your priority now."

"I will assist him," Juj said. "Come with me."

Mitch followed the alien. They went into a tower-like room with a wide spiral staircase. They went up and into a room that looked almost familiar. There was a wide bed with ivory blankets and square pillows. Two pieces of furniture took up the space on one side of the bed, one appeared to be a simple, wooden side table. The other was soft with a wooden frame that was covered with loose cushions of various colors. Juj walked to a nook built into the wall. A shelf rotated down with a tray of food on it. The alien took the tray over to the side table and set it down.

On the other side of the bed was a doorway. Mitch could hear water flowing. It sounded like a stream. He was beginning to question his sanity. It was such a surreal experience that he thought it was a dream.

"Food," Juj said, pointing to the tray, then at the bed, "rest, and in that room is a place for washing. You will find simple garments there that you may wear. There will be time to clean and mend your clothing, but for now please avail yourself of anything you need.

"Thank you," Mitch said.

Juj gave a little bow, then left the room. The door closed behind him, and Mitch dropped onto the sofa. It was comfortable, even for his oversized body. The food was some kind of stew. A large bowl sat on the tray, with several small loaves of bread and small blocks of soft cheese neatly arranged around it. There was a smaller bowl of fruit and a large mug. Mitch settled the tray on his lap and tasted the stew. It was rich, with a touch of spicy heat. He could see stewed vegetables and some type of dark meat. There was no way to know what it was, or if it was natural or artificial. Most space vessels carried either vat-grown or protein imitation meat. Mitch didn't care though. After one bite his stomach demanded more, as much as he could get. The bread was soft and excellent at soaking up the stew gravy. The cheese was a cool contrast to the stew's spicy heat. And when he had eaten every last morsel from the bowl, he tasted the fruit in its own smaller container. It was fresh, perfectly ripe, and sweet. There were grapes, a plum, an apple, and even some blueberries. When he finished eating he returned the tray to the nook where the shelf rotated as it rose upward and out of sight.

"This place is a trip," Mitch said.

He pulled off his armor. It was rank, spattered with dirt and gore on the outside, and soiled with his sweat on the inside. He carried it into the bathroom, which was nearly as large as the bedchamber. He hadn't been wrong about the water either. It was a stream that started high on one wall and then flowed across a narrow channel that looked as if it were made of stones. The artificial stream wrapped around three walls before ending in a pool that looked deep enough to bathe in. Mitch bent down and touched the water. It was warm. There was a bar of soap on a bundle of towels. It made Mitch wonder how the aliens knew he would join them. Maybe he didn't have a choice? Maybe they had gone to New Terra to harvest humans? Sure, they seemed nice enough, but it could all be an act. Yet try as he might, he couldn't see Arq, Qwii, and Juj as a threat to him. He took a bath, scrubbing his entire body and letting the tension drain from his muscles in the warm water.

The clothes he found were simple. Linen pants that cinched at the top with a silky belt. A long, sleeveless tunic that slipped over his head and hung to his knees. The clothing was comfortable, and so was the bed. It was soft and warm. His oversized body sank into the soft mattress. The blankets were lightweight and wrapped around him. He didn't even have time to ponder his strange circumstances before sleep overtook him. No dreams disturbed his mind as he rested from his labors. It would not always be so peaceful for him. Mitch wasn't built for peace, but for war, and it was sure to find him, even on an alien ship in a system on the far side of the galaxy.

CHAPTER 2

SERGEANT MARA JAMES was perched on the edge of her bunk. She was one of the lucky SSO Marines. At only six and a half feet tall after the LE Protocols had altered her body, she could still fit on a standard bunk. Across the narrow bunkroom of the S.F. *Marathon,* her squad mates Flash and Jingo had to curl up on their sides and still, they barely fit on the Space Force bunks.

"That hurt?" Estelle "Hawk" Flemming asked as Mara flexed her foot. It was part of the physical therapy assigned to her by the ship's doctor after her broken ankle had been scanned.

"Not really," Mara said. "It was just a fracture."

"By the time they scanned it," Flash pointed out.

"It looked pretty bad on the ground," Jingo added.

"It's fine," Mara said. "I'll baby it a few days. They didn't even keep me in the med bay."

"No room for us," Ninja said.

He was standing up with his shirt off. He had a small, hand-held shaving mirror in one hand, and his other lightly probed the bruise on his chest.

"I'd say we were lucky," Flash announced. "Only one casualty. Kilo Squad is no more."

"You hear something about Joker?" Jingo asked.

Flash shook his head. The run through Alpha Colony had been difficult and frightening. They were Marines, trained to put away fear and run toward danger, but giant spiders in the dead of night were stressful. They had succeeded in reaching the airfield for exfil only after one member of Kilo Squad was killed in action, and another severely wounded. The six-man team had already lost two members before joining Leo Squad for the run through the city. What would happen to the remaining two members was up to someone with a much higher pay grade.

"We've all lost people," Mara said. "And we always move on. They'll be okay."

"Damn shame about the LT," Flash said. "It was nice to have an officer I didn't have to bend down to look in the eye."

"What was he thinking?" Ninja said.

"He was thinking about that little girl," Jingo said.

They had all seen Mitch Murphy jump from the shuttle as it began to lift off. And they saw the colonist with his little girl who was practically tossed inside the ship as the hatch began to close up.

"Wish he'd given us some notice," Hawk said.

"You would have gone with him?" Mara asked.

She had been thinking the same thing but didn't know how the other members of the squad felt. They were all fiercely loyal to one another, but Mitch Murphy had been their new lieutenant. He was the first, and to her knowledge, only officer to have gone through the LE Protocols. But he had barely been in charge of Leo Squad for a week. The field survival training exercise had been their first time together off Alpha Base. So maybe the others weren't as attached to Mitch as she had been. But it appeared her thoughts on that score weren't exactly on target.

"Hell yeah," Jingo said.

"For sure," Flash added.

Hawk only nodded. She was a naturally quiet person.

"I wouldn't have liked it," Ninja said. "But I'd rather be down there in the mud and blood with him than safe up here without him."

"They'll go back for him," Flash said. "Right?"

Mara shrugged. Never before had she cared what her commanding officers did when they weren't barking orders at her. She was the highest-ranking NCO on Leo Squad, but even she wasn't privy to what the brass would do if one of their own went missing.

Before she could answer someone in the room shouted, "Officer on deck!" There were four SSO squads crammed into the bunk room normally occupied by a single regular platoon. Everyone was clustering together, and Mara hadn't seen the officer come in, but she jumped up onto her good foot and stiffened into attention like every other Marine.

"Sergeant James," a gruff voice called out.

"Sir, yes sir!" Mara replied.

"You're with me," the man at the hatch snapped. "Let's go."

"Dang, Mara's in trouble," Jingo said.

"Told you not to kiss the sailors, Sergeant," Ninja joined in.

She ignored them as she slipped her bad foot back into the support boot and tightened the Velcro straps. Pain was starting to throb in her ankle, but she ignored it and hurried after the officer. She didn't recognize the man, but the Lieutenant bars on his collar were easy to see. That meant he could tell her to do just about anything, down to and including scrubbing toilets with a toothbrush.

The man led through a narrow corridor. The Marine section of the ship was like a labyrinth. Every hallway was little more than a maintenance corridor with conduits running along the walls near the ceiling, and access hatches for various engineering spaces along the way. The rooms were sandwiched between other essential parts of the ship. They came to a stairwell, which was little more than a glorified ladder. She climbed it easily, despite the boot on her bad foot. At the top, they turned quickly into a series of offices. Captain Frank Marcs was waiting inside one.

"Captain, I've got Sergeant James," the lieutenant said.

"Very well," Captain Marcs said as he set his computer tablet down and looked up at Mara James, who stepped into the small office. "Have a seat, Sergeant."

"Yes, sir," she said. "Thank you, sir."

For a moment there was silence between them. Mara was starting to feel uncomfortable. It was impossible not to feel like she was in some sort of trouble, although, to her knowledge, she had done nothing wrong. Then Captain Marcs sighed and leaned onto his elbows, reclining slightly in his desk chair.

"What was Lieutenant Murphy's state of mind before we left New Terra?" he asked.

"State of mind, sir?" Mara repeated. "He was focused on completing the mission, I know that. It was his first taste of combat, and if I'm honest, sir, I think he liked it."

"Yeah, that's not surprising, is it, Sergeant? A lot of new SSO Marines want to see what they're made of."

"True, sir, but that doesn't really describe Lieutenant Murphy. He was more disciplined than that."

"You found him disciplined?"

"Extremely sir. Not fanatical, but very self-aware. He wasn't rattled, not on the training mission and not when the Lymies attacked. His orders were concise and on point. It didn't seem like his first command, sir."

"Would you describe him as happy in the Corps?"

Mara thought about that. She was close to Mitch. Over their week together, she had tested him both socially and more importantly, professionally. He listened and learned quickly. He could take everyone's input and then decisively make decisions that showed he had heard the collected wisdom of the group. Physically, he was their equal in nearly every way. Not as strong as Jingo, or as fast as Flash, but unlike the rest of them, he could do it all. He had the flexibility and stamina to keep up with Mara and Ninja when they sparred, and he could even give Hawk a run for her money on the sniper range.

"Extremely happy, sir. I got the impression it was a real step up from his old life."

"Did he talk about that much?" Captain Marcs asked.

Mara shook her head. "None of us do sir. We all had our reasons for volunteering, and the transformation is such a change that we just don't talk about what came before very often."

Captain Marcs sighed. "We have a problem, Sergeant. I'm going to ask for your opinions, and then I'm ordering you not to talk about this meeting to anyone. Is that clear?"

"Sir, yes sir," she replied.

"Good. I was there when Murphy jumped ship. Hell, I didn't even blame him. He wanted to fight and to be honest, I did too. But orders are orders, Sergeant. We all answer to someone, and the mission always comes first."

Mara nodded, not sure what to say. Jumping off the shuttle at the last minute was a heroic thing to do. Mara certainly respected it. And had it not been for her broken ankle she would have followed Mitch right off the transport. But in technical terms, it was a dereliction of his duty. They had been ordered to evacuate the planet, and staying behind could be considered Absence Without Leave.

"We've been in contact with Murphy," Captain Marcs continued. "He was doing everything we asked. Not always the way we asked, but ..."

"Is he in some kind of trouble, sir?"

"More trouble than being left on a planet that was bombarded from orbit with kinetic warheads, Sergeant?"

"We bombed the colonies?"

"What do you do when you have an infestation? You have to

fumigate the place, or burn it down and start over. Orders to use the nuclear option came from the Sol system, Sergeant. One kinetic warhead from orbit should have been sufficient to kill everything in Alpha Colony."

"Is he ..." she couldn't bring herself to say the last word.

Mara James wasn't an overly emotional person. And she didn't usually have trouble controlling herself, but she found her body trembling at the idea of Mitch Murphy being killed.

"Alive," Captain Marcs said. "Some strange things went down on New Terra. Most of it is classified, which is why I'm ordering you not to tell anyone what I'm about to tell you, Sergeant."

Mara nodded, her mouth suddenly dry. She was gripping the edges of her seat with both hands and leaned forward slightly, the pain in her ankle completely forgotten.

"Aliens, not Lymies, these were something different, something we haven't encountered yet, were on site when the bombs fell. And for some reason we can't explain, the warheads missed their targets."

"Missed?"

"They dropped between the colonies. We checked and rechecked the data. It wasn't an error on our part. The warheads themselves are dumb, nothing about them can go wrong, and the fact that they all behaved the same way, and at the same time, suggests something outside the bombs themselves."

"Strange," Mara said.

"In the extreme," Captain Marcs said. "We don't have good visuals of what took place on the ground. Our surveillance feeds were blocked by the debris kicked up by the bombs. But we have this on thermal imaging."

He spun his table around and lifted it so that Mara could see the picture. It was a paused frame from a video feed, all gray except for several blobs of bright color.

"Are you familiar with SSO Marine armor's thermal output?" Captain Marcs asked.

She was. Mara nodded.

"So then, you can see that Lieutenant Murphy is there with the aliens."

"Yes, sir," she said, her throat tight from the tension gripping her body.

He tapped an icon and the blobs began to move. Three of them led Mitch away until they disappeared.

"What happened to them?" Mara asked.

"This," Marcs replied as he turned the table around, tapped a few commands, then swiveled it back so she could see.

On the screen was another video feed, this time of an alien ship rising from the dust clouds. It was dark and-shaped like a crescent moon on its side. It rose up until it disappeared from sight.

"They took him?" she asked in horror.

"Or he left with them willingly," Captain Marcs said. "That's what we're trying to determine."

"He wouldn't leave us, sir," she insisted. "The Lieutenant wouldn't just abandon everything we fought for."

"And yet, he abandoned ship despite being ordered to retreat," Captain Marcs said. "Technically, he follows orders, but he does things his way. It's possible he left with the aliens because they enticed him to."

Mara didn't need to say that after the fleet had bombed the planet, Mitch Murphy didn't have much left to feel loyalty to. His own people were abandoning New Terra and would have murdered him from orbit if things had gone their way.

"Anything is possible, Captain."

"Obviously," he replied. "And you're sure he wasn't suffering some form of depression?"

"None," she said confidently.

"Did he ever complain about orders? I was his commanding officer. Did he talk about me with you, Sergeant? He won't be in trouble and neither will you. I need the truth."

"Never sir. Like I said, I think he loved his job. He certainly loved training with the squad. PT, range time, and sims all seemed to jazz him up. Lieutenant Murphy was the first one up and the last one to leave at night, sir. If you're trying to ask if he was a disgruntled Marine, the answer is no."

"Very well, Sergeant. Thank you for the information. Your job is to forget this meeting ever took place. That's an order."

Mara stood to attention. "Sir, yes, sir!" she said, snapping out a tight salute.

"Dismissed, Sergeant."

"Thank you, sir."

Mara walked out of the little office and started a slow return to the bunk room, where she knew the rest of Leo Squad would be waiting. Her mind was a whirlwind of competing thoughts. Mitch was gone. Not dead, but not on New Terra anymore. She didn't even know if Captain Marcs knew where he was. The ship on the video had just disappeared. She guessed maybe it had broken orbit, but she had never seen any ship fly like the one on the video. It didn't even look real.

There were too many unanswered questions. And she knew they were going to haunt her for the rest of her life.

CHAPTER 3

MITCH DIDN'T KNOW how long he had slept. He could have checked the chrono on his data cuff but it was in a pile of his stinky clothes in the bathroom. He woke up feeling good. It had been enough sleep to rejuvenate him, which was all he could hope for.

He was only on his feet in the bed chamber a few moments when a soft chime sounded and a tray of food descended in the nook built into the wall. He walked over and eyed the small feast with appreciation. There was what looked to be a stack of five very large pancakes, a bowl of scrambled eggs, and a saucer that had what appeared to be real bacon and sausage. There were also bowls of fruit, yogurt, and granola. Along with the food, there was a glass of orange juice and a mug of coffee. Mitch had just picked up the tray when the door to his bedchamber swished open.

"Will you take food with us?" Arq asked.

"Sure," Mitch said.

The white-furred alien gave a slight bow, then turned and began walking through the ship. Mitch stayed behind him, observing his host. There was no reason to be wary, but Mitch thought it was best if he stayed cautious. The aliens obviously wanted something from him. Maybe it was okay, maybe not. He would have to wait and see, but when the ask came, he wanted a clear mind when he answered.

Arq led Mitch to a room with a round table in the center, and several decorative tapestries hanging from the walls. Mitch wasn't sure what they were about, but it seemed like more of the religious philosophy that his hosts espoused.

"Welcome. Did you rest well?" Qwii asked.

"Very well, thank you," Mitch replied, setting his tray down on the table. The aliens each had large silvery bowls that were filled with what appeared to be a green salad of some sort, along with smaller bowls of water.

"We thank the Creator for this repast," Arq said softly.

"Thank you," his two companions said in soft unison.

The aliens didn't use utensils or their hooves to eat with. They bent forward and ate straight from the bowl, and lapped up water to drink. It was a surreal experience, but hunger overrode Mitch's wonder at his companions. His pancakes were excellent and his big body was eager for food. For a while, they ate in comfortable silence, but once their hunger had been satisfied they slowed down and began to talk between bites.

"How far are we from our destination?" Mitch asked.

"Two Earth days," Juj said.

"Normally, we would travel faster, but we wanted to give you time to acclimate," Arq said. "You are the first human we have invited into the order."

"Can you tell me more about it?"

"The Order of Scion is an ancient association of individuals from a variety of species," Arq explained. "Each dedicated to the principles outlined by the Creator for the universe. It is hoped that as we carry on the restoration it will elevate and unite our people."

"There's so much of that I don't understand," Mitch said. "Who is the Creator?"

"The source of everything that is," Qwii said.

"The first of all living things," Juj said.

"And a mystery," Arq added. "Yet one that is recognized by every intelligent species in the galaxy."

"How's that?" Mitch asked.

"You tell us," Arq said. "What do humans believe about how they came to be?"

Mitch shrugged. "No one knows," he said. "For a long time it was believed that we evolved from simpler forms of life over millions of years."

The aliens chuckled but in a polite way. "How inventive," Arq said.

"But that is not the prevailing thought any longer?" Qwii asked.

"I'm no scientist," Mitch said. "But I was taught that the evidence no longer supported the theory."

"Back to square one," Juj said.

"Are there other prevalent theories?" Arq said.

"Sure, but no real proof of anything," Mitch said. "Most people believe we were seeded on the Earth, that's our home world, by an advanced race."

"No belief in the divine?" Arq asked.

"Well, yeah, sure, there are plenty of people who believe in God. Is that what your Creator is?"

"A divine being in the sense that it exists outside our reality," Arq said. "One who initiated the creation of the universe. We call him Creator. The beliefs of our order run deep, and there will be plenty of time for you to study them in detail. For now, it is enough to know that we believe the universe was created, and finely tuned for life, but that creation was marred. The wonderfully diverse races were separated by vast distances of empty space. Many of the systems were misaligned, resulting in worlds that are completely inhospitable to life. It is our work to help restore what the Creator made so very long ago."

"Restoration," Mitch said. "What do you mean by that?"

"Long ago the first of the order were taught the means to control the power given by the creator," Arq explained.

"Gravity manipulation," Mitch said.

"That is one description of it," Qwii said.

"There are forces in the universe at work all the time," Arq said. "Gravity is the weakest, yet the effects of it are the easiest to see. Planets in motion. Light, attraction, even time itself is acted on and affected by gravity."

"When we understand the Creator's intent in giving us access to the Power, what we call the Knowledge is essentially knowing how, when, and why to use it," Juj said.

"All this you will learn," Arq said.

"Why me?" Mitch asked.

"You are the first who is ready," Arq said. "We have been watching. Every intelligent species grows in knowledge and abilities. Humans have long been in a phase of rapid growth. Your technology is phenomenal. And you have discovered the expansion portal left in your star system. Once you passed through it, the Terra system was discovered. First by you, then by others who were watching."

"The Graylings," Mitch said.

"They are one, yes, but there are others," Arq explained. "Hence the struggle for control of that system."

"If the aliens fought us for New Terra, will they invade the Sol system too?" Mitch asked.

"Eventually," Juj said. "For now, your military resources are formidable enough to secure your home system, but that will change."

"Every race goes through periods of strength and weakness," Arq continued. "It appears as though your people are pulling back. Perhaps they focus their technological resources, or perhaps they fall into apathy in their own system, believing they will never be threatened."

"Not a comforting thought," Mitch said.

"Nor should it be," Juj said.

"It is the work of the Order of Scion to share the Power and Knowledge, first to our own people, and then to others, as we work to restore the universe."

"How exactly are you doing that?"

"Only the most advanced of our Order can do the work," Arq said. "It takes decades of practice."

"What does?"

"Outline the levels of mastery for him," Qwii said.

Arq nodded. "Those who learn to use the Power and the Knowledge grow in stages. Many train to become Scion Warriors. They use the Power and Knowledge to protect the innocent."

"Protect them from who?" Mitch asked, wondering who would be foolish enough to fight these strange, alien wizards.

"There are many enemies of the Way," Juj said.

"Anyone who uses violence to take what does not belong to them is outside the truth," Arq said. "Is it not the same on your Earth?"

Mitch nodded. Stealing, of any form, had always been illegal as far as Mitch knew. Violence, be it via an individual or a nation, was seen as barbaric.

"Warriors grow in strength," Arq continued, "becoming Navigators, or what you might think of as space benders."

"What?" Mitch asked.

"Those with enough mastery over the Power and Knowledge can bend space time, and open portals like the one from your Sol system to the Terra system. A race with a True Navigator will have access to a wide array of worlds."

"Where they may grow in the truth," Qwii said. "Under the tutelage of a True Navigator."

"It is possible, although rare, for Navigators to grow into World Movers," Arq said. "These incredibly powerful members of the order can correct the orbit of planets, pushing them into what your scientists have coined the *Goldilocks zone*. Entire atmospheres can be pulled from gas giants to worlds and moons that allow life to thrive. Their control is both powerful and precise."

"Is that the highest level?" Mitch asked, realizing just how incredible the aliens were. To be able to move planets would give the human race unlimited space. Nearly every star system had planets, but the number of worlds that could support life of any kind was nearly zero. A habitable world, like New Terra, was one in a trillion. A world like Earth was more than anyone dared hope for. But if planets could be moved, their atmosphere manipulated, any system had the potential for a vibrant planet.

"There is one more," Arq said. "But in the history of our order, only a handful have ever reached it."

"The Star Savers," Qwii said, his voice hushed with awe.

"None in a century," Juj said.

"A Star Saver?" Mitch asked. "What does that mean?"

"Stars are delicately balanced, self-contained systems," Arq said. "The weight of the hydrogen drawn to the molten core eventually fails. The star grows weak, but exponentially bigger as the hydrogen expands into a red giant, before it all collapses back down, forming a unique gravity phenomenon your people call a black hole."

"And the most powerful members of the order can stop this?" Mitch asked.

"In some cases," Arq said. "The stress on a person is so great that few who attempt it survive."

"Wow," Mitch said, leaning back. "That's incredible."

"And it is yours," Arq said, "should you accept it. But the training is not easy. Many attempt the training and fail. Perhaps you will succeed."

"I think it is time for a demonstration," Qwii said.

"Excellent," Juj agreed.

"I believe your people say, there's no time like the present," Arq added.

Mitch nodded. The entire conversation felt surreal. He was on an alien ship, with furry creatures who claimed they controlled gravity. He missed his squad and wished he could share his adventure with them. Especially, Mara. He couldn't help but wonder how she was feeling. Mitch even missed Major Swift with her inquisitive mind. Of all the people he had met since volunteering for the LE Protocols, she would be the most fascinated by the Nagani.

"I'm game," Mitch said.

"Wonderful," Arq said.

They all three stood up and Mitch followed suit. They left their bowls and dishes behind. Mitch stayed with them, but kept an eye out for whoever else might be on the ship. Someone was cleaning up and cooking his meals. Mitch decided that he wanted to talk to that person. If he wanted the real scoop on who his hosts truly were, the hired help would be the ones to know. All he had to do was find them.

CHAPTER 4

THEY CAME BACK to the observation deck, only this time Qwii and Juj both had what looked like rubber balls. One was a big, blue ball, slightly larger than a basketball. The other ball was smaller, and red, about the size of a softball. Mitch stood beside Arq who gave the lesson, while Qwii and Juj stood several meters apart, each holding a ball out in front of them respectfully.

"Gravity, as I'm sure you know, is a fundamental attraction between any two objects that have mass," Arq explained. "It is both a very weak force, and an essential part of what makes the universe suitable for life. Without it, there would be nothing but microscopic bits of matter crashing into each other as it spreads through the void. This is all well known to your species, is it not?"

"Yes," Mitch said. "We understand how gravity works, just not where it comes from, or why it exists."

"Part of the grand mystery," Arq said. "We will answer those philosophic questions in due course. For now, allow us to show you what the True Navigators are capable of. Qwii, if you would drop your ball, please."

Qwii did. It bounced several times, and rolled on the floor for a moment. Then it suddenly floated up into the air.

"How are you doing that?" Mitch asked.

"I have surrounded the ball with an anti-gravity bubble," Arq said. "Give it a nudge."

Mitch reached out and tapped the ball with a finger. It spun in midair, floating slowly upward.

"It is within our ability to reduce gravity," Arq explained, "or increase it."

The ball suddenly dropped, only this time it didn't bounce. It hit the polished floor of the observation deck and stuck there, half compressed, as if a giant invisible hand were pushing down on it.

"This entire vessel is controlled by Qwii's influence over gravity," Arq said, as the ball slowly began to rise up into the air again. "With gravity, we can manipulate the ship through space, just as I am manipulating this ball."

Suddenly the ball swerved to the side, it shot upward so quickly Mitch could scarcely keep track of it. The ball made a wide turn, then shot straight toward Mitch, moving faster than a bullet, only to stop an arm's length from where Mitch stood.

"You can do all that?" Mitch asked in awe.

"We can do all that and more," Arq said. "If you complete the training, you will be able to control your own ship. You will be able to navigate between star systems."

"How fast can you go?" Mitch asked.

"Faster than you can calculate."

"Faster than light?"

"Of course," Arq said. "A True Navigator operates outside the laws of the physical universe. And as you can imagine that sort of power is not for everyone. It must be protected, and fostered, for the good of all. Otherwise ..."

"What?" Mitch asked.

It was Juj who replied. "Otherwise, there would be no end to the destruction."

He tossed the small red ball to Mitch, who caught it easily enough.

"Hit him with the ball," Arq said.

"What?"

"Throw it at him," Qwii said. The alien was so excited his voice was pitched higher than normal.

"I don't think I should," Mitch said.

"We could demonstrate with your sidearm," Arq told him. "But this is probably better for now."

"What?"

"Just throw the ball," Juj said. "Throw it hard. Try to hit me with it before I'm close enough to touch you."

Juj started walking toward Mitch, who looked at Arq. He had no way of knowing the ages of his hosts, or who was in charge. But Arq did most of the explaining, and Mitch instinctively thought of him as being the elder of the trio. Arq nodded, and Mitch looked back at Juj. The alien was four meters away, walking boldly toward him. Mitch reared back and threw the ball. It flew straight and fast, right toward Juj's chest. Only just before it reached him the ball suddenly dropped to the ground.

"You see, we can control our environment," Arq said. "The bombs your people dropped on New Terra were taken off target."

"You did that?"

"No," Arq said. "The Fray we fought there did that."

"Why was he there?" Mitch asked.

"To seize control of your world," Arq explained. "With the Power and the Knowledge an individual can do just about anything."

"Including enslave entire worlds," Juj said, as his red ball floated back up to his hand.

"And destroy whole civilizations," Qwii added.

"There are those who would use this marvelous ability, gifted to us by the Creator to steward the universe, for their own selfish gain."

All three of the aliens were staring at Mitch, who suddenly felt uncomfortable.

"There are those who do not want humans to have access to the Power and the Knowledge," Juj said. "And some who do not wish for your kind to ever leave the Sol system."

"It is the task of a True Navigator to lead their people forward," Arq went on. "While also protecting them."

"From others, and from themselves," Qwii said.

"In time, you will learn to do what we have demonstrated to you," Arq said. "You will have the answers to your questions, and see the possibilities available to your people. But you will also face the temptations of the enemy."

"What enemy?" Mitch asked.

"*The* enemy," Juj said. "The Fallen, the Saboteur, it is known by many names."

"Every intelligent creature wrestles with good and evil," Arq said. "Right and wrong are not mere constructs as some would have you believe. They are woven into our DNA and into the universe at large. When you see a system of planets that are slightly off the optimal orbits, barren, lifeless, completely uninhabitable, you will feel the wrongness of that system. It was not intended to be so empty and useless."

"The Creator made a vast universe for his children to explore," Qwii said. "But it was meant to be lush, vibrant, full of life."

"But the enemy marred it," Juj said. "And scattered the races to the far-flung reaches of what was made into a hostile, deadly universe."

"Eventually, the knowledge of the Creator began to fade from memory," Arq said. "So, the Creator raised up the Order. He sent his son to show us the way."

"The Creator has children?" Mitch asked.

"We are all his children," Arq replied. "Many kinds, in many places, but all originating from him. But the son is different. We call him Scion because he was not created as we were created. The son was always extant with the Creator."

"But it's his son?" Mitch asked.

"That is how we relate to him, yes," Qwii said.

"And it was this son that taught you to use gravity the way you do?"

"That is correct," Arq said. "The son gave us the Power and the Knowledge. The Order of Scion exists to bring the universe back into harmony with the Creator."

Mitch stepped back. He was in shock. Maybe it was all an elaborate parlor trick, but he had seen the aliens do things that defied explanation. They knew things he didn't. Mitch had never thought of himself as a religious person. He had known people who believed in all kinds of things, from conspiracy theories to beliefs that they were in a gigantic, digital simulation. The talk of a Creator didn't bother Mitch. No one knew where humanity came from. DNA and cellular science had proven that we had an intelligent origin. There was just too much complex information in the simplest cells for it to have arisen by chance. But who that original programmer was, no one knew for certain. It could have been the Nagani Creator being, or something else completely.

"You need time to contemplate what you have seen and heard," Arq said. "There is no rush."

"Everyone believes this?" Mitch asked. "Everyone believes what the Order of Scion teaches?"

"No," Juj said, "not everyone."

"It is our mission to illuminate," Arq said. "True Navigators use the Power and the Knowledge to protect their people, and move their race forward in harmony with other forms of life."

"But the universe is hostile," Mitch said. "Every race we've encountered has nefarious intentions."

"Your people on New Terra have encountered only a handful of intelligent beings," Arq said. "They seek the good of their own, often at the expense of others. Not every intelligent species is ready for the Power and the Knowledge."

"And you decided which ones are and which aren't?" Mitch asked.

"That is an astute observation," Qwii said. "It seems that way to you in this circumstance, but it is not so. We do not withhold the Power or the Knowledge from any."

"We have Navigators assigned to every intelligent species," Arq said. "Their mandate is to protect that race until they are ready to hear and accept the truth."

"It is our burden to protect those who are not ready," Juj said, "even from themselves."

"I can tell what you are thinking," Arq said. "You wonder what gives us the right to withhold the Power and Knowledge?"

"It seems like a lot of responsibility," Mitch said.

"Indeed," Qwii agreed.

"It is our wish for every race to have the Power and the Knowledge," Arq explained. "Only then will we be able to fully restore the universe. Those with the Power and the Knowledge seek to live in harmony with the other races, to learn from and grow with other intelligence species. But you do not let a toddler drive a transport. More to the point, you do not give children guns. Even on your planet, this is universal wisdom."

"Not every race is ready," Juj said. "The Power is dangerous without the Knowledge for which it was given."

"And everyone agrees with you?" Mitch asked.

"Sadly, no," Arq said. "At times, even within the Order of Scion there are struggles, disagreements, and misunderstandings."

"And there are the Fray," Juj said. "You must never forget that."

"What are the Fray?" Mitch asked.

"False Navigators," Arq said. "Blind guides that seek only their own gain."

"Those who embrace the Power, but reject the Knowledge," Qwii added. "They are our arch enemies."

"But you have the power to wipe them out," Mitch said. "Just levitating them right off the world or whatever."

"The Fray also access the Power, which nullifies our ability to stop them in that way," Arq said. "Nor do projectile weapons avail against them."

"The alien you killed on New Terra," Mitch said. "You used bladed weapons."

Arq nodded, but there was a sadness in his eyes. "It is sometimes necessary."

"We gave him a chance to retreat," Qwii said. "We urged him to surrender."

"I saw it," Mitch said, knowing the lone alien on New Terra with the double-ended spear had chosen to fight to the death. He was outnumbered, and overmatched, but he was relentless. Mitch didn't know if it was valor or stubbornness. The alien chose to die, and that was a powerful statement against the Nagani. Their explanations seemed reasonable enough, but something drove the other alien to fight a losing battle with them. He kept that fact in mind as he tried to absorb what the aliens were teaching him about the Power and the Knowledge as they called it.

"Some cannot accept the truth," Arq said.

"If he hadn't been there would you have still approached me?" Mitch asked. "Was I just in the right place at the right time?"

"We saw the sacrifice you made," Juj said. "You left the safety of the transport so others could live."

"You risked your life to protect a few innocent people," Qwii added. "That is the sacrifice necessary to wield the Power and the Knowledge."

"But not just courage, or selflessness," Arq said. "You also have the physical strength that many of your kind do not possess."

"It was the right blend of talents and character," Qwii said.

"And what if I don't believe the way that you do?" Mitch said. "Will I be excluded if I can't buy all the Creator stuff?"

"The Knowledge is what sustains us," Juj said.

"And guides us to make good choices," Arq said. "Everything the Order of Scion has done in the universe is based on what we believe. But everyone's faith is personal. Lack of it will not keep you from utilizing the Power to benefit the human race."

Mitch bent down and picked up the red rubber ball. It flexed easily in his hand. He tossed it up, and it fell back down. Catching it was simple.

"If you can manipulate the balls, you can probably levitate people too," he said.

"With your permission," Arq said.

Mitch nodded, and suddenly his stomach flipped. It felt like he was on an elevator that started down. But he was rising up. He could feel the hair on the back of his neck and on his forearms rustling as if in a breeze. He waved his arms and legs, but they didn't move him through the space. Letting go of the ball he watched it float beside him.

"It isn't levitation," Qwii corrected Mitch. "We simply cut off the gravity that holds you down."

"So, I'm in an anti-gravity bubble?" Mitch asked.

"Correct," Qwii said. "And if I increase the gravity in front of you it will propel you forward."

"Think of walking down a hill," Arq explained. "It takes almost no effort. You simply keep your legs moving ahead of you, and gravity does the rest."

"A ball rolling down a hill will pick up speed the longer it rolls down," Juj said. "It is the same for you, and even for the ship."

Mitch was flying around the room by that point. Not headfirst like a superhero, and not because of anything he was doing. The aliens had him in motion, first slow, then fast, then slowing him down again.

"That's amazing," Mitch said as he came back to stand on his feet by the white furred trio. "That's what's powering the ship?"

"Powering is not the right term," Qwii said. "But I have a gravity bubble around us."

"It is, much like the atmosphere of a planet," Arq said.

"Is that opening, an actual opening?" Mitch said, pointing to what he thought was a massive window.

"It is," Qwii said. "There is no need to encapsulate us inside a structure. The gravity bubble keeps us safe."

"From hard vacuum?"

Qwii nodded.

"What about the cold?" Mitch asked. "How do you keep out the cold?"

"By retaining the heat," Arq said. "What we are feeling is the residual air temperature. It will eventually get colder, but we will be back in a civilized system before then."

"And you can travel like this between systems?" Mitch said. "It's really fascinating."

"Your own scientists have studied the idea for decades," Arq said. "Anti-gravity engines would work essentially the same way."

"But we can't get the science right," Mitch said. "Or protect our ships from space debris at high speeds."

Arq nodded. "Learn the ways of the order, Mitch Murphy, and you will be able to do all that and more."

He was in, even though he hadn't told his hosts, or even admitted it to himself yet. He knew he couldn't turn away. He couldn't just ignore the ability to do the things they had shown him. Whatever it took, he would learn their skills. And he couldn't wait to get started.

CHAPTER 5

"ALL SHIPS HAVE LEFT THE SYSTEM," the radar operator said.

"Fascinating," Admiral Darcy Wilcox said.

General Stanley Mercer didn't find it fascinating, but he was intrigued. Their orders were to bomb the colonies from orbit and pull back to the portal. But he couldn't help but wonder if they were missing an opportunity on New Terra with the other ships gone from the system.

"They followed the crescent-shaped ship," the weapons controller said.

"Some left before it did," the ship's commander, a short, broad-shouldered officer named Michael Hughes pointed out.

"Yes," the Admiral agreed. "The crescent ship entering the atmosphere was what started the exodus from the system. What do they know that we don't?"

"Maybe the crescent-shaped ship did something to the planet," the radar operator suggested. "Maybe they poisoned it somehow."

"They didn't stay long, whatever the case," Hughes said. "And we're certain they killed the other alien?"

General Mercer and the rest of the *S.F. Marathon's* crew had watched the thermal imaging video from the surveillance drone circling over the airfield at the edge of Alpha Colony. The entire area was shrouded with dust and debris from the kinetic warheads dropped by the *Marathon's* sister ships *Zama* and *Hastings*. But the thermal image had shown two unknown alien ships landing near the airfield. From the first a single being had emerged. They had no photos of the alien, just the heat signature. Three others had exited the larger, crescent-shaped spaceship. General Mercer and the other officers had seen the beings fighting. They didn't use conventional weapons. Instead, they chose to fight hand to hand. From the video feed it appeared the three from the crescent-shaped ship stayed on New Terra long enough to kill the other alien, and then captured Lieutenant Mitch Murphy. It immediately left the planet and the system, using technology so advanced the Admiral with all the *Marathon's* advanced sensors and radar arrays couldn't discern what powered it.

"It hasn't moved," Mercer pointed out. "And the body is cooling before our very eyes."

The alien had begun as a bright orange blob, but was rapidly cooling from yellow to blue. The *Marathon* was a full two days from the planet, and still gaining speed on their run across the system toward the portal that would take them back to the Sol system. But it appeared that Admiral Darcy Wilcox was about to make a command decision. One that General Mercer had been gently manipulating her to do since the crescent-shaped vessel left the planet.

"All right," she said at last. "We need eyes on the ground. General Mercer, do you have a team you can send?"

"I have several," he said confidently.

"Commander, have a drop ship prepped for transport," Wilcox ordered.

"It won't make it back before we leave the system," Hughes pointed out.

"We aren't leaving," Wilcox said. "I'll record a message for the brass. I want the armada at the portal, but we'll stay in system until we get solid intel on what took place on the ground."

"What about the aliens?" the weapons operator asked.

"We'll send a single team," Mercer announced. "Enhanced operators, they can be our eyes and ears until the brass decides what to do about the planet."

"Can we retake the colonies?" Wilcox asked.

"We'll need another regiment of Marines," Mercer said. "Maybe two. As long as more reinforcements don't show up, we could retake the planet."

"I'll make that clear in my report," Wilcox said. "Meanwhile, get a team prepped and ready."

"Aye, aye, Admiral," Mercer said.

He left the Command Center and headed to his private wardroom. Officially, General Polk and his staff could use the space, but they weren't doing so. General Polk had been caught unprepared; the evacuation had shocked him, and would be the end of his career. Under his watch the most valuable asset outside of Earth itself had been lost to alien invasion. It wasn't the kind of mistake a military man could recover from.

"We're sending a team," Mercer said as he barged into the room where his staff were already gathered. "Long term recon, no support, I don't want anyone who isn't enhanced on the mission. This could be a one-way trip, only time will tell. Who's ready to go?"

"We've got a dozen teams that could do it," Captain Frank Marcs replied. "But if it were my call to make, I'd send Leo."

"They don't have a CO," Lieutenant Colonel Jerome Banks said.

"And some minor injuries," Major Elaine Swift pointed out.

"But they'll want to know what happened to their lieutenant," Marcs said. "They won't mind waiting for him on the planet.

Finishing what he started with the other survivors. And if we lose them ..."

"I see your point," General Mercer said. "Get them ready. The Admiral wants them headed back down ASAP."

"What about the Lymies?" Major Swift said.

"Every other ship has left the system," Mercer said.

"What? Why?" Colonel Banks asked.

"That's what Leo Squad is going to find out," Mercer said. "Maybe it was our bombs. They can look like nukes from a distance."

"But they have people on the ground," Major Swift said. "Surely they'll be back to give them support."

"That may be the case," Mercer said. "But with the rapid change in the situation we can't afford to abandon the planet. Not without knowing exactly what happened down there."

Captain Marcs got to his feet and left the wardroom. General Mercer poured himself a cup of coffee and settled into his seat at the head of the table. Major Swift leaned forward onto her elbows. He knew what she was going to ask before she said it.

"No, Major," General Mercer told her.

"But sir, if there is a new species down there you'll need an expert to do the study."

"Leo Squad can bag the body," Mercer said. "I'll have their transport land nearby. They can bag it and send it back up to us."

"What about the alien ship?" she argued.

"We'll have a video of their search. It will have to suffice for now. You can't go, Elaine. You aren't trained for that sort of operation, and you can't keep up with the squad."

"Don't they need leadership?"

"Not to simply be our eyes and ears on the ground," Mercer said. "They train for missions like this constantly. They conduct a search of the airfield, then find a place to wait and see what happens next. I can't have them looking after you, Major. The answer is no."

She wasn't happy, but being in command wasn't a popularity contest. General Mercer didn't mind pissing his people off every once in a while, if for no other reason than to remind them he was in charge.

"Everyone is going to be watching our every move on this one," General Mercer continued. "Brass, politicians, even the general public depending on how much intel the Command Staff decides to leak to the media. We have to show them that SSO is the future. That the program is worth the investment the Marine Corps has made."

"Haven't we proven that already?" Colonel Banks asked. "We led the evacuation, protected the transports, got everyone off world before the Lymies invaded.

"Not everyone," Major Swift pointed out.

"We got everyone who followed instructions," Colonel Banks said. "No one is going to blame us for not waiting for the stragglers."

"The Enhancement program has shown excellent results, but we need more. We need to show, in every situation, that the SSO can do anything we ask. I want all the information coming out of that planet going through us."

"What if it's bad news?" Captain Lindsey Priss, the logistics officer, asked.

"Then we can spin it," General Mercer said. "And if it's good news we'll ride the wave of support all the way to the budget meetings. That is our mission."

"Even if it costs lives?" Major Swift said.

"We're Marines. Dying is part of the job description."

Of course, General Mercer didn't see himself as a Marine. He was, at least in his own mind, a natural born leader. The Corps was just a steppingstone to bigger and better things. And he would use the Latent Enhancement Program to boost his star and solidify his legacy in the Marines before stepping into civilian politics, where he had every intention of rising to the top post as well.

†††

"You aren't kidding, sir?" Sergeant Mara James asked.

"No, Sergeant," Captain Marcs said. "You sure that ankle is up for the challenge."

"Positive sir," she replied. "The boot is just a precaution for the medical pukes."

"Good. Get your team assembled. You'll be taking down a full communication load. Recon only. Search the airfield for alien artifacts, then go to ground. We'll be in constant communication with your team."

"Outstanding, sir. We're on it."

"Very good. I'll see you on the flight deck in half an hour."

"Sir, yes sir!" she said, snapping to attention and saluting.

Captain Marcs returned the salute and left her in the narrow corridor outside the bunk room Leo Squad was sharing with a few other SSO teams. Her heart was pounding as she hurried back inside. Of course, any mission assignment was exciting, but Mara was especially anxious to find out what had happened to Lieutenant Murphy. There were rumors of course. A spaceship is a boring place, and rumors are often the only source of excitement. So, it was no surprise that the news of Lieutenant Murphy's departure from the planet on an alien ship was being talked about in every nook and cranny of the *Marathon,* and probably on the other ships in system as well.

"What's the word, Sarge?" Flash asked her.

"We're going back," Mara said in a low voice. "Grab your gear and head to procurement."

"Are you serious?" Ninja asked.

"They want a recon team on the ground," Mara said quietly.

The mission wasn't classified. She hadn't even been given orders to keep things quiet. And she had no doubt the other SSO teams in the narrow confines of the bunk room were listening in.

But that wasn't her mess to clean up. She bent down, unfastened the latches on the support boot, and pulled her leg free.

"How long?" Jingo said.

"Long as it takes," she replied. "We're being prepped for an extended stay on site."

"Beats the hell out of being stuck in this tin can," Flash said. "What about the aliens?"

"We see 'em, we kill 'em," Mara said. "But recon is priority one. We're going down with a communications suite. We'll have surveillance drones, recharging gear, and lots of cameras to set up."

"Don't they have techs for that kind of work?" Hawk asked.

"Not on contested ground," Mara said. "Am I wrong in thinking you'd all rather be headed for the planet rather than staying on board the *Marathon*?"

"No," Hawk said.

"Just getting a feel for expectations," Ninja said. "Who's our CO for this one?"

"We don't have one," Mara said. "Not on this op. We'll get instructions via the hotline."

"And what happens if we lose communications?" Jingo asked.

"Then I guess we'll have to make some decisions for ourselves," Mara said.

That got a laugh from the rest of her squad. They were anxious to get moving. Mara got her combat boot laced up. Her ankle was tender to the touch, and the weight of her boot made it ache a little when she lifted her foot, but it would support her weight just fine. And she guessed that after two days of flying back to the planet it would be completely healed.

"All right class, time for a field trip," Mara said, standing up straight.

She led the rest of Leo Squad out of the bunk room and to the armory, which was a small room near the flight deck of the battleship. The Sergeant at Arms supplied them with weapons. They choose their usual gear, including full packs with survival supplies, and extra rations. It was enough to get them through a couple of weeks, after that they would have to supply their own food. In addition, they all got battle armor, and powerful sets of binoculars.

From the armory, they went to the flight deck and found Captain Marcs overseeing the gear being loaded onto a jump ship.

"You touch down and unload this gear," he ordered them. "Sergeant James and Corporal Gustav, you will secure the alien body and get it loaded into the freezer unit in the drop ship."

"Could be a real mess," Jingo said. "It's been dead a while, sir."

"You get as much as you can," Captain Marcs said. "Once the ship dusts off, you will be completely on your own. I want an initial assessment upon arrival. If you see bugs in and around the airfield, we may have to abort. In that case, you set up an omnidirectional camera and launch the drones before taking off again."

"Roger that, sir," Mara replied.

"Keep in mind, even with the transmission buoys there will be a slight delay in communications. Once the drop ship leaves, your first objective will be to find a defensible position and get the communications gear running."

"Any orders regarding survivors if we find any?"

"Do you best to keep them alive, but that is not your mission objective," Captain Marcs said. "This a recon op, and depending on what we find it could last a while. You all good with that?"

"Sir, yes sir!" Jingo said.

"That's what we do, baby," Flash said.

"We won't let you down, sir," Ninja added.

"Very well," Captain Marcs said. "Get all the rest you can on the flight over. After that, I want you on alert status 24/7. No excuses, Leo Squad, everyone will be watching."

"Roger that, sir," Mara said.

"Good luck, Leos."

They all snapped to attention, and Captain Marcs saluted in return. Then he watched as the five large special operators climbed onto the jump ship. He stepped away as the rear hatch closed, and then watched from the edge of the flight deck as the ship was lifted by a deck crane that maneuvered the small, armored transport into the airlock. By the time he got back to the wardroom with his report, the drop ship had launched and was making its way back to New Terra.

CHAPTER 6

MITCH DIDN'T NEED a lot of time to rest. But he recognized and appreciated that his alien hosts were giving him time to process what he was learning. He spent much of the afternoon touring the ship. It was not what he expected. Unlike human interstellar vessels which were built for utility, the alien ship was more like a mansion. There were all sorts of luxuries on the vessel, including a library with books and scrolls in exotic languages. There was an exercise space, several salons with huge openings that gave a person extensive views of outer space. There was furniture of all kinds, for different body shapes and sizes. There were a variety of entertainment systems as well. Perhaps most impressive was a planetarium. Mitch found himself studying the various star maps of both the Milky Way galaxy and the universe at large.

The aliens gave him time and privacy, but were always nearby to answer his questions. Juj found him in the planetarium late on the evening of his second day on the ship.

"Are you a student of astronomy, Mitch Murphy?" Juj asked.

"Not really," Mitch admitted.

"Were you always a soldier?"

"A Marine," Mitch corrected the alien, even though he didn't know if Juj knew the difference. "No, I was a businessman for a long time."

"A businessman? What is that, exactly?"

"I was in finance," Mitch said. "On earth, many people buy and trade ownership shares in public companies. I was a facilitator."

"I see," Juj said, settling into the reclining seat next to Mitch. "I find your race fascinating."

"We must seem pretty backward to an advanced race like yours."

"No, not at all. Each race develops in their own way. Yours is very technologically astute."

"How long have you been watching us?"

"I was assigned the human race eight of your earth years ago," Juj explained. "It is an honor to help you progress."

"What did you do before you were assigned to humanity?"

"The Nagani have had many True Navigators," the alien explained. "I spent a long time as a protector, helping curb the destruction of the Fray."

"You fought? You were a soldier?"

"Of sorts," Juj said. "The Fray are not like an army. They have no organization. And they can appear just about anywhere."

"Were they all trained by the Order?"

"Not all of them," he said. "But most. Sometimes the Fray take on apprentices, but it is rare. The Power and the Knowledge drive some people insane. Others are simply greedy. It can be difficult to work with lesser beings."

Mitch understood that. He had been given orders by people who weren't as strong, or as physically enhanced as he was in the Marine Corps, short though his time was. And in the business world he had seen many people rise through the ranks around him because they went to a certain school, or knew the right people. Some of them were complete idiots in Mitch's opinion, and taking orders from them was always a challenge.

"Is the training hard?" Mitch asked.

"It is not physically as taxing as you might expect, but it requires mental strength, and discipline. Some races are especially sensitive to the Power, others struggle to tap into it. Only time will tell with you, as you are the first human to be shown the Way."

Mitch felt both honored and afraid. What if he failed? What if he went crazy? The last thing he wanted was to become some type of super villain that kept the human race isolated and alone because of his failures.

"I am from Liganti," Juj said. "It is one of almost a dozen Nagani worlds."

The holographic star map expanded until it showed just one star system.

"Did the Order terraform the system for you?"

"What is this word terraform?" Juj asked.

"It means to manipulate a planet to make it hospitable to life," Mitch said.

"Ah, yes, the Liganti System was barren. The Grand Master Yark corrected the orbits of the worlds and moons. There are two planets where our people live, and four moons, each one with thick atmospheres and natural resources."

"Do you get back there often?"

"We in the Order rarely have emotional bonds. I have visited a time or two since joining the Order, but there is little to draw me back there."

"Now that you've found a human for the Order, what will you do?"

"Once you have mastered the Power and Knowledge, we will help you protect and develop the human race. There may be others of your kind fit to join us. And you will need counsel."

"No doubt about that," Mitch said.

"But eventually Qwii and I will be reassigned. Arq will stay with you until his time in the universe ends."

Mitch nodded. They were talking about some pretty heavy

stuff, and he didn't want to take it lightly. Still, he had a lot of questions.

"Arq is the oldest?"

"He is. Our kind live longer than many humans."

"How much longer?"

"Almost twice the average lifespan," Juj explained.

"Wow, and you do that without a mate?"

"Our species does not mate as yours does," Juj explained. "We come together to procreate a few times, but that is all. Most of our species are solitary. We steward the worlds, and help foster growth."

"Sounds noble," Mitch said. "Humans were once mostly farmers, but as our cities grew more and more people settled into different ways of life."

"Yes, I have studied your history. It is rich. There is much warfare, but also so much art, poetry, song, and story. Humanity has so much to offer the universe."

"I'm glad you see it that way," Mitch said. "I doubt everyone would. We have plenty of flaws."

"Every race has flaws. Every individual too."

"Can I ask a question?"

"Sure," Juj said. "Anything."

"The alien you fought on New Terra, who was it?"

"A Salamantor," Juj said. "They are pawns of the Fray."

"Pawns?"

"Many trade access to the Creator's Power in exchange for fighting members of the Order. His presence in the system forced us into action."

"What would he have done if you hadn't stayed?"

"No one on the planet would be safe. They come to enslave. Those that resist are murdered. The Power can be incredibly destructive. It can stop a heart from beating."

"Oh," Mitch said, realizing for the first time just how potent the gravity force the aliens wielded really was.

"A person with mastery of the Power can destroy entire armies. If one reached the Sol system, it could destroy your fleets, and take control of your planet easily."

"What's stopping them?" Mitch asked.

"The Order," Juj said. "We are the protectors of the innocent."

"Most people would say humanity isn't innocent."

"Those who have yet to learn the Power and the Knowledge must be protected. They must be allowed to develop and grow in their own time. It is part of the Order's mandate to keep them safe."

"But once we venture out of our system?" Mitch wondered.

"The ability to leave one's home system is an indication that they are ready to face what the universe has to offer, good and bad. We do not interfere, but we cannot let those without the Power and Knowledge to become enslaved."

"So, you stop them?"

"We try," Juj said.

He brought up a larger map of the galaxy his home world was in. Several systems glowed with a bright green color, and several more were dark red.

"Not every attempt at defense is successful," Juj continued. "We can do many things, but we cannot read the minds of our enemies. We cannot know where they are going or keep tabs on every one of them."

"And sometimes they win," Mitch said. "The systems in red?"

"Correct. They are under the control of the Fray. Eventually, if the Order has enough warriors, we will take those systems back and free the native peoples."

"But you don't have enough people now?"

"As you can guess we take the training seriously. It is not a process to rush though. And we are selective in who we recruit. Even then, the failure rate is high. Many do not complete the training, and even those that do must face the temptation to fall away. It is a trap that some never escape."

The thought of it made Mitch's mouth go dry. He didn't think of himself as an especially strong person. He wasn't weak, but was he good enough to wield the kind of power the aliens possessed without it going to his head? He didn't know. And that thought frightened him.

"Come, we will eat soon," Juj said. "Tomorrow, we will reach Vodex and your training will begin."

CHAPTER 7

IT WASN'T that Mitch didn't trust his gracious hosts, but he felt he was only getting one side of the story. Of course, the members of the Order of Scion would claim to be the good guys. Mitch didn't disbelieve them, but he felt sheltered. He had explored the upper levels of the ship, but that evening, when his hosts retired, Mitch decided to see what was below the grandiose levels of the magnificent ship.

He started in the dining room, looking at the wonderful tapestries that hung on the walls. He was interested in the story they portrayed in pictures, and it wasn't hard to see the image of a wise creator bringing the universe into existence. Nor did it take a lot of imagination to spot the various characters in the story. The Son was smaller than the Creator, but just as light and beautiful. The enemy, Mitch had learned, was called by many names. Deceiver was just one of them, but it resonated with Mitch, who was himself on a mission to find the truth about the incredible power the aliens possessed. The Deceiver was presented on the tapestries as both beautiful and sinister. Another of the flowing fabrics showed a fragmented universe, and another showed the

Son sharing the Power and Knowledge with the founding members of the Order of Scion. Mitch was more interested in what lay behind the tapestries than what they displayed. He found the door he was looking for, a narrow doorway that led to set of stairs. Mitch went down the stairs, hoping that he wasn't breaking some sort of unwritten rule. Of course, if his alien hosts grew angry with him for snooping, it wasn't a very good sign that they were on the up and up. *A person who is doing the right thing doesn't fear scrutiny*, Mitch's business ethics professor had always said.

The stairs led to a food preparation area. Mitch still had no idea how the ship, if it could even be called that, was powered. But he found a clean prep area with a wide table, and several appliances built into a counter that ran around the edges of the room. He was a little shocked to see the General Appliances logo he was so familiar with on the stove and refrigerator. Somehow the aliens had gotten their hands on human technology. He opened the refrigerator and found several common items sold in just about any grocery store in the solar system.

He went through a connecting door and found what appeared to be a hydroponic garden. A variety of leafy plants were growing in floating baskets, and on the floor grew grass of different shades of green and blue. Mitch understood where they got the food his alien hosts ate from their big stainless steel bowls. But what he really wanted to know was who was preparing the meals.

He passed through a series of small rooms with various cleaning supplies, and eventually came to what looked like a break room. Mitch was reminded of how small and untidy the breakroom in the Sterling Finance offices was for the lowest tier employees. His immediate supervisor had a real office, and a lounge with a free coffee stand run by a barista instead of a break room, while Mitch only had access to vending machines and a few plastic chairs. The higher executives had an actual dining room that was rumored to be as fancy as any upscale restaurant in the city. Mitch had no way to know if the rumor was true or not, it was on the second highest level of the building and he wasn't allowed up there.

Still, the break room on the ship was well appointed. There was a table that seemed to be made of the same material as the ship itself. Mitch wasn't sure if it was stone or some kind of crystal, but the entire ship seemed to be cut from a single massive block. Around the table were the same type of chairs in the dining room upstairs. There were cabinets with labels he couldn't read, and a refrigerator with a glass front. Inside was a wide variety of bottled drinks.

He had just been looking at the drinks when he heard something behind him. He turned and found a short, humanoid creature. It wore the same kind of flowing robes that the aliens wore, and that Mitch himself was wearing. Its skin was dark brown, and it had glossy black hair that was grown long and tied back into a ponytail. Its eyes were big, the nose was very small, as was its mouth.

"Hello," Mitch said.

The short being cooed gently, sounding a lot like a dove.

"I'm Mitch," he said, unsure of what else to say. "I was hoping to talk."

The big eyed, brown skinned creature bowed, then hurried away. Mitch wasn't sure what to do, and was still trying to decide when a female was ushered into the room by the first alien. It was cooing at the female, who had longer hair, and wore her robes more like a dress. Mitch didn't move. He was afraid of doing something that might offend the aliens, or make them go running to the Nagani on the upper levels.

"Hello," he said again.

"How do you do?" the female said slowly. She carefully pronounced each word, and had a heavy accent that Mitch had never heard before. He was taller than most humans, and she was shorter.

"My name is Mitch," he said. "I was hoping to talk to you."

"To me?"

"Well, not you specifically," Mitch said. "Just someone down here."

"Is something wrong?" she said in the same slow diction.

"No, nothing is wrong," Mitch said. "You are the ones cooking and cleaning?"

The female alien nodded.

"It's excellent. My compliments to the chef, really. It's all been fantastic. Thank you. But I was wondering who you are? And why do you work here?"

"It is good," the female said. "Very prestigious."

"Working on this ship?"

"Working for the Order of Scion," she said with a little bow. It was a subtle attempt at modesty. She wasn't bragging, but it was obvious that to her, working for the Nagani was a big deal.

"And you volunteer?"

"We train ... long time," she said. "I am Uri. I am chief."

"That's excellent," Mitch said. "Congratulations."

She smiled, obviously very pleased.

"Is the Order of Scion good?"

She frowned as if she didn't quite understand the question.

"I mean, are they good people. Do they do good things where you come from?"

"They are the light-benders," she said slowly. "They protect us. My kind cannot use the Power and the Knowledge. So we serve."

"I see," Mitch said. "Was that your idea, or theirs?"

"We volunteer," she said. "Train special. Is very big honor."

"I see," Mitch said. "And you're happy doing all this?"

"Happy, yes. Very happy."

"Good," Mitch said. "I didn't know. I was afraid they were just telling me what I wanted to hear."

"You can trust them," she said. "You are in good hands."

"Thank you," Mitch said. "You've been a big help. I won't bother you anymore."

"You first," she said, beaming with pride.

"First what?" he asked.

"First guest come down to visit Uri. We learn much about humans. We watch and listen. We taste food. It is very good."

"You tried Earth food?"

"Yes," Uri said. "We like candy. And coffee. Very good."

"I can't argue with that," Mitch said. "I like candy and coffee too."

"Would you drink coffee with Uri?"

"Sure," Mitch said. "I'll drink with you and all your staff if you like."

She turned, cooing at the big-eyed alien who had brought her in. Then he ran off, while Uri showed Mitch to a chair. It was a bit small for his wide frame, but he made it work, while Uri prepared a pot of coffee. She had a bag of roasted coffee beans, scooped some out, and ground them fresh. Then she added hot water to a glass pot with a press inside. Soon four other aliens arrived. They all looked excited. Uri began pouring coffee for everyone.

"You take sugar?" Uri asked.

"Sometimes," he said. "Usually I drink it black."

This resulted in a giggle of excitement from the others.

"Does anyone else speak English?"

Uri shook her head. "Just me," she said. "I work for Arq long time. I study."

"Your English is excellent," Mitch told her.

"Thank you," she said, as she added a lot of sugar to her small cup of coffee.

"Can I ask where you got all this?" Mitch asked, waving his hand toward the coffee and the bottles of soda in the glass front refrigerator.

"Delivery," was her response, and the other aliens cooed and giggled.

Mitch spent the next hour and a half with the ship's crew. None worked to operate the ship. They were custodians, not maintenance members. There simply wasn't much technology on the ship, certainly not enough to warrant maintenance personnel. Mitch left the group feeling reassured. Sleep that night came easily. A full five hours and he woke feeling refreshed. He also found that his clothing and armor had all been cleaned. He dressed in his Marine fatigues, but left the armor and his pistol behind. When he came to the observation deck he found that they were already in orbit around a bright planet with dark clouds over a series of rugged mountain chains.

"This is Vodex," Qwii said. "We'll land soon."

"What's down there?" Mitch asked.

"A training center at the base of the mountains," Qwii said. "The opportunity for you get more answers and see how receptive you are to the Power and the Knowledge."

"What will you be doing?" Mitch asked.

"Arq and Juj will be returning to the human systems," Qwii explained. "I will remain here to help you."

An hour later, after a hearty breakfast, Mitch said his goodbyes to Juj and Arq.

"I want to thank you," Mitch said. He started to extend his hand but the Nagani had no hands to shake with. Their arms ended in split hooves, which were capable of many things, but not a human handshake.

"We will meet again soon, Mitch Murphy," Arq said with a slight bow. "Until then, may be blessed as you seek the Way."

"Thank you," Mitch said.

A small ship came and docked with the crescent-shaped vessel. Arq and Juj left on the smaller craft, then the bigger ship descended from orbit. Half an hour later Mitch was the first human to set foot on Vodex. Looking around, Mitch was surprised to find brilliant blue skies, and white puffy clouds. There was no sign of civilization on the wide, grassy plain that stretched away from the mountains. But on the hillsides were what appeared to be adobe houses built into little clefts in the rock and connected by narrow trails.

At the bottom of the mountains was a larger building. The architecture looked almost like ancient Japanese. The building was made of timber and stone, with walls that were honey combed with openings. A cool breeze was blowing, but in the distance Mitch could see dark smoke billowing over the mountains.

A group of aliens approached. There were more Nagani, and several other races that Mitch didn't recognize. They all stood upright, and wore the same type of loose fitting, lightweight fabric material that Qwii was draped in.

"Welcome to Vodex," a voice sounded in Mitch's head. The leader of the group from the big structure was tall, with a bulbous head. He had narrow, slanted eyes, and no discernable nose. His mouth was long, with very thin lips. Mitch didn't know how, but the alien was speaking to him without using sound.

"Thank you." Mitch replied.

"And welcome to the Order of Scion," the same voice said. "I am Doss. I have been entrusted with teaching you the Way."

"Okay," Mitch said, still not sure how he was hearing the alien's voice.

"Doss is a very learned instructor," Qwii said. "He is speaking to you via a telepathic link."

"Oh, I see," Mitch said, not really happy that someone was inside his head.

"He cannot read your thoughts," Qwii continued. "Only project his voice. And not even in his own language, but your brain translates it."

"You can understand me, though?" Mitch asked.

"My brain translates your words," Doss said. "I admit, you are the first human I have ever met. You are a physically impressive being. Are all your kind so large?"

"No," Mitch admitted. "Most are not."

"You chose well, Qwii. Come, let us go inside and your training can begin."

The alien didn't waste time, and Mitch could appreciate that. The interior of the structure wasn't like a temple, but it did have a big main room with a sweeping ceiling. Inside the air was cool, and Mitch saw aliens in the Order's robes lounging on wooden furniture. Doss led the way to a smaller room with a window that looked out toward the crescent-shaped ship.

"When you are not training, it will be our pleasure for you to stay with us," Qwii said. "Uri and the crew are quite taken with you."

"Oh, okay," Mitch said. "Thank you. Thank them for me."

"It is our pleasure," Qwii said.

When Mitch turned around, he saw that most of the aliens with Doss had settled onto the floor, their backs against the wall. He wasn't happy having an audience, but he was a guest and they had their ways. None of the other aliens were introduced to him personally, so Mitch did his best to simply ignore them.

"Arq is an excellent teacher," Doss said. "He will have explained much to you."

"I guess so, yes," Mitch replied.

"Then we will start with the practical. Please feel free to ask any questions you have, Mitch Murphy, but as we focus on specific lessons, try to keep your mind fully engaged in the moment."

"Yes, sir. I can do that," Mitch said.

"Excellent. We will begin with a simple exercise that will help you identify and recognize the Power. It is all around you. It holds you to the ground on this planet, and connects everything from one galaxy to another. It is the fabric of the Creator's power made manifest in creation. It is both invisible and visible. It is both weak and powerful. Close your eyes, Mitch Murphy. Relax your body as much as you can, and open your perceptions to the waves moving in this place."

Mitch did as he was told. He had never been a spiritual person.

Prayer was foreign to him, and he had never meditated before, although he had seen people doing it. At that moment he felt awkward just standing in the room with his eyes closed. But it only took a moment for him to become aware of his body. Since the LE Protocols he could feel his heart beating, and the blood carrying sweet oxygen to his muscles. His bones felt strong, his muscles like coiled steel springs, his nervous system sensitive to anything going on around him. He could feel his clothing against his skin, and the soft breeze wafting in through the big windows. The sounds of beings going about their business was a soft hum in the background.

For several minutes that was all Mitch felt. He felt his blood pumping with every beat of his heart, heard his lungs expanding with every breath he took, but nothing else. He was starting to fear that Arq had made a mistake. Or that maybe Doss was trying to get him to do something he wasn't capable of, when suddenly he felt something. It was like his mind rising on a wave. As a child he had visited a water park with a large pool capable of generating waves like the ocean. He had spent hours in that pool, just rising and falling with the waves. He could stand in chest deep water and let the waves lift him just a few inches from the concrete bottom of the pool. It was both exhilarating and relaxing at the same time. And the feeling Mitch had in the Order training facility reminded him of that. His body didn't move, but the sensation of movement was the same in his mind.

It happened one time, one mental wave, and everything went back to normal. He immediately questioned if he had actually felt anything at all. There were plenty of documented cases of people believing something had happened just because a persuasive person in their life suggested it. Mitch had always been the kind of person who confined himself to what he could see, taste, touch, smell, and hear. The invisible, the supernatural, that was the stuff of movies. He didn't believe in magic, or superpowers, despite the fact that he was living proof that humanity had untapped potential.

"Don't resist it," Doss said softly. "It's there. It's always been there. You've just trained yourself not to notice. You must open yourself up to the possibility that you were meant to work in cooperation with the Creator's power."

That was another sticking point that was hard for Mitch to get past. He didn't subscribe to the belief in a Creator. There was no doubt that humans, and probably every other living species in the galaxy, came from somewhere. Mankind had spent hundreds of years desperately trying to prove evolution, despite the fact that spontaneous complexity was found nowhere in the universe. Eventually, the evidence against evolution simply couldn't be ignored, but did that really mean there was a God who had created everything? If so, why? And where did he come from? And where had he been for millions of years? To Mitch, that theory was just as full of holes as evolution.

Except ... the feeling of rising on a wave hit him again. For just a moment Mitch felt the swell of something around him, maybe even passing over him. It made him feel giddy, just like when he was a kid in the water park. Then it was gone, and the doubts came rushing back in. He thought about what he had seen Arq, Juj, and Qwii do. It seemed supernatural. They had some sort of power. The crescent-shaped ship was proof that it was more than just a parlor trick. He might not fully understand how the ship operated, but he was certain there were no engines on board.

The wave came again, and this time he embraced it with his mind and it lingered. He felt an almost magical ebb and flow. At first it was just the movement in his mind, but after a few moments he began to feel more of it. It was like being on a trampoline. When the other beings in the room moved, he felt it. Doss was on his feet, moving around Mitch. The gentle, invisible waves moved between them. He could even feel the gentle tug from the wave wanting to pull Mitch and Doss together. With a little effort he could feel the walls of the room. The structure had weight and he could sense how sturdy it was. The other beings were sitting along the wall, but

Mitch could feel them. They were disturbing the waves somehow, interacting with them.

"Remarkable," Doss said. "You feel it?"

"I do," Mitch said. "Like waves in an ocean."

"Exactly," Doss said. "We sometimes think of straight lines and right angles, but gravity is a wave, just like light. It is in motion. Let yourself feel the motion. Notice how it reacts to you, to your movement, to the things around you."

Mitch did. It was, in some ways, overwhelming. His mind struggled to cope with the feeling of gravity in motion around him. Everything with mass was connected. He could feel himself drawn to the surface of the planet under him. He could feel the wide-open expanse beyond the building he was in. He could feel the mountains too. It was like going from perpetual night, to seeing things in broad daylight.

"Your task is to acclimate," Doss told him. "Over the next few days, you will learn to feel the Power around you all the time. It is gentle, never overwhelming, like the Creator himself. The Power will not do anything you do not request that it do. It is always there, but never pushes itself to the forefront, never insisting that you take notice or action, but always available. It is like the air you breathe and must become second nature to you."

After the short lesson, one of the other members of the Order, a tall, thin being with feline facial features called Bess led him around the complex. She was one of a handful of instructors who had been tasked with learning his language. They stopped often so that Mitch could reconnect with the sensation of the gravity waves. It was easy to forget about them when he was learning something new, or seeing something he hadn't seen before. And there were plenty of fascinating things to see in the complex. Beyond the big building was a narrow yard, before the ground started sloping up to form the mountainside. In the yard were dozens of members of the Order, training to fight.

"What's this?" Mitch asked.

"Martial training," Bess said. She had a soft, velvety voice and a thick accent. "We must fight to defend the weak."

Mitch was no expert, but he had trained in hand-to-hand combat. First on the *Wellington* as they traveled to New Terra, and then with his squad. Ninja and Mara were experts in close combat, both with weapons and without. Mitch saw members of the Order doing basic moves, and others training in advanced techniques with strange weapons. Mitch had nearly forgotten seeing them on New Terra. Arq, Juj, and Qwii all had weapons but they didn't flaunt them. The weapons were hidden inside their robes. He remembered the black blades. They looked almost like shadows, but they sounded real enough. And Arq had run his short sword through the Fray they had fought.

"What are their weapons made of?" Mitch asked.

"Cidian," she replied. "It is a unique element, found in only a handful of places. Vodex is one of those."

"Cidian, is it like rock or something?"

"No, it different. You learn more about it as your training progresses."

The lesson for the day ended in a time of focused meditation. Mitch sat with Doss in the training room, feeling the gravity waves, as his mentor instructed him.

"You can sense the Power," Doss said. "But it is nothing without the Knowledge."

"What if I don't believe in the Creator?" Mitch asked, his eyes closed, his mind trying to simultaneously sense the gravity waves, and engage in the conversation.

"It is not necessary," Doss said. "The Creator believes in you. He has made you aware of the Power, and he will lead you into the Knowledge as well. Patience is all you need. The answers you seek will come to you. For now, it is enough to hear the truth."

"Why did the Creator give us the power?" Mitch asked. "Why not just clean up his own mess?"

"That is an excellent question," Doss said. "You should ponder it tonight. Our lesson is complete for today."

"That's it?" Mitch asked, opening his eyes. "I'm not tired. I could keep going."

"I see that. Your kind has great stamina, but I need rest."

"Oh, I'm sorry," Mitch said. "I didn't mean to push."

"Your enthusiasm is welcome, Mitch Murphy. It is refreshing to this old Quyzar. In the morning we will continue. Until then, may the Creator bless you."

"Thanks," Mitch said.

He left the big building, what the others were calling the academy, and walked through the gathering dusk toward the crescent-shaped ship. It was the first time he had been alone in hours, and he decided that what he needed was a run. Exercise helped clear his mind, and it was crowded with new knowledge and wild ideas. After checking in with Qwii, Mitch set out in a slow jog away from the mountains. He fell into a rhythm, his legs pumping, arms swaying, and his mind began to slowly organize all the new things he had experienced.

At some point he turned around, pushing the pace as he returned to the ship. He stopped running a few hundred meters out and walked the rest of the way in, organizing his thoughts along the way. One thing was certain in his mind. He felt good about where he was. No matter how everything shook out in the end, or what he was able to believe about the Knowledge, he had discovered something about himself and the universe that would change his future for the better.

CHAPTER 8

"PLANET FALL IN THIRTY SECONDS," the pilot announced.

Leo Squad had comlinks built into their battle helmets, giving them access to the pilots in the cockpit.

"Anything on the scanners?" Mara asked.

"There's a lot of debris in the air," the pilot said. "It's fogging up the scanners. Radar is blank too. It's a crap shoot, Sergeant."

"Roger that," Mara replied. "We won't be long."

As soon as the drop ship was close enough to the ground, Jingo and Flash jumped from the open rear hatch. All around them the dust kicked up from the orbital bombardment was swirling. It had been nearly a week since the bombs fell, yet in those five days the air remained choked with dust, dirt, and debris. The jet engines on the drop ship made it swirl. The two Marines on the ground could only see a few meters in any direction.

"Clear," Jingo announced.

"As far as we can see, that is," Flash added. "Which ain't much."

"Touching down," the Pilot announced.

Mara led Ninja and Hawk out of the ship. Flash remained on

guard, while the others went to work. Hawk and Ninja carried crates of equipment out of the ship, while Mara and Jingo moved to the body of the slain alien.

"Over here," Jingo announced. "Found it. Looks like we're not the first either."

"Let's get it bagged and into the freezer. The eggheads can take their time with it after that," Mara said.

She felt a shiver of fear just looking at the alien. Its head and lower body seemed intact. Whatever wound had killed it, the vermin had gotten into. Most of the alien's upper body was ripped and torn. Bones with gnaw marks were visible in what Mara thought of as the chest cavity. Organs had turned black. There were maggots writhing around inside the body cavity.

"I think I'm going to be sick," Jingo said.

"You've seen worse," Mara said. She was thankful that her helmet filtered out the dust in the air, and most of the stench from the putrefying flesh.

They spread out the triple layer, bio-toxin-safe, body bag. Once it was open, Mara lifted the alien's shoulders, while Jingo lifted the feet. Black blood oozed out as they lifted the body. The backbone held both ends together, but the middle was eviscerated. Organs protruded, and strings of sticky, black jellied flesh stretched from the ground to the body.

"Disgusting," Jingo declared.

They set it in the body bag, then sealed it up. It was impossible not to get the blood and gore on the outside of the sack, which they lifted and carried back toward the ship, setting it down just outside the ramp.

"We've got the body," Mara said. "But we're double-bagging it."

"Thanks for that," the pilot replied.

Mara ran on board. Ninja and Hawk were carrying off the last of the equipment. She grabbed another body bag. It took less than sixty seconds to get it spread out and open. The other fit neatly inside, and they got the second bag sealed without getting any gore on the outside. Then she and Jingo carried the alien body into the back of the drop ship and stored it in a chest freezer that had been put into the ship for that very reason.

"You're good to go," Mara said, as she followed Jingo down the ramp. "Leo Squad is clear."

"Roger that Leo Squad. Good luck down here."

The ship lifted off easily on the powerful repulser engines. The jets roared as it flew away.

"What now?" Flash said, as the group huddled around the mound of equipment.

"The tower," Mara said. "It's as good a place as any to get started. Jingo, Flash, you guard the comms equipment. Try to get one of the cameras set up. Hawk, let's get a drone in the air."

"It won't be able to see much in all this dust," Estelle Flemming replied, even as she popped open the hard case with one of the surveillance drones inside.

Mara knew that was true, but the drones had thermal imaging. As long as it could get airborne, it should be able to alert them if anything alive was moving toward them. She hesitated for a moment, listening to the sand and tiny bits of grit flying into her helmet. It was like being in a sandstorm in the desert. Fortunately, the kinetic bombs weren't radioactive. In fact, they had no explosive elements at all. They were just big, tungsten steel rods that were shot toward the surface of the planet from orbit. Gravity did the work, and the kinetic energy released on impact was significant, but clean. Eventually the dust would settle, and life would get back to normal, even in the big craters created where the bombs hit.

"Get one up and set to thermal," Mara ordered. "We have to know if we're not alone out here."

She didn't mind taking the lead. It was better than being barked at by a puny little officer who couldn't keep up with her team. And Mara had been a Marine long enough to know what needed to be done in just about any situation. She had earned the rank of

Sergeant, and with it came the responsibility of looking after her squad, with or without a CO on the ground.

"Let's see what we can find, Ninja," Mara ordered.

They set out in the direction where they knew the fallen control tower would be. The airfield was a large compound, with a few long runways and several buildings. Most had taken damage from the bombing, even though the impact had been nearly twenty-five kilometers away. The hangars were simple buildings, metal supports covered by thin sheet metal, which had crumpled and blown away from the shockwave during the bombing. It hadn't been a single impact either. The bombs had missed the colonies, and hit the ground between them. So approximately twenty-five kilometers on either side of Alpha Colony a heavy kinetic rod had sent shockwaves in every direction. The airfield had been hit, perhaps only a second apart, from two different directions.

"I got a bug," Ninja said.

He was slightly ahead of her. The dead Lymie appeared out of the fog of dust and debris a second later for Mara. It was on its back, the four long spindly legs curled in on top.

"Dead," Mara said. "Keep moving."

"Ever see one playing possum?" Ninja asked.

"No," Mara said. "You?"

"Negative."

They still gave the dead alien a wide berth. Soon the ruins of the control tower came into view. It was mostly intact, but had toppled over. The roof had been covered with radar dishes, antennae, and radio transmitters. From a glance, Mara guessed that some of the old equipment could be salvaged, but she was more interested in using the downed control tower to hide their own communications system.

"Let's do a quick perimeter sweep," Mara said. "Then I want to be sure it's clear inside."

"Roger that," Ninja said.

They split up, each of them going in a different direction around the fallen tower, and meeting up at the lower section.

"I got nothing," Ninja said.

"Same. If anything is around here, it's staying out of sight."

"Can't blame 'em," Ninja said. "Without our armor we'd be in world of hurt in this weather."

"If there's something close, it'll be inside," Mara said, checking the safety on her automatic shotgun.

"Marauder, the bird is in flight," Hawk announced over the comlink, which was laced with static even though Mara was less than a hundred meters from Hawk.

"Is it picking up anything?" Mara asked.

"The signal is crap," Hawk told her. "We need to get our receiver and signal boosters set up."

"Just keep that bird circling," Mara ordered. "Ninja and I are checking the tower now. Standby."

"Copy that, standing by," Hawk replied.

"After you," Ninja said.

Mara went first into the ruins of the tower. The lower floor was missing, which formed a sort of artificial cave. The side of the tower on the ground was crumpled and uneven. But there wasn't much debris inside, although there were small drifts of sand and dirt from the dust clouds. Mara found the stairwell, and proceeded to the next section. It was a wreck, with furniture piled up on what was once a wall, but had become the floor.

"Might find some rations in there," Ninja said. "It'd be worth doing a search at some point."

"I'm more interested in aliens," Mara said.

Their helmets boosted the light coming in from the windows, most of which were still intact. Glass was a difficult item to manufacture, and a fragile commodity to transport. Most of the windows in the tower were made of transparent polymer. Mara and Ninja used flashlights to do a visual search of the second floor. It wasn't very big, and there was no sign of the spidery aliens.

"Next floor," Mara ordered.

The third floor was offices and took longer to search. But it was empty too. The top floor was where the controllers had done their work. The walls were all transparent, some shattered, others popped from their frames but still intact. The equipment had been mounted into consoles, which stood out halfway up the floor, which was now a wall.

"Not much left," Ninja said, shining his flashlight beam into the darkened corners.

"Nothing functional," Mara said. "But who knows what we might be able to salvage? The tower will give us shelter. We can set up the comms equipment just outside and run the controls back in here. At least we'll be out of the wind."

Overhead there was a thick pall of dust and debris. Mara could see it through a bank of windows straight up. They were still intact, while most of the windows on either side had been knocked out.

"Leo Squad, the control tower is clear," Mara said. "Let's start hauling the equipment over here. We'll make this our base of operations."

"Copy that," Jingo said, his voice crackling through the static.

"Ninja, see if you can climb up there and get a lay of the land," Mara said. "Shoot out one of the windows and get topside."

"We still won't have much visibility," Ninja said.

"This dust storm won't last forever," she told him. "And if anything is moving in this direction I want to know about it."

"Roger that," he said, rotating his Garrison Assault Rifle around to his back before he started climbing the built-in consoles.

Mara slipped out one of the busted windows. She moved around to what had been the top of the tower. A few seconds later Flash, Jingo, and Hawk appeared. Each of them was carrying a piece of equipment.

It took a full hour to get everything moved. An hour after that they had their communications unit set up. It expanded the distance and clarity of their comlinks, but couldn't break through the clouds of debris.

"We need more power," Hawk said. "I've got the drone at fifty meters, but that's as high as it can go before we start losing signal."

"The important thing is that we don't get ambushed," Mara said. "There's still plenty of equipment to salvage from around here."

"Speaking of that," Jingo said. "I don't think we're the only ones who have done that."

"Someone's been here?" Mara said.

"Looks that way," Jingo said. "I took a look back at the foundation of the tower. Some of the batteries have been taken."

"Maybe they were blown away during the bombing?" Flash pointed out.

"They were bolted down," Jingo replied.

"So, the whole damn tower was knocked down bro."

"My point is that the bolts were left on the ground. And almost all the solar cells are missing. The only ones left are too busted up to be much good."

"Someone salvaged the power system," Mara said. "Probably the survivors Murphy was helping. We'll have to make contact with them sooner or later."

"You think they know what happened to the LT?" Jingo asked.

"If anyone does," Mara said. "For now, let's see if there's any juice in the batteries they left behind. I want to utilize the signal boosters on the tower roof. We have to get a word to the fleet."

"Copy that, I'm on it," Jingo said.

"I'll make sure no boogeymen get him," Flash said with a smile.

They moved off, and Mara looked around. Hawk was focused on the equipment, trying to finesse a signal through the cloud of dust that hung thick in the air. She reminded herself that their mission was a marathon, not a sprint. And while the dust storm was a pain in her backside, it was also good cover. When it cleared they could get more done, but they would also be at a greater risk of being discovered. She decided that she was thankful for the chance to get her people settled. They would establish a base in the old tower and then branch out to explore their surroundings, the most important of which was the alien ship. But they couldn't report their findings yet, so that adventure would have to wait. She just hoped that once they got their communications established, that they wouldn't run into any unwelcome surprises.

"Marauder, we have contact," Hawk said. "Something big."

"Headed this way?" Mara asked.

"This way, adjacent," she answered.

"Where?" Ninja asked. "I got nothing."

"It's still half a klick out," Hawk said. "Due south. Coming through the forest."

"Jingo, Flash, get back over here," Mara ordered. "Whatever it is, we need to present a united front."

"Copy that," Jingo said.

"On our way," Flash added.

"Is it headed toward the tower?" Mara asked.

Even though the control tower had fallen over, it was still on the far east side of the airfield. Looking west, they could see the runways and landing pads, but the other buildings were lost in the dust cloud, which was thicker the higher up one went.

"No," Hawk said. "Not unless it changes course."

"Which it might do once it's in the clear," Ninja said.

Mara knew that was true. The only thing that had occurred at the airfield was their arrival. She stepped up behind Hawk and looked at the display screen. It wasn't clear. There were lines of static and the entire imagine jumped occasionally. It was the video feed from the surveillance drone. The thermal imaging showed a huge, dark red blob.

"It's moving pretty fast," Hawk said. "I had the bird staying close, doing sweeps through the other buildings."

"Anything?"

"No, we're the only living things on the airfield from what I can see," Hawk explained. "But when I widened the search I ran into that."

"Wonderful," Mara said.

"We're back. Want us to gear up?" Jingo asked.

"Negative," Mara replied. "Let's go to ground and hope this thing, whatever it is, passes us by."

It was a big risk, but she wasn't looking for a fight. Not so soon, and not against something so huge. They had set up surveillance cameras on either side of the tower, and another right on top near where Ninja was on guard duty. She called him back inside, and they waited to see to what the huge thermal bloom was that was headed their way.

CHAPTER 9

NIGHTS ON VODEX WERE SHORT, barely seven hours. After Mitch got cleaned up from his run, Uri and her team had a feast waiting for him. He ate and slept, and was up with the sun ready for another day with the Order of Scion.

Doss met him at the main doors of the academy. He was calm, and welcoming.

"Good morning, acolyte. Are you ready for your first full day of training?"

"I am," Mitch said.

"Very good, we begin with the simplest of tasks."

He led the way through the grand lobby, past the other members of the Order and the various students. Mitch was the only human. The other aliens varied in appearance, from humanoid to slightly horrific. There were rarely two of the same species, although the members of the Order wore the same billowy robes that gave them a sense of similarity, at least to Mitch's mind. There were moments when he felt extremely lonely. Not that he was ever alone. Qwii seemed to be always available and had dined with Mitch the night before. Uri and her crew were around as well.

Having made contact with them, the ship's stewards didn't try to hide from his sight. While Mitch slept, they washed his clothing and had everything ready for him by morning. Still, he felt a little out of place. There was nothing overtly alien about Vodex or the academy, but Mitch was new, and hadn't yet fully bought into the ideas that were being espoused.

Back in the training room, Doss had Mitch sit on the floor, cross-legged, while the instructor held up a feather.

"Please observe this delicate feather," Doss said as he held it up over his head and dropped it.

The feather floated down toward the floor, just as it would have done on Earth. Mitch watched it fall. There was a grace to it, the feather rocked back and forth, flipping over a time or two, before settling easily onto the floor, which Mitch decided was solid stone, highly polished, and very clean.

"I want you to try to feel it," Doss said. "Feel the mass of the feather. Even something so delicate and light has a place in the Creator's power."

It took several tries to really get a sense of the feather. Doss raised it and dropped it over and over. He could feel the movement, but it took time to feel the feather's shape, but eventually he could sense every part of it, even the wispy tendrils.

"You have it?" Doss asked, holding the feather over his head.

"Yes," Mitch said, his eyes closed, his attention focused on the feather.

"Good," Doss said. "I want you to press it down. Crush the feather, make it weigh a hundred pounds."

"O—kay ..." Mitch said.

"You can feel the gravity waves," Doss said. "Call them together in your mind. Attach them to the feather. Increase the connectivity of those waves around the feather. It's not as difficult as it sounds. The Power obeys your will. It's all there, all available, just channel it onto the feather."

Mitch failed in his first attempt. Not that he didn't affect the feather as it fell, but he didn't crush it.

"This is an essential task for a Scion Warrior. You must feel everything, and control everything. Every bullet fired at you must be stopped. Every laser bent. And it's all within your grasp. Take control of the power. Own it. Make it part of you."

On the second attempt, Mitch crushed the feather. It wasn't easy, but he made the connection. The feather didn't just fall, it dropped like a stone.

The lesson took half a day. Afterward, Bess took him up on a trail that wound around behind the academy building. They sat on a flat rock and Mitch practiced connecting to the gravity waves until he could feel the other members of the Order in the yard below, and the movement of the trees on the hillside in the soft breeze. Mitch even connected with the tiny insects buzzing round the wildflowers and through the swaying grass.

By evening he was mentally exhausted. The training was not physically arduous, but mentally it took a toll. For all the increase in his physical size, it was his mental strength that needed to increase. He needed to increase his awareness to include the gravity waves he was constantly surrounded by. That evening he took another long run, and slept a full four hours before going at it again. The next day Doss came to him on the ship. They flew up into orbit around the planet. Whoever said that gravity is empty space had no idea of the reality. On the surface of the planet, everything was pulled down toward the enormous mass of the vibrant world. But in space, beyond the pull of Vodex, gravity was everywhere, the ebbs and flows had no order, it was like being caught in a raging white water rapid. He was pushed and pulled in a chaotic fashion, but there was nothing competing with the gravity to hold his attention. The ship was an oasis around him, and Mitch could feel Qwii's strong control of the gravity waves.

For a week he practiced adding weight to objects. By the end of that week, he was gaining a mastery of the practice, and Doss introduced a new idea. He met Mitch with a stone in hand.

"Remove the gravity from the rock," Doss said. "Free it from the bonds holding it down."

It took time. It was as if he had spent all his time building his biceps, only to discover that his triceps were weak. Freeing the bonds of gravity was actually more difficult. Even the slightest gain of weight on the feather had been noticeable, but unless Mitch removed all the gravity from the stone, it wouldn't move.

Hours bled away. Mitch was so engrossed in the training he hardly noticed. Day after day he was getting stronger, and capable of doing more. At the end of the second week his combat training began. And where he struggled with mastering the basics of controlling gravity, he excelled in fighting. His body was eager for a challenge. Even his opponents, using gravity as a weapon, had trouble subduing Mitch. He was fast, agile, and exceptionally strong. And as he learned to use the lessons he was being taught in the mornings to enhance his combat skills; he quickly became unstoppable. Even the most experienced members of the training staff struggled when sparring with Mitch.

At the beginning of the third week Doss brought in a new object for their training. He held out a small silvery lump of metal.

"Do you know what this is?" Doss asked.

Mitch shook his head. He knew it was lightweight, he could sense that much. But at a glance he had no idea what it was.

"This is solid hydrogen," Doss said. "I've studied your race's scientific knowledge in this area. Are you familiar with the Periodic Table?"

"Familiar yes," Mitch said. "I never took chemistry in school though."

"Essentially, it is a list of all the elements known to your race."

"There are more?" Mitch asked with a smile.

"Indeed, but that is a study for another time. Our focus today is on what your scientists call atomic mass. They created your periodic table of elements around the mass weight of one atom of a given substance. Hydrogen, for example, has an atomic mass of one. I'm generalizing here, but essentially, hydrogen has one proton or neutron, whereas other elements have more. Some of them, much, much more. I want you to feel the object, Mitch. The metal hydrogen has a gravitational weight to it. You will get to know each element by the way gravity waves naturally adhere to them."

Mitch could feel the lump of metal. It was incredibly light, and in some ways that made it almost invisible. The gravity waves were hardly even drawn to it. Levitating the object would be simple, and adding weight would be more difficult. Mitch was still pondering the lump of metal hydrogen when Doss pulled out another nugget of metal.

"Can feel this one?" he asked.

"Yes," Mitch said immediately.

The lump of metal was exactly the same size as the hydrogen, only it had much more presence in the gravity waves.

"What is it?" Mitch asked.

"Gold," Doss said. "Pure gold. It feels different, yes?"

"Very different. It practically shines."

"Indeed. And it has a unique presence within the Power that can be identified."

They spent the entire morning going through the most common elements in nature. The next day they went back up into space where Mitch was tasked with feeling the various elements in the system star, and then in the atmosphere of several of the gas giants. It wasn't something he could do from memory alone. Discerning the differences between the various elements was possible, identifying them from feel alone was more difficult. His training progressed, and soon Mitch was becoming adept at controlling the gravity waves around him.

"You have proven to be one of my finest students," Doss told him at the end of the first month of training. "There are only two tests remaining. First, you must fly Qwii's ship into orbit and keep it there for twelve hours."

Mitch felt a tremor of fear. It wasn't just a test; it was a matter of life and death. The crescent-shaped ship was little more than a huge structure with big openings at various places that served as windows. Lifting something so large was difficult enough, but holding it firm in a bubble of gravity in the hard vacuum of space would be even harder. If he failed, even for a second, the results would be catastrophic.

"You've spent time, entire days, immersed in the Power," Doss said. "But you must learn to live with it. To be comfortable with controlling it even when you are doing other things."

"And the second test?"

"We will discuss that when you are ready," Doss said.

Mitch didn't feel ready. He felt strong, and capable, but not all that confident yet. What really worried him was keeping up the level of control it would take to protect the ship and everyone inside it for twelve straight hours.

"How do you do it?" Mitch asked Qwii that evening.

"It is second nature to me," Qwii said. "Even when I'm sleeping, part of my mind is functioning to hold everything in place. Eventually, you will feel it too. It will become like breathing, not completely involuntary, but something that is rooted deep within you."

"I hope so," Mitch said.

The next morning Doss met Mitch with Qwii outside the ship. He seemed excited, but Mitch felt stressed. He had never really struggled with testing. In college he learned quickly how to prepare for exams, but no test he ever took had life or death consequences."

"Are you ready?" Doss asked.

"I'm ready," Mitch said.

"Good. Let us begin."

"Wait," Mitch said. "What about the crew?"

Doss and Qwii both looked at Mitch with questions in their eyes.

"Shouldn't they disembark?" Mitch said. "What if I fail? They could be killed?"

"Then don't fail," Qwii said, walking back onto the ship.

"Good advice," Doss said, following the Nagani on board.

Mitch watched them for a moment, realizing he would have all their lives in his hands. It wasn't something he was looking forward to. Their presence would only add more pressure to an already high-pressure situation. But he had no option. It was time for the test, and it was pass or fail, with failure being death. Mitch didn't want to die. He didn't even want to damage his friend's ship. Qwii had become a good companion. The Nagani was always available to Mitch, and always quick to listen. He gave good advice too, and was always encouraging.

Thinking back to when he had first made the decision to join the CMC on what was the absolute worst day of his life, he realized that so much had changed. When he signed on for the LE Protocol, he didn't care if he lived or died. But that had changed. Mitch wanted to live. What's more, he wanted to return to the CMC, to his friends in Leo Squad. He wanted to share his new abilities, and the hope that came with them. There was so much he wanted to do, but first he had to pass the test. And he didn't have to wonder what the Order of Scion would do if he failed. In that case, he wouldn't live long enough to find out.

CHAPTER 10

IT WAS A GRUMBLER. Mara had heard of them, and seen video of the giant aliens, but hadn't seen one in person.

"Look at the size of it," Flash said.

"Never thought I would ever feel small again," Jingo said.

"That thing is bigger than a dinosaur," Ninja said.

They had heard the Grumbler's footsteps before they saw it. The huge alien crunched through the forest south of the airfield. Even with the dust and debris in the air, they saw him from several hundred meters away, and heard the reason why his race was called Grumblers.

"Is it talking?" Flash said.

"Sounds like it," Jingo replied. "Can't make out what it's saying though."

"It's just mumbling," Mara said. "Even if it's saying words, we wouldn't understand its language."

"That's why she's in charge," Ninja said. "She's a thinker."

The ground shook with each step the Grumbler took. They had weapons trained on the alien, but didn't need them. It stepped on one of the hangars, destroying what was left of the building and anything inside. The sound was deafening. The alien was forty feet tall, with a humped back, stooped shoulders, and long arms that hung nearly to the ground. Its legs were shorter than Mara expected, but the feet were long and wide, almost like duck feet rather than human. It carried a long, curved sickle in one hand, but no visible guns or other weapons. A patchwork bag hung from one shoulder, and a thick fabric cap was pulled low over its eyes.

"It's used to looking down," Hawk pointed out.

"Just keep going," Mara urged the giant alien.

And it did keep going. It missed the airport building, and trudged on toward Alpha Colony.

"Man, that thing's going make a mess of town," Flash said.

"Follow it," she ordered him. "Don't get too close. Record what you can, but don't get too close to town. I don't want the Lymies knowing we're out here."

"Roger that," Flash said.

"Jingo, you're back on battery retrieval. Take Ninja with you."

"You don't want me back on top?" Ninja asked.

"We have cameras up," Mara said. "Until this dust clears, we can't see enough to make it worth having someone up there. Contacting the fleet is more important."

Mara and Hawk set up the control room. There were some chairs that weren't bolted down to sit in. The communications gear and surveillance controls were set on top of the empty crates the equipment came in. They had two ninety-six-hour, rechargeable battery generators that were beefy enough to run all the equipment they had carted down from the *Marathon*. But that was only enough to keep them in power for a week. If they couldn't salvage more supplies from the airfield, they would be forced to make runs into the colony. And despite the bombardment, which had surely caused damage in the colony, Mara feared the presence of more Lymies. Not that Leo Squad couldn't fight the spidery aliens, but she didn't want to. They had limited supplies, including just two crates of ammunition. They would need more if their mission stretched from weeks to months. But only time would tell, and their first priority was getting word back to the fleet.

"I've more power," Jingo announced. "A few rechargeable power cells at least. It's all in good shape. We just have to move them."

"Good, let's get them over here," Mara said. "We'll worry about getting solar panels to recharge our generators later."

It took two hours to splice the large radio antenna and signal booster to the portable system they brought. But once their system was connected, and boosted via the tower's battery generators, they managed to get a signal through the dust cloud and into orbit.

"What's your status, Leo Squad?" a voice from space asked.

"We are secure at the airfield, *Marathon*," Mara replied. "Visibility is extremely low. And there is hostile traffic in the area. A Grumbler is headed toward Alpha Colony. We are staying out of sight and recording as much as possible."

"Signal strength is minimal, Leo Squad," the voice replied. "Save everything you get. Weather patterns should help clear the air in a few days."

"Roger that," Mara said. "We are proceeding to search the airport building. Leo Squad out."

"Time for some fun?" Ninja asked.

"I suppose so," Mara said. "Hawk, you remain here and keep an eye on things."

"The drone has six hours of power left. That should be enough time to check out the airport."

"And keep a line open for Flash," Jingo said.

"As soon as you hear from him, report everything to the *Marathon*," Mara said.

"Will do," Hawk said, settling her body into one of the reclaimed desk chairs.

"You boys ready?" Mara asked.

"Born ready," Jingo said.

"Always," Ninja added.

"All right, be prepared for anything. There could still be aliens in that building."

The airport was divided into two sections. The passenger lounge/concourse was much larger than the austere baggage area. But the passenger section was down to bent support beams and debris. Nothing was intact. Fires had burned and explosions from grenades had destroyed it all. The baggage area, on the other hand, was still intact. It was a large room with concrete walls, big conveyor belts, and a few small rooms made of painted cinder blocks. The team searched them all.

"This was clearly a break room," Ninja said. "There's still snacks in the vending machines."

"Now, we're talking," Jingo said. "Let me at 'em."

"There's some furniture too," Ninja continued. "Nothing's in great shape, but we could base our operations here. There's a bathroom and plenty of space for storage."

"What's in the other room?"

"It's a maintenance room, some tools, mostly cleaning supplies," Mara said. "Let's check the stairs."

A metal staircase lined one wall and led up to the roof. The section over the main concourse was unstable or missing completely, but the roof over the baggage area was still strong.

"It'll take some time," Jingo said. "But we could move what we need from the control tower up here. It's more stable."

"Safer too," Mara said.

"Can't argue with that," Ninja said.

"All right, we've got a plan," Mara said, before leading her companions back to the fallen control tower.

"What do we do now?" Jingo said.

"We hunker down and wait for the storm to pass," Mara said. "Once the dust clears, we'll see about moving what we need from the tower."

Everything in the airfield was quiet. The only things that moved were the swirling clouds of dust. Flash kept tabs on the

Grumbler, which made a straight line for the colony. The giant alien smashed his way across the city, destroying buildings and anything that was in his path. Flash saw Lymies too. Dozens of them tried to stop the giant, but it was a waste of effort and life. The Grumbler stomped on the Lymies, or cut them down with his sickle. The giant wasn't fast, but he was extremely powerful. The spidery Lymies leaped onto the Grumbler, trying to stab through his thick skin with their stingers. A few may have even succeeded, but either their toxin wasn't strong enough, or it simply had no effect on the giant alien. He crushed some of the Lymies with his bare hands, and flung several away, sending them sprawling down the streets to crash into buildings. The big alien even ate a few of them. Flash didn't think the alien enjoyed the Lymies, but he devoured them anyway.

The Grumbler tore straight through what remained of the city. The outer edges had taken damage from the bombing. The shock-waves from the orbital, kinetic strike had ripped off rooftops, and knocked down several buildings and structures. But the outer edges of the town took the brunt of that damage, and left the central interior intact. The Grumbler stumbled and stomped his way straight through it all. It knocked down the tallest buildings, and left a wake of destruction that was hard to believe.

Leo Squad couldn't send the video up to the *Marathon* until the storm cleared and their signal strength improved, but the rest of the squad watched the video that Flash had recorded on one of the monitors they had set up inside the wrecked command center of the flight control tower.

"It's unbelievably strong," Jingo said.

"The Lymies can't stop it," Ninja said.

"How many are left in the town, do you think?" Mara asked Flash.

"Hard to say. They were holed up in the buildings before the Grumbler came along. Could be a lot more, but they've taken a beating."

"We killed a bunch before we left the first time," Hawk pointed out.

"I think the LT killed even more," Flash said. "I didn't go into the city, but I got close enough to get eyes on Alpha Base. There were dozens of dead aliens all around it."

"He would have had to get resupplies," Mara said. "The base would have been an ideal place to get what he needed."

"We'll have to do the same thing," Jingo insisted. "I hope there's something left. Did you see any Lymies in there?"

"None that were alive," Flash said.

"We killed some, Lieutenant Murphy killed more," Mara said. "And any that were exposed when the bombs hit were probably killed by the shockwave. There's plenty of evidence of that right here in the airfield."

"So, unless they had reinforcements ..." Ninja said.

"They won't be at full strength," Jingo said. "We might be able to sneak in, get what we need, and get back out again."

"Can't hurt to try," Mara said.

"Unless we get killed doing it," Flash said with a chuckle.

"If it gets hot we'll pull back," Mara said. "We can move in slow, make sure we have plenty of cover fire if we have to make a run for it."

"The dust storm should make us less conspicuous," Flash said.

"Tomorrow," Mara said. "For now, we settle, secure our position, and get some rest."

Which was exactly what they did. Hawk landed the drone and got it recharging. Mara set a rotating watch. The others salvaged what they could from the tower, including some mattresses and furniture cushions. None of them needed a lot of sleep, but there wasn't much else to do. They took turns standing watch through the night, but it was impossible to see anything. Their battle helmets had low light amplification, but all they revealed once the sun set was the dust in the air. The surveillance videos were no better. But there was little to fear in the night. And when dawn came, they began formulating their plans.

The city was six kilometers away from the airfield, and the open ground would normally have made the squad of SSO commandos vulnerable. But the first thing they did was launch the surveillance drone. The dust in the air was too thick for normal visuals, so they relied on thermal. There was nothing between the airfield and the colony proper. And a quick circuit over the city showed only a handful of Lymies.

"Any chance they could be blocking our scans?" Jingo asked. "They have some kind of signal jamming effect, right?"

"That's true," Hawk replied. "But I don't think there are enough of them left to block us."

"Where are they hiding?" Mara asked.

"Mainly the business district," Hawk said. "And the school."

"None on Alpha Base?" Flash asked.

"No," Hawk explained. "Unless they hear you or have some type of way to sense movement, you should be able to get in and out easily."

"We have to try then," Mara said.

She led the team to the city. They ran the six kilometers in under ten minutes, then took up positions near what was left of the outer ring of buildings.

"I still don't see anything," Hawk said. "Thermal imaging is clear."

"There could be traps," Mara said. "Just because the enemy isn't close doesn't mean this will be a cakewalk."

But that's exactly what it turned out to be. Leo Squad salvaged two armored transports and filled one with weapons and ammo, the other with food. There was no sign of the Lymies, and they left the city on the transports without incident.

"We could probably reclaim the city," Jingo said. "It might be messy, but we could sweep through and take out the Lymies hiding there."

"That's not the mission," Mara said. "Besides, once we took the city we couldn't defend it. We'd need a regiment of Marines to do that, and from what I saw, there wasn't much of value left."

There wasn't room in the ruins of the control tower for all the gear and food they had salvaged. They stored all the munitions in the old maintenance room of the airport baggage area, and organized the military rations in the break room. All the communications equipment was moved over, including several components from what had been the roof of the flight control tower. They mounted the big antenna onto the roof right beside the entrance to the stairs, along with the signal booster and the big parabolic receiver dish. Next, they moved whatever comforts they could from the tower to the airport. Mattresses, furniture, tables, and chairs were all moved. The transports were low on power and without major charging capabilities. They were parked in front of the baggage loading doors, making the structure a little more secure.

Over the next several days they made improvements. Wind turbines were salvaged from the colony and mounted on the airport roof. They produced enough electricity to keep the communications gear functioning, but not enough to power the transports. Surveillance cameras were set up around the airfield and on the roof of the baggage area. A few were even taken out to keep visual tabs on the city, but the signal was weak and the dust storm made them ineffectual.

The weather prediction turned out to be true. On the fourth night a storm rolled in. The dust was pounded with heavy rains. And when the sun rose on their fifth day on New Terra, the air was much clearer. A yellow pall of smog still tainted the sky, but they could see for several kilometers in every direction. The surveillance drone could use regular video, and the signal back up into orbit was strong enough that everything the group had recorded could be sent to the *Marathon*.

"It's a good thing we moved," Jingo told Mara, as they gazed out at the control tower. "Everything is flooded."

It wasn't a major flood, but there was standing water around the fallen watch tower. The airfield looked more like an abandoned junkyard, only instead of derelict vehicles, there were carcasses of dead aliens. The squad set to work moving them to the far end of the airstrip. The spidery bodies weren't all that heavy, and could be dragged away. The only signs of life were the vermin that were feasting on the dead.

Ten days in they got their first assignment. Leo squad was being sent to Bravo Colony. They geared up with weapons and drones. Hiking the fifty kilometers to Bravo Colony could have been done in about fourteen hours. Even with their weapons and supply packs, the physically enhanced Marines could have made the long hike in a single day. But Jingo found a baggage cart. It was electric, but ran on wheels. The vehicle's battery was not nearly as robust as those that powered the armored transports. Hawk managed to get it fully charged using the wind turbines, and the group set out on a road trip to Bravo Colony.

There was a road, although it wasn't paved or maintained. It was little more than a track across the open grasslands between the colonies, but it was reassuring, nonetheless. The baggage cart was most efficient at just over twenty kilometers an hour. And a little over an hour into the trip, they came to the impact crater from the kinetic bomb dropped from orbit.

"Would you look at that," Flash said.

"Fifty tons of tungsten steel ain't no joke," Jingo agreed.

"That's gotta be what?" Ninja asked. "Two kilometers in diameter?"

"Looks about right," Hawk said.

"And no sign of the steel rod," Flash said. "It must have been completely destroyed on impact."

"Go around it," Mara said. "I don't want to get stuck."

More rainstorms had followed the first. The ground wasn't muddy, but it was soft, and there was standing water in the center of the crater. They went around it, and kept going. An hour later, Bravo Colony came into view.

"They aren't kidding around," Ninja said.

"What is that?" Jingo asked.

Hawk had her long-range optical scope on her LRRG rifle. She was looking through it.

"They're covering it with webbing," she said. "There's hundreds of them."

They could see movement even from ten kilometers away. The Lymies were moving on top of the webbing they had used to cover the city.

"Launch the drone," Mara said. "We'll stay here until we get a better understanding of what's going on."

"You think they're all like that?" Flash asked.

"The other colonies?" Jingo said.

Flash nodded. "Yeah, you think they've all been overrun?"

"Probably," Jingo said. "We didn't put up much of a fight anywhere but Alpha."

Bravo Colony was smaller than Alpha, but still a sizable settlement. The outer buildings showed some damage from the orbital bombardment, shattered windows, missing roofs, walls knocked down. But just like Alpha Colony, the interior of the city was intact, only Bravo was covered with silky webbing and crawling with Lymies.

The video from the surveillance drone showed the same thing. Several hundred aliens in the city, some nesting, others patrolling the webbing. Very few were on the ground, but there did seem to be some scouting units.

"What do you think they're looking for?" Hawk asked.

"Food," Mara said.

"You think they see us?" Jingo asked.

"We have to assume they do," Mara said. "And we have to start preparing for when they come."

"You saying they'll come for Alpha Colony?" Flash asked.

"Makes sense," Mara said. "They've got Bravo wrapped up tight. Tomorrow we'll check Charlie Colony, but my guess is it's the same."

And they have all the other cities under their control, why not Alpha?" Jingo said. "Hell, there's not even much in the way of resistance."

"Not much left worth taking though," Flash pointed out.

"It's about control," Mara said. "They're taking control of the planet, and they won't want to leave anything untouched that might suggest someone else has a claim here. Let's set up a surveillance camera and head back."

They made it home without incident. And the next day they made a similar trip, only in the opposite direction. The colonies were built along the planet's equator; what the scientists called the Warm Belt. After Alpha Colony was established, the colonists spread out to the east and west. Bravo Colony was built fifty klicks away to the east, and Charlie was built fifty kilometers to the west. Delta Colony was then constructed fifty kilometers east of Bravo, and Epsilon was fifty west of Charlie. By the time of the Lymie invasion there had been nine colonies in total, four on either side of Alpha. Charlie looked exactly the same as Bravo colony, a smaller city with damage to the perimeter structures and everything covered in webs. They weren't neat, geometric pattern webs like a spider on Earth would spin to catch prey. It was more of a rough covering over the city, the Lymie way of staking their claim.

"I'm glad we aren't being ordered in there," Flash said. "Even if the aliens were gone, cutting through that webbing would be creepy."

"Let's just hope they take their time marching against Alpha Colony," Jingo said. "That happens and we're screwed."

They all knew it was true. The airport, as sturdy as it was, couldn't hold back the Lymies who could scale the walls and drop in from above. Even with all the weapons and ammunition they had salvaged, there were just too few Marines to hold off the aliens if they decided to attack. The next several days were spent planning and preparing for the inevitable. An escape route into the forest was the only reasonable option. Food, weapons, ammunition, and survival supplies were cached inside the forest. The thick timber made good cover and the squad had plenty of mines and explosives for booby traps. The Grumbler had stomped a path through the thick forest, leaving an opening the Marines could use to quickly get deep into the woods before hiding themselves among the big trees.

Eventually they had to trek out and explore the alien ship. It had set down nearly thirty kilometers to the north, close to where the plains turned into swampland. They took the cart on wheels and reached the alien vessel in less than two hours.

Their first impression was that it looked like a castle. Perhaps it was the gloom of the low hanging storm clouds, or the eeriness of being all alone on a hostile planet, but the sight of the alien ship was creepy.

"Looks like it came right from Villains-R-Us," Jingo said.

"Doesn't look like it should fly at all," Ninja added.

"Let's find out," Mara said.

She put Flash and Hawk on guard duty, one by the cart, the other by the entrance to the strange ship. Mara led Ninja and Jingo right up to the side of the vessel. And the closer they got the more she agreed with Ninja. She had expected the hull to be some sort of fabricated material made to look like stone, but when they got close she realized she was wrong.

"It's actually made of stone blocks," Ninja said.

"That's impossible," Mara said, suddenly feeling numb all over.

"I'm no builder, but look at the stones," Jingo said. "They're all irregular shapes, but they're fit together perfectly."

"You couldn't get a hair between them," Ninja said. "No mortar either."

"It would have to be airtight to fly in space," Jingo said. "Maybe it's sealed on the inside."

The ship looked like a castle, or more accurately, like a medieval fortress. The base was square, but the two front corners were actually round towers that rose up higher than the others. The stone was dark blue, with traces of some lighter material streaked through it. It was constructed of huge blocks, but they weren't squared off. There were no regular shapes. Each stone was a multi-sided polygon, yet somehow they fit perfectly together. She ran a hand over the rough exterior, still not really believing what she was seeing.

"Make sure your helmets are recording this," Mara said. "Command will want to see it."

"We could chip off a bit of it," Ninja said, "maybe ... you know, to take a sample of it."

"Perhaps at some point," Mara said. "Right now, we don't have any means of testing it, or getting it to the fleet. Hawk, do you read us?"

"I've got you, Marauder," Hawk replied. There was static but she was understandable.

"We're going to check the perimeter of the ship. Any sign of trouble from our friends in the south?" she asked, referring to the Lymies in Alpha Colony.

"Negative, you're all clear," Hawk said.

"All right, gang, let's see what we can find," Mara said, leading the way around the alien vessel.

What they found didn't make sense. There were no exhaust ports, no engine mounts, or power systems that were visible from the outside. But there were windows with no glass, or coverings of any kind. Jingo boosted Mara up to look into the first window they came to. Inside was what looked like a sleeping chamber of some kind. There was a massive cushion in the middle of the room. It was covered with colorful blankets, and what appeared to be a wooden pole. The upper portion of the pole was bare of bark, and had deep scratch marks on it. There was even a table with a wide bowl and what appeared to be a jug of water.

"What do you see, Sarge?" Ninja asked as Jingo lowered her back down.

"It looks like a bedroom of some kind," she said.

"No window glass," Jingo said. "No shutters. Could you see how they seal it up?"

Mara shook her head. "It looks old and like some kind of house, not a ship."

They continued circling. The ship was strange, and when they reached the front they found a wide opening with no door.

"How is that possible?" Ninja said.

"It's not," Jingo said as he tapped on the stones around the opening. They were massive blocks. "This thing has to weigh hundreds of tons, maybe thousands. And there's no way it could stay together even if it could somehow fly into orbit."

"Captain Marcs said it did," Mara said. "He said it flew into the system, and landed here."

"Had to have come from somewhere," Ninja said. "It wasn't here before."

"Nothing about it makes sense," Jingo said.

"Maybe the answers are inside."

They went in and spent nearly five hours searching the ship. It was empty. Just a big structure, with strange furnishings, but no power plant, no life support systems, and no engines of any kind. There was no basement, no engineering spaces that they could find. When they stumbled out several hours later, they had more questions and no answers.

They returned to the airport and uploaded all their video to the *Marathon*. It was all they could do, and until Marine Corps researchers could come out and examine the ship, it was left abandoned. Weeks passed and Leo Squad fell into a routine.

"A month in and not much has changed," Estelle "Hawk" Flemming told Mara as they stood watching the sun rise on top of the airport's baggage area.

"It's getting colder," Mara pointed out.

"Is that a good thing?"

"Maybe the Lymies don't like the cold," she said. "A girl can hope."

"We've done all we can do," Hawk said. "The fleet should come and get us."

"We haven't found any survivors."

"Maybe there aren't any," she argued. "Maybe we're the only people left alive. And you know that sooner or later they'll decided to bomb the colonies again. All but Alpha I would think. The other colonies are already gone."

Mara shrugged. "You're probably right."

"And when that happens the survivors will turn toward Alpha Colony," Hawk continued. "Even if just fifty from each of those colonies comes here, it would be more than we could handle."

"Maybe so," Mara said. "But we're ready."

"It just seems like a waste. Why do we even care about this stupid world?"

"Thousands of colonists call it home," Mara pointed out. "If we leave the system, what do we do with all the refugees?"

"Not my problem," Hawk said. "It just seems stupid to risk my life for something I'm not even sure we want."

"We'll just have to wait and see," Mara told her. "I feel like things are changing."

"For better or worse?"

"Can't tell yet," Mara said. "But when it happens we'll know."

They looked out toward the forest. The other direction lay the city that had once been thriving, but had since the invasion fallen dark and derelict. Alpha Colony was a depressing sight. The forest seemed vibrant, alive, and completely unfazed by the destruction of the human towns. Mara couldn't help but wonder if the humans themselves were as resilient and hardy as the massive trees not far away. Only time would tell.

CHAPTER 11

MITCH HAD NEVER LIFTED anything as large as the crescent-shaped star ship. He had encapsulated many things, including himself, severing gravity's hold and letting them float freely. But the ship was massive. He could feel the mass of it, the thick waves of gravity holding it fast to the surface of the planet.

He settled himself in the observation deck, sitting on the floor, letting his senses pick up the waves of gravity around him. Once he had a good feel for the ship, he began to free it. Getting the big ship moving wasn't easy. Every last connecting wave had to be severed. The work wasn't hard, but it was like a chess match, his mind racing to see any and every contingency and possible outcome. He had been at the work for ten minutes before the ship moved. Doss and Qwii stood watching. Neither spoke out loud, but Mitch knew that Doss never did. He could communicate telepathically with Qwii, and for all Mitch knew, the white-furred Nagani could as well. He was aware of their presence but not distracted by it.

The ship began to slowly ascend. Mitch was content to go slow. It was a marathon, not a sprint, he reminded himself. He had identified the elements around him, not so much by name as by feel.

The ship was made of a singular substance, some type of crystal and he worked to keep the ship moving while also holding the air inside. The big opening at the end of the observation deck ensured that if Mitch failed in his task he would be sucked out into hard vacuum, where he would freeze to death before his brain had time to shut down from lack of oxygen.

But he didn't fail. The ship rose higher and higher, eventually breaking into orbit. Mitch could feel the bubble around the ship. He could feel the air pressure inside, and the complete lack of it outside. He could even sense the cold just beyond his protective measure. But holding the ship wasn't difficult. Not like he had expected it to be. It was a lot like holding something in his hand. He was aware of it all the time, and yet he didn't have to constantly think about not letting go. His mind had become strong enough to hold the bubble around the large ship, protecting it and controlling where it went. By removing the gravity on any side of the ship, the vessel moved in that direction. His task was to fly the ship, and that was what he did. He took the vessel out of orbit and into free space. He moved around, flying one direction then turning on a dime to move in another. And even the sudden change in direction had no effect on those inside the ship. They were held in place by the gravity he directed inside the bubble. It was both exhilarating and simultaneously empowering to have so much control.

As the day went on, they moved from the observation deck to the dining hall. Lunch was served, and Mitch ate while still controlling the ship. Eventually, Doss and Qwii retired to take naps. Mitch flew around the moons of Vodex and raced out to where the system star warmed the ship. When the day was over, Mitch was tired, but more from the stimulation of what he had discovered about himself than the work of flying and protecting the ship. When he landed, he found releasing the ship a little difficult to do. It took an act of will. His mind had become accustomed to holding and protecting the ship.

"You did well," Doss said. "Better than I had hoped."

"He is an excellent student," Qwii pointed out.

"It is a compliment to your race," Doss said. "But the task I have set for you tomorrow will be much more difficult. Meet me at the academy building at dawn."

"I'll be there," Mitch said.

Doss left and Mitch went for a run. Normally the exercise helped him to relax, but despite the run he continued to worry about the final test the next day.

"What can you tell me about it?" Mitch asked Qwii over dinner that night.

"Very little," the white furred alien replied. "You have great aptitude, and have moved quickly through your training."

"That's good though," Mitch said. "Isn't it?"

"It has left you with little practical experience I'm afraid. Most acolytes have twice the amount of time in training that you have put in. The final test will be difficult."

Mitch could hardly sleep. When he did manage to doze off, he had nightmares of failing his test. He didn't really know what would happen to him in that event. They couldn't just send him off and tell him to never use the Power they had helped him to develop. Not that the Power came from him. He had simply learned to tap into it. The Power was always there, and in his mind was probably the best argument for the Order's belief in a Creator. The power came from somewhere, and he had no other ideas of what the source might be.

The next morning, he skipped breakfast. He was too nervous to eat. He arrived at the academy just before sunrise and found Doss waiting there for him.

"This is your final test," Doss told him. "Should you pass it, you will be considered a warrior and given the chance to join the Order of Scion in an official capacity. But I must warn you, Mitch Murphy, this is not merely a test of ability. It is symbolic of your grasp of the Knowledge. You will be tested in many ways over the next several days. Before we begin, I have one final lesson for you."

Doss stepped back, and from some hidden fold of his robe he drew what looked like a long, serpentine dagger. The blade was made from dark black material. The guard was made of polished stone, and the handle was contoured wood. He handed the weapon to Mitch.

"Do you know what this is?"

"It's a dagger," Mitch said.

"It is a weapon of the Order. To become a warrior, you must fashion a weapon of your own from the depths of the great Tyrantus volcano."

He waved one arm toward the mountains and Mitch could see in the early morning light a plume of smoke rising from one of the peaks.

"It is a dangerous journey," Doss continued. "One cannot reach the summit without the Power, and the way is filled with obstacles. You will see things you do not expect, Mitch Murphy. The mountains are the home of the enemy's forces. You will not see them, but they are real. And they will do all in their power to stop you."

"What am I supposed to do?" Mitch asked, wondering if Doss was expecting him to kill something with the dagger.

"The Order of Scion is a protective fellowship. There are many dangers which we must face. I have little doubt that you are a being of great courage. Arq would not have selected you for training otherwise, but there are things in the mountains you have not imagined."

Doss took back the dagger. "This is made from Cidian. It is only found in the hottest part of the volcano, and never in its pure form. You must gather it, atom by atom, and bind it together using great force, molding and shaping it into the weapon you will carry as your badge of authority into contested systems. There is no time limit on this test. It should take you several days. Go into the mountains, retrieve and forge your weapon, then return. If you do, you will have passed the test. If you fail ..."

He didn't say Mitch would die, but it was implied. To flee from whatever horrors were waiting for him in the mountains would prove him to be a coward. He couldn't imagine anything keeping him from the task. The Power he had been taught to use was so incredible that Mitch was anxious for the challenge. If he came back without a weapon he would be helpless. The other members of the Order would mostly likely kill him. The alternative was to allow him to become an outcast with no accountability and absurdly great power.

"I won't fail," Mitch said.

Doss put a hand on Mitch's shoulder. "You have great potential. Good luck."

Bess appeared. The feline alien had a satchel woven from the same material as the billowing robes she wore. She handed the bag to Mitch.

"Food and water," she said. "Enough for three days if you are careful."

"Thank you," Mitch said.

"The journey there is perilous," Doss said. "The journey back is even more so. Hold fast to the Knowledge of the Creator, Mitch Murphy. It just might save you."

Mitch nodded, then set out at a slow jog. It felt good to be moving and burning off some of the nervous energy that had plagued him all night. The morning was cool, and Mitch enjoyed the climb. The trail was easy to follow, and for the first several hours he made good time. But once he crossed over the first mountain pass, the trees grew close together, and closer to the trail. Tall, dark trees,-shaped like evergreens, only they weren't green. The trunks were black, the needles a dark gray, and they cast shadows over the trail. The climb became steeper too, and by early afternoon there was no more trail. He crossed icy streams and trudged up the steep mountainside of the Tyrantus Volcano. It was the tallest and widest of all the surrounding mountains. A band of snow covered the upper third of the peak, except for the very top, where steam and smoke billowed up from the open cone.

Mitch's body was made for physical exertion. His lungs sucked in the cold, thin air, and his heart pumped the warm blood through his cold arms and legs. He was thankful for the combat boots and rugged fatigues he had been issued by the CMC, but he dreaded nightfall. Late in the day he came to the snow line, and for the first time he stopped to eat and drink. The meat consumed on Vodex was not an animal that Mitch was familiar with, but it provided a satisfying meat that was similar to shrimp in taste and texture. There was a small bag full of the meat nuggets, a few loaves of crusty bread, some soft cheese, and a thick bar of chocolate. There were also two canteens of water. Mitch sat on a rock and looked out over the mountains. There was a rugged beauty to the landscape. He had ascended to where no trees grew, and he had an unobstructed view. The academy was far below and to his right. Mitch could even see Qwii's crescent-shaped ship in the distance.

You should just leave and go back to your people.

The thought was not his own. It was as if he had heard someone else speaking, but there was no one else on the high mountain.

Look at those pathetic losers down there. They're not half the man you are.

Mitch didn't like what he was thinking. Judging people, especially those that were different, had always seemed wrong to him. Since being physically enhanced by the LE Protocol program, he found the temptation to look down on regular people was strong, but he always fought it. If he kept in mind who he had once been, and how helpless it felt to be overlooked, cheated on, and written off, it was easier to keep his new-found abilities in perspective. And since arriving on Vodex he had been awed by what the members of the Order were able to do. He could keep up with the best of them in combat, and had even learned to nullify their attacks using the gravity power, but they could do things he dared not attempt. So, it surprised him that such hateful, negative thoughts were suddenly popping into his brain.

You don't owe them anything. They're using you. They need you. But their backwards, bigoted beliefs will only hold you back.

Mitch shook his head, and glanced at the canteen of water. He wondered if it was laced with some sort of hallucinogen.

They sent you up here to die? Who does that? They must be evil.

"No," Mitch said, thinking of Doss, and Qwii, and Bess. They were his friends. They didn't want him to die.

If you go back to them, they'll kill you. They're waiting to kill you.

A shiver went through his body. Mitch looked at the setting sun and guessed he had maybe an hour of daylight left. The climb up the last third of the mountain would be the hardest, and the slowest. He decided to wait and rest before pushing on.

With the last of the daylight, he went back down into the tree line. He found a wide trunk on a relatively flat spot to lean against. His first task was cutting some soft, flexible boughs from some saplings. He piled them in front of the tree to sit on. They acted both as a way to soften the hard ground, but also as insulation to keep the cold from seeping up into his body during the night. After gathering an armload of fallen wood, he kindled a small fire using a ferro rod that he kept in his pocket. The trees blocked most of the cold wind, and as night fell so did the temperature. Mitch built up a little fire, and used some rocks to bank up behind the flames. It wasn't much, but it was enough to warm his hands and keep the worst of the cold night at bay. Sleep came in short bouts between adding more wood to his little blaze. The fire burned hot and fast, requiring more fuel about every hour, but Mitch didn't mind. He wasn't on the mountain to rest. And his enhanced body didn't need a lot of continuous sleep to renew his strength.

When dawn came, Mitch made sure the fire was out, then started up the mountain again. As soon as he reached the snow line the voice was back in his head. It seemed louder and angrier than the day before.

This is a ridiculous task. Why should you risk your life? You already have the skills to protect your people. The Order just wants to control you. They want you to do their dirty work. They're scared. You don't owe them anything.

Mitch knew that wasn't true. He had yet to meet any being that was a member of the Order of Scion who was afraid. They were patient and persistent, but not fearful. And he did feel like he owed them. Perhaps he could have learned all he had been taught over the last month on his own. But he knew he couldn't do it as fast. And without their instruction, he doubted he would have ever opened himself up and discovered his new senses.

The climb was more difficult than he expected. He was big and strong, but also heavy. His thick muscles required a lot of oxygen as he climbed the almost vertical mountainside. Only there wasn't much oxygen to sustain him. At one point he felt lightheaded, and nearly lost his grip on the mountain. But he knew what to do. It required concentration and mental effort to find a pocket of oxygen in the air below him. He used the Power to pull the oxygen together and formed a bubble around it, which he settled over his head. Instantly he felt stronger. He kept climbing, assisting himself with the Power whenever he could. Just going weightless wouldn't help him reach the summit. He had to direct his body, and move where the mountain allowed him to go. At one point he floated up a tall, sheer cliff face. At other times he just lightened himself so that the climbing was easier and he felt more secure.

Whenever he stopped to refill the air bubble with pure oxygen, or to rest his freezing arms and legs, he heard the voice in his head.

This is insanity. What are you doing up here? You're going to die. Turn back before it's too late.

But Mitch had no intention of turning back. He was only a few hundred feet from the summit. He pushed himself onward. And it wasn't long before he began to feel the heat from the cone of the volcano. The snow was melting beneath him, and the stones he was climbing over were wet. But they were also warm to the touch. He kept climbing, pushing himself higher and higher until, early in the afternoon, he reached the precipice. There was no oxygen in the air, and the heat coming from the volcano felt like a sauna.

Wonderful. What a beautiful place to die. No one will ever find you way up here.

Mitch considered climbing down into the cone, but it he feared it was too hot. The smoke was choking out any oxygen that might have settled inside the volcano. Mitch had to gather more from outside the mammoth of a mountain. And then he focused down into the depths of the volcano. It was dark, but he could make out the soft glow of molten rock down deep. He let his senses go down into the craggy opening, and was surprised at the number of competing gravitational forces. There were waves coming from every direction, pushing and pulling the interior of the volcano -- squeezing up the molten rock, and venting plumes of gas that were trapped beneath. There was a ton of pressure, and a sense that it was growing stronger every minute. Eventually, he knew, it would give and whatever lay below would come flooding up and out of the volcano. It was a dangerous place.

Those lying bastards sent you up here knowing how insane it was? What kind of sadistic person could do that? Why do you feel any kind of loyalty to the people who would throw your life away so easily? What you should do is go back, take Qwii's ship, and get what you deserve. With the power you possess, you could rule Earth. They need you. You would be so good at it. The endless debating and backstabbing would end if you were in charge. Think of how many people you could help! And if the aliens came into the system, you could stop them. You could destroy their ships and kill them all. It would send a message to the entire galaxy not to bother the humans. Why are you wasting time here?

Mitch settled onto a flat portion of the rocky precipice and searched the interior of the volcano for the mineral that Doss had shown him. He didn't resist the voice directly. It was making some interesting points. But he wanted a weapon like the other members of the Order carried. Mitch had seen them cut through logs of wood with the black blades. He had even seen them cut metal.

He focused his mind on the tiny bits of Cidian he could find. Doss hadn't lied. There was hardly any in one place, and it was all fused with other minerals and buried inside solid rock. Mitch had used the gravity waves to make things weightless, even himself at times. He had used it make things extremely heavy, stopping anything that was thrown at him. He could form a bubble that gave him air to breathe in the harsh hard vacuum of outer space, but breaking stone was a new task. It took Mitch a solid hour to break free the first small bit of Cidian. He had to use pressure, carefully applied to the surrounding rock right at its weak points. It was a bit like flint napping, only instead of using a tool to snap off flakes of stone, Mitch used the power of gravity. He increased it so much, and in such a focused way, that bits of stone began to fall down into the molten rock below. When a bit of Cidian was exposed, he broke it free, then quickly made it weightless so that it floated up to him. It took hours, but by dusk he had enough of the rare material.

He formed the raw bits of Cidian, which were like coal dust, into a solid shape. He chose a simple, slightly curved blade. It was three fingers wide, angled to a cutting edge on just the belly of the blade, with a short clip point at the tip. It looked like a Japanese Katana, only the Cidian wasn't smooth like steel. It was rough and uneven on the broadsides, but the cutting edge was perfectly aligned along the slightly curved sword's length. Mitch lowered it down into the volcano, getting as close to the molten rock as he dared, using the intense heat and all the gravity force he could manage, to compact the material in the blade. It transformed the separate atoms into a solid piece. He could feel the strength of the blade, the unyielding hardness. And the cutting edge was so fine that he could feel the individual molecules along the sharpened surface. It was dark by the time he finished. When he raised the blade out of the volcano it was smoking. He let it cool slowly, then took it in hand. There was no handle yet, no guard, just a bare blade, but it felt natural in his hand.

It was time to leave, but the climb down would be difficult, and made even more dangerous by the extremely sharp weapon he was carrying. Normally Mitch could do physical labor all day and not be over tired after fourteen to sixteen hours. His newly enhanced body from the super serum was capable of great strength and stamina. But forging his sword had taken a lot of concentration. His head wasn't hurting, but he could tell he was low on oxygen, and he needed to eat. Holding the sword with one hand, he carefully descended the mountain. The snow, as bitterly cold as it was, felt good to him at first. And the voice in his head had vanished the moment he took hold of the Cidian blade.

He felt a sense of pride at what he had accomplished. After moving down through the snow-covered hillside, he stopped at midnight. The climb down, even being extremely careful, was much faster than climbing up the mountain. And he had gotten out of the snow before stopping to eat just where the trees began to grow. Unfortunately, he was wet and cold. The food was dry in his mouth, the water burned his throat. He managed to gather some wood and start a fire, but it wasn't enough to dry his clothing. The night was miserable. He was exhausted, but couldn't stop shivering. When the sun finally came up he was already on the move. Not in an effort to cover a great distance, but simply to force his blood to pump and warm him from the inside out.

Eventually he found what he hoped for in the forest. A branch from a dead tree, long enough to make an excellent sheath for the sword. He stripped the bark away, and split the branch in a clearing where the sun shone bright and warm. He built a fire and melted globs of tree sap, which he mixed with ashes from the fire, to form an epoxy. After cutting a blade-shaped notch on the interior sides of the tree branch, he used the epoxy to carefully bind the two sides back together. He had to keep the glue from getting into the sword's slot. The work took nearly two hours, but he completed the scabbard. There was plenty of metal in the rocks on the mountainside. Mitch gathered enough titanium to forge a guard for the sword. The bright metal contrasted with the matte black blade. And a bit of animal horn that had been shed in the forest became the long, two-handed handle of the sword. He would add some finishing touches to it later, but the weapon was ready for action. And just in time, as he continued his descent and discovered he was not alone.

CHAPTER 12

MITCH HAD SEEN SO many aliens that the sight of something vastly different from a human no longer shocked him. The sight was of eight skeletal figures, each with a weapon of black Cidian, their heads looking like masks from a Día de los Muertos parade. They spoke, but in a language Mitch didn't understand. He realized he should have been afraid, but for some reason he wasn't. Fighting had become something he enjoyed. His size, strength, and speed allowed him to dominate most other species in close quarters. Mitch had been sparring for weeks by that point, and was ready for a real fight. Plus, he felt a bit like a kid with a new bicycle. All he wanted in that moment was to use his sword the way it was meant to be used.

"Looking for me?" Mitch said. "I'm right here."

One of the skeletons gave orders. It and two others held back, while the remaining five spread out.

Mitch had the high ground. He had just stepped into a clearing. There were trees behind him, a steep little ravine behind the skeletal aliens. They moved stiffly. As they got closer he could see their thin skin stretched tight over an almost human-shaped skeleton. He was nearly twice their height. The aliens had muscles, but they were thin and barely protruded from the bones that stuck out of their pale skin.

He wasn't afraid, but his mind kicked into tactical mode. He knew if he stayed put and allowed them to attack they would come at him from two sides at once. To even the odds he needed to attack first, but not in the open where they could circle around behind him.

"Come on then!" he shouted. "Come and get me!"

It didn't cross his mind to use the Power he had learned to wield from the Order of Scion. Not when he had a new sword in hand. He drew the weapon. It was well balanced and sturdy. The sword practically begged to cut something. Mitch turned and ran back up into the trees. It was a calculated move, one meant to evoke a certain response, which it did. The five aliens shouted in surprise, then rushed up the hill after him. Only Mitch hadn't gone far. He was just a few meters into the trees, waiting for the fastest alien to catch up. When it did, Mitch jumped out from behind a tree and swung his sword. He had no training, just natural instinct. It was enough.

The blade hardly slowed as it passed through the alien's neck and backbone. Mitch barely felt the impact, but he saw the skeleton head fly up into the air. The alien had a short sword, thicker than Arq's, but of a similar design. It dropped from its bony hand, and surprised Mitch when the Cidian flew apart. The hardened blade, which had surely started as dust the same way that Mitch's had, returned to powder as the weapon fell.

The alien behind the first thrust out with a spear on a long white pole. The blade had a hook on the back side. Mitch managed to deflect the thrust, but the alien expected as much. It twisted its spear, turning the hook around and catching Mitch's sword blade. The alien tugged down, but wasn't strong enough to rip the weapon from Mitch's grasp. He stepped forward, still uphill from the alien, and kicked out with a long leg. The ball of his foot, sheathed in the thick leather of his combat boot, smashed into the alien's face. It flew backward, bright green blood gushing from the holes where its nose should have been.

Mitch dipped the end of his blade down and let the spear slide off. It made a grinding sound, and another of the aliens was in range. The third skeletal creature had two long, delicate-looking blades. He had to get close to use them and the best he could manage was to dive at Mitch's foot. The Marine saw the tactic and raised his boot. The alien slashed at nothing but air, and Mitch shifted his weight, bringing it all down on the back of the alien's head. His boot slid off the bulbous skull and onto its neck. Mitch heard the bones snap, and out of the corner of his eye he saw the knives dissolve into dust.

The final pair of assailants were smarter than their companions. They both stopped out of reach of Mitch's sword and they spread out. One had a short, curved sword, the other had a fighting axe. Mitch stuck his toe under the edge of the spear at his feet and flicked upward. He caught the spear just behind the blade. It was heavy and clumsy, but he was strong. He spun the weapon around and hurled it toward the alien on his left, then jumped toward the one on his right. The alien on the left had the curved sword. It managed to swing the sword and bat the spear aside. Meanwhile, its companion was slashing and chopping at Mitch with its axe. It was the size of a hatchet, with a curved blade on one side, and a spike on the other. The alien was skilled with the weapon, but it didn't have the reach of Mitch's sword. He stepped back and stabbed down at the alien. The tip of the sword ripped into the skeletal alien's shoulder, severing bone and tendons before sticking. The creature wailed in pain, dropping its axe. Mitch pulled it close, then kicked the alien from the end of his sword. The creature flew backward and smashed into a tree before falling into the gnarly roots completely unconscious.

Turning, Mitch barely had time to avoid an arcing slash that would have cut open his stomach. He avoided the attack, but stumbled in the process. The alien, sensing weakness, rushed forward, sword held high, ready to chop down and end Mitch's life. But while Mitch wasn't trained with the sword, he was trained in combat. He lashed out with one boot and swept the alien's legs out from under it. The skeletal alien fell hard, and bounced down the hill, losing the grip on its weapon. Mitch rolled to his knees, grabbed the axe one of the aliens had dropped, then rose up to his feet in one fluid motion. The last three aliens were at the tree line. Mitch threw the axe. It flew end over end. An alien with a short spear never saw it coming. The axe buried itself in the chest of the alien, who dropped dead at the feet of its leader.

"Cra'tach lorr asta!" the leader shouted.

It had a sword as well, a one-handed, double-edged sword with a blade that tapered from the guard to the point. It pointed the sword at Mitch as it shouted orders. The other alien had two curved blades, each with a wooden handle. It carried one in each fist, like a deadly set of brass knuckles. The alien charged up the mountainside. Mitch took a step back and raised his sword. The alien continued running forward, straight at Mitch, who stabbed forward with his sword, point first. The thrust was aimed at the alien's thin chest. It made a simple blocking motion with one of its weapons. The blades met, clashing in a rough, grinding sound. But the alien didn't get Mitch's weapon completely deflected. Instead of impaling it in the chest, the sharpened blade cut a gash in the alien's neck. It took the charge out of the skeletal being and caused it to stagger backward as green blood gushed over its shoulder. It cried out in alarm, turning toward its leader, who snarled as it smashed in the side of its companion's head with a wicked chop of its sword.

"Just you and me now," Mitch said. "No one left to do your dirty work."

The alien screamed in rage and stepped closer. Unlike the others, it was skilled with its weapon. Mitch on the other hand, was not. The alien feinted one way, then lashed out with its sword.

Mitch managed to parry the slash, but it wasn't pretty and he was left off balance. The alien immediately followed with a thrust that should have split the flesh on Mitch's thigh, but he managed to spin away.

The alien didn't let up. It moved forward up the hill until it was even with Mitch, who was still coming out of his turn. The only thing that saved his life was a tree. The alien slashed, Mitch stumbled, but the sword caught on a tree trunk and halted the blade. Mitch recovered his balance just as the alien tugged the sword free. It wasn't until that moment that Mitch remembered he could do more than just slash and chop with his new sword. As the alien closed in on Mitch, it suddenly dropped to one knee, then onto its face. The alien was crying out, its arms and legs flailing. Mitch kicked the alien's sword hand. The weapon went spinning down the hill and he released the alien from the crushing gravitational pressure he had used to pin it to the ground. He could have killed the creature. They had attacked him after all, eight to one. No one would have blamed Mitch for defending himself however he could, but Mitch didn't feel right about using the gravitational wave power to kill.

He stood over the alien and put the blade against the alien's neck.

"Surrender," he said.

The alien looked up. There was a dim flicker of pure hatred in its eyes. Mitch stepped back, and waited to see what the alien would do. It rolled to its knees and grabbed a rock. Perhaps it wasn't planning to attack Mitch with the stone, but he couldn't imagine what else the alien would do with it. He flicked his sword down. It hit the rock, severing three of the alien's fingers. The rock fell, and the alien dropped backward into a sitting position. It stared dumbly as green blood pumped out of its severed fingers.

"All right then," Mitch said.

He turned his back on the alien. It was wounded, but still alive. Mitch let the gravity waves flow around him. He felt the trees, the slope of the mountain, the water flowing beneath the surface of the ground. And he felt the aliens. The leader was back on its feet, swaying, unsteady, but moving. Mitch didn't have to guess what the alien was doing. And he didn't have to turn around and look. He could feel the Cidian in the short spear that had dropped to the ground when its bearer took the axe in his chest. Mitch kept walking. He was back in the clearing. Perhaps he was taking an incredible risk, but he needed to test himself. He felt the alien behind steady itself against the trunk of a tree. He felt the spear go back, then flash forward as it was hurled toward him. Mitch caught the spear in mid-air. Not with his hands, but with his control of the gravity around the weapon. He severed the gravity bonds and sent it flying up into the sky. It whisked harmlessly over his head. Mitch turned around, saw the look of fury on the alien's face. It was already a hideous visage, but twisted in pain and contorted in fury, it looked like a nightmare. Mitch used his power to lift the alien's own sword into the air, then sent it rushing toward the enraged being. The tip punched through its back, slicing and cutting as it drove forward under the pull of gravity. The alien arched its back, grunting in pain, then toppled forward. The sword in its back fell to dust, and a breeze made the trees sway.

The fight was over, and Mitch felt happy to be alive. But it wasn't the same battle rage he had experienced fighting the Lymies on New Terra. He had no hatred in him for the skeletal aliens. He didn't even know what they were or why they had attacked him. Still, he didn't regret having fought or killed them. Ultimately it was self-defense. Perhaps he had wanted to fight, to test himself, to try out his new sword, but that didn't mean he went looking for violence. Still, there was a sense of futility that settled over him. Killing seemed wasteful to Mitch. He wiped the green blood from his black Cidian blade on the grass, then continued his trek down the mountain.

CHAPTER 13

GENERAL STANLEY MERCER was waiting in the *Marathon's* teleconferencing room. The battleship had returned to the wormhole that linked the Terra System to the Sol system. Resupply ships had taken the colonists and regular Marines off the battleship, and resupplied them with everything needed to continue monitoring the planet. It had been over four weeks since the sudden attack that led to the evacuation of the planet, and the senior officials were anxious to re-establish control of the planet.

"We're all here," Admiral Darcy Wilcox said as she entered the room. "Send word that we're ready."

"Already done, Admiral," the communications officer said. "The link is established. There will be some lag from Sol, but not too much."

"Very well," Admiral Darcy Wilcox said. "You are dismissed."

No one but senior staff was staying for the teleconference. That included General Mercer and his second in command, Lieutenant Colonel Jerome Banks. On the fleet side was Admiral Wilcox and the ship's Commander Michael Hughes. Across the small table two holograms appeared. Each one was a glowing face of a person linked in for the meeting. Commander-In-Chief of Space Force and the Colonial Marines was Fleet Admiral Alexander Nance, and the officer in charge of the Terra System Defense was General Hinto Wan.

"We're ready to begin," Admiral Wilcox said. "Welcome to the S.F. *Marathon* Admiral Nance, General Wan."

It took nearly a minute for the reply.

"Good to see you, Darcy," Admiral Nance said. "You've done fine work this last month. I won't beat around the bush though. We want New Terra back. I want to hear your opinion, and yours too, General Mercer, on the best way to accomplish that."

Mercer looked at Admiral Wilcox who nodded. Then he began to speak.

"As you both know we have a team on the ground," Mercer said. "There isn't much left of Alpha Colony, and the others are completely overrun. But we've been observing as best we can. Surveillance drones over the cities, and eyes on the ground. We even have thermal imaging of the aliens in our colonies. What we're not seeing is reinforcement of any kind. My xeno-biologist Major Elaine Swift tells me that the Lymies on New Terra are warrior caste. We believe they took control of the colonies for two purposes. One, the readymade shelters, and two, the colonists are food for the aliens. We believe they were expecting more of their kind to arrive once we had been neutralized. But that has not happened. No one knows why exactly, only that all the alien ships in the system fled."

Admiral Darcy Wilcox spoke up. "We're the only vessels still in system. The *Zama* and the *Hastings* have set up surveillance satellites and radar beacons through the system. If anyone shows up we'll know about it instantly. We've also got satellites in orbit around the planet. More than we've had since New Terra was first discovered."

"All that to say," General Mercer continued, "we are in a prime position to take down the Lymies and re-establish human control of the planet. The system is ours; we only need the go-ahead to take down the enemy."

The wait for a response lasted nearly sixty seconds. The video from the *Marathon* was beamed through the wormhole, and across dozens of communication buoys at the speed of light. The response from Space Force headquarters in orbit around Saturn was exactly what General Mercer expected.

"We've crunched the numbers here," General Wan said. "I believe taking the initiative at this time is the right move."

"But the colonies are lost," Fleet Admiral Nance said. "We're starting over, is that correct?"

"Yes," Admiral Wilcox said. "The best strategy at this point is to bombard the colonies. The Lymies are concentrated there, and we can hit them from the air."

"We suggest using conventional munitions," General Mercer said. "The orbital kinetic bombs are the biggest bang for the buck, but they create a disturbance in the atmosphere that leaves us blind to what is happening on the ground."

"We'll start by landing the SSO squads led by Captain Frank Marcs," Admiral Wilcox continued. "Meanwhile, drone bombers can be programmed with targets and set up to run autonomously. They will hit all eight auxiliary colonies at once. That should minimize their numbers significantly. Our teams will be able to sweep them easily after that."

The teleconference room fell silent again as they waited for the reply.

"I don't like it," Fleet Admiral Nance said. "Those colonies represent trillions of dollars of investment and decades of work. I've studied the surveillance imagery and had the very best people in the system giving me advice, including some of the colonists themselves. Everyone is convinced that if we draw the enemy out and defeat them on open ground, we stand a very good chance of reclaiming all eight colonies. The Lymies have infested them, but they are still in good physical condition. Homes, factories, warehouses, that's worth saving. We should at least try to coax the enemy out of our towns. Then we bomb them and sweep them up with ground forces."

"It's a feasible plan," General Wan said. "We know the Lymies are aggressive. Let's kick the hornets nest and see what comes out."

General Mercer thought that was a stupid saying. Getting close enough to a hornet's nest to kick it, without knowing exactly what was in it, was dangerous. But Mercer knew what was in the colonies, namely hundreds of hostile aliens. Throughout history there had been decisive battles when entire armies met on the battlefield, or when small groups of high-ranking officials were caught unaware and slaughtered. Every general fantasized of leading an army into battle and being so completely victorious that the enemy was slaughtered and the course of history was changed. But Mercer didn't think the Lymies would leave the towns very easily, and if they did it would be to their advantage. By his estimates there was approximately twenty-five hundred aliens on New Terra. If they united it would take a lot of work to wipe them out. Even with drones and ground artillery, the aliens were fast and strong. They were effective at jamming signals, including drone controls. Without having pre-fixed targets that could be programmed into the drones so that they operated independently, there was little chance of success.

"You've got the best Marines ever trained," Fleet Admiral said. "Let's run a test. Have your squad on the ground hit one of the colonies. We'll see if that draws them out. And if so, we'll know how to proceed."

"That could be costly, sir," Mercer said. "Leo Squad is just a five-member team. They won't last long against a hundred Lymies. At least let me land the other SSO teams to back them up."

"Negative," came the reply. "I would think you could see the folly of that way of thinking, General. It's better to lose one squad and learn your enemy's tactics, than to risk the entire LE program. What happens if all the aliens mobilize before we're ready? Our forces would be overrun. Five Marines is an acceptable risk. The entire SSO program is not. Send one team, study the enemy, and let's draw up a plan of action guaranteed to end with us in control of the planet. Is that clear?"

"Absolutely," Admiral Wilcox said.

It took General Mercer a moment to reply, but in the end he nodded. "Yes sir," he said. He didn't like it, but not because he felt any kind of compassion or sympathy for Leo Squad. In fact, he would have gladly sacrificed their lives to get what he wanted. And what he wanted was a pristine record. Leo squad getting wiped out wouldn't necessarily equate to a failure on his part, but if the SSO program was going to rise in importance he needed victories, not defeats.

The holograms vanished, and Admiral Wilcox turned to General Mercer.

"I'll leave the details to you," she said. "We'll begin our run back to the planet immediately."

"Very good," General Mercer said. "I'll make sure the Fleet Admiral's orders are carried out."

Admiral Darcy Wilcox left with Commander Hughes in tow. Mercer turned to Colonel Banks.

"Start prepping the SSO teams. I want them ready for rapid deployment as soon as we're in orbit."

"Eight days," Jerome said.

"Yes. In eight days we go to war."

"It's a shame about Leo Squad," Banks added. "They've proven to be good operators, even without an officer on the ground."

"They're a means to an end, Colonel. They'll follow orders, I'm sure of it."

He didn't add the fact that it would almost certainly mean their deaths. General Mercer stood up and tugged at his uniform. Weeks on board the spaceship had led to some bad habits. He was eating more and exercising less. His stomach pressed against his shirt, which made the uniform ride up when he moved certain ways. He would have to rectify that issue. When he returned to the Sol system as a conquering hero, he wanted to look his best.

CHAPTER 14

MITCH DIDN'T GO FAR before the stranger appeared. It was an alien that stood at least as tall as Mitch, but on three legs and with a wide tail. The body was covered with a long coat, and it wore a hat over its head, shading the face. Mitch saw it standing and staring at him. The alien carried what looked like a rifle. It had a long, high pressure, gas tank for a stock, and no grip on the barrel. It looked more like a tool than a fighting weapon, but Mitch didn't take anything for granted.

When the stranger disappeared into the trees, Mitch hoped that it wouldn't bother him. But he kept his head on a swivel and picked up his pace. He also tried to expand his sensitivity to the gravitational waves. It was a simple matter to feel everything that was close to him. Anything with mass was acted on by the gravity waves. Any two bodies were drawn toward each other, even though the force was so weak that it was rarely felt, or had any effect. But Mitch needed to expand his awareness, stretching it out beyond what he could see. It wasn't second nature to him, and he remembered what Qwii had said. Excelling at his training was good, but it left him with a deficit of experience he had no way of filling.

An hour passed. Going down the big volcano was much faster and less taxing than going up, but he still had to be careful. There were slick places where the soil was loose or soft. With so many trees he couldn't always tell what the ground under his feet was doing. He had a Cidian sword, he had survived the climb into thin air at the peak of the volcano, and used his powers to get the materials he needed, but to pass the test he still had to get back to the academy in one piece. Doss had warned him the journey back would be more difficult than the journey up the volcano. So, he wasn't surprised when the stranger reappeared.

The alien looked civilized, but when it raised its wide tail over his head, Mitch felt certain the strange being was up to no good. Fortunately, Mitch had a good sense of everything around him. The stranger launched a barb from the end of its tail. The attack was unexpected, the stranger seemed relaxed and gave nothing of his intentions away, other than raising its tail. But Mitch felt the barb leave the tail. Time seemed to slow down and all it took was a simple command to increase the gravity between himself and the stranger. The barb flew halfway to Mitch, then plummeted suddenly to the ground. The stranger made no sign of disappointment, he simply slipped back into the trees. He had been directly in front of Mitch, and when Mitch continued on his way down the mountainside, there was no sign of the alien.

"Yeah, you better run," he said softly, but what he really wanted was a straight-up fight. Paranoia was plaguing the Marine. He didn't like having to worry that the stranger would appear when he least expected it.

Another half hour passed before Mitch noticed anything. And when he did, it wasn't the stranger he felt at the bottom of the ravine between the massive volcano and the chain of mountains around it. Instead, he felt several small but heavy creatures. They carried some type of weapons. Mitch could sense that much before he saw them. The weapons were made of different types of materials, each with a different weight to it. Mitch wasn't so well versed that he could identify elements simply by feel. He could focus in one thing that he wanted, and tell the difference between it and other things the way he had done in the cone of the volcano when he identified and drew out the Cidian. But to be able to say that something was made with a certain kind of metal, or contained a certain type of gas, was beyond him. Still, what he did know was useful.

He had two choices. He could go around the small creatures waiting to ambush him. But that probably wouldn't stop them, and he didn't like the idea of being pursued. The advantage of surprise had shifted to Mitch. He knew where they were, how many of them there were, and what they were planning. The only thing he didn't know was how. If they were carrying firearms or projectile weapons he could deal with that. But what if they were flame throwers or lasers? Could he protect himself faster than the speed of light? No, he knew better than to think he was that strong. Still, he could get a bubble of gravity going around him even before the group of aliens attacked, and hopefully that would be enough to keep him safe.

Which led to the other option. He could go right at them. Spring their trap, and take the fight to the aliens. That felt like a better option to him in that moment. As long as he wasn't overrun by the creatures, he felt confident he could survive. Mitch drew his sword. It made a unique sound coming out of the scabbard. It didn't hiss like steel; it was more of a dry whisper. Mitch thought it was even more menacing, a low, dangerous noise that few would recognize.

He started up into a narrow pass. It wasn't really a trail, but it was one of the few places that could be used to move up into the thick trees that grew a dozen meters up the hillside. It crossed Mitch's mind to use the gravity power on the short beings waiting to ambush him. That would be an acceptable way to combat an enemy, but Mitch felt the need to test his defenses. And he didn't have to wait long. He was halfway up the steep slope that led to the trees on the mountainside proper, when a pair of short aliens with laser rifles came rushing toward him. They were screaming. Their large, hairless heads had tiny eyes and big mouths filled with pointed teeth. Their ears were pointed, and their bodies were the size of children.

Mitch immediately increased the gravity around him. He could feel it pulling down so hard that the loose stones caught in the bubble shield were grinding against the rocky mountainside. The aliens didn't hold back. A flash of laser light hit the wall of gravity around Mitch. He was safe inside the bubble, and only had the gravity increased at the edges. To his surprise he saw the laser beams hit the invisible bubble and alter their trajectory. The aliens kept up a steady rate of fire, and more joined them. Some had projectile weapons. Small, pointed darts were stopped in midair and crushed to the ground before they could reach Mitch. Nothing could touch him.

It was a life-altering moment. He wasn't invincible, but he suddenly realized just how incredible the Power he had been taught to access really was. He could have stood before an army and they wouldn't have been able to shoot him. It was a heady realization, but it did nothing to stop the aliens. To do that, he had to alter the gravity around them. Suddenly, the short aliens with big heads started floating straight up into the air like they were helium balloons. They were screaming and chattering. Mitch couldn't understand a word they said. Their noises reminded him of the sounds troops of monkeys make when they're threatened. But he didn't need to understand their language to recognize the fear in their voices. They lifted straight up, nearly ten meters. Then he added gravity to each of them. They fell hard. Bones broke and the screaming abruptly stopped. Mitch didn't know if the aliens were alive or dead, but he knew they wouldn't be a threat to him any longer.

He continued his climb, keeping his senses ready, and expecting an even greater test. So far he had learned a lot about the

Power, and about himself. Mitch didn't like to kill, especially since his control over gravity made him so much more potent in a fight. The Order of Scion taught that the Creator gave them access to the Power in order to protect and restore. It was what they called the Knowledge, or their mandate. Those that rejected the Knowledge were considered Fray, not because they were hostile, but because they disrupted and tore down what they had the power to restore and build up. The lessons he had been taught seemed almost childish when he had been practicing in the academy, but out in the mountains everything was making a great deal of sense.

He pondered his place in the Order, and his responsibility to his own people, as he ascended the mountain ridge that was the last terrain obstacle between him and the academy. The stranger reappeared just as he was about to cross the saddle and regain the path that led back down to where he started the test. The stranger seemed to appear out of nowhere. One moment the path was clear, the next moment he was there, blocking Mitch's way back. He didn't say anything. The thick tail swayed behind the stranger, but didn't come up to shoot more barbs at him.

Suddenly, Mitch felt light. His hair extended out and his body began to rise up off the ground. He shifted his control over the power, feeling himself severed from gravity. It was like stepping outside into sub-arctic temperatures. One could go from feeling warm to suddenly shivering and wondering what happened to the heat that had only a second ago surrounded his entire body.

But Mitch wasn't in a blizzard. He was still in control and quickly brought the gravity back to bear on his body. His feet had gone only a few inches off the ground when they touched down again. To his right a tree snapped in half, the breaking sounded like a bolt of lightning, and the top half of a tall evergreen type of tree started to fall on Mitch. It would have crushed him under its stiff branches, but Mitch used the Power to pull the tree back behind him where it hit the ground and lay still.

"You'll have to do better than that," Mitch said.

"Rool gath," the stranger hissed. He also drew a sword of black Cidian. It looked like the oversized blades from a video game. It was long and straight, the blade nearly as wide from cutting edge to spine as Mitch's forearm. He couldn't believe the stranger could lift such an unwieldy sword, but he did. Mitch drew his own blade, but held it low.

"I have no wish to kill you," Mitch said.

Suddenly the sword in his hand felt like it weighed a hundred pounds. He had to push the stranger's gravity off his weapon. The three-legged alien moved forward, slowly at first, brandishing the huge sword. Mitch was a big man and knew how intimidating size could be. He also knew that in many people, size made a person slow and often less agile. The big sword was frightening, but Mitch knew there was only so much the stranger could do with it. The blade extended from a wide guard out nearly two meters. It was not the kind of weapon one used to fence with one's opponent. Mitch had no intention of trying to block the big weapon. He would rely on speed, agility, and movement to either stay out of reach, or dodge the big sword.

He tried his own power against the stranger. It felt odd to have the gravitational force he was commanding rebuffed. The Power which was so potent against other beings who couldn't control it, was nullified completely by something that could. It crossed Mitch's mind that if he had a gun he could just shoot the three-legged alien. But he realized that projectile weapons would be useless against an opponent with the Power. They would stop those projectiles the same way that Mitch had stopped the tree from crushing him. The only way to fight was to get close, hence the old-style weapons. And Cidian blades were stronger than steel, sharper, and lighter too. Mitch brought his up parallel with his upper body and held out to his right as he moved toward the stranger.

The big sword flashed up, the black Cidian didn't reflect the sunlight, but it made a stark contrast to the light of day. Mitch kept moving forward, knowing what was coming. As soon as he was in range of the big weapon, the stranger slashed down in a chop meant to cut him from shoulder to the opposite hip. But Mitch was faster than his opponent expected. He ducked to the side, felt the wind from the thick blade as it swished past him, then he countered with his own sword. He made a fast, flicking stroke that cut across the stranger's left forearm.

Another hiss. The alien staggered back, looking down at its arm. It sounded like an animal, its breath rumbling in its wide chest, as it hissed a warning. Dark blood welled to the surface of its arm. Mitch hadn't cut it deep. He might have been able to sever the arm above the wrist if he had swung his blade hard. But he was opting for speed and agility. To swing hard meant bracing his feet, and putting a lot of strength into the slash. It would have been slower, and had he missed he would have been left off balance. Instead, he just flicked his sword up at the stranger, letting the Cidian do the work.

"Borgah!" the stranger shouted as it hefted the big sword for another strike.

Mitch waited for it, then jumped back out of range. Then he feinted toward the alien. It staggered, trying to swing the big weapon back around to defend itself. The stranger would have fallen if not for its third leg. It lashed out with its wide tail, but it wasn't close enough to make contact with Mitch. The movement was intended to drive him backward and give the stranger the split second it needed to regain its balance. But Mitch could feel the trajectory of the stranger's thick tail. His awareness of the gravity waves, which were always moving around him, allowed Mitch to understand that the tail wouldn't hit him unless he moved into its path. Instead, he waited, the tail swished harmlessly past him, and he slashed at it with his sword in a one-handed strike that used the tail's movement to generate the cutting power. A long strip of flesh was severed along the side of the tail before the stranger even realized the danger. Instead of regaining its balance it staggered, shrieking in pain.

Mitch saw his opportunity to end the fight. All he had to do was step forward and thrust his sword into the stranger's neck. But he didn't want to kill the alien. He couldn't say why in that moment, only that it seemed wasteful. So, he hesitated for a second, and when the stranger whirled around, Mitch slashed at the stranger's right arm. The tip of his sword caught on the stranger's right arm, just below the elbow. Mitch felt a slight jerk as the sword severed tendons and even bone. The big sword fell out of the stranger's hands and it scurried backward. Its right arm hung down, too damaged to use. The look on the alien's face was pure fear. Mitch could have chased him down and run him through, but he just stood still, waiting and keeping his mind open to the gravity waves around him.

He felt the portal open. There was no other way for Mitch to describe it. Gravity suddenly disappeared in an oval space beside the stranger. Mitch couldn't see the portal, but he could feel it. There was a void in the air just beside the alien, who stepped into the void. For a moment Mitch wasn't sure he was really seeing what happened. The stranger simply vanished, and a split-second after stepping through the portal, it closed. Gravity returned to the space and everything was quiet. Mitch turned around in a full circle. There was nothing else there, nothing he could see or feel other than the trees and the mountain. He looked down at the big Cidian sword. There was blood on the ground too. He hadn't imagined the fight. It wasn't a hallucination, or a simulation. The stranger was real, but it was a being so vastly different from Mitch that he could hardly understand what happened.

"Another dimension maybe," he said out loud, as he bent down over the huge sword. It was starting to break down into dust, like the others had done. Mitch could feel the particles breaking apart.

Mitch focused his attention on the Cidian. He used his power to hold it together. It was like sweeping up tiny bits of Styrofoam.

He had to be gentle to keep it from sending the Cidian dust flying away. The work wasn't easy and took all his concentration, but he was grateful for that. Doing something so focused grounded him in a moment when he felt untethered from reality. After combining the Cidian into a block he increased the gravity exponentially. He didn't have the heat of the volcano to help him weld the material into shape, but the more gravity he applied, the more pressure was compounded on the block. He could feel the material bonding on an atomic level. He took his time, making sure he didn't lose any of the precious material. He had no idea what he would do with it, but he knew it was a valuable resource and one he wanted to keep.

When he finished, he bent down and picked it up. The block was solid, but seemed lighter than it should have been. He put it into the satchel with what was left of the food he had been given by Bess. Then he continued down the mountain, his mind pondering what the stranger had done.

There were certainly other dimensions. Human scientists had known about them for a long time. They didn't know much beyond the fact that they existed, but it was theorized that it could be possible to move in and out of the four dimensions humanity existed in. Maybe other intelligent species could do it. Maybe the stranger could step into and out of the plane of existence that Mitch perceived. It was fascinating to think about. He remembered the voice in his mind telling him to quit. It wasn't the first time in his life he had been tempted to do something. Nor the first time in his life thoughts had come to him unbidden. Normally, they seemed like his own thoughts. When he heard a voice in his head it was usually his own, even if he hadn't conjured up the words himself. Humanity had given up on the supernatural thousands of years in the past. Anything they couldn't explain was either ignored or disbelieved. But if there were other beings in other dimensions, who could say what they were able to do? It was possible they could speak to a person, influence their thoughts, tempt them to do stupid things. He realized he still had a lot to learn.

There were no more attacks as he descended the mountain. The path was steep, but much easier to traverse than the places without a trail. The sun was just beginning to set when Mitch reached the academy building. Doss was there waiting. He bowed as Mitch approached.

"You have returned," Doss said, his voice entering Mitch's mind and making him wonder about the voice in his head on the mountain. It was really no different.

"I have," Mitch said.

"That is wonderful. And you are not empty-handed. May I see the weapon you forged?"

Mitch had the rough scabbard stuck through a belt loop. He pulled it out and handed it to Doss. The alien instructor drew the blade.

"Very nice," he said. "Strong, but graceful."

"Thank you. I got this too," Mitch said, pulling out the block of Cidian from the satchel.

"Indeed. That is a treasure. Cidian is an exceedingly rare element. It is hard to retrieve and harder still to separate from the surrounding material. Did you take this in combat?"

Mitch nodded. "It was breaking down. It didn't seem right to just let it blow away."

"It will be useful to you, I predict. At some point down the road, you will know what to do with it."

"Thank you," Mitch said. "What happens now?"

"It is late," Doss said. "Return to Qwii's ship. Refresh yourself. Tomorrow, there will be an assembly. You will be presented and given the chance to join the Order of Scion."

"I still have a lot to learn," Mitch admitted. "You think I'm ready?"

"It is the fact that you understand how much you still have to learn that confirms that you are ready," Doss said, sounding pleased. "Your next steps will be taken in a practical field, Mitch Murphy. A place where you can learn by doing. And as long as you continue to learn, you will continue to grow in the Power and Knowledge. They are intrinsically linked."

"Thank you," Mitch said.

"Training you has been an honor. I will meet you at Qwii's ship in the morning."

"Looking forward to it," Mitch said.

Before his last test he wasn't sure about anything. He didn't know what he believed, or if he wanted to be part of the Order of Scion. He had gone with Arq and the other Nagani because they asked and he was curious. They were clearly very advanced beings, and his own people had left him stranded on New Terra. So, it was an easy decision. But joining the Order of Scion clearly came with a lot of responsibilities. He hadn't known if taking on those responsibilities was a good idea or not. But after his encounters on the mountain, he knew two things. First, he knew he was capable of using the Power that he had been taught. He could do all the things he had seen the Order of Scion do. Surely there were things he couldn't do yet, but he felt that eventually he would be able to. Second, he knew there was something to the Knowledge, call it mythology or religious belief, but there was something undeniable about it. The Power didn't exist for selfish reasons. It made sense that a benevolent Creator would gift his creation with the ability to make the universe a better place. Mitch knew he wanted to dig deeper into that Knowledge, to plumb its depths so that he could use the Power as it was meant to be used. And the Order of Scion seemed to be on the right track. Joining them would allow him to continue learning.

As he walked out toward the crescent-shaped ship that was beginning to feel like home to Mitch, he realized that something had led him here. All the things that had gone wrong in his life up until he joined the CMC, perhaps they had happened for a reason. He had thought it had been because he failed, because he wasn't strong enough or smart enough, but looking back, he couldn't help but wonder if there were things happening behind the scenes.

Maybe there were things at play that he couldn't see, and couldn't explain, but that had a very real impact on his life. It was something he was going to have to think about. He had been given the chance to improve himself and everything around him. He was going to embrace that opportunity with all his strength, and see where it would lead him.

CHAPTER 15

"WE'VE GOT a pair of bogeys, three o'clock," Mara announced.

They were in Alpha Colony proper, making their way toward the middle of town.

"Almost in position," Hawk said. "Sixty seconds."

"We could take these bugs down," Flash said.

"Just hold your position," Mara said.

She was in the lead, with Jingo, Ninja, and Flash behind her. The goal was to take down as many of the Lymies as possible, and see if they could draw out the rest into the open space between the town and the airfield. No one really liked their orders, but there was nothing unusual about that. They weren't called grunts for no reason. Their job was to carry out orders, if even they seemed asinine to the Marines on the ground.

"We stick to the plan," Mara said. "I don't want them knowing we're here."

"They won't know anything if we hit them fast enough," Flash said.

That made sense if the enemy was a couple of human beings. But the briefing Mara had gotten from Major Swift suggested it was highly likely that the Lymies shared a hive mind. If that was the case, anything the two bugs approaching her position knew, even seconds before they died, might be accessible to the others. And while Leo Squad had a clear mission objective, Mara's priority was to get them all out of the city alive. Perhaps the officers in orbit didn't care if they lived or died, but Mara certainly did.

"Just hold your position," Mara ordered.

"Almost there," Hawk said.

"They're less than a block away," Mara said. "Closing in. I don't think they know we're here, and I'd rather not start shooting at this stage of the game."

"Copy that," Hawk said. "I've got them. Standby."

They didn't have to wait for long. The first shot made one of the spidery alien heads explode. Black blood flew in all directions. The body scrambled forward several meters before flipping over and deflating, its long legs curling up.

"That's one," Jingo said.

The second Lymie stood frozen in shock for a split second, then it turned to run. Hawk's second shot shattered one of its legs, but didn't penetrate the thick hide on its body segment.

"Damn, they're tough," Flash said.

The kinetic impact from the sniper rifle knocked it over, but it immediately began scrambling to get back on its feet. The only problem was the shattered leg. It took the Lymie a moment to get its bearings on three legs instead of four, and that moment was all the time Hawk needed to make a kill shot. The bolt from the Long Range Rail Gun split the alien's head wide open.

"They know we're here now," Ninja said.

"But they don't know where we are," Mara said. "Ninja, hold this position. Flash and Jingo, on my six."

"Copy that," Jingo said. "We got your back."

"Let's go, double time it."

They ran to the corner of the street. The blood from the dead

Lymies was pouring onto the pavement. Mara looked through a building window. The street ahead was clear.

"Go!" she ordered, as she stepped around and covered her companions.

Flash and Jingo dashed across the road and took covering positions behind the nearest building.

"We're set," Jingo said.

Mara followed them across the street. They were approaching the rubble made by the Grumbler. The giant alien had started down one road, but the city was laid out in concentric circles. Few of the streets ran straight for very far, and the giant didn't bother going around the buildings.

"Advance," Mara said, once more taking the lead as she hurried past Flash and Jingo.

"You know, while we're here, I could use a new stereo," Flash said.

"How 'bout a new game system," Jingo replied.

"That would be tight!" Flash said. "Tunes, games, you think the brick oven place is still standing?"

"Movement, movement, movement," Hawk called. "The bugs are on the move."

"Where?" Mara asked, raising one fist to halt Flash and Jingo. They all three went to one knee, their weapons held to their shoulders ready to fire. There was a wine shop to their left. Mara was still facing north, Jingo turning to cover their rear, and Flash watching the buildings across the street.

"One block east of your current position," Hawk said. "It's a group of them. They're rallying together. I count eight."

"Where are they coming from?"

"Looks like that old cannery on Front Street," Hawk replied.

"Check the bird's-eye view," Mara ordered.

"One sec," Hawk said. "Thermal imaging is picking up heat signatures in the cannery, and the hovercar dealership. The only place on your side of the Grumbler line with any signs of life is the worship center on Kinder Lane."

"Copy that," Mara said. "Jingo, fall back to the corner. Flash, run to the worship center. You know it?"

"Sure," Flash said. "I been there a time or two."

"Get inside and find out what's in there. But don't do anything stupid."

"That really narrows down the options, Sarge."

"Exactly," Mara said. "Remember they can be hard to kill. If there's more than one in that building wait for backup."

"Roger that," Flash said, before he started sprinting down the street.

He was an impressive runner. At just a hair under eight feet tall, his long legs gave him a huge stride. He ran faster than any professional athlete and was quickly out of sight.

"Bogeys are moving south," Hawk said.

"Jingo, get some grenades ready," Mara said.

"Oh, yeah, now you're talking," the big man replied.

"Can you get to the rubble without being seen?"

"I think so."

"Do it," she ordered. "I'm moving around behind them."

Hawk interjected. "Thermal shows two more groups still under cover," she explained. "We hit this bunch; you could have dozens more right on top of you in a matter of seconds.

"Let's try to coordinate," Mara said. "Flash, you copy?"

"Loud and clear," he replied, his voice tinged with static on her comlink.

There were still several dozen Lymies in the city, enough to create a static fog that their radio signals suffered from. But it wasn't enough to completely block their transmissions.

"What's the situation at the worship center?"

"Just one alien, but it's a big nasty brute," Flash said. "There's a lot of bodies in here too. All wrapped up in spider webs ready to eat."

"And there's only one Lymie guarding them?"

"Just one that I can see," Flash said. "The auditorium is wide open, but there are a lot of smaller rooms in back and off to the side. A children's area, offices, that sort of thing."

"All right, on my mark you take out that bug," she ordered. "Jingo, are you set?"

"Found me a nice slab of concrete to hide behind," he said. "I can hear the bad guys coming."

"Prepare to engage," she said. "Hawk, as soon as the grenades go off start mopping them up."

"Copy that, team leader."

"All right, here we go. On my mark," Mara said. "Three, two, one, mark!"

She was watching the aliens. They were two blocks away, moving quickly down the path that the Grumbler had taken. They stopped abruptly and turned in her direction, but it wasn't Mara they were keyed in to. Mara could only guess, but they must have been reacting to Flash killing the alien in the church. And if they recognized the danger from the grenades that Jingo tossed toward them they made no move to escape.

The grenade detonated two seconds after the group stopped and turned. They were standing still, legs stiff, and the concussion grenades knocked them down like a bowling ball hitting the pins. Three were wounded by the grenades, their legs broken by the shockwave. The others were just knocked down. Mara had her fully automatic shotgun at her shoulder, the recoil absorbing pad was pressed tight. The weapon had two pistol grips and a round drum magazine with thirty shells loaded inside. They were soft lead slugs, big bullets the size of her thumb. They didn't have the penetrating power of the depleted uranium-tipped explosive rounds the GARs fired, but they had more kinetic power, especially at close range.

One of the spidery heads exploded. Hawk was on top of a flour mill on the edge of town. The tower had taken a beating from the orbital bombardment shockwave, but was still intact. It stood fourteen meters high, and had a decent view of the city. Jingo rose up from his position and started blasting out three round bursts. The depleted uranium could penetrate two inches of solid steel, but it just bounced off the bodies of the Lymies. They had molted soon after the initial attack on the city, only instead of shedding their old skin it had hardened to form a type of armor over their body segment. The head wasn't as tough, which was why Hawk was taking headshots. Jingo didn't make as many kills as he expected to, but he wounded two and killed another. The last pair were attempting to hurry away from the scene of the slaughter. Four aliens were wailing from the pain of their shattered legs. Mara leaned out and fired a single shot at one of the aliens. It hit the creature's head and blew a saucer-sized chunk out the far side, spraying its companion with black blood.

The dead Lymie dropped and rolled over. The blood-covered companion jumped. The Lymies could really move when they needed to. And they could jump ten meters high. The nearest building was only five meters tall. The alien jumped up onto the roof, and was skittering toward the far edge of the building. The sniper rifle wasn't loud. The rail gun made a pop when fired as the launcher slid forward and hit the stops. The six-inch-long tungsten steel bolts it fired were pointed on the nose, and had tiny fins on the back that spread out once the bolt was launched. It had an effective range of five to six kilometers, depending on the atmosphere and weather conditions. Hawk was perched on the flour mill just three kilometers from the ambush. The bolt flew silently, hitting the alien in the top of its skull and blowing the entire face off. It tumbled from the top of the building and into the street.

"Clear," Mara said. "Jingo, take care of the stragglers."

"Copy that," he said. His GAR made a loud pop with every shot. The tactical rounds had explosive gas propellant that was loud and echoed off the buildings in the street as he shot the wounded in their big, pumpkin-sized heads.

"Flash, what's your status?"

"Just clearing the church offices," he said. "It's empty."

"Good, let's begin pulling back," Mara ordered.

"What about the people in those web sacks?" Flash said. "Has to be forty, maybe fifty of them in there."

"It's been over a month since the attack," Mara said. "There's nothing we can do for them now."

"Damn," Flash said. "All right. I'm on my way."

"We kicked the hornet's nest all right," Hawk declared. "North end of town is filling up fast."

"OK. All right, I want to move back in a controlled manner," Mara said. "Cover fire. Leap frog positions. We don't want to go too fast."

"Faster's always better," Flash said as he came sprinting into view.

"That right there is your problem in life," Jingo said.

"Cover us," Mara ordered. "We're moving to your position."

Flash outran her. Mara knew she couldn't keep up with the big man. But she wasn't slow either. She sprinted back to the corner of the wine shop.

"Gotta remember this place once the city is clear," Flash said.

"Jingo, fall back," Mara ordered.

"Roger dodger," he said.

They waited, looking north, knowing the horde would catch up to them soon. Jingo sprinted from the ruins left by the Grumbler back to the wine shop.

"Sixty plus," Hawk said. "They're spreading out. Some on the rooftops, some on the ground."

"All right, we all know the drill," Mara said. "You two start running. I'll cover you."

Jingo and Flash sprinted back down the street they had come up just moments before. Mara was waiting on their verbal acknowledgement that they had reached the end of the block, but all she heard was static. Suddenly the aliens were in view. Dozens of them. They skittered back and forth on the road in an evasive manner. She could hear the aliens on the rooftops too.

Mara brought her weapon up and pulled the trigger. It chugged out a dozen rounds. Two of the aliens that were closing in on her went down with broken legs, and another took a hit, fell, but immediately bounced back up.

"What's going on back there?" Mara shouted.

She didn't have time to turn and look. There seemed to be aliens everywhere. They were closing in fast. There was no reply on the comlink, but her squad mates began to shoot. She turned and ran. Jingo and Flash were on one side of the road, Ninja was on the other. They used the nearest buildings for cover, but were firing at anything that moved except for Mara.

"Grenades, grenades, grenades," she shouted as she slid to stop just past Jingo and Flash.

She had two on her belt. They were round, baseball-sized concussion grenades. She dropped her automatic shotgun, letting it dangle on the harness around her neck and shoulders, while she pulled the two grenades, flicked out the safety pins, and pitched them back down the street. Flash threw his two onto a rooftop. Ninja threw one on the street, and one on a building top. They had all taken hold of their weapons again when the grenades went off with echoing booms.

"Go," she ordered. "Comms are down. Leapfrog, block by block. Move, move, move!"

Flash and Jingo started running. Mara emptied her thirty-round drum, hit the release and let it bounce on the pavement at her feet. She hooked another one into place and rotated the loading lever to feed a round into the breech.

As soon as Jingo and Flash started shooting, Mara and Ninja started running. They stayed on opposite sides of the street. Black blood and Lymie flesh were flying. The aliens weren't stupid, but they had to close the distance to attack the Marines. They scampered around, using what cover they could get in an effort to get close. But Mara wasn't having it. She shot at anything she saw moving.

"Looks like they're wising up," Hawk said. "The bugs are spreading wide. Attempting to flank you."

"Discourage them," Mara ordered. "Flash, get to the transport and come get us."

"Roger," he said, sprinting away immediately.

"This could get ugly, Sarge," Jingo said. "I'm getting low on ammo."

She had just one drum of shotgun shells left. They weren't especially effective against the aliens either. There was no time for precision shots. And her handgun would be useless against the spidery aliens.

"We keep moving," Mara said. "The plan is working."

"Too good," Ninja said. "We need air support."

"There is none," Mara said. "You two get moving."

Jingo and Ninja sprinted back and Mara fired several bursts from her shotgun. The spiders were squealing and chittering. She could hear more than she could see. Few were stupid enough to get into her field of fire. Instead, they were trying to circle around behind her. She turned and ran. There was no more time for a controlled retreat. It was time to run for their lives.

"Go! Go! Go!" she shouted as she sprinted past Jingo and Ninja.

They didn't need much encouragement. Both men turned and ran. It was a footrace. Thankfully, Hawk kept the Lymies from getting too close. When one did, she took it down. But Mara knew that if she didn't get clear soon the aliens would find her. Scaling the flour mill would be no problem for the four-legged aliens.

"I see you," Flash announced over the comlink, but his words were lost in static.

He raced up in the armored transport. He had both sides open. The armored doors slid on tracks opening up the passenger compartment. He slowed, hitting the reverse thrusters and turning.

The transport drifted sideways down the street toward the fleeing Marines. Mara turned, emptied her magazine, and gave her companions time to get on board. Then she turned, grabbed a handle at the back corner and screamed for Flash to drive.

"Punch it!" she shouted.

The armored transport wasn't built for speed, but it responded quickly enough. The ensuing turn nearly made Mara lose her grip.

"Hawk, get the hell out of there," she ordered.

"Co...at," was all she heard around a burst of static.

But they all knew the plan. The fleet wanted to see if Leo Squad could draw out the Lymies. There were less than a hundred of the aliens in Alpha Colony. What would happen once they were in the open was anyone's guess. And if it worked at Alpha, it would probably work at the other colonies. Mara didn't care, she just wanted to survive with the rest of her squad.

"They're fast," Ninja said, reaching out and helping Mara into the passenger compartment.

Several of the aliens had spun out long webs and were drifting up into the sky. Without letting go of the support post that ran down the center of the transport, Mara pulled a mini-rocket launcher from the weapons rack.

"Ninja, get in the turret," she ordered.

The armored transport had weapons capabilities, but didn't have anything mounted in the turret when Leo Squad acquired them. They had gotten a twin barrel, high-capacity machine gun set up in the turret before setting out on their mission. As Ninja hurried up the steps to the turret, Mara leaned out and fired a rocket at one of the aliens dangling in the air on a long ribbon of spider silk. She had to keep the small weapon trained on the Lymie so that the laser mounted on the rail above the barrel of the weapon could guide the mini rocket to the target. It hit, exploded, and sent the wounded alien plummeting toward the ground. Mara saw it ejecting more silk in an effort to stop its fall, but it wasn't high enough. It hit the ground, bounced, then lay still.

The turret began to chug out rounds in a violent staccato. Jingo was still shooting his GAR, having gotten fresh magazines in the transport. He leaned out the far side of the vehicle, firing his rifle one-handed.

"I'm getting ready to make a hard right turn," Flash announced. "Everybody hold onto something."

The turn was fast and would have knocked them all off their feet, but they were braced for it. Regular Marines might have buckled under the centrifugal forces, but the members of Leo Squad were all enhanced. They were bigger, stronger, and faster than normal people. They held on while the transport slewed around, then corrected itself and raced forward.

"Hawk?" Mara called out over the comlink.

"Rail gun's jammed," she said. "I'm coming down the emergency ladder."

"Hurry," Mara said. "These bugs are out for blood."

"Maybe shooting the big food guard was a bad idea," Flash said.

"Something made them mad," Jingo agreed.

"There's Hawk," Flash announced. "Damn' they're right on top of her."

Mara turned to look forward. Estelle "Hawk" Flemming was hurrying down the ladder that was built onto the outside of the flour mill. She was still pretty high up, and there were three Lymies racing down toward her. Mara didn't know if she should shoot at them or not. The mini-rocket might knock the entire building over.

Before she could decide what to do Hawk slipped. She fell, and hit the ground hard, rolling her ankle in the process.

"Hawk!" Mara shouted.

"Kill the bugs!" Jingo added.

His GAR rattled out three round bursts. Mara saw Hawk get up and try to run, but she couldn't put weight on her injured foot. She was hopping away. Mara fired a rocket at one of the Lymies just as it reached the ground and started bounding toward Hawk. The rocket raced past her and hit the alien. The explosion knocked the alien backward, but it also flattened Hawk. She immediately began to crawl. Jingo leaped out of the transport and was running to help her as Flash hit the reverse thrusters to stop.

One of the Lymies that was still on the building jumped. Mara racked a new rocket into the breech but she wasn't fast enough. Neither was Jingo, who lifted his GAR one-handed and began shooting at the bug. It landed on top of Hawk, its legs spread wide, its body bending as it thrust its toxin filled stinger into her back. Hawk screamed. The alien was hit by multiple bursts of gunfire from Jingo. It topped back and died, but the damage to Hawk was done. Jingo picked her up like she was a rag doll, flopping her over his shoulder and continuing to shoot his Garrison Assault Rifle in the process. He ran back to the transport.

"Go!" Mara shouted.

She dropped to her knees and pulled Hawk's limp body across the deck. Jingo braced himself with his feet and rammed a fresh magazine into his rifle. Hawk's eyes were open, but she wasn't responding.

"Can you hear me!" Mara shouted. "Estelle, you stay with me!"

"They're falling back to the city," Ninja announced.

"Keep hammering them," Jingo said.

"Stop the transport," Mara ordered.

All she really cared about was her friend, but she was too disciplined to ignore the mission. Flash stopped the transport. Mara looked out. There were nearly three dozen aliens left at the edge of the city. They were loath to leave the safety of the structures.

"They're afraid," Jingo said.

"Maybe just not completely stupid," Ninja said, still in the turret. "They know they're sitting ducks out in the open."

"Which is why we need air support," Mara said. "Jingo, get the shoulder cannon."

"Got it," he announced, pulling the big laser cannon out of the transport.

It was a powerful laser, but like all lasers it didn't have kinetic energy release on contact. And it would take several seconds of steady output to burn through the thick bodies of the spidery aliens.

"Aim for their legs," Mara ordered.

"No problem," he replied.

Green light shot from the cannon in a steady beam. Smoke billowed from where the laser hit the buildings behind the aliens. They scampered around, but all Jingo had to do was wave the weapon back and forth. The beam scorched their bodies, but it burned clean through their spindly legs.

"Oh, that's got 'em," Flash said.

"Finish them off," Mara ordered. She was sitting on the deck of the passenger compartment, holding Hawk on her lap.

The injured Marine lay unmoving, her eyes staring straight up. She was alive, but just barely, her body paralyzed by the Lymie nerve toxin. It was all Hawk could do to keep breathing.

"Stay with me, Estelle. You're going to make it. You hear me? You're going to make it."

The turret gun began to rock. The aliens that couldn't run away were chewed to pieces by the continuous rapid fire from the twin barreled machine guns. Another two dozen Lymies died on the edge of town.

"How is she?" Flash asked from the driver's compartment.

"Bleeding a lot," Mara asked.

"We're clear," Jingo said. "No more movement."

"The sky?" Mara demanded.

"It's clear too," Ninja said.

"Ninja, you keep eyes out for the Lymies. Jingo, take control of the drone. We can't lose it."

"Signal's good," Jingo said, activating the drone's flight controls on his data cuff.

"Should be," Flash replied. "We killed enough of the Lymies today."

Mara wasn't listening. She rolled Hawk over and tried to get a look at the wound. The stinger had stabbed beneath a plate of armor on her back and angled up.

"Gotta get this off," Mara said.

Jingo didn't know if she was talking to him, or to Hawk, or just to herself, but he bent down to help. Mara unfastened the armor and Jingo pulled it off. Hawk's fatigue blouse was soaked with blood. Ripping open a packet of quick-clot powder, she poured it into the wound, and then stuffed in gauze.

"Where are we?" Mara demanded.

"Almost home," Flash replied. "I'm taking us right to the front door."

"Ninja, stay with Flash. The two of you make sure the castle is secure."

"Copy that, Marauder," Ninja responded.

"Jingo, carry Hawk straight up to the common room. I'll get the med supplies."

"Yeah, no problem," Jingo said.

"Flash, as soon as the front of the castle is secure, get up top. I want to know if the enemy is planning a counterattack."

"I don't think there's enough of 'em left to try it," Flash said.

"The aliens in Alpha Colony aren't the only ones we're contending with. Jingo, get to the control center and send that drone out to check Bravo and Charlie Colonies. The goal was to draw the enemy out, and we have to know if it worked."

"If it worked we're screwed," Ninja said.

"I say bring it on," Flash replied.

"We just got pushed out of the city by a few dozen aliens," Ninja said. "What chance do we have against a few hundred?"

"We're in a good defensive position here," Jingo said. "We might not make it, but we'll sure as hell make them pay through the nose if they want to kill us."

"Upload everything we've got," Mara continued. "If we're going to die down here, it can't be for nothing."

She was thinking more of Hawk than herself. The transport

pulled right up to the big opening on the front of the alien castle they had taken residence in. Jingo snatched up Hawk and jogged inside with her in his arms. Flash closed the outer door of the transport, while Mara hurried to collect their medical supplies.

Standard procedure for any unit in hostile territory for any length of time is to bank blood. With the wind turbines producing energy, the squad of Marines had salvaged several useful items from the airport's main building, including a small beverage cooler with a transparent door. They used it to keep the blood they had drawn in bags marked with their names. Every two weeks they each put back a liter of blood. The LE Protocol had increased their overall blood volume, and their enhanced bodies could replace the blood supply faster than a regular person, but they could only store so much. Mara grabbed a liter of Hawk's blood from the cooler, along with the medical supply kit, and raced to the common area.

Jingo had Hawk on the table and was cutting her shirt off. He had a worried expression on his face.

"She's still bleeding," he said.

"We'll have to run a scan," Mara said, setting the hard medical case on the ground. It was the size of a standard piece of luggage and had all sorts of medical devices inside. She flipped open the lid and pulled out the telescoping IV stand. Setting it on the table, she grabbed a needle and tape for the IV, along with the plastic tubing. She had practiced battlefield triage many times. It was what the Marines did. If they weren't deployed on a mission, they were training, honing their skills, preparing for whatever might come their way.

"I'll get some water," Jingo said.

Mara set the IV supplies on the table, then pulled out the medical scanner. One cuff went around Hawk's upper arm to monitor her blood pressure. A little clip went on the end of one finger to monitor her heart rate and pulse oxygen. A strip on her forehead monitored her brain waves, body temperature, and respiration rate. The hand-held scanner had a digital readout. The vital signals were wirelessly transmitted to the device. All came back in the red.

"Everything is down," Mara said. "Blood pressure, heart rate, respiration, blood oxygen, it's all low. And her temperature is one oh two and climbing."

"We have to cool her down," Jingo said. "Get that blood going. Her heart is working too hard."

Mara scanned the puncture wound. The device showed one kidney as non-functional, and there was a lot of tissue damage. The toxicity of the venom was causing the area around the wound to die. She pulled a can of antiseptic spray from the medical kit and saturated the wound with it. After that she filled the wound with medical foam. It helped clot the blood and seal off the wound from outside germs that might infect it. Her last task was to stick an adhesive bandage over the wound, further sealing and containing the puncture.

Jingo had a basin of cold water. He soaked several strips of fabric in the cool water and laid them gently across Hawk's forehead, throat, and chest. Mara turned to her friend's arm and got the IV started.

"That cold blood should help," Jingo said. "It's her best chance."

"I can't believe how bad she's hurt," Mara said, fighting back tears. "How much venom did they inject her with?"

"I don't know," Jingo said. "But she's tough. She'll pull through."

"We've done all we can," Mara said.

"Her ankle is swelling," Jingo pointed out. "Let's elevate it."

The squad had salvaged blankets, pillows, and sofa cushions from the watch tower's lounge. Mara grabbed a thick cushion and elevated Hawk's foot. It took a few minutes to get her boot off. They had to unlace it, and Mara held it still while Jingo worked the boot. They had chemical ice packs in the medical kit. Mara folded one until the chemicals inside mixed and grew cold. Jingo scanned the ankle.

"High ankle sprain," he said. "Nothing broken."

"That's the first good news we've got," Mara said. "Just control the swelling."

"Yeah, it'll heal on its own in time," Jingo said.

"Sarge!" Flash shouted as he hurried into the room. "It's all quiet for now. How's Hawk?"

"Fighting for her life," Mara said. "Just like the rest of us."

CHAPTER 16

THE BIG LOBBY of the academy building was packed. Members of the Order lined the walls, with the highest-ranking members in seats at the far end. Acolytes and the throngs of aliens who worked at the academy were lining the balcony overhead. Mitch had to admit he hadn't even known there was a balcony. He walked in with Doss, Bess, and Qwii just a few hours after dawn. He was still in his worn but freshly cleaned military fatigues. The dark green camouflage pattern stood in contrast with the light, billowy robes that the members of the Order wore.

Doss led the way in. Mitch's only instructions were to stay beside Doss. Bess and Qwii joined the other members along the sides of the large open space in the center of the big structure. Mitch could feel the eyes of hundreds of aliens on him. His shock at seeing all sorts of aliens had diminished. He still noticed the differences, but the appearance of the vastly different species no longer acted on his mind like the wrong notes being played in a symphony.

"Fellow members of the Order of Scion," Doss announced, his voice sounding loud and officious in Mitch's mind. "I present for membership, Mitch Murphy, human from Earth, in the Sol system. The first of his kind."

There was silence. Mitch stood at attention. He wasn't sure of anything in that moment. He felt out of place and on display. His nature was to eschew attention, but that hadn't gotten him far in his former career. And he had sworn not to make the same mistakes again. Part of him wanted to run away. It seemed like things were happening so fast, and yet he also felt like he was finally whole. There was something about being able to wield the gravitational power that made him feel complete. Looking back, something had always been missing. Getting out of a bad marriage hadn't fixed it. Getting the physical enhancement by the Latent Technology program hadn't fixed it. Not even taking command of Leo Squad had made him feel complete, but when he was on the mountain, facing danger, using the things he had been taught, it all came together in a way he never imagined.

"I am Thorn Isska Malchais Sonso, Planet Mover, eighty-year member and ninth of my kind," a small alien with six arms and thick wrinkles on its face said in a small voice. "You have learned the skills necessary and passed the tests required, Mitch Murphy. But do you believe in the Creator's mandate?"

The alien spoke in his own language. Mitch heard it with his ears, but Doss was translating in his mind, so that he understood what was being said. It was a good question. Mitch felt like he was leaning toward belief, but hadn't quite gotten there yet.

"I believe in doing good," Mitch said. "On the mountain, I discovered what was really capable with the Power, and I feel like the Knowledge is our guide to becoming what we should as beings with such incredible capabilities."

"That doesn't answer my question," Thorn said.

"He is young," a humanoid being with long, golden hair. "I have looked into the human race. They have stepped back from anything supernatural. It will take time for Mitch Murphy to fully embrace the truth."

"Well spoken, Hash Tier," another alien spoke up. "Mitch Murphy has completed training faster than anyone in recent memory. He obviously has great potential. But that may be for good or for harm, only time will tell."

"Who is sponsoring Mitch Murphy?" Thorn asked.

"That would be me, sir," Qwii spoke up. "Arq selected him. But I am taking the full responsibility."

"Very well," Hash Tier said. "Humanity is ready. And the Order has need. I see this as the Creator's will."

"You would see the Creator's work in everything," Thorn rebuked the younger member.

Mitch could only watch and wait. He had no idea what they would do to him if he was rejected.

"Because he is always at work," Hash said. "He does not sleep. He never grows tired."

"Yes, you are a great proponent of the Creator and of the Son, but we should be careful today," Thorn said, his voice booming around the big lobby. "Humans have great potential; none can argue that. But it is potential for good and for harm. Their own history is laced with those who have abused their power."

"They are quick to violence," another member said.

"And yet Mitch Murphy acted with mercy on the mountain," Hash said. "He could have caused great harm. Yet he chose to show kindness, and held back when he could have killed those who clearly sought his own demise."

"Why didn't you kill the Shade from the outer dimensions?" Thorn asked Mitch.

He didn't have to ask for clarity. Only one of the creatures he fought slipped through a portal and disappeared. The three-legged creature with the barbed tail and the huge sword was a Shade. Mitch had wondered what sort of being it was.

"It felt like an abuse," Mitch said. "When I use the Power it is wonderful. I didn't want to taint it by killing if I didn't have to."

"He has shown great ability with the Power, and an innate understanding of the Knowledge we hold dear," Hash said.

"Yet he is not fully devoted," Thorn said.

"Was any first-of-their-kind fully devoted?" Doss asked. "It is my opinion that Mitch Murphy will grow in his understanding and commitment to the Knowledge as he progresses."

"Hear, hear!" several of the members said.

"Most are in agreement," Thorn said. "And I would welcome Mitch Murphy to the Order, with only one request."

"Name it," Mitch said.

Looking back, he wasn't sure why he volunteered so quickly. He hadn't realized how much he wanted to be accepted by the Order of Scion. Had they all unanimously voted to accept him right away he might have felt differently. But seeing them argue, he found his own desire growing along with the debate.

"It is my opinion that it would best for you, Mitch Murphy, not to return to your people," Thorn said. "At least for some time."

Mitch hesitated. The request felt loaded, as if the members of the Order knew something he didn't. He turned and looked at Qwii, who wouldn't meet Mitch's eye.

"I'll gladly serve wherever I'm needed," Mitch said. "But if there are things that need the Order's attention on Earth, or New Terra, I would like to be involved."

"As is your right," Hash said.

"This is a terrible risk we are considering," Thorn insisted.

"I won't let you down," Mitch said.

"Time will tell," Thorn said, his native voice squeaking like a broken speaker.

A vote was taken, no one dissented, and Mitch became a member of the Order of Scion. Robes were presented to him, and his first assignment was issued.

"Help is needed on Bispee," Doss said. "Qwii and Bess will be your mentors. Do all you can to stop the Fray, Mitch Murphy. You are a Scion Warrior now."

"I'll do my best," Mitch assured him.

There was no party. The assembly broke up as everyone returned to their tasks. Mitch and Qwii were joined by Bess in the crescent ship, and it took off without fanfare. In his quarters on the elegant craft, Mitch removed his fatigues and combat boots. He replaced them with simple trousers and tunic of the Scion Order. Over them he wore a robe made from a single, long strip of the lightweight fabric. With his clothing changed, he saw to his weapon. Uri brought paint and a spool of material that looked to Mitch like leather. It was long and narrow, sort of like a shoelace. He used the leather to wrap around the handle of his sword. The black paint was quickly brushed over the scabbard and set to dry. It felt like a proper weapon once he had seen to the handle and sheath.

"Mitch," Bess called from just outside his room.

"Yes, come in," he replied.

She stepped into the room, and gave a nod of approval. "You look good, Scion Warrior."

"Thanks," Mitch told her. "Did I do the robe right?"

"Yes," she replied. "Qwii requests for you to come and see the flight to Bispee."

"Oh, okay," Mitch said, following her from his room.

They met Qwii in the observation deck. Mitch could see that the ship was near the edge of the system. It was a flight that would have taken a human ship an entire week to accomplish.

"I'm going to bend space," Qwii said. "You should observe."

"Bend space," Mitch said. He had heard of the concept, but it still seemed impossible.

"That is correct," Qwii said. "To facilitate our passage to the Bispee system."

Mitch and Bess stood back, watching. Visually, nothing seemed to be happening, but as Mitch opened his senses he could feel an incredible amount of gravitational energy building up.

"Space is best described as a fabric," Qwii said. "It was

stretched out by the creator, making room for the vast wonders of his work. Using the Power and Knowledge, we can bend the fabric to make short jumps across great distances. It is why we are called the True Navigators."

Mitch could feel space moving. The ship seemed to be stationary. Out the wide opening in the elegant vessel nothing could be seen, just the vast empty stretch of the cosmos. But Mitch felt it moving. It was very much like a piece of fabric on a smooth surface. Gravity was summoned by Qwii, concentrated, much in the same way that Mitch had applied pressure to the Cidian, first to form his blade, then to form the block of material that was with his other belongings. The fabric of space was pushed and began to ripple. When two points touched the spaceship leapt forward, jumping from one spot in the universe to another. The jumps happened five times before Qwii stopped bending space. And instantly the view through the ship's wide opening revealed an entirely new star system.

"This is Bispee," Qwii said. "A group of Fray have invaded."

Mitch could see a tiny green dot in the far, far distance. The ship was already moving toward it, but the dot was only the size of a grain of sand. He couldn't tell much about the world yet.

"A group of the Fray?" Mitch asked. "I thought they worked solo?"

"They work apart from the Order," Bess explained.

"This is a group of Cadish that broke with the Order decades ago," Qwii said. "Their leader is a Planet Mover called Wezzor. He rules their home world and trains acolytes to enslave other planets. The last report from Bispee reported five Fray had landed."

"Five?" Mitch asked with a touch of surprise. "And how many members of the Order are down there?"

"None," Qwii said.

"We are answering their call for help," Bess said.

"There are no Bispees in the Order of Scion," Qwii continued explaining. "Their race is content where they are. It's a resource rich planet, which is why the Cadish want to control it. We are all that stand between them, and total global domination."

Mitch felt a shiver at the thought of what they were about to attempt. There were just three individuals. He understood the Power and Knowledge were vast, but they were outnumbered and facing a hostile force. His military training wanted more intel and a solid battle strategy before going down range to face the enemy.

The crescent ship made the journey through the system in less than half an hour. It was easy to forget just how powerful the gravity force was. Without friction, the ship could attain any speed. All Qwii had to do was shut off the gravity directly in front of the ship. Their vessel essentially fell forward, while retaining perfect gravity inside the ship.

Once they entered the atmosphere and began to descend Mitch was amazed. Bispee looked like the set from a fantasy movie. There were huge mountains covered in gorgeous forests, rivers, waterfalls, colorful birds, and golden grasslands in the valleys. The ship held altitude at just a few hundred meters above the surface. As they traveled across the planet Mitch saw massive herds of animals, and small villages built into the trees.

"This place is paradise," Mitch said.

"It's no wonder the Bispees don't want to leave," Bess said. "They have found balance with the natural world."

"All planets could be this way," Qwii said. "There are entire systems finely tuned to make every world as lush and beautiful as it can be. We will visit them in time."

Bess gave Mitch a nod. Just the thought of a star system with every world habitable and thriving was stupefying to him. He had never been to Mars or one of the lunar colonies, but he had seen documentaries on all of them. They were barely livable, most in bio domes that were dirty and cramped. Even Earth wasn't what it had once been. Hundreds of years in the past, before the industrial revolution, Earth had been a vibrant, lush world. Not that life was easy in those primitive times, but cities were small, there wasn't so much pollution, and there were hundreds of animal species still living wild that were currently extinct.

"I can't wait," Mitch said, once more feeling the rush of excitement that he had been chosen to learn the ways of the Order of Scion. It felt like the greatest privilege and like winning the lottery at the same time.

"The Fray have gathered against us," Qwii said.

It was an unnecessary comment. Mitch and Bess could see just as well as Qwii. The beauty of the planet had diminished greatly, and in the distance was a huge mining pit. Dark smoke rose from the center of it. Worse still were the bodies of the Bispees. They were short, thick bodied bipeds with fur, and long antennae that stuck out of the tops of their flat heads. As the ship slowed, it also descended. Mitch could feel the ground beneath them, and the gravity that pulled on the ship. Worse, he could feel the bodies left splayed in death on the fields below them.

"The Bispees fought," Bess said.

"It was a futile resistance," Qwii said. "The Fray are without mercy."

In the distance Mitch could feel thousands of Bispees moving like rows of ants inside the mining pit. The golden grass was either scorched black or gone altogether. In front of the big pit were three small ships. They looked like aircraft, only bigger, with strange holes like a sea sponge. Spread out before them were five beings in dark clothing.

Qwii settled the ship on the ground, and Uri brought out three sets of weapons. Mitch's Cidian sword, Qwii's pair of short, curved Kama, and a spear for Bess with a curved, double-edged collar where the spear head met the staff. It was taller than she was, the curved cross piece angled up, and was just above the round feline ears on the top of her head.

"We will give them the chance to surrender," Qwii said.

"And when they refuse?" Mitch asked as he slipped the wooden scabbard into his robe at his waist.

"If they will not leave peacefully, we will fight," Qwii said.

"Shouldn't we have a plan?" Mitch asked.

"It's not a bad idea," Bess said. "They're bound to try and over-power us."

"You're the most experienced," Mitch said to Qwii. "Stay behind us and fend off their attacks with the Power. We'll deal with them up close and personal."

"I'm not helpless," Qwii argued.

"Oh, I'm certain of that," Mitch said. "I've seen you in action."

"But we're supposed to fight," Bess said. "That's what warriors do."

"Very well, but only if they refuse to surrender," Qwii said. "The Creator gifted us the power to defend the helpless, not to slay our enemies with impunity."

Mitch liked the word impunity. He knew plenty of powerful people on earth who thought of themselves as above the law. And for the most part it was true. Some wielded vast corporations with enough resources to take over small countries. Others were from wealthy families and felt that the rest of mankind was beneath them. Mitch had come to learn the meaning of true power. He didn't conjure it, and he hadn't earned it. The Power and Knowledge had been gifted to him, handed over to his stewardship for the purpose of restoration and protection. It was his hope that he could foster the growth of the human race, not just to advance them across the galaxy, but to help them see a greater purpose than self-gratification.

But first he would have to survive his initial battle as Scion warrior. And they were outnumbered. In truth, he was the weakest link in their three-person team. And yet he was anxious to see what he could accomplish physically. The LE Protocols had given him increases in size, strength, and speed. And he was still learning what he was truly capable of.

Mitch stepped out of the crescent-shaped ship and onto the surface of an alien world. The ground crunched beneath his feet.

Across a short expanse were five tall aliens. They stood on two feet, and had long, skinny arms. Their faces were flat. Wide jowls held oversized teeth, and their noses were just horizontal slits. Each of them carried weapons. From their belts hung firearms of some type. They were bulky, and Mitch guessed they fired some sort of projectiles. They also had short, double-edged swords that reminded Mitch of a Roman Gladius. They were arranged with three aliens slightly in front of the other two. The three in front drew their swords. Mitch recognized the black blades as Cidian.

One of the aliens in the back barked out something in a language that Mitch couldn't understand. Bess leaned close and said softly, "He claims we're too late. The planet is already theirs."

When Qwii replied it was in the same rough language.

Bess translated again: "He's telling them to surrender."

The laughter from the aliens was clear enough. Their leader barked an order and the first three moved ahead, spreading out, waving their swords to loosen up their shoulder muscles. Mitch glanced at Bess. She stood leaning on her spear and didn't move. Mitch didn't know the protocol, but he wasn't going to simply wait around for the three aliens to attack. He drew his sword, the black Cidian whispering against the scabbard.

Qwii placed a hand on his shoulder. "Not yet," he said softly.

Suddenly the leader spoke in English. It was shocking to Mitch, but not to Bess or Qwii. It was almost as if they were expecting it.

"Hello, human," the Cadish leader said. "Are you the first of your kind?"

Mitch felt uneasy and didn't reply.

"It matters not," the Cadish leader said. "I am Fors'No and I was sixth of my kind. My forebears opened the universe for my people, but died in service to the Order's false god. I no longer serve their twisted aims. Are all humans as weak and foolish as you?"

Mitch glanced at his companions, but they just stared across at the five Cadish warriors.

"Surely they told you that not everyone believes in their fairy tales," the alien continued. "You'll have to decide what's best for you. Is the human race a subservient species? Or do you have grander ideals. Step aside, and I will show you a better path. I will teach you the meaning of true power and knowledge. You will be free to do as you wish. You can return to your kind and reveal to them the secrets of the universe that have long been held secret by the Order of Scion. Just think of what your kind might accomplish."

Mitch felt a sudden sense of doubt. How much did he really know about the Order of Scion? What if they were holding him back? Fortunately, he managed to remember what had really happened. The Order had come to him. They had protected New Terra from a threat humans didn't even know existed. They had taken him to Vodex where he was taught to sense and control the Power and the Knowledge. They hadn't coerced him. Instead, they offered him a place among their ranks.

"I'm happy right here," Mitch said. "But I will not hesitate to stop you from hurting these people. Even if that means killing all five of you."

The leader of the aliens laughed, but it was forced. The others clearly didn't understand what was being said. They looked around nervously. Mitch realized they were scared. Perhaps it was the sight of him and his companions. Mitch was taller than the aliens, and much, much thicker. Their muscles were thin and wiry. His were thick and impressive, even in the loose-fitting robe he wore. And Bess was fierce looking. She didn't look exactly like a human / lion hybrid, but that was essentially how Mitch thought of her. And the spear she held was frightening too.

Qwii spoke up. "This is your last chance, Fors'No. Surrender and return to the Order."

"So they can murder me?"

"So you can atone for the crimes you have committed," Qwii said. They were speaking English, perhaps for Mitch's sake, or maybe out of some convenience he didn't know about. Either way, he was thankful to understand what was going on. "Wezzor is not here. Why do you think that is?"

"He has a planet to protect," Fors'No said.

"Or he sends you out to do his dirty work, so that you take all the risk and he reaps all the reward," Qwii countered. "Your companions are poorly trained. They will not overcome us in a fight. Surely, you must know this. Lay down your arms and you will live. All of you."

"This world is ours," Fors'No snapped. "The Order has no business here. Flee, or face my blade, Qwii."

"So be it," the white furred alien said. "Now, Mitch Murphy."

It was the command he had been waiting for. Mitch jumped forward with a battle cry and took the fight to the enemy.

CHAPTER 17

MAJOR ELAINE SWIFT STOOD TRANSFIXED. She was in a wing of the medical bay that was sealed off for xeno-biological research. The *Marathon* was a battleship, but it had quarantine capability, as well as medical research equipment. After getting the body of the new alien, the one that had landed on New Terra and subsequently gotten itself killed by the three aliens who left with Mitch Murphy in tow, she had been studying it. A week was spent on physical examination and recording of its intact body. The cause of death was some sort of stab wound to its lower chest. Major Swift had photographed, recorded, and scanned the body. After that came the more time-consuming internal anatomy procedure.

The frozen body was sliced up in tiny slivers ten micrometers in width. The resulting slide was then photographed from both sides, and scanned into a special computer that put everything back together in a holographic display that showed every organ, bone, tissue, blood vessel, and nerve bundle in the alien's body. Most fascinating of all was the creature's brain. Unlike a human's brain that is two halves equally divided, the alien had a long, cylindrical brain. The computer had run DNA analysis, as well as tests on the creature's blood and several tissue samples. Major Swift had no idea what race the alien was, or why it had come to New Terra in its strange ship, but she knew a great deal about its body and anatomy.

All the frozen slides of the creature had been reassembled and locked away in a frozen container. Entire teams of researchers would spend their careers studying the alien. It had already been shipped back through the portal on a supply ship, but Major Swift had the holographic data, and the alien's strange clothing. Most importantly, she had its weapon. A simple, wooden shaft made of something akin but not exactly like birchwood. It was light weight, but strong. Unfortunately, it had been cut in two during the alien's fight with the trio from the crescent-shaped ship. But what was really intriguing were the two blades, one at each end. They were simple, almost primitive looking blades. Not forged or cast like Earth's metals. In fact, it looked like it was flint napped from some kind of stone, only without the grooves and chip marks that come from striking a stone to shape it. Instead, the blades were molded, and consisted of an element that wasn't on the periodic table.

The weapons had been scanned, photographed, and recorded in a variety of ways. All that data had been sent back to Earth with the alien's body, but Major Swift kept them. An alien material, both primitive and deadly. What fascinated her most as a military officer was the fact that the blades on either end of the spear were sharper than any razor. Scans showed the cutting edges on either side of the leaf-shaped blades were honed down to a single atom, allowing the material to cut through practically anything when applied with enough force. There was no chipping or flaking of the material either. She had hit the sharpened edge with a hammer made of high carbon steel. The alien blade was undamaged, but the hammer head was severed in two. She hit it with a combat knife made of tungsten steel. The alien blade dissected the combat knife in a single blow. It was, perhaps, the most dangerous hand weapon Elaine Swift had ever heard of. Nothing was as deadly, or as sturdy, as the alien blades made from the unknown element.

Her data cuff buzzed with a message. She glanced at it. General Mercer was ready to give some orders. He always called his staff together before making the big decisions. Major Swift hadn't agreed with his plan of action since it was decided that they should stay in the system. But she hadn't put up much of a fight. As fascinating as the enhanced Marines under their command were, and as loath as she was to throw their lives away needlessly, she was much more interested in the new alien. With a sigh, she left the hologram she had been studying in the converted research wing. She alone had access to the space, even though the alien and any contaminants it might have contained, were already off the ship. Still, it was her own little kingdom and she didn't want to give it up.

"On my way," she said, the data cuff converting her words to text and forwarding them on to the General.

Normally, Major Elaine Swift didn't enjoy being on a naval ship for extended periods. It didn't take long for the cramped spaces and lack of privacy to start bothering her. She sometimes felt a sense of claustrophobia that made it difficult to breathe. Unlike commercial transports, there were very few luxuries on the *S.F. Marathon*. There was no observation deck with grand views of outer space. There were no social gatherings to attend. Her berth was smaller than a closet, with just enough space to open her locker, or fold down the table with its narrow stool. Her bunk was recessed into the wall, and sometimes felt like she was sleeping in a shoe box. The narrow corridors were crowded with machinery that she appreciated, but didn't understand. And just the thought of hard, cold vacuum on the other side of the ship's hull made being on a star ship even more dreadful.

But since fleeing New Terra during the Lymie invasion, Elaine felt like she was on the front lines. Not literally, but from a command standpoint. She wasn't safe in an office in the Sol system reading about what was happening in the Terra system. She was where the decisions were being made, and the discoveries were happening. She walked into the Wardroom and found the rest of General Mercer's command staff already seated. Major Swift poured herself a cup of coffee and sat down just as General Mercer entered. He settled at the head of the table and glanced at his second in command, Lieutenant Jerome Banks.

"You've read the report?" the general asked.

"As soon as it came in," Banks replied. "Leo Squad did a hell of a job."

"And without proper leadership," Captain Frank Marcs replied.

"We'll discuss that later," General Mercer said. "I just came from the CIC. The Lymies are mobilizing."

"It worked?" Captain Lindsey Priss asked.

"So it would seem," General Mercer said. "The question now, is what orders we give next."

"Is there time to land our SSO Squads?" Captain Marcs asked.

"I suppose," Mercer said. "But I'm not sure I see the benefit of that."

"You don't want to fight the Lymies?" Lieutenant Johnny Tosh asked.

"What I want is to catch them off guard and unprepared," General Mercer said. "Landing our forces and going toe to toe with the enemy seems foolhardy to me."

"We don't have enough Marines to retake and hold the colonies," Colonel Banks said. "Catching the enemy out in the open is our best chance of defeating them."

"Maybe, but we won't have the option of air support," General Mercer said. "That many aliens will block our control signals. We need to entice them to a certain place at a certain time so that we can preprogram our drones."

"That's risky," Captain Marcs said.

"Which is why I'm not committing our other SSO squads. The Lions have done well enough up to this point. I say we keep using them. Once we've put a dent in the enemy's numbers, the other squads can drop to the planet and retake the colonies. Once we have control of the world again, the Brass will send in reinforcements."

Elaine didn't say what she was thinking, but she knew what General Mercer had left unsaid. Namely, that reinforcements could be brought in after he had all the glory of retaking New Terra and riding the wave of success as far as it would take him. She knew what he was proposing was to sacrifice Leo Squad. She was familiar with the members because she had vetted the team before recommending that Lieutenant Mitch Murphy be given command of the Lions. They were highly capable, and all of them veterans of multiple enemy engagements. She thought throwing their lives away was dishonorable and wasteful. But she wasn't in charge of military operations. Her job was to study the enemy and give General Mercer advice when and if he asked for it.

"They have a wounded team member," Captain Marcs pointed out.

"Lance Corporal Flemming was stung by one of the Lymies," General Mercer said, turning his full attention to Elaine Swift. "What will that do to her?"

"Tissue damage," Major Swift replied, "paralysis that could last anywhere from forty-eight to seventy-two hours. And even then, she'll be weak. Blood loss could be a factor from the wound itself. And there's the possibility of infection. If an alien pathogen gets into her system, it could be fatal."

"They will have to leave her behind if she can't keep up," General Mercer said. "It's an acceptable loss."

Elaine looked down. She didn't know how anyone, senior officer in the Colonial Marines or not, could so callously order another person's death.

"They won't leave her behind," Captain Marcs said. "Those teams are incredibly loyal to one another."

"That's the way we've trained them to be," Colonel Banks said.

"I don't want us dropping ordnance onto the airfield," General Mercer said. "Let's get them a game plan to lure the bugs away."

"They'll be coming from two fronts," Colonel Banks said, "east and west."

"North is no good," Captain Priss said. "Not if you have any desire to try and save what is left of Alpha Colony."

"South," Captain Marcs said, "through the forest. There's open ground on the far side, before they hit the swamps in the southern hemisphere."

"Set a rally point for Leo Squad south of the forest," General Mercer said. "Let them lure the enemy out into the open where we can hit them from above."

"We could send people down to set mines, and IEDs," Captain Marcs proposed.

"No, I don't want the bugs to be discouraged from coming out into the open," General Marcs said. "If they start triggering land mines they'll just retreat to the trees."

"Where our air support will be much less effective," General Banks said.

"Not to mention the damage it would do to the ecosystem," Captain Priss pointed out.

For a second General Mercer stared at his logistics officer as if she were the alien. Then he shook his head. "Tell Leo Squad to get ready to move. But they can't go until the aliens arrive at that airfield. They need to chase our people through the forest and into the open ground on the other side."

"That's pretty much a suicide mission," Captain Marcs pointed out.

"And that's why we're paid to make the hard decisions, Captain. Nothing is gained without sacrifice. We get one shot at this. Our entire future is riding on this mission. If it fails the Brass could lose confidence in our ability to wage war on the enemy. They could pull the plug on the entire mission. Besides, the enhanced Marines are resourceful. If anyone can survive this mission its them."

Elaine didn't agree, but she didn't have to. Her job was to keep her mouth shut unless she was asked a direct question. But it still took all her willpower not to call the entire plan a heinous waste of good Marines.

"I'll convey the plan to Admiral Wilcox," Mercer said. "And get her people busy programing the drones."

"How much time does Leo Squad have until the enemy arrives?" Captain Marcs asked.

"They're joining forces," General Mercer said. "At least that's what the eggheads in the CIC are telling me. The satellite feeds are only able to pick up areas of signal interference. But I'm told those areas are moving. The admiral has her radar people watching the enemy. Large groups are converging on Bravo and Charlie Colonies. I'd say Leo Squad has twenty-four hours to prepare."

"I'll make sure they're ready," Marcs assured the General.

"I'll set the rally point," Colonel Banks said.

"The rest of you stay available," General Mercer said. "We may need your expertise, Major Swift. You have the best insight into the minds of these alien bastards."

"Yes, General," Elaine Swift replied. She didn't want to do it. She considered herself a scientist first, and a Marine second, but she knew that following orders wasn't just a recommendation. If the General was ordering to have a front row seat to what was sure to be a terrible slaughter, she would have to do it. All she could hope for was that when the end came for Leo Squad, that it would come quickly.

CHAPTER 18

MITCH DIDN'T RELISH KILLING, but he was enthusiastic about battle. The thrill of challenging another person, alien or human, was something he loved since the LE procedure that had altered his body so much. The Cadish were humanoids, tall and slender. They had very pale skin, almost translucent and long hands with six fingers.

Two spread out as Mitch charged forward. They looked uncertain. Mitch could see what looked like veins pulsing through the skin on their neck and face. The Cadish had sunken eyes, and thin, limp hair that hung to either side of their faces.

Mitch feinted to his left, then swung his sword at the alien to his right. The Fray blocked the slash, but was bowled over by Mitch's strength and enthusiasm. The tall alien fell back, staggering at first, then tripping and crashing to the ground on his back. His companion hissed and thrust his own short sword at Mitch, but he easily dodged away and brought his own curved sword down on the alien's forearm. Brilliant blue blood spurted from the wound. The alien barked out a cry of alarm and dropped his sword.

Mitch spun around, expecting the third Cadish warrior to be

attacking from behind, but the third alien was circling Bess. Mitch felt a sudden surge of gravity. It was like an invisible hand pressing down on him. It took all of his considerable strength to remain standing. The first alien he had knocked down was back up, but giving him space. Mitch didn't know what Qwii was doing. Perhaps the alien was overwhelmed, but Mitch couldn't wait and hope that Qwii came to his rescue. He willed the gravity that was pulling him down to cease. It was just what Fors'No had expected him do. Mitch saw the alien staring at him, one hand raised as if reaching out for Mitch. As soon as Mitch blocked the gravity pressing him down toward the ground, Fors'No changed tactics and made him weightless, pulling him up into the air. In just the few seconds it took for Mitch to get his bearings he was forty meters above the ground.

Once more, Mitch had to intervene, using the Power and his skills to block what his enemy was doing. The truth was, he should have been ready for that type of attack. When he fought the stranger on the mountains of Vodex he had been forced to fight both physically, and with the gravitational abilities at the same time. His mistake on Bispee was expecting Qwii to protect him. For a moment Mitch allowed himself to hover, weightless in the sky. He could see the fighters below him. Fors'No and his Cadish partner were well back from where Mitch had fought the two warriors, and where Bess was engaged with the third alien. He could also see the mining pit in the distance, and Qwii's crescent-shaped vessel. Qwii was still on board, standing calmly, watching the battle. Mitch wasn't sure what he was doing if anything. He let his sense of the invisible gravity power flow out. Bess was fully engaged, fending off both the warrior and the unseen power being directed against her. Fors'No was focused on Mitch, their powers canceling one another out. But there was no sense of anything happening with Qwii, or coming from the crescent ship.

Mitch directed himself down, and let a light strain of gravity pull him back toward the ground. He had to project a bubble of control around himself to keep Fors'No from using the Power to harm him. Mitch came down to the ground easily, and was only a few meters from the warrior he had first attacked. The Cadish fighter launched himself into the air, using gravity to flip himself upside down in a super powered leap. Mitch brought his sword up and blocked the chop his opponent aimed at his head. Mitch let the alien land before spinning around. He didn't have a lot of sword skill, but he had strength and speed. The alien blocked his initial slash, but was once more staggered by the blow. Mitch followed up with a lightning-fast flick that opened a shallow cut on the alien's leg. He bent down, grasping the wound with one hand. Mitch could have severed his head from his shoulders, but once more he felt a hesitation to kill. He stepped close, blocked the alien's clumsy thrust one-handed, and with his left hand he punched the alien in the face. Blood exploded from the alien's nostril slits. His eyes rolled back and he dropped to the ground.

Mitch felt Fors'No rushing toward him. He slid to the side and raised his sword defensively. Fors'No was the complete opposite of the other aliens. He was fast, confident, and just as thrilled to be in the fight as Mitch had been. He feinted like he would slash at Mitch, and shifted into a thrust that Mitch barely managed to dodge. Fors'No used the same double edged short sword as the other Cadish warriors, but he was clearly skilled with the black Cidian sword. He came at Mitch with a flurry of blows the human barely managed to block or evade. Fear was creeping into Mitch's mind. He simply didn't have the experience or skill with the sword to defeat the alien.

"You are strong," Fors'No said while still attacking Mitch. "But clumsy."

Mitch realized the alien was right. He wasn't going to beat Fors'No in a sword fight. Instead, he threw himself at the alien, lowering his shoulder and smashing into the leader of the Cadish invaders. Fors'No hadn't been expecting it. He was knocked to the ground, but scrambled back up quickly and stayed out of reach of Mitch's longer sword.

"There's more than one way to fight," Mitch said.

"I underestimated you," Fors'No said. "Perhaps you are ready to learn the truth."

"Everyone's got their version," Mitch said. "I'll stick with what I know."

"You know the Order protects the Power, dolling it out to newcomers in dribs and drabs. I can show you the full power that the strong were meant to wield," Fors'No said. "Without the need to believe in an invisible Creator, or carry out whatever missions the elders decide to send you on. I took their boot off my neck, and I can help you do the same."

"From the looks of things here," Mitch said. "The only people with the boots on anyone's necks are yours on the Bispees."

"We are improving their backward, stagnated civilization," Fors'No said. "They thank us for it daily."

"Sure..." Mitch said.

Of all the things the alien proclaimed to know or be about, the Bisbees thanking the Cadish invaders was too much for Mitch to swallow. He stepped forward, feinting one way, then kicking up a cloud of dirt toward Fors'no. The alien used his gravity power to fling it all back in Mitch's face. The big man swung his sword to keep the alien at bay, but Fors'No wasn't attacking. Bess had the third warrior pinned to the ground with her long-hafted sword-spear. Fors'No and the other Cadish alien were fleeing.

"Stop!" Qwii called out.

Mitch had been about to chase after his adversaries. But the order was clearly for him. He stood looking around. Two of the aliens sat on the ground, one holding his wounded arm, the other his swollen, bleeding face. Bess stood over her opponent, one foot on the alien's chest.

"We can catch them," Mitch said.

"They are fleeing this world," Qwii said. "That was our mission."

"But they'll just come back," Mitch pointed out.

"Perhaps, but if they do we shall return as well."

Mitch wanted to ask what the Nagani had been doing during the fight. Maybe he had rushed into the conflict a little too soon, but Qwii was supposed to be keeping the Cadish invaders from using their power against him. And from what Mitch had seen and felt, Qwii had been merely a spectator.

"Bind up the prisoners," Qwii continued. "And take them aboard the ship. Bess can watch over them. We must speak to the Bispean leaders."

The fight was completely out of the defeated aliens. They didn't speak to him, but he got the sense that they were never really convinced of their abilities in the first place. They seemed morose. Mitch thought they should be grateful for the mercy they were shown. He doubted they would have been as quick to let him and his companions live if they had won the fight.

The conflict in his mind about killing was starting to worry Mitch a little. He certainly felt that killing others with the Power was wrong. It was a gift from some higher power, whether it was really the Creator that the Order of Scion claimed it to be, or something else, it still felt wrong to kill using the amazing gravity abilities. But Mitch also knew that when someone was trying to kill you, taking it easy on them was not smart. When he had sparred on New Terra with Ninja and Mara, they never held back. He knew a split second of hesitation, from indecision or as an act of mercy, could cost him his life. But he didn't feel bad for not killing the aliens. He never felt like sparing a life was a bad thing. He hoped he never did.

CHAPTER 19

"HOW BAD IS IT?" Flash asked as he made his way into the series of storerooms that the team had set up as their base of operations inside the airport.

"Don't know," Jingo admitted. "The wound won't kill her, but the toxins might."

"She's struggling to breathe right now," Mara said. "She lost a lot of blood, but we're replacing it now. Time will tell. I want you and Ninja on watch."

"Copy that," Flash said. "I've been checking the drone. The bugs didn't follow us."

"Don't mean they won't," Jingo pointed out.

"Good, we need a breather," Mara said. "A couple of days laying low would go a long way for Hawk."

She was cleaning the blood off her hands when Ninja came into the room. He looked concerned. "Sarge, Captain Marcs is on the horn. He wants to talk."

"Probably just wants an update on how things went down," Jingo said.

Mara hated debriefs. After action reports were fine, but having officers pick apart every decision she made in the heat of battle was infuriating. She left one of the small cinderblock-walled rooms and made her way to the communications setup under the metal stairs that led up to the roof. Cables that they had salvaged from the old flight control tower hung down the wall, connecting their communication gear to the antenna they had set up on the sturdy part of the roof above the baggage area of the airport building.

"Captain Marcs," she said, putting on a pair of headphones that were already plugged into the console. "This is Sergeant James."

"Excellent work in Alpha Colony," he told her. "How's Corporal Fleming?"

"Alive," Mara said. "Fighting the toxins, but it's touch and go, sir. She needs medical evac ASAP."

"That's not going to happen Sergeant," Marcs replied. "The *Marathon* is still a few days from orbit. Please upload all the data from your armor. That will have to do for mission debrief. The Lymies are mobilizing."

"Can't be more than a couple dozen of them left, sir," Mara said. "If they move on the airfield we'll cut them down before they get close."

"Not the bugs in Alpha Colony," Captain Marcs explained. "The other colonies. They're all on the move."

"The other eight colonies?" Mara asked.

"Affirmative. We can't tell how many they're sending. The Lymies still scramble the signals from our satellites, but we know the aliens are converging at Bravo and Charlie Colonies."

"For a strike here?" Mara asked.

"Looks that way from up here, Sergeant. We want you to draw the Lymies south, through the forest, to a designated location for an aerial ambush."

"Won't the drone operators lose control of their birds when they get close to the Lymies, sir?"

"They won't be remotely operated," Captain Marcs said.

"We're preprogramming them to hit a specific piece of ground. You job is to get the enemy there."

"The only way to do that is to draw them in," Mara said. "We'll have to be there too."

"We've run the numbers, Sergeant. If your people are at an exact location, you'll be clear of the blast waves. In armor, you'll have an eight-five chance of surviving the bombing with no injuries."

Mara almost laughed. It was a suicide mission no matter what Captain Marcs or anyone else said. The eggheads in orbit could run calculations all day long, but it wasn't their neck on the line. She knew that whoever was setting the odds of survival at eighty-five percent would quickly change their tune the instant they were informed that they would be joining Leo Squad. Not that the engineers on the *Marathon* would ever be put into harm's way. That's what grunts were for, Mara knew. Officers made plans, and her team would carry them out. It was up to her to find a way to survive the mission. Her and no one else.

"If you say so, Captain," Mara replied. "How much time do we have?"

"So far, the Lymies are holding just outside Charlie and Bravo Colonies," Marcs replied. "Giving the bugs from the outer colonies time to reach them."

"We're only fifty kilometers from Bravo and Charlie," Mara said. "Once they start this way it'll only be a matter of hours before they converge on our location."

"That's right," Captain Marcs said. "You need to get ready to move ASAP. I'm sending the mission parameters to you. We'll be watching from up top, but once you make your move from the airfield the clock will start. You'll have twenty-four hours to lead the Lymies into the kill box."

"How far is it?" Mara asked.

"Twenty klicks from your current position. You bloody their nose, Sergeant, and they'll follow you right into the trap."

Mara didn't need to ask if the bombardment would be sufficient to take out the aliens. Either it wouldn't and her people would have to fight the survivors, or the bombardment would be so massive that they had no chance of survival.

"You're not using orbital kinetic bombs sir?" Mara asked.

"No, the brass decided against it. They want the planet back, which means a more focused offensive away from the colonies."

"Sir, I don't mean to be contrary, but there will still be aliens in the colonies."

"We understand that," Captain Marcs said. "Leo Squad will initiate phase one of our efforts to retake the planet. Get your people through this first battle, Sergeant. Mission guidelines are in the pipe. You'll be receiving them shortly. Good luck."

"Thank you, Captain," Mara said, but the feed was cut before she got the words out.

It was a slap in the face. A suicide mission with no backup. She was down to just four Marines in fighting shape and the Lymies could be on top of them within hours. Fury boiled inside her. She hit the wall with the side of her hand, but it didn't make her feel any better. Fortunately, her enhanced strength and size made her bones less fragile. Nothing broke in her hand, but she felt broken just the same. They were an experimental squad in an experimental regimen. She could have had the word *expendable* tattooed on her forehead because that's what she was. Following orders would almost certainly lead to her death. But what choice did she have? The Lymies were mobilizing to hunt her down and kill her. If the Fleet was planning an ambush, she could at least lead the bugs into it. She would probably be killed in the process but she would die knowing she had killed as many of them as possible.

The only unknown to her, as she stood up and activated the cameras Leo Squad had set up to keep tabs on Bravo and Charlie Colonies, was if the brass would have sent them to die if Lieutenant Murphy hadn't bugged out with the aliens? There was no way to know for sure, but she had a feeling that if Mitch was still around, they might not be tasked with a suicide mission.

The cameras showed no movement. There was no sign of the Lymies massing near Bravo or Charlie colonies. The cameras were mounted on weighed tripods and stuck up nearly five meters into the air. They could be rotated or zoomed in. From their vantage point, both cities were clearly visible. If the Lymies were mobilizing, it was being done on the far sides of the cities. Mara wondered briefly if there was any chance the aliens might not be massing their forces to come after Leo Squad and re-establish their hold on Alpha Colony. She could speculate, but the facts were pretty unwavering. The only thing that the Lymies needed an army to do was to fight the humans still near Alpha. Nothing else would require a show of force. Maybe, if there had still been Lymie ships in the system, she could fool herself into thinking they were picking up the warriors no longer needed on New Terra. But there were no Lymie ships in the system, and as far as Mara could see, the only enemy they needed to fight was her team of SSO Marines.

She started back into the old airport break room. Jingo, Flash, and Ninja were waiting. They all three stood around the table where Hawk was laying, but there was nothing they could do to help her. They all looked up when Mara stepped inside. The room wasn't that big. They had each taken small areas to make sleeping mats on. They used their backpacks for pillows, and some of the furniture cushions from the flight control tower were spread out to make a bed. It wasn't much, but it was better than sleeping on the concrete floor.

"What's the word?" Ninja asked.

"We have a mission," Mara said. "The Lymies are mobilizing from the other colonies, and congregating at Bravo and Charlie."

"To attack us?" Jingo asked. "How many bugs we talking about?"

"Hundreds," Mara said, "approaching from east and west, probably at the same time. A coordinated attack on our position and to retake Alpha Colony."

"Damn," Flash said. "We must have really pissed them off."

"Hundreds of bugs against one squad," Jingo said, shaking his head in disbelief.

"They mean business," Ninja added.

"Reinforcements?" Flash asked.

Mara shook her head.

"Evac?" Jingo suggested.

"No," Mara said. "We're going to lead the enemy to a designated position where bomber drones will wipe them out."

Flash chuckled and Jingo frowned.

"You're kidding, right?" Jingo asked.

"Come on, man," Flash said. "This is exactly the kind of mission they would send us on. You know that."

"What I know is that mission sounds more like suicide than a plan," Jingo said.

"The brass can't tell the difference," Ninja said. "It's always been that way."

"After all we've done, they're going to hang us out like bait?" Jingo said. "That's bul—"

Mara cut him off. "It's what we've been ordered to do," she said. "And so, that's what we'll do. How's Hawk?"

"No change." Flash said. "Her breathing is still labored. She's showing signs of poor oxygenation. Blue lips, pale skin, but her eyes are moving. You can see that."

"Flickering back and forth behind her eyelids," Ninja added.

"She needs time," Mara said.

"Time we don't have," Jingo snapped. "How far is the ambush site?"

"Twenty kilometers south through the forest," Mara said. "Probably on the far side of it. Out in the open."

"Nice," Jingo said. "The perfect killing ground. And we'll be right in the thick of it."

"So, what's new?" Mara asked. "That's what we get paid for."

"I didn't sign on to just throw my life away," Jingo replied.

"You scared of dying?" Mara asked.

"Not scared of it, but I ain't looking to speed it along either," Jingo said. "Tell me you've got some brilliant alternative."

Mara shook her head. "Not this time," she said. "I can't see any other alternative. We could run, but the aliens still want us dead. At least this way, we can take as many out with us as possible."

"It ain't much, but it's something," Flash said.

"We need someone monitoring Hawk," Mara said. "The transport needs to be prepped and the battery fully charged."

"We don't have a charger with enough juice," Flash pointed out. "Sun and solar can keep the communication gear working, but it isn't enough to charge the deep batteries on the personnel carrier."

"So rig something up," Mara said. "Use everything we've got. The eggheads on the *Marathon* claim they can keep us from getting caught in the bombardment. I think we all know that's wishful thinking. But either way, we're not coming back here. We set some surprises for the enemy, just enough to get them good and mad."

"Then we run like hell," Flash said.

"As long as we can stay ahead of them," Mara said. "We could get lucky."

"Outpacing the bugs in the transport won't be too tough," Ninja said.

"Once we leave here, we'll have twenty-four hours," Mara said. "We use guerilla tactics in the forest, keep them engaged and moving south. Then we make our stand and pray that the bombs land in time."

"Before we're wiped out?" Jingo said with a grim shake of his head. "You know the bombs will do that right? They'll drop everything on the enemy and we're just collateral damage."

"We can rig the transport," Mara said. "Take shelter inside it when the bombing starts."

"Even an armored personnel carrier won't survive a direct hit from a bomb," Ninja pointed out.

"It won't even survive a close hit," Jingo said. "They're made to stop bullets, not bombs."

"What choice do we have?" Flash said. "We draw the enemy to the ambush then go to ground. We've survived crazier missions before."

"Not like this," Jingo said. "Tell me this doesn't feel like we're the bait in their massive extermination plan."

"Oh, it definitely feels like we're the bait," Flash said.

"But we've got surprise on our side," Ninja said. "At least we'll go down swinging."

"Marine Corps style," Mara said.

"Yeah, who wants to live forever anyway?" Flash added.

"Not forever, but I thought we'd live a bit longer than this," Jingo said.

"Flash, you see to the transport," Mara said. "Jingo and I will gear up in full battle rattle, comlinks tied into the main system here just in case we get a call from up top."

"You're seeing to the welcoming party?" Ninja asked.

"A few land mines wouldn't be unwelcome," Mara said. "You up to that, Jingo?"

He nodded. "Yes, I'm with you."

"Then it's settled. We pack as many guns and as much ammo as possible into the transport. The video feed isn't showing the armies near Bravo or Charlie colonies. That could change at any minute, but for now we've got some time."

"Best to make the most of it," Flash said.

"Yeah, when the bugs come we'll be ready," Ninja agreed.

Hawk made a gurgling sound, almost a gasp, as if she were chiming in on the conversation. Then she exhaled her last breath, and died.

CHAPTER 20

"WILL THEY RETURN?" Bess whispered. She was acting as the interpreter for Mitch. They were gathered with a group of Bispeans near the rock-breaking equipment. It was perched near the side of the huge crater that the aliens had dug. Some of those who had been enslaved to dig up the precious minerals that were native to Bispee were still climbing out of the gigantic hole. Mitch could see even from a distance how weak they were. The long trail that led out of the mine would be difficult to ascend under the best of conditions. And the short, furry Bispee aliens with their antenna drooping, looked ragged.

"Eventually," Qwii said. "Your planet is rich in resources."

"Resources we have worked to protect," the leader of the Bispee party said. They spoke in whispery sighs and what sounded to Mitch like whimpers, but they could speak what Mitch had learned was called Common, a simple language known on many planets. Common sounded more like a language than any alien dialect he had heard. And he made up his mind to learn it as quickly as possible. In the meantime, Bess continued to translate for him.

186   TOBY NEIGHBORS

"We choose to honor our world, not harvest it," the Bispean leader said.

"As you should," Qwii said. "Bispee is a jewel among the worlds of the universe."

"But we cannot protect it from the Fray."

"That is our job," Qwii said. "The Order of Scion will always fight the Fray, no matter where they turn up."

"We owe you a great debt."

"Your friendship is all the payment we desire," Qwii said. "We must leave soon and take the captives back to our rehabilitation facilities in the Ashyn system."

"On Bispee, murder is a high crime, one that requires retribution, not rehabilitation."

"I understand," Qwii said. "But if we were to leave them here it would put your people at further risk."

The aliens all bobbed up and down in clear agreement with Qwii. They may have wanted the Cadish invaders dead, but they knew they weren't in any position to do the executing personally. Mitch felt sorry for them. They had a wonderful planet, and what seemed to him like a great society, but they couldn't protect themselves. It made Mitch wonder just how prepared the human race was to protect itself. He remembered the kinetic bombs aimed at the colonies on New Terra. They should have all been obliterated, but the Fray had knocked nine fifty-ton metal bombs off course. He had no idea how fast they were falling, or exactly how they were aimed, but he couldn't help but wonder if he was strong enough in the Power and Knowledge to save even one colony from such weapons, much less nine.

"So be it," the Bispean leader said. "Take them and go. The Order of Scion will always be welcome on Bispee. Your intervention will not be forgotten. We must see the restoration of our world, and those families that lost loved ones."

"We are honored," Qwii said. "Should you need us, you have

only to send word. My brothers will soon secure a portal for your people so that you can contact us easily."

The group of short, furry aliens all bowed, their antennae waving gently in the air over their heads. Mitch and Bess stood up. Qwii followed suit a moment later. They turned back and headed toward the crescent-shaped ship.

"Does your ship have a name?" Mitch asked.

"A name?" Qwii asked. "It is just an object. Why would it have a name?"

"Among my people we name our ships," Mitch asked.

"Cities have names," Bess said. "Planets, systems ... why not ships?"

"Do you have a suggestion?" Qwii asked.

"It's your ship," Mitch said. "You should name it."

"It's my home," Qwii said. "Flying is secondary."

"How about *Luska*?" Bess suggested. "In Common it means moonlight."

"Looks like a crescent moon," Mitch admitted.

"It does suit the structure," Qwii said. "*Luska* it is."

They took their time. Mitch was a tall man, with a long stride. But his companions were shorter. He had to slow down and take his time. He used the slower pace to allow his senses to spread out. It was a new habit he was working to develop. Everything was affected by gravity. Even the insects in the ground were operating in the planet's gravity, but also emitting their own gravitational fields. It was strange, yet in a way it was like part of his mind was waking up to a reality he had never noticed before. It was walking out of a cave and being able to see again.

They walked onto the ship and went directly to the observation deck. Mitch felt very somber as Qwii formed a gravity-free bubble around the *Luska*. It rose up into the air, giving the three individuals at the opening a great view of the planet. The mine was like a scar upon the world, but the higher they rose the less prominent the mining pit became. If the Bispeans were diligent, it would be filled in and brought back to the natural state along with the rest of the planet.

"The prisoners are rousing," Bess said.

"We will make the leap to Ashyn within the hour," Qwii said. "The two of you will have no issues keeping them in check."

Mitch gave Qwii a little nod, then followed Bess to a different part of the ship. Mitch felt at home in the main gallery, the dining room, and the area he thought of as the observation deck. It was actually more of a lobby, or a really big foyer, mainly just a large empty space with a massive opening. Mitch was still staying in the room he had first slept in. The room had furniture that seemed custom made for him. And Uri did an excellent job of keeping everything clean. Mitch wasn't a naturally neat person, but joining the Marines and always feeling as if he weren't in his own space, caused him to work a little harder to remain tidy.

The Cadish captives were kept in a small chamber with no furniture. It looked more like a storage compartment than a prison cell. But like everything on the *Luska* it was spacious and light. There were no shadows, no racks of cleaning supplies or tools. The floor, walls, and ceiling all looked exactly the same, as if the entire ship was carved from one big block of whatever substance the ship was made from. It reflected light, which made the walls and floors seem to glow. The prisoners were laying down inside the room. Mitch and Bess paused outside the chamber's only door. Mitch could feel the Cadish prisoners moving around inside. Two were nursing their wounds, the other starting to pace. What surprised Mitch the most was that they didn't seem to have any Power, or Knowledge. They were just people, not humans, but not gravity masters either.

"They don't have power?" Mitch asked.

"What they can or cannot do is yet to be seen," Bess said. "Some Fray are very powerful. Others are simply useful tools."

"Pawns," Mitch said. "Fors'No was using them."

"Some are lured into evil by the promise that they will be taught the Power and Knowledge."

"Not the Knowledge," Mitch said. "Fors'No claimed it wasn't true."

"Their own twisted version of Knowledge," Bess said. "From my experience the Fray are great imitators of truth. They don't do anything on their own, but only what they see and hear. They take the Knowledge and pervert it."

"Okay, so we have three pawns with no real power," Mitch said. "What will happen to them?"

"It depends," Bess said. "If their knowledge and ability really is minimal, they could be rehabilitated and sent home. Those with greater skill must be carefully contained to ensure they do no more harm."

"Is it possible that they had no control?" Mitch said. "Can the Power be used to control people?"

Bess thought about the question for a moment, her feline features pinched in thought. "For some races it is possible," she replied. "Although such use of the Power and Knowledge would be a great injustice."

The trip didn't take long. Mitch still felt like the day had just begun, and he had already traveled to two different star systems and defeated a group of Fray. Ashyn was a strange planet that cycled between warming and cooling periods every thousand years. The cities were built on massive pylons so that when the warm cycle was in full swing and the surface of the planet was covered in water, the cities were still above the deluge.

The *Luska* landed on a platform beside a series of towers linked together with bridges every few stories. It was an impressive sight. All the pylons had round landing platforms built around them on all sides, like flower petals.

"This is Ashyn," Qwii said. "The Order of Scion is based here."

"And the prisoners will be kept here?" Mitch asked.

"Processed here," Qwii explained. "Then taken to a separate

facility to be guarded. Here every member of the order can find rest, healing, counsel. It is a sanctuary for the True Navigators."

They were met by a group of aliens that looked almost like dogs. They had four legs, and canine faces, but they spoke the common language and wore what looked like leather clothing. They even had tails. They took charge of the three Cadish prisoners who didn't resist. Mitch guessed they were grateful just to be alive, and maybe even out of the control of their ruthless masters.

"What's next?" Mitch asked.

"Now, we present you to the High Council," Qwii said. "It will not hurt to spend a few days here. There is still much for you to learn."

"Got it," Mitch said. "I could stand to learn that language you've been using."

"Tutoring is available here," Qwii said. "In Common, and much more."

Bess was silent. She walked behind Mitch and Qwii. They still had their weapons tucked neatly into their Scion robes, which were arranged to conceal them. Mitch wasn't sure how Bess got her Yari spear sword tucked into her robe, but he knew it was there. They walked across a bridge. Dark blue water with whitecaps surged below them. There was no railing on the bridge, and nothing to keep you from tumbling down into the deep water. Occasionally a wave would slap against the pylon hard enough to send spray flying up into the air. Little rainbows formed in the spray.

Looking up, Mitch could see towers that were so tall their tops were lost in the clouds. The buildings were constructed in all kinds of shapes, from round towers to polygon-shaped buildings that seemed to defy logic. Mitch was used to cities that were built from glass and steel, but the buildings on Ashyn were more like the *Luska* and built from some type of alien material he couldn't identify. It was more organic than the structures he was used to.

The bridge from the landing pad led into a massive building. The entrance was grand, the ceiling at least twenty meters high, the floors polished to a gleaming shine in the light from glowing orbs that floated in the air above their heads. There were statues in nooks built into the walls, and large plaques with strange writing were mounted between the statues.

"This is the Hall of Honor," Qwii said. "To commemorate those who devote their lives to restoring the Creator's order in the universe."

"It's impressive," Mitch said.

"We do it to remember those who have come before us," Qwii said. "From the very first members of the Order, those who were taught the Power and the Knowledge from the Creator's own son."

"How long ago was that?"

"Thousands of generations," Qwii said.

They went up a staircase at the far end of the Hall of Honor. Mitch wasn't bothered by the climb, but Qwii was breathing heavily by the time they reached the top. It opened to an ornate hallway that curved off in both directions from the staircase. There was signage on the wall that Mitch couldn't read.

"This way to the council chamber," Qwii puffed. "But give me a moment to catch my breath."

Bess touched Mitch's arm. "Farewell, Mitch Murphy."

"What? You're leaving?"

"Our paths separate here," she said.

"Wait, are you leaving for good?"

"I must," she explained. "There is work to be done. You do not need my help."

"Are you kidding?" Mitch asked. "I can't even understand Common. And there's so much left for me to learn from you."

"Learning is a lifelong endeavor," she said with a smile. "Helping you on your journey was my pleasure, but there are other needs that I must attend to. Farewell."

"Okay," Mitch said. "I'll see you around ... I hope."

He watched her move off down the curving hallway. Qwii

nodded at Mitch and then set off in the opposite direction from Bess.

"Did you know she was leaving?" Mitch asked.

"I didn't ask," Qwii said. "It is customary for Scion Warriors to cross the galaxy with True Navigators. They come and go as needed."

"Will we see her again?"

"If the Creator wills it," Qwii said.

"How many members does the Order of Scion have?"

"That is an excellent question. And one I cannot answer. The numbers change. Some leave us to devote themselves to study, or to serve the Creator in other ways. Some fall away, it is sad, but true. Not all who receive training in the Power and Knowledge keep to our Mandate. There are many temptations in life. And some pass away. There will be time for learning this and much more."

The hallway ended in a plush room with a variety of comfortable furniture. There were sofas of varying heights and sizes, round chairs with no backs, large cushions that sat right on the polished floor, and even a few wooden railings that looked like something a bird would perch on. There were already several beings in the room. Mitch thought maybe they were the High Council, but Qwii corrected that error.

"The High Council meets in the next chamber," Qwii said. "Here we wait until called in."

He walked over to what appeared to be a touchscreen device, next to a set of massive doors wrapped in dark material that looked like leather, with padding underneath. Mitch guessed they were made that way to block the sound from the council chamber. Qwii tapped at the touchscreen, then settled onto a couch nearby. Mitch joined him. They waited for nearly an hour. Mitch spent the time studying the other members waiting to see the council. Some were called in before them, others left waiting. None seemed worried or nervous the way Mitch felt.

"Why do I need to go before the High Council?" Mitch asked.

"You are a member of the Order," Qwii replied. "These are your leaders now. You have the right to be seen, and to bring the council information as needed. That is our way, Mitch Murphy. We are all devoted to the Creator's mandate, and none is more important than another."

"Okay, but what's going to happen in there?" Mitch asked.

"You will introduce yourself and your species," Qwii said. "It isn't something to be nervous about."

Mitch disagreed, but didn't argue. When they were called in, he stood up and adjusted his robes. Then he followed Qwii through the massive double doors.

CHAPTER 21

THE COUNCIL CHAMBER was smaller than Mitch expected. Nine aliens sat behind a horseshoe-shaped table. No two were alike. Some were big, some small. Two looked as though they came from aquatic worlds. Some had multiple arms, another had none and looked like a giant worm. The three directly in the center of the curving table were more like Mitch than the others. One was a Nagani like Qwii. Another was tall and thin, with long, white hair that flowed down from the top of his oval-shaped head. The third had big, dark eyes, and a long tapering head. Its hands had three fingers with little suction cups at the tips.

Qwii spoke first, then stepped back so that Mitch was in the center of the room.

"Um, Hi," Mitch said, clearing his throat nervously. "My name is Mitch Murphy and I'm from Earth, in the Sol system."

The alien with the long head spoke in Common. Qwii translated the question.

"He wants to know if you're a human," Qwii said.

"Yes," Mitch said. "I'm a human, although my physiology is

different from most of my kind. I was given a serum that enhanced my physical traits. I'm taller and stronger than most humans."

The alien with long, white hair spoke.

"This is Germantus," Qwii translated. "He wants to know why you've been enhanced to be bigger and stronger."

"My race discovered a portal to a system we call Terra," Mitch explained. "After working for centuries within our own system, we ventured through the portal and into the Terra system where we found a habitable world. But we weren't the only ones to find it. My people have long been protective of what we have. I joined the Colonial Marine Corps, a military organization formed to protect the colonists on New Terra."

"So, you are a fighter," Germantus said. "And now you are a member of the Order of Scion. Do you believe as we do, in the Creator and his mandate of restoration?"

"I do," Mitch said. It wasn't the whole truth, but it wasn't a lie either.

"We welcome you, Mitch Murphy," the Nagani member of the council said.

Qwii continued translating.

"You are the first of your kind," Germantus said. "That is a high honor."

"I am honored," Mitch said. "And thankful to the Order of Scion for accepting me."

"We will be watching your career with great interest," the Nagani council member said.

Qwii gave a brief bow and Mitch did the same. When they left the chamber Mitch breathed a sigh of relief.

"See, that wasn't so bad," Qwii said.

"No one seems to think I believe in the Creator," Mitch pointed out.

"Do you?"

"Yeah ... I haven't worked out all the details yet, but I'm getting there."

"Good. Power without Knowledge is dangerous," Qwii said. "Entire worlds have been lost in the struggle for Power without the guidance of the Knowledge."

"Really?" Mitch asked.

"Yes," Qwii said. "My own home world, for instance, was ravaged by fighting when the Fray went to war against the Order."

"There have been full scale wars?" Mitch asked.

"It is inevitable," Qwii said, leading the way to a bank of elevators. The doors swished open and they stepped inside. "There are many historians who can teach you of the past, but today, we will focus on the future."

The elevator rose up quickly. When the doors opened again, it was to an elegant space with tables and various kinds of seating. The aroma of hot beverages and baked goods made Mitch's stomach growl. Qwii led the way to a counter where a group of aliens was busy working to prepare food and drink. Mitch was given a hot, sweet beverage. It was like hot chocolate for adults. And he received a small green loaf that was a mix of bread and cake.

"This is Yashini," Qwii explained about the loaf. "Made from sea vegetation. It is naturally sweet and very sustaining."

"Looks delicious," Mitch said.

They sat down at a table where an alien with a long neck, small head, and watery eyes was reading a computer tablet of some sort. The creature spoke in Common, which Mitch didn't understand but was starting to get a feel for. At first the language had seemed all garbled together, but having heard it multiple times, from various aliens, he was starting to pick up on individual words.

"Mitch Murphy, this is Hollis Dai, a gifted teacher and nine-year member of the Order," Qwii said. "Arq convinced Hollis to learn your language so that she could teach you Common."

"That would be fantastic," Mitch said. "You understand me?"

"I do," the alien said in an almost hypnotic voice. "I would be honored to teach you, Mitch Murphy."

"That would be great," Mitch said. "I'm eager to learn."

"Good," Hollis said. "We can begin now. You are sitting on a *dosk*. Repeat it please."

"Dosk," Mitch said out loud.

"Good. Put your hands on it and think about the dosk. Imagine it in your mind's eye. This will help you remember it."

"Dosk," Mitch said again.

Hollis put her hands on the table. They were more like animal paws, than human hands, only the digits were longer. She had blonde fur on the backs of her hands, and instead of fingernails, she had thin, curving claws at the tip of each of her four fingers.

"This is called a *jusit*."

"Jusit," Mitch said, putting his hands on the table. "Jusit."

The lesson went on for another ten minutes while they ate their meal. The sweet loaf of bread reminded Mitch of carrot cake, only it was denser. The outside was flaky, the interior soft, and the small item was much more filling than Mitch expected. Once their meal was finished, they left together and made their way back down to the ship. Hollis went to fetch a few more belongings and Qwii met with another member of the Order to get their next assignment.

"Where to now?" Mitch asked. He was feeling good, even a little arrogant. Life with the Order of Scion seemed easy and fun. But he had barely even dipped his toe into the reality of life across the universe.

"The Osterious system," Qwii said. "And from there, we will join the other Scion Warriors helping the Grostu people transition to a new planet."

"Sounds good," Mitch said. He couldn't imagine anything better than seeing more of the galaxy and helping people in need. The Power he had gained access to was so amazing that he couldn't wait to see what needs might come up that he could help solve.

They stopped on their way back down at the observation level. The entire floor was one big open space. The walls were completely transparent. Mitch could see for miles and miles out across the open expanse of water. The sun was going down and the ocean reflected the dazzling red color.

"This is spectacular," Mitch admitted.

"Wait until you see it in a storm," Qwii said. "The waves get so high and crash hard against the pylons. Lightning fills the sky overhead. The wind howls. My planet had nothing like it."

"Had?" Mitch asked. "You said your planet was destroyed in a war?"

"Nagin Prime," he said. "The Nagani have long been supporters of the Order of Scion. The first of us to be accepted by the Order was Urk the Peacemaker. He returned to us and opened our eyes to the true knowledge of the Creator. My people embraced the truth and lived at peace. Every generation more members were added to the Order, and we grew in understanding that was much like your industrial revolution."

"You know Earth history?" Mitch asked.

"I have studied your race along with Arq and Juj for many years. It was an honor to be selected for that prestigious service. I am the twenty-second of my kind. But in helping you, I am helping a new race discover the truth of our Creator and making the universe a little more like what it was intended to be."

"But you lost your world?"

"The Fray banded together nearly a century ago," Qwii explained. "And began attacking worlds protected by the Order. Nagin was one such planet. We fought back of course, but the Fray were ruthless. They couldn't defeat us, and instead they destroyed what we were committed to protecting. They combined their strength and sent our moon, Javini, crashing into the surface of Nagin. I don't have to tell you what the gravitational power of two such large bodies did to each other. Nagin was ripped apart. The plate tectonics shifted so much that everything we had built was destroyed. Without the moon, the planet was unstable. Our people were forced to flee. Fortunately, by that stage we had dozens of other worlds in different systems colonized. But Nagin was lost forever."

"Couldn't a Planet Mover have saved it?"

"In theory," Qwii said, staring out at the endless waves. "But none were there in time. The collision of the moon into the planet's surface destroyed it, and there is no way to restore that."

"I'm sorry," Mitch said. "That sounds awful."

"It was, but that is in the past. I never knew life on Nagin. But we were all taught as cubs about our precious home world. I have visited that system many times. The destruction is great, but there is still a beauty there. The planet is wild and unstable. So much of the liquid water on the surface was vaporized, filling the atmosphere with steam that then fed savage storms. Nothing lives on Nagin now. It is a constant reminder of how destructive the Power can be apart from the Knowledge that guides our use of it."

The lesson was sad, but one that struck a chord with Mitch. He understood how dangerous unchecked power could be and didn't want to fall into that trap. It was another reason he felt that joining the Order of Scion was a good thing. The other members gave him a sense of accountability to help combat the temptation to use his power for personal gain.

When they reached the Hall of Honor, Mitch was surprised to find Hollis waiting for them. She had a bag with her. It was long and narrow, hanging from one shoulder. In her other hand was the tablet she had been reading when Mitch first met her.

"Are we ready to leave?" Qwii asked.

"I am at your disposal, Navigator."

"Very good," Qwii said. "By the time we return, you'll be reading and speaking Common, Mitch Murphy."

"Sounds like a plan," he replied.

They walked out over the bridge. The smell of briny ocean water was strong. Mitch remembered it from trips to the bay when he worked at Sterling Financial. San Francisco wasn't a beach town, and he couldn't afford to live in the city, but there were several parks with views of the famous bay. The smell of salt water was the same on Earth as it was on Ashyn.

They entered the *Luska* and Qwii was met immediately by Uri. She seemed concerned.

"What's wrong?" Mitch asked.

"It is nothing," Qwii said. "Just news from home. Nothing to worry about."

Mitch didn't know how much the Power affected his mind, or what the LE Protocol had done to increase his mental acuity, but he knew without a doubt that Qwii was lying to him in that moment. He didn't need Uri's look of doubt to know that he wasn't getting the full story. But he didn't want to call out his mentor in front of Hollis.

"Uri will get you settled, Hollis. We will be in the Osterious system in a few hours."

"Very well," Hollis said, with a bob of her head.

"I think maybe I'll get a little rest too," Mitch said, even though he wasn't tired and didn't need to rest.

"I will wake you when we are approaching the planet," Qwii said.

Mitch made his way up to his room and waited for nearly an hour before Uri arrived. When she did, she looked nervous.

"I know he wasn't telling me the truth," Mitch told her. "But I won't let on that I heard it from you. He doesn't need to know that."

"I would never disobey the master of the ship," Uri said. "He is a venerated member of the Order of Scion."

"Yes, he is. But this news pertains to me, doesn't it?"

She nodded, looking down.

"Then I think I deserve to know the truth."

"A message came in from Arq," Uri said. "He's requesting that you join him in the Terra system."

"That's not so bad," Mitch said.

"There's trouble on the planet."

"I'm not surprised. There were several hostile species on that world when we left."

"Arq implied that your race is in danger. That is all I know."

Mitch felt an icy cold void in the center of his body. Humans in danger wasn't news, it was a story repeated daily in the Sol system. But Arq wasn't in the Sol system, he was in Terra. And the only people there were colonists and Marines. Mitch thought they were gone, taken out by the Space Force fleet. So why was Arq calling for Mitch's assistance? He didn't know, but he knew it was imperative that he find out ... before it was too late.

CHAPTER 22

IT WAS FOLLY, but they took the time to bury Hawk at the edge of the forest. The ground was soft but rocky. They spent half a day digging the grave, making sure it was deep enough. Mara washed her friend's body. Estelle Flemming had been her companion for years, the only other woman on Leo Squad. Mara had seen Marines come and go, some were reassigned, others killed. She had always thought that she would die herself long before Hawk did.

While Mara cleaned the body, Ninja and Flash cleaned her armor. Jingo saw to the LRRG sniper rifle. He broke it down, cleaned and oiled every part. The barrel was lined with metal hydrogen which had almost no friction, but made the weapon very expensive. That one weapon cost more than a family-size hovercar. When Mara finished cleaning and dressing her friend, they put on her armor, including the helmet, and wrapped her arms around the long rifle before swaddling her in clean sheets.

"Damn, this is harder than I thought," Jingo said.

"Can't believe she's gone," Ninja said. "We had plans."

"Tell us," Flash said as they lifted the body onto a door that Jingo had pulled free from one of the other rooms in the airport.

The four remaining members of Leo Squad lifted the door by the corners and started walking across the building. It was little more than a shell. In the main concourse the roof had been torn off, the windows were all shattered, the furniture smashed, and the ticket kiosks destroyed. Only the old baggage area remained intact. It had two big overhead doors. One was blocked by the armored personnel carrier. The other was open for the group to walk through. No one had their armor on, no helmets or in-ear comlinks. It didn't matter to any of them if the Lymies showed up while they carried their friend to her final resting place. Nothing could disturb that sacred final act.

"We had a little thing going," Ninja said. It wasn't news, the entire squad knew about Ninja and Hawk, even though they kept it private and didn't flaunt their relationship. "She really loved the Corps. Didn't ever want to leave, but you know, sooner or later they'll find a reason to discharge us."

"Ain't that a hell of a thing," Flash said.

"True," Jingo said.

"So, we made plans. We were both saving as much of our pay as we could. We were going to build a hunting lodge. A nice place for the rich fat cats to come and play at being the hunter. We were going to have a little place for ourselves too. An apartment over the garage maybe. Let the guests stay in the big house when they weren't in the bush. It would have been just the two of us. We could take guests during the hunting season, but the rest of time we could be together."

"Sounds nice," Mara said.

"Peaceful," Jingo added. "You think she would care if we came to visit?"

"She talked about it," Ninja explained. "She would have put you all up in the big house. It was her dream to have her friends close."

They reached the grave and carefully set the door with Hawk's body on top of two long cargo straps that Flash had pilfered from the airport wreckage.

"Things rarely turn out the way we hope," Mara said. "I never knew Estelle to be religious, but she believed in something that was bigger than all of us."

"She used to say the guy upstairs was watching out for her," Ninja said, fighting back the tears.

"Wherever she is I know it's gotta be better than here," Jingo said. "If anyone deserved it, Hawk did."

"Never said a cross word and always had your back," Flash added.

Mara knelt down beside the body. "I'll miss you and I'll never forget you." Standing up, Mara took up a strap. The others followed her lead. Ninja was weeping openly, but no one faulted him for it. There were tears in all their eyes.

"My mother used to sing this old gospel song when I little," Mara said. Then she began to sing with a strong, clear voice.

I love you, Lord.
For your mercy never fails me.
All my days, I've been held in your hand.
From the moment that I wake up
Until I lay my head
Oh, I will sing of the goodness of God.
Cause all my life you have been faithful.
And all my life you have been so, so good.
With every breath that I am able
I will sing of the goodness of God.

By the end she was struggling to sing through her sobs. The three huge men with her were crying too. They weren't religious, but they understood death. They knew there was something that animated a person other than a beating heart and neurons firing in a person's brain. That spark, or spirit, or soul, or whatever one chose to call it, had taken leave of Estelle "Hawk" Flemming's body and had gone on to some other place. She was beyond their reach and it was comforting to think that she was in God's hands.

They moved her over to the grave, the body hanging from the cargo straps as they carefully lowered her down into the hole. The crying continued as they shoveled the dirt down onto her body. When it was done they covered the mound of dirt with the larger stones they had pulled out of the ground when they were digging the grave. And Mara used a small laser pistol from the armory they had taken weapons from in Alpha Colony to inscribe her name on the largest of the stones.

It felt good to have done the work of burying their friend the proper way. And they were all mentally tired from the exercise. They walked back to the airport building in silence and began the work of preparing for war. Mara went to the communications console under the stairs. There were lights flashing with missed messages from the ships in orbit. But one glance at the video feeds from the cameras monitoring Bravo and Charlie Colonies told her what she needed to know. The Lymies were on the move. Not that she could see them. Both feeds were nothing but static. The screen was a blur, not an out of focus image, but one completely scrambled by the spidery aliens.

Mara picked up the headset and hit the transmit button.

"*Marathon* actual, this is Leo Squad. Do you read me? Over."

The response was instantaneous. "We read you Leo Squad. We've been trying to reach you. Stand by for Captain Marcs."

"Standing by," Mara replied.

The wait was nearly four minutes. Then the captain's gruff voice came through the headset.

"Leo Squad, this is Captain Marcs. You have bogeys on the move. I repeat, the Lymies are headed your way."

"Copy that," Mara said. "We're getting ready."

"You've been offline for nearly six hours, Leo Squad. What is going on down there?"

"We were burying Corporal Flemming," Mara said. "She passed. The toxins were too much for her body."

"Damn, I'm sorry, Sergeant. But her death won't be in vain. We will get the planet back. And we'll make every last one of the bugs pay for her death."

"Roger that, Captain. We are gearing up and should be in radio contact until the bugs get close. Do you have an estimate on when they might begin to arrive?"

"You could see the first of them in a little over an hour from the west," Captain Marcs said. "The weather pukes are saying there's a pretty good wind blowing west to east. If the bugs take to the air, they could be at the colony pretty fast. Otherwise, we're guessing three hours. I wish it were longer."

"That's enough time," Mara said. "We aren't holding this position for long. I'm needed Captain. Is there anything else?"

"Negative, Sergeant. Give 'em hell."

"You can count on it, Captain. Sergeant James, out."

She flung off the headset and let the tears flow. It was turning into the worst day of her life and the only good news was that she would soon get to kill some Lymies. She wiped the tears from her face, put on her battle helmet, and suited up.

Once she was in full battle rattle, she checked her weapons. The automatic shotgun was loaded with solid slugs. She had one barrel magazine on the heavy weapon, and three more on her belt. She slung a Garrison Assault Rifle over her back, and strapped tactical webbing with ten magazines for the GAR over her armor. She had a Desert Eagle .45 caliber automatic pistol on one hip, with several clips of ammo for the pistol on her belt. She also had no less than five knives clipped to her armor.

Flash was working nearby, loading up the transport. He already had the battery swapped out with one from the fallen flight control tower. Ninja was setting mines to the east of the airfield. Jingo was rigging explosives near the trees which they would be running for when the Lymies got close. Mara picked up a bag full of land mines. The small devices were round and said *this side up* on the top.

She slung the bag over her shoulder and started running. There was no need to tell the rest of her companions what she was doing. They all knew what was coming.

"You in a hurry, Sarge?" Flash asked.

He was still in the transport and she was already out of the building, but his voice came to her via the comlink. Her helmet had tiny speakers beside her ears, so she could hear him clearly even with bombs going off all around her.

"The bugs are on the move," she replied. "We've got anywhere from an hour to three hours before they show up. Don't dawdle."

"Yeah, copy that," Flash said. "Slow is the one speed I don't do."

"Any idea where they'll come from first?" Ninja asked.

"The wind is blowing east," she said. "The brass says the fliers could be coming from that direction soon."

"I'll be finished here before that," Flash said. "I'll get up top and cover you, Marauder."

"Sounds good," she replied. "Until we see them, everyone keeps working."

"Copy that," Jingo said.

Mara wondered how much longer she would live. Part of her wanted to just make a stand and kill as many bugs as she could before they overwhelmed her. But she had a mission to complete and like it or not, she was the de facto team leader. The bombing would probably kill the entire squad, if they lived long enough to lead the bugs to the ambush site. The clock wasn't ticking yet, but once they headed south they would have twenty-four hours. She didn't want to die, but she was glad she could see it coming. Her family traced their heritage way back to the native tribes of North America. It was all a bit fuzzy, the records weren't clear, and Mara had never cared all that much about it, but she related to one idea she had read as a child. It had to do with how a person faces death.

She wasn't going to shy away from it, or try to hide from it. Mara James was ready to go out and meet death. She would face it on its terms and if it chose to take her to whatever came after, she was fine with that. At least then the pain she was feeling over the loss of her friend would end. And while she might not be buried, she could rest knowing that she died on the same world as Estelle. It was cold comfort, and thin at that, but it was better than nothing.

She dropped to one knee and started digging a hole for the first land mine.

CHAPTER 23

MITCH LEFT his room and went down to the Observation deck. Qwii was there. The ship had already made the transition through space and was in the Osterious system. Mitch could see several gas giants in the distance. He walked up beside Qwii and stood with his hands behind his back.

"You can tell me what's really going on now," Mitch said.

"I don't understand what you are asking me," Qwii replied. "We're going to the Osterious system to help the Osters in their struggle against the Lomtuc Raiders."

"I've heard of them," Mitch said.

"They've long troubled the Osters. Of late their efforts have intensified."

"But they're not the Fray," Mitch said. "Right?"

"That is correct. They have not been found worthy to be taught the Power and Knowledge. Perhaps in the future that will change."

Mitch nodded. It was interesting information, but not what he had come to talk to Qwii about.

"So, what was the message you got?" Mitch said. "There's no sense in lying to me about it. We both know it was bad."

"I do not know that it was bad," Qwii replied.

"Come on," Mitch argued. "You don't have a strong poker face."

"Poker face?"

"It's a card game that sometimes involves bluffing. What I'm saying is that you are not a good liar."

"That should be a compliment."

"Qwii, please, tell me what the message was. I know you well enough to know that you're hiding something from me."

His shoulder sagged a little and for the first time since Mitch had arrived he glanced over at him.

"There were no details," Qwii said. "Just a recommendation from Arq that you return to the Terra system."

"So, what's the big deal?"

"Do you not recall what Thorn Isska Malchais Sonso told you before your confirmation?"

Mitch had to think a moment, then it came back to him: *It is my opinion that it would best for you, Mitch Murphy, not to return to your people, at least for some time.*

"He doesn't want me going home," Mitch said.

Qwii nodded. Every race is different. Yours has a history of conflict. There have been many tyrannical leaders in your human history. That is a temptation best put off until you are well grounded in the Knowledge of the Creator's mandate."

"Okay, I understand that," Mitch said. "But shouldn't we at least find out what's going on?"

"What good would that do?" Qwii said. "It will only make staying away more difficult. I think it best if we busy ourselves with other tasks."

"I understand," Mitch said. "But if my people are in danger the way the Bispeans were, or even the Osters, and I could help, I want to."

"Arq and Juj are there. They will not let your people be destroyed."

"But I was chosen, not just to fight, but to lead my race into the Knowledge of the Creator. That's my task, not Arq's or Juj's. It's my responsibility, Qwii. I need to know what's going on. And if necessary, I need to go and do whatever I can to help."

"That's exactly why I didn't tell you. I have found you to be a person with strong compulsions to do what you feel duty bound to carry out. You could have stayed on the shuttle that bore your companions away from New Terra, but you gave up your seat for others. You came with us when the opportunity was presented to you, and threw yourself into the training. I have no doubt that you will become a great member of the Order one day, Mitch Murphy, but I cannot allow you to return to your system."

"Terra isn't my system," Mitch said.

Qwii turned and looked at him again. Mitch returned the gaze.

"Technicality," Qwii replied.

"What were the human ships doing when we left the system?"

"Running for the portal back to the Sol system."

"Exactly. We had given up all claim to the planet. For all we know I wouldn't be returning to my people. You're not breaking any rules. We can go there and back in less than a day, am I right?"

"It is possible," Qwii said. "We took our time leaving your system to allow you the opportunity to acclimate to the ideas we were presenting."

"So we go, see what Arq needs me for, then come back," Mitch said. "It might be no big deal."

"Arq would not have reached out otherwise."

"Does he even know that I completed the training?"

"I sent him word, yes."

"Okay, well, I owe him. I owe my people. And I owe you most of all. I won't let you down."

Qwii shook his head, his fur rippling with indecision. Mitch waited. He had presented his case and it was all he could do. If Qwii denied him, Mitch would have to accept it.

"You can be very persuasive," Qwii said. "Once our task here is complete, we will journey to the Grost system by way of the Terra system."

"That is all I ask," Mitch said.

They stood side by side and remained silent for a long time. Mitch was itching to get back home. He wanted to help, whatever the situation was. The Knowledge didn't discourage him helping his people. In fact, leading them to peace and protecting them was part of his mandate. Eventually, he would have the strength and skill to operate his own ship the way that Qwii flew the *Luska* between star systems. He could help the human race expand across the galaxy and teach them about the Creator. Mitch had no illusions about the reception his message would have. Some would embrace it; others would reject it. But none would be able to deny the Power, which in turn would be proof that what he was sharing was true. At least that was what he hoped. Humanity had a habit of martyring people who worked to bring peace and stability. Still, Mitch knew that no one had ever had such incredible power before. If someone tried to harm him, he would have to show them just how bad an idea that really was.

The Osters were tall beings. Incredibly thin, with long arms and legs. They had no discernable head, just eyes and mouth on the top of a long skinny body. Mitch was reminded of a walking stick, only the Osters weren't insects. They lived in small villages and subsisted on whatever they could find. Some were hunters, but mainly using traps to catch small game. They all foraged. Their world was thick with edible plants, berries, and fruit. When Mitch stepped out onto Osterious he found the air thick and sweet with the scent of growing things. There was thick grass covering the ground like a carpet, and small colorful flowers sprang up everywhere. Most of the trees were short and laden with exotic fruits that Mitch had never seen before.

Hollis joined Mitch. If the tutor had a weapon Mitch couldn't see it.

"Listen when people speak," she instructed. "I will translate for you, but try and pick out some of the words you hear."

"Okay," Mitch said.

A crowd of the Osters was gathering. One stepped forward and bowed. It was a surprising gesture. The figure was very stiff, and had to bend his long legs to bow. Qwii copied the gesture, and then spread his hands. When he spoke in Common, the crowd hung on every word.

"We are from the Order of Scion," Qwii said. "We are here to help you in your struggle."

The chief of the village spread his hands. "It is too late. The Lomtucs have taken Larmyr, the great city. They have weapons that strike us down from a distance. We have no choice but to do as they tell us."

"The Lomtucs are hostile people, but they cannot stand against us," Qwii said. "We will drive them back to their starships and send them away from your planet."

"If that is possible, we would forever be in your debt."

"The Order of Scion will always help. It is our mandate."

Qwii bowed and then turned back to the ship. Mitch was a little surprised. He was expecting to confront the Lomtucs head on.

"What are we doing?" Mitch asked.

"We will fly in low," Qwii said. "Let the Lomtucs see us. That may be enough to send them fleeing from this world."

"Oh," Mitch said. "Okay. What if they try to shoot us down instead?"

"I guess you'll have to defeat whatever weapons they employ. And convince them that we mean business."

Mitch nodded. It sounded like a plan, only he feared he might not be able to stop the attack. On New Terra, the Lomtucs mostly raided human farms. They sometimes stole entire crops. His information on the aliens had talked of them using firearms, but not necessarily rockets or anti-aircraft weapons. Of course, that could have been because as a Colonial Marine, he would be confronting them with his boots on the ground. They might have all kinds of nasty surprises, and Mitch didn't know if his control of the Power was enough to stop a missile.

They returned to the Observation deck and Mitch stood close to the opening. Qwii took the ship into the air, and made straight for the city the chief had mentioned, Larmyr. How Qwii knew where it was confounded Mitch, but he would leave that question for another, less dangerous time. Instead, he let himself feel the gravity waves around the ship. He could sense the pull from the planet, and the forests of fruit trees. Soon they passed another village. Mitch could feel the people in it, hurrying to look up at the beautiful, crescent-shaped aircraft. There were no vehicles in the villages, no technology that he could sense. The Osters lived a primitive lifestyle, harvesting what they needed to survive from the land. And the planet was rich with life, Mitch could feel animals moving in the yellow grass, and through the treetops.

It wasn't long before they approached the city of Larmyr. It was different from the villages. There were a dozen structures made of stone. From the shapes of the buildings Mitch thought the city was maybe some kind of religious center. There were a couple of store-houses. Mitch could sense the Lomtucs looting the goods in the city. He noticed wine and oil presses, a mill powered by a small but fast running stream, and several ornate structures right in the center of city that were currently filled with Lomtucs. The raiders were strong beings, wide-bodied with four arms and two thick legs. They had no heads, just a pair of antennae that stuck up out of the muscular bodies.

Some began to run from the city as the *Luska* approached. Qwii was slowing down. Mitch felt the Lomtucs getting weapons. It was like he was one with the ocean of gravity and could feel everything in and around the city. He could feel the aliens, feel the food they were feasting on, feel the tables they were gathered around, feel the long rifles they were rushing to retrieve. The first shot fired toward them seemed almost comical. The raiders had good weapons for general fighting, but they weren't powerful enough to bring down an aircraft. It made Mitch wonder why the CMC wasted time with ground forces, when a gunship would have been much more efficient.

He could also feel the bubble around the *Luska* that Qwii was projecting. Inside the bubble was peaceful, but outside it Qwii marshaled strong gravity forces to move the big ship. In space it was enough to block gravity in the direction they wanted to go. That technique worked in atmosphere too, but the speed was too much. Instead, Qwii was pulling the ship around slowly, using strong gravity to move the vessel where he wanted it to go. Mitch projected his own strong gravity field between the ship's bubble and the city. The bullets fired by the Lomtucs were pulled back down to the ground by Mitch's force long before they could hit the ship.

"They don't seem interested in fleeing," Hollis pointed out.

"They will be," Qwii said. "Mitch, you must convince them."

Maybe it was a test. Mitch had the power to rip the buildings apart and smash the Lomtucs to death with the stones. He could crush them with a wave of powerful gravity that would pin the aliens to the ground and choke the life out of them. In the CMC his task had been to dispatch an enemy in whatever way was available. And the Lomtucs had a history of savagery against humans. On New Terra, farmers were sometimes found skinned, gutted, and carved up like game meat. It was not unusual for men to be killed in front of their wives and children. The Lomtuc Raiders took what-ever they wanted and destroyed things with no regard for the people living in the villages and farms. When they attacked the colonies they would often set it aflame before fleeing from the Marines marshaling against them. To almost anyone Mitch could have been justified in massacring the aliens, but he didn't want to do that. Instead, he lifted them up, just a meter off the ground and then dropped them. Some even landed on their feet, but most collapsed on the ground, expecting to be hurt. Mitch focused his power on their weapons, pulling them from the hands of the raiders and sending them flying from the town. And within two minutes of his counterattack, if it could be called that, the Lomtucs were running away. They fled from the city to get away from the big ship and the incredible power of the Order of Scion.

"Interesting," Hollis said. "You could have gone another way."

"Didn't seem right to hurt them," Mitch said.

"They hurt the Osters," Qwii said. "This isn't the first invasion."

"I understand," Mitch said. "And I'm not afraid to fight, I think you know that. But this wasn't a fight, not when they had no power to touch me. Killing them wouldn't be right. There's a lot I don't know about this life, but one thing stands out to me. The Creator didn't share this power with us so we could slaughter people."

"Well said," Hollis agreed.

"There were those among the Order who feared your kind would see things differently," Qwii said.

"They were right," Mitch assured him. "I think there are a lot of humans who wouldn't care about the Creator, or our mandate."

"But you do?"

Mitch nodded. "I do. The Power is great enough to destroy just about anything, but it seems even more impressive to build with it. That's what I want to do. To help people, not hurt them."

"Arq chose wisely," Hollis announced.

"He was right about you, Mitch Murphy."

They spent the next five hours running the Lomtucs out of the villages and camps where they were raiding from. There were thousands of them. For many, just the sight of the *Luska* was enough to send them running for their ships. By nightfall, there didn't seem to be any left.

"Our work here is complete," Qwii said.

"Another successful mission for the Order of Scion," Mitch said. "And I've worked up an appetite."

"We will meet with the elders at their city, Larmyr," Qwii said. "Then continue on our way."

Mitch looked at Qwii, who gave a slight nod. It was all the confirmation that Mitch needed. He was excited to go home. Not that New Terra was his home exactly, but it was as close as he had. It was familiar territory, and he hoped he would have a chance to help. But before he could head for the dining room, where he was certain Uri would have a wonderful meal waiting for him, Mitch saw Qwii stiffen. Hollis saw it too. She was a teacher and a historian, a member of the Order of Scion, but she was a devotee to the Knowledge, rather than the Power. She noticed Qwii's reaction too, but the look of surprise on her face made it clear she didn't know what had startled him.

"Qwii?" she asked.

"We are no longer alone in the system," he said quietly.

"But the Lomtucs are leaving," Mitch said. "Aren't they?"

"They are fleeing, just as we intended them to do," Qwii said.

"Who is it?" Hollis asked. "Can you tell?"

"It is the Fray," the white furred alien said. "But I cannot discern who. They are blocking my efforts."

"Are they coming here?" Mitch asked.

"Yes," Qwii replied. "They are coming for us."

CHAPTER 24

THE LYMIES CAME from the west within an hour of Captain Marcs' warning. Most were high off the ground on long ribbons of silky webbing.

"Bogeys, nine o'clock high," Mara announced. She stood up, dusted the dirt from her hands and took hold of her rifle, but the aliens were too high and completely out of range.

"I see 'em," Flash said. "They're way up there."

"What are they doing so high up?" Jingo wondered.

"Reconnaissance," Mara said. "Flash, get our bird down."

"Already on it, Sarge," Flash replied.

"Wrap it up, gentlemen," Mara ordered. "And get back to the rally point."

"Copy that," Ninja said.

"On my way," Jingo added.

The rally point was the airport baggage area. Mara had started putting down landmines nearly a full kilometer from the airfield, and slowly worked her way backward so that she didn't accidentally set one off when she needed to hurry to the rally point. She had buried fourteen mines. It wasn't enough to stop the ground attack they knew was coming. It probably wouldn't even slow the Lymies down, but it would kill some of them, and wound more. And that was all Mara was focused on. She wanted to spend the last twenty-four hours of life killing as many Lymies as she could.

"What's the status on our ride?" Mara asked.

"She's charged up and ready to go," Flash said. "I had to get creative with the power, but I think we're good."

"Outstanding," Mara replied. She trusted her team implicitly. If Flash said it would work, she believed him. There was no need for him to explain his work to her.

"Are we heading out now?" Ninja asked.

"Negative," Mara said. "We'll wait on the ground attack."

She looked upward. There were several dozen Lymies drifting by overhead, but they didn't seem concerned about her. Maybe they were expecting bigger human resistance. If they had descended on the airport, that could have been difficult for the Marines to deal with. Hitting targets in three-dimensional space was harder than hitting targets on the ground. The Lymies had extremely tough bodies, which made killing them difficult even when you could shoot them. Those in Alpha Colony had only been vulnerable to direct head shots. Their legs could be hurt, but they were even harder to hit than the spidery head segments. It didn't bother Mara that the Lymies in the air weren't descending to fight with her squad.

"They'll know we're here," Jingo said. "Might even know about the surprises we set up for them."

"Nothing we can do about that," Mara said. "Our job is to draw them in, then lead them to the ambush site. Maybe it works, maybe not."

"Ain't no such thing as a perfect plan," Flash said.

They met at the baggage section of the airport building. Jingo and Ninja joined Flash in loading magazines. They already had dozens loaded and on their armor, but there wouldn't be time to load more once the fighting started. Mara went up on the roof and watched.

The Lymies in the air drifted away, leaving the airport quiet. It was the calm before the storm. Mara was filled with tension. She had felt it before, a fear mixed with anxiousness. The closest she could come to describing it was when she had been sent to the principal's office as a child for beating up Billy Wondrun. The boy had been trying to kiss her, and Mara had punched him in the nose hard enough to make it bleed, and kicked him between the legs just the way her daddy had taught her. Looking back, she understood the crude flirtation. They were children, and for some reason Billy got it in his head that chasing the girls and forcing his lips somewhere on their face was acceptable. Mara had disagreed, but getting into trouble and having to wait for the principal was difficult. So was waiting for a battle to begin. The minutes could wear a person down if they let them. She had seen Marines defeated before the fight ever began, but she wasn't that type of person. Instead, she used the time to relax her body and focus her mind.

It was a full two hours later before she spotted the enemy. They were still far out, just a smudge on the horizon. When she turned and looked the other way, she could see movement there too.

The rest of Leo Squad had joined her on the rooftop. They were as ready as they could be. Jingo and Flash had eaten and were dozing, their big bodies stretched out on the roof's gravel surface. Ninja was quiet. He hadn't eaten or slept. Mara knew he was thinking about Hawk and she didn't disturb him. So, it was surprising when he spoke up.

"A coordinated attack," he said. "Two fronts. They'll hit us at the same time."

"Fine by me," Mara said. "We're ready for them."

"We could have spent a month getting ready, and we still wouldn't be in a good position to fend off that many aliens," Ninja said. "There has to be a thousand of them in each group."

"True, but fending them off isn't our mission," Mara said.

"Even if we can get them to the ambush site, what then?" Ninja said. "If the fleet bombs the area, how are we supposed to survive?"

"We aren't," she said simply. "But take as many of the Lymies with us as possible."

"And you're good with that?"

"I'm not happy about it, but I'll die fighting. We can't ask for more than that."

"Even if it's a senseless battle that will change nothing in the long run?"

"Even then," Mara said. "You want to try something else, Ninja, I won't stop you."

"Hell no," he said. "I ain't running, if that's what you mean."

"Those are our only two options," she said. "Run or fight."

"I'll fight," he said. "But I have to say it. These orders are bull-shit. If the fleet really wanted to defeat the Lymies, they would have landed a thousand Marines. We could have dozens of machine gun nests set up around here. When the Lymies came in, we could just hose them down."

"Only our bullets aren't always effective," Mara said.

"I'll take my chances with a thousand Marines," Ninja said. "Give us a fighting chance, that's all I ask."

"You'll get your chance on the other side of the forest," she said. "That's where the real battle is taking place."

"Four Marines against two thousand Lymies," he said. "It won't be much of a fight."

"That's what the Persians said about the three hundred Spar-tans at Thermopylae."

"Yeah, I guess so," Ninja said. "This how you saw your life ending?"

"Not exactly," Mara said. "But I never wanted out of the Corps. I didn't have a plan B, or a dream for what came next in life. I sure as hell didn't want to die alone in some old folk's home."

"Yeah, me either," Ninja said. "But I can't stop thinking about what life could have been like if Hawk hadn't died."

"I'm not sure anything would be different."

"I might have a little more to fight for," he said.

Mara nodded. That made sense. She was thinking about Mitch Murphy and wondering if things had turned out differently if the two of them would have had a chance together. It was hard to imagine. Flings in the CMC were common enough, especially when they were stuck on an interstellar spaceship between deployments. There wasn't much to do on those ships, and people stuck in such tight quarters often gave in to temptation. The Corps didn't even forbid it. But Mara had always hoped she might find someone that was more than just a fling. To her, romance wasn't just a casual way to pass the time. And she had begun to think that Lieutenant Murphy might just fit the bill. He seemed cautiously interested in her as well, right up until he leaped off the transport. She obviously hadn't cast a spell on him. And sometimes she wondered if he stayed on New Terra just to get away from her.

"Wake up the children," Mara told Ninja. "The neighbors are almost to the first line of defense."

"Wake up you oaf," Ninja said, nudging Jingo. "Man, you snore like a wounded elephant."

"Do not," Jingo said.

He gave Flash a shake. "Time to earn your pay," Ninja growled.

"With pleasure," Flash said, sitting up.

They had just enough time to shake off the lingering fatigue and check their weapons. Mara had her automatic shotgun slung over her back and was using a standard semi-auto 30.06 with a Keebler optical scope. It was a sniper rifle for the average Marine, and could hit a target well over three kilometers away.

"I've got the western front," she said. "Flash you and Jingo get to the transport. Jingo, man the turret guns. Make sure your coms stay connected. Ninja, you take the eastern front."

"Copy that," he replied.

"Ya'll good up here?" Jingo asked. "Need anything?"

"We're fine," Mara said. "Just get that transport ready to rock."

"You know it, Sarge. We got this," Flash said.

"No heroics, yeah?" Jingo reminded them. Then he and Flash hurried down the metal stairs, past the communications equipment and into the personnel carrier.

The first of the land mines went off on the eastern side. Ninja had spent more time putting them down and had over twenty placed directly in the path of the swarm of aliens.

"That's a beautiful sight," he said.

"Might as well jump right in," Mara said.

She had an alien in her sight, but she had to compensate for the distance. Gravity would pull her shot down, and the wind was blowing straight at her. Friction would slow the bullet she was about to fire. She raised the barrel just a little above her target and fired. It took the shot a full two seconds to reach the alien. She lowered the rifle, and watched her handiwork through the scope. Half of the alien's head pod disappeared on impact. It was a good shot and the last one she would wait and watch. She began firing more quickly. A Lymie stepped on a land mine. It exploded up and out, ripping the unlucky alien into bits and wounding all the spidery creatures around it. Dust flew up too, Mara kept shooting. More mines were going off, but the Lymies were undeterred. They didn't try to evade the sniper fire, or get to cover. There were hundreds of them. More than she could count. She would have given anything for mortars or, like Ninja had suggested, a full battalion of Marines at her back. But there were only four Marines left on New Terra. And if the Space Force was going to help, it wouldn't be for a full twenty-four hours.

"Time to move," Mara said.

"They're still two klicks out," Ninja argued.

"We're drawing them in, remember," she said, dropping the sniper rifle and rotating her shotgun around on its sling. "Get moving, Ninja."

He dropped his rifle too, and ran for the stairs. In that moment Mara heard the feet of the alien army. They were thumping into the ground, thousands of feet, marching together, it sounded like a rumble. It was a frightening portent of the danger they were in.

She raced down the stairs and ran out to the transport. Ninja was settled on the far side, the door locked halfway open. He was connecting his armor to a safety tether that hung from the ceiling. Mara did the same on her side of the transport. The Lymies didn't use firearms. They had to close the distance to attack. That meant Mara and Ninja could stand in the open doorways of the passenger compartment and continue to fight.

"Flash, you ready?"

"Born ready, Sarge," he replied.

"Get us to stage one," she said. "Jingo, wait to start shooting on my command."

"Roger that," the big man said from inside the rotating turret.

The armored personnel carrier activated with a hum. It lifted off the ground and hovered about a meter in the air. Flash drove the vehicle forward and moved them into position in the center of one of the airport landing strips. The mines had all been detonated. Dozens of Lymies had been blown apart, shot, or wounded in the carnage. Maybe as many as a hundred, it was impossible for Mara to estimate. All she knew was that their wounded, however many they were, was only a fraction of their total number.

"Wait for it," Mara said softly, her voice carried to the other three members of Leo Squad via their helmet comlink.

The Lymies had a kind of natural scrambling sensory projection that disrupted radio waves and blocked all sorts of transmissions. But with the squad in close proximity their comlinks would continue to operate.

"Wait for it," she said again, as the first of the aliens skittered onto the ends of the long runways. Some were moving to circle around the ruined airport building. If they stayed too long the aliens would attempt to flank them front and back, cutting off their escape toward the forest. Flash had wisely settled the transport facing the airport building, not the forest. Mara didn't want to do anything that might tip their hand.

"They're getting close, Marauder," Ninja said.

"Stay cool, Ninja," she ordered. "Just a few more seconds."

She waited until the closest alien was only a hundred meters away, then she called it.

"Now!"

Her shotgun chugged out round after round in a violent barrage of thick, lead slugs. They didn't have the penetrating power of the GAR explosive rounds, with their depleted uranium-tipped ammunition. But her shotgun had stopping power. The Lymies on her side of the transport went down in a wave. She fired all forty rounds from the drum magazine in one vicious barrage.

"Flash!" she shouted.

"Rock and roll," he replied as he spun the transport around.

The movement gave Mara time to reload. She hit the release button and let the empty ammo drum fall. It bounced on the deck of the transport then flipped out onto the tarmac. She rammed a fresh one into place and tugged the charging lever. By the time Flash had the transport turned, she was ready to fire. The Lymies were closing in on both sides. Flash sent the transport racing for the trees. If not for the harness tether Mara would have fallen. Above her, Jingo opened up with the spinning twin barrels of the belt-fed machine guns in the turret. The empty brass rattled out across the roof of the transport like a metallic rain. While her automatic shotgun chugged out its bullets, the spinning barrels fired with a whir that was loud above her, filling the transport with noise. She saw the tracer rounds in the flow of firepower from the machine guns in the turret. They made her shotgun seem like a children's toy. But the Lymies reacted to it. They jumped and scurried out of the line of fire. Those hit weren't killed immediately. Their tough hide was almost impenetrable, but the twin machine guns were firing so many bullets, some laced with phosphorus, that the aliens were chewed to pieces. Their spindly legs shattered; big chunks of their hard outer flesh were torn off. If their heads were hit, they exploded in clouds of bloody vapor. It was a savage fight, but still the aliens surged forward. They had the numbers and were desperate to stop the carnage. Some jumped for the transport. Mara and Ninja fired up at them. A few were knocked out of the sky. Some fell short, or missed wide. But a few landed on the transport. Fortunately, they were all on the rear section, directly in the line of fire of the twin machine guns. They were torn to pieces under the barrage of fire.

"Almost there," Flash said.

"Jingo, prepare to come down," Mara ordered. "Lock that turret down."

"Copy that," he shouted.

The transport reached the tree line and stopped just inside. There were still hundreds of Lymies rushing toward them. Mara leaned out and opened fire with her shotgun. Ninja did the same out his side of the ship. Jingo dropped to the deck and rushed to rear of the transport. He slid open a panel that was designed to shoot out of. He stuck his GAR into the opening and pulled the trigger. More Lymies were being wounded every second, but the others didn't seem to care.

"Say the word, Sarge," Flash said.

"Not yet," Mara ordered. "They need to get closer."

"She's lost her mind," Jingo shouted.

Ninja was just screaming as he fired away. Mara ejected her ammo drum and put another in place. She wanted to keep fighting but she saw movement in the trees.

"Now, Flash," she shouted. "Go! Go! Go!"

He didn't say a word, he just hit the accelerator and raced off into the trees.

CHAPTER 25

"IT'S BEGUN," Lieutenant Colonel Jerome Banks announced.

It wasn't really necessary. They had lost contact with Leo Squad as the Lymie armies approached from the east and west of the airport. They had no real intel as the *Marathon* reached orbit, only that two large alien forces were converging on the SSO squad's position at the airfield that used to service the human colonies on New Terra.

"How can you know that?" Major Elaine Swift asked. She and the rest of General Mercer's staff were in the *Marathon's* CIC along with Admiral Darcy Wilcox and her crew.

"Energy surges disrupt the jamming frequency," the Weapons Control Officer said softly. "Something is blowing up down there."

"That would be our people," General Mercer said. "They are highly trained and motivated."

"Doesn't take much motivation not to want to die," Major Swift whispered.

She was sitting at a console between the ship's radar and weapons control station. There were no other ships in the system, which meant there wasn't much for the Space Force officers to do. It was General Mercer's show, and he was loving every second of it.

"Start the clock," he announced. "Let's get the drop ships prepped and ready. I want the drone bombers loaded and ready to fly. Do they have the coordinates?"

"Aye, General," one of the Space Force officers said. "Our technicians will have to program the route once they're on the ground, though."

"Have them ready, we have a tight timeline and we can't make any mistakes. We'll only get one shot at this."

There was nothing to see. The satellites that should have given them a bird's-eye view of the battle returned nothing but static. All they could say for certain was that there were still Lymies in the colonies, enough to scramble signals from there. Elaine Swift was a smart woman. She could have been a full professor at any university on earth, or a VP of product development at any number of Fortune 500 companies. But her passion was alien life forms. She had dedicated her career to learning all she could about the intelligent races who had appeared in the Terra system. That left no room for understanding how a video signal that originated in orbit could be scrambled by aliens on the ground. She knew the Lymies had a type of mental telepathy. That was proven once again when Leo Squad attacked Alpha Colony, which triggered a response from the other colonies hundreds of kilometers away. The aliens seemed to act in concert despite the distances. Major Swift believed it was the same telepathy that scrambled radio signals, and disrupted human technology.

That left nothing for General Mercer's staff to track except blurry spots on a map. As long as the blur kept moving south, it was an indication that Leo Squad was alive and carrying out their mission. She stood up, stretching her back and wondering what she should do.

"Twenty-four hours," Admiral Darcy said. "Give us four hours to get the drop ships all launched and two more to make planetfall. That's six hours. How long will the programming take?"

"Not long, Admiral, say an hour, two at the most," one of the drone pilot operators in the CIC replied.

"That's eight hours," the Admiral said. "We get them airborne and moving to the target, say another four to six hours."

"Don't forget that each of the bomb clusters have to be activated individually," General Mercer said. "They have safety pins that have to be removed before they can be armed."

"What happens if the aliens disrupt the drones?" the Weapons Control Officer asked.

"In that case we have wasted a lot of time and energy," General Mercer said.

"Not to mention lives," Major Swift said. "Leo Squad is taking a huge risk and relying on the air support. If it fails ..."

"Yes, of course," General Mercer said. "That goes without saying."

"Leo Squad is resourceful," Captain Frank Marcs said. "Don't count them out."

"Another detonation!" Colonel Banks announced.

"Looks like it should be right at the tree line," the radar operator said. She had a map overlay so that she could pinpoint what lay underneath the static haze caused by the aliens.

"Leo Squad has put together a hell of a plan," Captain Marcs said.

"Twenty-four hours," General Mercer said. "Then we take the planet back. And this time we're going to hold it. I'll have SSO Squads prepped and ready at a moment's notice. If anything gets through the Space Force blockade, we'll hit them the moment they land."

"We aren't blockading the planet," Admiral Wilcox said. "We don't have the resources to keep other ships out completely."

"But we're in a position to know what enters the system," General Mercer said. "We can pinpoint and track them. Identify who they are and what they're capable of. My SSO squads will hit them so hard they won't know which way is up. They won't want any part of us."

Major Swift knew braggadocio when she heard it. Of course, Marine officers were supposed to be supremely confident in their ability to make war, but General Mercer was forgetting that anything could come into the system, be it an armada of aliens they already knew about, or one vessel of beings so powerful they might wipe out every human in the system with ease.

"All right, people," Admiral Wilcox said, "we've got a job to do. Let's get those drop ships prepped. I want them touching down a hundred kilometers from Indigo Colony."

"That'll give the drones a little over three hundred kilometers to the target zone," the drone pilot said. "Average flight time with full capacity is eighty klicks in good weather. Say four hours in the air."

"A lot can go wrong in four hours," Elaine Swift remarked.

"The Autonomous Ordnance Aerial Delivery Systems are state-of-the-art," the pilot said. "Anything short of a hurricane and they'll find a way to make it work."

"It has to be on time," Captain Marcs said. "Each bomb has to come down in a designated spot, otherwise the Marines on the ground will be in danger."

"We'll be ready," Admiral Wilcox said. "Commander Hughes, see to the drop ships."

"Aye Admiral," the Commander replied immediately as he headed for the door.

"This is our moment," General Mercer said. "History in the making. Let's not fumble the ball at the goal line."

Major Swift didn't reply. She hated sports metaphors and wasn't needed in the CIC. Perhaps in twenty-four hours, if the plan was still in motion, she would return. At the very least she could stand witness to the final heroic acts of Leo Squad before they were sacrificed on the altar of General Mercer's ambition.

CHAPTER 26

"JINGO, BLOW THE EXPLOSIVES," Mara ordered.

They were only forty or fifty meters into the trees. Hundreds of aliens were in pursuit. It was all part of the plan. Leo Squad had to stay close enough to draw the aliens after them. But not so close that they got caught. It was a fine line. Jingo had set old-school explosives inside the tree line. They were backpack-sized devices that were strapped to the tree trunks. Each had a small motion sensor built into it that would detonate the explosive automatically. They were sometimes remotely controlled, but with the interference produced by the Lymies, Jingo hadn't bothered with setting the remote detonators.

"They're set for motion sensors," Jingo said. "Can't control them from here."

"The aliens are almost on top of us, bro," Ninja said. "They should have gone off already."

It was true, but the spidery aliens weren't running along the ground. Jingo had set the explosive less than a meter from the roots of the trees. When the aliens jumped into the forest, they bounded from tree to tree, never touching the ground at all. It was an over-sight on Jingo's part, but one he couldn't have foreseen.

"I know," he replied.

"Maybe their interference," Mara started to say, but before she could finish the first explosive went off. It was followed immediately by several more. She looked out the open door on her side of the transport. Smoke was billowing through the trees, and she caught glimpses of orange flame. Looking up, she could see the aliens slowing down. They were looking back, then looking around. Maybe they feared running into an explosive, or maybe they weren't as brave without an army behind them.

Flash had been forced to slow his progress as he navigated through the forest. There were no roads. The transport was a big vehicle and couldn't slalom through the trees at high speed. Mara fired at a Lymie that was closing in from above them. The fat shotgun slugs knocked the alien out of the tree and sent it crashing into the underbrush. The team had already marked three rally points along the way through the forest using detailed topo-graphical maps. The first was a hill just six kilometers into the woods.

"Sounds like all our surprises have been found," Jingo said.

"Good," Ninja said. "I hope they suffer."

"The fire and threat of death is slowing them down," Mara said. "We keep this up for twenty-four hours, team, and we're home free."

"How far to the first check point?" Mara asked.

"Three kilometers," Flash said.

"Status?"

It was a team-wide order. Everyone began to check themselves and their surroundings.

"Transport is good," Flash said. "Plenty of juice in the new batteries."

"Turret guns are fine, but we spent a little over half of our ammo for them," Jingo said. "Otherwise, we're looking good."

"Ninja?" Mara asked.

"I'm fine," he said. "They didn't get close."

"All right, Flash, stop the transport," she ordered. "Ninja, you take over. Jingo, you stay with the transport too."

"I don't like us splitting up," he said.

"Me either, but we don't have a choice. We need intel on the enemy's movements and there's only one way to get that."

"We might need to urge them on too," Flash said. "Bait them into following us into the forest and beyond."

"He's right," Mara said. "You two move on to the checkpoint. Flash will be our eyes, and I'll cover his back."

"I got a bad feeling," Jingo said.

"This is a crap mission even if it goes off without a hitch," Flash said.

"You both know what to do if we don't make it back," she reminded them. "Keep moving, try to draw them to the ambush site."

"Or, we keep moving," Ninja said. "All four of us. If the enemy doesn't keep up, so be it. The brass can try something else."

"Yeah, something that doesn't get us all killed in the process," Jingo said.

"None of us deserve this," Mara said, stepping out of the transport and checking her weapon. "If you want, I'll do it myself."

"You know we won't let you do that," Flash said. "You go, we go."

"Oo-ya!" Jingo said. "Leaving you behind ain't gonna happen, Sarge. But I don't think this is a good mission."

"It's too dependent on the Space Force drones, and so far, they've failed every time they went up against the bugs," Ninja said.

"Why are we throwing our lives away?" Jingo asked.

"Ain't no fight ever easy," Flash said. "But we're the ones who run toward danger, not away from it."

Mara nodded. "This may be a pointless mission, but it is our mission. Leo Squad is here and we've got an objective. Our reputation means everything to me. I'd rather die trying than give up."

"Can't argue with that," Jingo said.

"Yeah, you're right, Marauder. Hawk would have said the same," Ninja agreed.

"So, we're all on the same page. Ninja, Jingo, get to the checkpoint. Flash baits the bad guys and I'll cover his six. We'll meet you in a couple of hours."

"Don't be late," Jingo said.

"Hell no," Flash said. "We'll be there."

"Look for us in two hours," Mara said. "And stay alert. We know where the other checkpoints are. If need be, we'll catch up to you on foot down the trail."

There were nods all around. Mara could see the urgency in Jingo and Ninja's eyes, willing them not to die. Not just Mara, but Flash too. They were taking a huge risk, but it was the only way to ensure the mission. They couldn't just run to the ambush site and hope the aliens showed up.

Jingo climbed back into the transport passenger cabin, while Ninja settled into the cab. Mara turned to Flash. "Go see what you can find out," she ordered. "But don't take any chances. I'll be here. You get into trouble come running. I'll keep the bugs off you."

"Copy that," he said. "Be back in a second."

She watched him jog away into the woods. Flash could jog faster than most people could sprint. He could keep it up for hours too. His long stride and strong core made him agile and fast. She felt a shiver of fear but shook it off. Yes, they were in a dangerous situation, and Flash was running back toward the enemy. But it was necessary, and it was what they were trained to do. She moved off the trail. Not that they had been following a defined pathway, but she moved to a denser part of the forest, and put her back to a big tree. She had her automatic shotgun ready with a drum nearly full of thick, lead slugs. Another hung from her belt, and her GAR was on a sling so that it hung down under her left arm. Her head was on a swivel, alert for any signs of danger. She knew it was out there, and that it was getting closer. The battle of her life was approaching. Death was breathing its frosty breath down her neck. But she was ready for it, ready to face the enemy and die if necessary. All that mattered was the mission. Not because it would strike a blow against the enemy, or because her superiors had ordered it, but because it was Leo Squad's mission. And that was enough for Mara to see it through, no matter the outcome.

CHAPTER 27

THE FRAY SHIP didn't waste time. It was too far away for Mitch to feel it. He could tell that he was growing more sensitive to his gravity power, but he couldn't project out like Qwii yet. Nor could he focus his senses to pick up certain things, and ignore others. When he let his sense of gravity expand, he felt the powerful pull of the planet, and that of people walking around, structures, landmarks like mountains and water. But he was nearly overwhelmed by the tiniest of creatures. Insects crawling through the grass. He could be all alone in a wide-open field, but with his senses expanding through the Power of gravity he could feel every bug and worm until he felt like he was standing in a crowd of people back on Earth.

"They are homing in on us," Qwii said.

"You mean they're here for us," Mitch said. "As in they're hunting for us?"

"Yes," Qwii said. "There are those of the Fray who seek our destruction over everything else."

"I will not be much help in a fight," Hollis said. "It has been many years since I was a Scion Warrior. And even then, I was not powerful like Mitch."

"Stay on board the ship," Qwii told her. "We will face the threat."

"What about the Osters?" Mitch asked.

"When they come I will send them away."

He landed the *Luska* on a hilltop overlooking a wide, grassy valley. There were small creatures grazing near a trickling stream. It was an idyllic environment, not the sort of battlefield Mitch expected. Half an hour later the Fray ship landed. It was small and dark with a cigar shape fuselage and engines in the back, although they were not powered on. Mitch saw movement through a wide transparent panel in the conical end of the ship, then a hatch lowered. It was more like a human spaceship than what Qwii operated from.

"Hannoi," Qwii said. "And his apprentice. Take care, Mitch Murphy. Hannoi is a powerful being. A skilled fighter. His apprentice will be as well."

"Yeah, I might need to take some sword lessons," Mitch said. "Do we do that?"

"There are those within the order who are masters of sword-craft. We will seek them out soon. Until then, trust your instincts. Arq chose you for this, not because you could learn to swing a sword, but because you have innate skills in a fight. You must let them out. Don't hold back."

Mitch nodded. His spine felt as though he had a heavy weight pressing him down, and his skin tingled all over. At first he thought it was a gravity attack from the Fray, but quickly realized it was just fear. Mitch had been afraid plenty of times in his life, but as he rotated his shoulders and loosened the muscles in his back, he remembered who he had become. He was a big man, strong, fast, agile. These were his natural abilities. He had failed to develop them in his younger years, but the LE Protocol had given him a second chance, and even more than that. The super serum had boosted his body to the absolute peak of its abilities. All he had to do was let himself do what he was naturally drawn to in the conflict. There was no need to hold himself back in any way.

Two beings came down the ramp from the cigar-shaped ship. One was a three-legged creature with a long, whip-like tail that curled over one shoulder and hung down the alien's chest. It had a wide, thin neck, sort of like a cobra, and its face was angular. It wore tight fitting dark colored clothing, and around its waist was a belt with a huge sword. It reminded Mitch of a scimitar.

The other being was shorter, only half of Mitch's height. It had short arms and bowed legs. With no shoes, the second alien's feet looked like hands. Mitch was reminded of a chimpanzee, but the alien had a head unlike anything Mitch had ever seen. It was small and pointed, angling from front to back, sort of like a rat's but with no fur. The eyes were small, the mouth tiny as well, but the ears were large. They curled around in concentric circles tight against its skull, and ended in a large cup that faced the same direction as its eyes.

"Qwii of the Nagani, at last we meet," the shorter alien said.

Mitch was surprised that he could pick out most of the words. He had been working with Hollis in short sessions, and was picking up the Common language fast. It was designed for that purpose, but it still seemed almost magical that Mitch could understand a little of what was being said. Still, if Hollis hadn't joined them from the ship, moving silently up behind Mitch and translating, he wouldn't have understood most of the conversation.

"Hannoi, you are not welcome here."

"No, I suppose not," the short alien replied. "But I wasn't looking for an invitation. I take what I want."

"And what have you come for?" Qwii asked.

"Your head," Hannoi said, his tiny eyes gleaming.

The sun was starting to set. The shadows were long and a golden light filled the valley. The cigar-shaped ship had settled below them, and the aliens were walking up the incline. Mitch was glad they had the high ground, but he still felt nervous. The aliens didn't seem timid or cautious like the Cadish had on Bispee. Mitch realized he was in for a real fight. It made his hand itch, and his mouth felt suddenly dry.

Qwii spread his robe and pulled his short, sickle-shaped weapons from his belt.

"If that is what you desire," Qwii said. "You will have to come and take it."

"Ah, you Nagani are so blunt. I forget that," the short alien said. "I've been all over the galaxy hunting you religious zealots. When I finally find you, I like to take my time dispatching you to whatever afterlife you believe in."

"You are a stain on the universe, Hannoi," Qwii said. "You are the son of Destruction, an abuser of the Creator's power. His justice will not be denied."

The short alien chuckled, then waved at his three-legged companion. "Allow me to introduce Flek. He is a powerful Fray and has joined me in my quest. Introduce yourself, Flek."

The three-legged alien drew the big sword. He held it in two hands, then began to twirl the sword around his body. Sometimes he flipped it up into the air and caught it as it dropped, at other times he flipped the blade around his forearms before catching hold of the handle again. Mitch knew the display was meant to frighten him. He also knew the alien was a talented sword fighter, but that just gave Mitch the idea to take the swords out of the equation.

The scimitar was made of Cidian just like Mitch's blade. And unlike the short, double-edged swords the Cadish had carried, Flek's thick blade was a work of art. It was obviously well balanced, but also clearly heavy. It was meant to overpower an opponent. But Mitch was no pushover. He pulled back the edge of his own robe to reveal the leather-wrapped handle and its simple round guard, but didn't draw the weapon.

"Shall we get down to business?" Hannoi asked. "Apprentice versus apprentice?"

"Mitch Murphy is not an apprentice. He is a Scion Warrior, a human, the first of his kind."

"It will be an honor to dispatch him," Hannoi said. "He shall be the first and last of his kind, eh?"

If you choose to fight us we will show you no mercy," Qwii said. "Surrender now, and you may live long enough to do some good in the universe."

Hannoi laughed. "Kill the human," he ordered his apprentice. "He is no match for your power."

The three-legged creature started forward. Mitch drew his sword, but Qwii put a hand on his arm.

"These are sons of destruction. Death is all they know. Do not hesitate."

Mitch nodded, and started toward the three-legged alien. They stopped with just a few meters separating them. The alien had a cold look in his eyes. He raised his thick sword high over his head, then he hissed. Mitch almost missed the long tail as it flicked back behind the alien, then lashed out from around the creature's thin waist. Mitch was holding the sword loosely, his weight on the balls of his feet. When the tail lashed out at him, he swayed to the side and flicked up with his sword at the same time. The tail cracked like a whip near his head, but hit nothing but air. The tip of Flek's tail was dark gray. It was recoiling behind the alien when the blade of Mitch's sword caught it. The Cidian edge was so sharp it severed the gray tip effortlessly.

Flek screamed in pain, as the tail jerked back behind his body, dripping blood. He jumped forward and chopped down with the heavy sword. Mitch brought his own blade up to block, and at the last moment released the handle with his left hand and braced his sword blade, palming the spine of the weapon close to the pointed end. The scimitar came down with terrific force. Mitch saw the muscles in the alien's shoulders and back bunching from the effort of the blow. His own muscles tensed as the swords clashed. Flek clearly expected Mitch to be knocked off his feet, but he was too strong. He checked the alien's chop, then lashed out with his right foot in the front kick that Mara James had taught him in their sparring session. Flek was downhill from Mitch, and his narrow chin was at the perfect height for Mitch's kick. His foot smashed hard into the alien's face, and Flek tumbled down the hill.

Remembering Qwii's advice, Mitch raced down the hill after his opponent. Flek lost his grip on the heavy sword. It tumbled out of reach, just before Mitch landed on top of the alien. To his surprise, even after getting kicked in the face and having Mitch's nearly three hundred pounds land atop him, the alien was still hard to pin down. Mitch flopped onto his side, laying across the alien's body just above the three legs. They were still on the hill; the alien's head was lower than its body. Mitch pressed his left elbow into the creature's chest and lifted his sword as he prepared to slash the blade across the alien's throat, when Flek kicked up with all three legs, bucking Mitch off his body and flipping over in the process. Mitch had been caught off guard. He scrambled up just as Flek lashed out with his tail. The whip-like appendage wrapped around the handle of Mitch's sword and tried to jerk it from his hand. But Mitch held tight. He was pulled toward the alien, off balance. He lowered his shoulder and dove toward Flek, who tried to dodge but was too slow. Mitch managed to wrap his free arm around one leg, and as they fell the limb twisted. The sound of the bone breaking was like a twig snapping under Mitch's foot. It didn't seem significant in that moment, but then the alien screamed in pain.

Mitch tried to raise the sword, but Flek's tail held it fast. Once more Mitch used the leverage created by the pull to draw him down onto his opponent. He rolled and flung out his left elbow, smashing it into the alien's face. His momentum carried him away from Flek, who released Mitch's sword. As he got to his feet Mitch saw Flek swaying off balance, but he had somehow managed to regain his sword. The thin tail didn't offer much support, but it snatched a tuft of grass to help. The alien had also gained the high ground. Mitch was no fool. He began to circle. Nearby, he could hear Hannoi and Qwii talking. He guessed it was about the fight, but he was too focused on Flek to try and understand what they were saying. Hollis was up the hill, behind Qwii, watching nervously.

Mitch's nerves were gone. The fight had started and all Mitch wanted was to end the threat. He actually enjoyed the contest, and the chance to use his strength. He walked slowly up the hill in a circling fashion. Flek must have known he should attack before Mitch gained the upper hand, but he couldn't. He was barely stable on just two legs. The third was bent at a painful angle. The heavy sword was not to Flek's advantage any longer. Mitch didn't wait to get uphill from the alien. Nor did he try to circle around and attack him from behind. He had never really thought about it, but if he was going to fight someone, he wanted to look them in the eye. When he got level with Flek on the hillside, he darted forward. Mitch was a big man, thick with muscle, but faster and more agile than people expected. His sword was slightly longer than Flek's, and Mitch had already learned that he could let the sharp edge do the work. All he needed was to get it in range. The sword came in and Flek tried to parry with his scimitar, only he was too clumsy and slow. Mitch's sword slid up Flek's left arm and into the elbow. The alien hissed and dropped the sword. His left arm fell to his side, dangling uselessly, the tendons at the elbow had been severed. Mitch hardly even felt any resistance.

Flek leaned hard on his sword, the blade tip down, digging into the soil. He was breathing hard and bleeding. It trickled from the nasal slits on the end of his pointed face, and ran freely from the deep laceration on his left arm. Mitch felt a surge of excitement. He had won the fight. Flek could no longer defend himself. Mitch raised his sword in both hands, ready to deliver a killing slash, but he hesitated. The alien was finished. Killing him seemed unreasonable.

Suddenly Mitch was flung backward. A strong gravitational force was pulling him backward, and bouncing onto the ground. It was like being a toy that had been picked up by a toddler. The surprise of it, and the shock of pain when he first hit the ground, left him reeling. It took a few seconds for Mitch to regain control of the Power and sever the gravitational tug. He had dropped his sword. It lay nearly several meters away and down the hillside. Without warning it shot from the ground and flew toward Mitch like a bullet. He slammed a bubble of heavy gravity down onto the blade, driving it into the dirt near his feet. Flek laughed, a wicked cackled that turned into a bloody cough. Mitch bent at the knees, picked up his sword, and started toward Flek. The alien turned, set his feet and lifted his sword with his good hand.

Mitch wasn't content to wound the alien. He had learned his lesson. His shoulder his bruised and he was struggling to catch his breath, but his mind was still in fight mode. He came at his enemy fast. A low feint caused Flek to twist away. He fell backward, caught himself in a gravity bubble and shot up over Mitch's head. The scimitar swung like a wrecking ball, and would have cleaved Mitch's head in two. But he dropped to the ground and let Flek sail past him. Then, with a boost of his own gravity power pulling himself up the hill, Mitch drove his sword point-first into Flek's side. The blade sank deep before the tissue caught hold of it. The alien hissed, dropped his sword, and collapsed. Mitch put a foot on Flek's chest and jerked the sword free. Blood flew in a wide arc from the blade. Holding it high, Mitch prepared to drive it down when the alien's tail coiled around his neck. It tightened. Mitch staggered, gagging, and slashed the tail in two. He was free of Flek's hold, but the end of the tail around his throat didn't loosen. He had to reach up and uncurl it.

Mitch felt Hannoi's attempt to save Flek. The alien was suddenly weightless and floating up. There was a tug of gravity, but Mitch had reacted too quickly. He didn't try to fight the Fray's gravity power. He only needed to hold Flek in place a second as he swung his sword down in a savage slash that severed the alien's head. The decapitated Flek flew back toward the cigar-shaped ship, but when Hannoi realized his apprentice was dead, he dropped the body. Both body and head tumbled down the hill.

"Mitch do not let him escape," Qwii called out as he stalked down toward Hannoi.

For a moment Mitch didn't move. He stood panting, the fight suddenly gone from his mind. He didn't feel good about what he had done, but he knew that he had come very close to being killed himself. The alien had been relentless. And Hannoi drew a thin, curved blade that looked a lot like Arq's weapon, only it had strange hooks and serrations on the spine. Qwii held his own weapons in a defensive position as he moved down the hill. Hollis had retreated back by the *Luska* and looked relieved that Mitch was still alive.

Qwii said something in Common. Mitch picked out the words *survive, both,* and *us* as he hurried down the hillside to cut off the alien's retreat to his ship. A huge rock suddenly rose up, tearing itself free of the soil. The rock hurled with great speed toward Mitch, but he jumped out of its path. It was swung wide, starting to move back, but then it dropped to the ground as Qwii engaged the alien.

They were close together. Qwii was still uphill which made him even taller than Hannoi. The white-furred Nagani rotated his arms in an intricate pattering, swinging the curved blades of his sickle weapons. Hannoi blocked a few blows, but dodged the rest. He swayed back and forth like a prizefighter, his own weapon dancing in his hand. The alien was just defending himself at first, but then the tip flicked up and Qwii was forced to jump back. He began slowly moving up the hill backward. Hannoi followed, his curved blade flicking and slashing until Qwii was completely on the defensive. Mitch didn't hesitate. He hurried around, moving in behind Hannoi. Mitch felt a surge of heavy gravity, but he countered it almost instantly. Hannoi turned, slashing his blade through the air. It wasn't close enough to reach Mitch. He was so much larger than the alien that he didn't need to get in Hannoi's range to strike at him. A fast stab forced the alien to spin out of the way, but Qwii immediately cut the alien off.

"Keep it up," Qwii said in English. "Don't let him escape."

Hannoi was slashing left and right, spinning, juking, trying to find a way past the two members in the Order of Scion. But they were determined not to let him go. Mitch leaped forward, stabbing at the smaller alien. The tip of his sword stabbed through Hannoi's leg and lodged in the bone. There was a grunt, but Mitch was forced to pull back to avoid Hannoi's reverse slash. When he pulled back, the sword pulled Hannoi's leg sideways before popping free.

The alien dropped to the ground, his big ears quivering in pain. Qwii stepped forward, pinning Hannoi's sword arm under his foot. He held one sickle under the alien's pointed chin.

"Yield," he ordered, and Mitch remembered the word.

Later Hollis told Mitch what the alien replied. *And let your kind put me on display like a prized animal before the slaughter. No, get it over with, coward.*

Qwii didn't say anything else. He swung his second sickle down and stabbed it through the middle of the alien's chest. It sent a spray of blood out of the tiny mouth and across the pale skin. Then Hannoi died.

"Excellent work, Mitch Murphy. That was no mean feat," Qwii told him.

"They would have killed us," Mitch said.

"They did their best to accomplish that, yes."

Mitch felt a little sick. It was his body purging the spent adrenaline, and it left him slightly shaky. He bent down, cleaned the blood off his Cidian blade and sheathed the weapon.

"What do we do now?"

"Now we go to the Terra system," Qwii said. "Arq needs our help and we shall supply it."

CHAPTER 28

THE EXPLOSIVES DID a lot of damage. Each one had been filled with hundreds of small tungsten ball bearings. When the charges went off, the explosion caught the trees on fire, but it was the violent expulsion of the ball bearings that really caused damage. The little balls were launched so hard and fast they tore through the trunks of the surrounding trees. Some fell, others were blown apart. It made good fuel for the fires, and created a barrier that held the Lymies back for several hours.

"They may call off the attack," Flash said as he met back up with Mara and explained what he had seen up and down the initial line of trees where Jingo had set the charges.

"Not if they know we're still here," she said. "Time to go commando mode."

"Any instructions?"

"Shoot to kill and don't get caught."

"That's what I'm talking about."

They moved toward the carnage. There were still Lymies probing the fire, searching for a way through the destruction. It was clear they were being cautious. Mara didn't think the aliens felt fear. She had seen them run over their own dead during an attack. She had seen groups slaughtered and it didn't seem to faze the survivors one bit.

She stopped behind the trunk of a wide tree. Ahead of her, through a gap in the smoke, she could see three Lymies. They were approaching slowly. She slid her automatic shotgun around to her back and brought the GAR to her shoulder. The Garrison Assault Rifle was a heavy weapon for most Marines. But Mara and Leo Squad were all enhanced via the LE program. They were bigger and stronger than most people. The heavy rifle felt natural in her hands. Unlike the shotgun, the bullets for the GAR had penetrating power. They were designed to punch through armor, and had small explosive charges inside the hollow tip that were engineered to cause maximum damage.

The bullets still wouldn't penetrate the thick, Lymie hide. Their bodies were covered in an exoskeleton that was like the tread of thick off-road tires. Even the uranium-tipped rounds she fired wouldn't punch through it. Sometimes they stuck in the strange armor and blew out chunks. Unfortunately, that didn't seem to hurt the Lymies. More often than not, the bullets just bounced off without doing any damage at all. But their heads were a different matter. They were still tough. The aliens had thick, bony skulls, but if a person had the time to target them carefully, the alien heads were vulnerable to attack.

Mara lined up her shot. The GAR had a standard, square sight, with a small fluorescent dot in the center. The end of the thick barrel had a simple V on the tip. Mara lined the dot up with the V right on the center of one of the Lymies probing the line of destruction in the forest. She took a breath, let a little out, then stopped. She was tense and tried to relax as she gently squeezed the trigger. The GAR barked a loud report that was muffled by the thick forest. It seemed to leap in her hands, but she was strong enough to hold it steady. The bullet hit the alien in the center of its head. A squirt of blood proceeded the Lymie's face-first dive into the underbrush.

She didn't wait to see it roll over in death. She was already targeting the next alien. In the two seconds after the first Lymie was killed, its companions were confused. They hadn't heard the shot from Mara's GAR. All around them fires were crackling, limbs were snapping, trees were toppling over. Another loud boom wasn't distinguishable in the din of the forest fire. She shot the second alien. The entire top of its head flew up into the air in a spray of dark blood. That got the third alien's attention. It retreated quickly, but Mara was planning to let it live all along. She needed it to communicate that the Marines were still close, still fighting. It was the only thing that would keep the aliens coming for them.

She moved quickly, searching for more targets, not worried about being seen. In fact, she wanted the aliens to see her. She made noise as she crashed through the underbrush. There were plenty of scrub bushes and leafy plants growing by the roots of the big trees. In the canopy above, birds were squawking in fear. Mara saw another alien, took aim, and put it down with a single shot. It was slow work as far as battle went. But she was safe from the Lymies on her side of the fire line. At least she thought she was. Some had made it past before the explosions. One dropped out of a tree and almost landed on Mara. It lifted a leg to stab down at her, but Mara was too fast. She spun around, dodging the thrust of the pointed leg, and fired her GAR one-handed. She was point-blank to the alien's face, close enough to see the pincer mouth, with its bony mandibles. Her rifle fired and the Lymie jumped backward, collapsed to the ground, and rolled onto its back in death. She was lucky and she knew it. When two more came scrambling down out of the smoky canopy, Mara was forced back toward the fire. A burning limb snapped off and fell beside her, singeing her left arm. She staggered away from the sparks and smoke only to have a Lymie leap toward her. Mara dove to the ground, rolled over her shoulder and fired up into the alien's belly. Maybe that portion of their body wasn't as thick and tough as the rest, or maybe it was because she was so close, but the three rounds she fired all penetrated, and sent the alien tumbling behind her. She didn't notice the root that had found the gap in her armor until after she had killed the second Lymie. It had hung back, hissing and chattering at her. Mara had shot it in the head, watched it flop over and then moved back away from the fire.

As she jogged she thought she felt a stitch in her side. It was odd. She hadn't felt a stitch in her side since the LE procedures. She could run for miles without getting tired, much less feeling a stitch in her side. Instinctively she reached down. The pain flared hot for a moment, then eased some. Mara felt something hot and sticky on her hand. When she looked, her palm was stained red with blood.

There wasn't time for first aid. That would have to come later. She began moving back, watching the tree tops for more Lymies. They were there, some moving on the trunks, others hiding in the leaves. She shot down three of them before meeting back up with Flash.

"You okay," he asked, glancing down at her side.

"Fine," she said. "I gouged myself on a tree root. You?"

"I'm good," he said. "Can't say the same for the Lymies."

"We should begin pulling back. The fire is dying down."

"It's getting dark too," he added.

The fire was still burning, but it wasn't spreading. There was very little wind, and the forest wasn't dry. The dead limbs and chunks of wood blown out of the trees were already consumed. They fell back and waited. It didn't take long for the Lymies to show up. They came in small clusters, probing into the forest. Mara's low light amplification came on. Her helmet's view screen went black and white which made judging distances difficult.

"We fire and they'll see the muzzle flashes," he pointed out. "They'll come right at us."

"Use your grenades," she recommended. "But let's wait until it's a little darker out."

In the forest twilight quickly became full dark. Mara and the other members of Leo squad all had six concussion grenades. She pulled one from the tactical webbing on her armor and flicked the safety pin off.

"Fire in the hole," she whispered, before throwing the grenade toward a group of approaching aliens.

The grenade wasn't lobbed, it was hurled like a fastball. It hit one of the aliens, flipped up and exploded. Mara had closed her eyes so the flash of the grenade wouldn't blind her. Losing her vision, even for a few moments, could be fatal. When she opened her eyes she saw the cluster of Lymies laying on the ground. None had been killed, but they were all in shock from the grenade's energy release right above them. A few had wounds from the shrapnel and some had even broken their spindly legs.

"Not bad," Flash said. "Might do more damage if it hits low."

"Agreed," Mara said.

They worked their way backward. Moving slow, letting the aliens progress with only a few setbacks. When Flash threw his first grenade, he let it bounce and roll under one of the spidery aliens. It tried to jump away but wasn't fast enough. The grenade ripped the alien's guts out, and wounded three more.

By the time Mara and Flash reached the first checkpoint they had used all their grenades.

"Ninja, Jingo, this is Mara. You out there?" she asked.

There was no sign of them on the small hill that was their first designated rally point.

"We're here," Jingo said. "Got you and skinny in my sights."

"Got plenty of aliens too," Ninja said. "The forest is crawling with them."

"Is the transport ready?"

"Affirmative," Ninja said. "We parked it behind the hill."

"Get it ready to go," Mara said. "Jingo, wait for us. We're going to give the bugs something to remember us by."

"Copy that," Jingo said. "It's about time."

Mara and Flash climbed quickly up the small hill. The wound

in her side was aching, but she didn't think it was serious. The bleeding seemed to have stopped and it didn't hinder her from fighting.

"All three directions," Mara said. "Full auto. Two mags. We want them to see us and feel us. As soon as your second mag is empty, run for the transport."

Jingo was on Mara's right side. Flash was on her left. They opened fire, spraying the forest with explosive rounds that made deep-pitched booms on contact. The muzzle flashes blinded them from seeing much beyond their little hill, but the attack was more of a statement than a tactical assault. It was a sign saying *we're still here, come and get us,* to the Lymies. Mara emptied her first magazine. She hit the release, let the spent canister drop at her feet, and shoved another one in the breech. Her movements were fast and smooth. The reload, including racking the first round into the firing chamber, took less than two seconds. She fired again, several wild bursts until that mag was empty too. Then she turned and ran for the transport. Flash was ahead of her, Jingo behind.

They jumped onboard the transport and Ninja pressed the accelerator levers forward. The transport zoomed away from the hill, crashing over saplings, snapping branches and scraping over shrubs. It wasn't a quiet escape, but it was effective.

"How far, Sarge?" Ninja asked.

"Stop three klicks from the second rally point," she said. "You can take my place. Cap a few of the bugs when they reach us."

"Roger that!" he said enthusiastically.

"You got hit?" Jingo said, bending over to look at the wound in Mara's side.

"Rolled over a root," she said. "It's no big deal."

"There's something in it," Jingo said. The lights on his helmet came on as he examined the wound. "You need some intervention."

"It'll have to wait until we get to the rally point," Mara said. "Then you can dig it out."

"Maybe we should stay together," Flash said.

Mara shook her head. "We stick to the plan. Keep them moving."

"We're nearly halfway through the forest," Jingo said. "There's no need to take unnecessary chances."

"Agreed," Mara said. "It's working, just stick with the plan."

Jingo took control of the transport. Flash and Ninja stayed behind to wait for the enemy and lure them deeper into the jungle. Mara was in the back of the transport with their weapons, ammunition, and supplies. She opened a first aid kit and took her armored vest off. She had a laceration in her side. It was already swollen. The bit of foreign matter was barely visible. It was smaller than her pinky, yet when she touched the wound pain shot through her entire body. She hosed it down with numbing antiseptic and waited for Jingo to stop the transport.

It wound through the trees and stopped at a clearing beside a river that flowed through the forest. The transport was a hovercraft. It easily glided over the rushing water and settled in the trees on the far side. It was a great place for an ambush. The Lymies would have to wade through the water with no cover. Mara knew they would need to let the enemy get close, but they could do some real damage while the aliens crossed the river.

"Doctor Jingo is in the house," the big man said with a grin.

"Good," Mara said. "Get this thing out of me."

They closed the doors on either side of the personnel carrier so that the light from Jingo's helmet wouldn't be seen by anything in the forest. He bent over her and examined the wound.

"Damn, Mara, it's already swollen."

"I know," she said. "You'll have to cut a little."

"You want a pain pill?" he asked. "Morphine injection? What?"

She shook her head and felt the damp padding inside her helmet. She hadn't known she was sweating so much. But battle took its toll, and she had been near the fire from the explosives.

"Just do it!" she ordered. "Cut it out of me. We don't have time to waste and I can't take anything while there's fighting to do."

"Dang, girl, you're one tough lady," Jingo said. "I'd be crying for my mamma."

It wasn't true. Mara knew that Jingo was just trying to bolster her spirits and she was thankful for him. He got a tool from the trauma kit that looked like needle nose pliers. It locked onto the end of the foreign matter. He gave a little tug and Mara groaned. The pain was intense and that made her worry. It had punched into her side, piercing the external obliques just above her hip. When she did her shoulder roll the edge of her armored shirt must have pulled away from the hip protector just a few millimeters. That was all it took for the bit of wood to stab into her like a giant splinter.

"All right, this is going to really hurt. But there's nothing else to do," Jingo said. "Better mute your helmet and the comlink. I don't want the others to hear you screaming."

His warning didn't make Mara feel better. Her hands were trembling a little as she took hold of the transport's side wall to brace herself. Jingo took out a disposable scalpel and leaned in close. His hands were steady as he made a small incision on either side of the big splinter. It felt to Mara like someone was touching her with a red hot poker, but she clenched her teeth and didn't make a sound.

"Moment of truth," Jingo said, putting in a reverse clamp to hold the wound open.

It felt to Mara like he was tearing her insides out. He pulled on the tool clamped to the wood. At first nothing happened. Then Mara screamed. She couldn't stop herself as the sliver of wood began to come out. Blood gushed around it and then Jingo pulled it free. Mara sagged to the floor of the transport, her side on fire. Jingo removed the reverse clamp and began spraying numbing antiseptic into the wound.

"We might have a problem, boss," he said.

"What?" Mara said, breathing heavy as the pain finally began to subside.

Jingo held up the bloody sliver of wood. It wasn't a splinter but a thorn with tiny barbs on the sides.

"Not sure what this is," he said. "But it ain't meant to come out."

"Hurt like hell," Mara panted.

"No doubt," he replied. "Thing is, a thorn such as this one, often has toxins. Might be something bad."

"If we're alive at this time tomorrow I'll worry about it then," she said. "Help me get my armor back on."

He filled the wound with a spray that turned to biodegradable foam that sealed the wound. Then he put a patch over it and taped it down securely.

"All done," he said. "Why don't you rest until we hear from Flash and Ninja? I'll keep watch. Ain't nothing to do anyway."

"Four eyes are better than two," she said. "Help me with my armor."

He shook his head. Of course she would have preferred to just climb into bed and rest. They were all exhausted from lack of sleep and constant stress. But Mara had endured much worse in the past. She got her armor back on, and picked up her GAR. Normally she would have slung the heavy shotgun over her back too, but decided it could wait.

"We used all our grenades," she said. "Let me get some more and I'll meet you outside."

"Copy that," Jingo said, shutting off the light on his helmet.

He slung open the door and nearly fell down. "What the ..."

Mara turned, bringing her weapon up ready to fire. But what she saw wasn't a target.

"Are you here to rescue us?" a young woman said.

She was flanked by men on either side. They looked nervous. All three carried CMC standard-issue rifles, the same kind that regular Marines were given.

"We are not," Mara said. "Pretty soon this entire part of the forest is going to be crawling with Lymies. Is it just the three of you?"

"No," the young woman said. "There are more of us. We've been hiding here, waiting for Lieutenant Murphy to come back."

Mara felt a pang of heartache for the young woman. They had no idea that Mitch had left the planet.

"Right now, we're luring the enemy into a trap," Mara said. "Gather your people. You'll have to come with us."

"All right," the young woman said. "We'll get the others."

They turned and disappeared into the trees. Mara looked at Jingo. "You see those rifles?"

"Yeah," he said. "The LT must have gotten them from the armory for them."

"This changes things," she said. "And it gives me an idea. We might have more of a surprise for the Lymies than we thought."

CHAPTER 29

THE *LUSKA* CROSSED a portal into the Terra system and began to slowly move toward the system star. Mitch had cleaned himself up and seen to his weapons. He was back on the Observation deck when they jumped into the system.

"Your people have been busy," Qwii said.

"What do you mean?"

"They haven't left the system as you thought. There are satellites and sonar buoys all through the system."

"Where is Arq?"

"Hidden in plain sight," Qwii said. "His vessel looks like an asteroid. He's been drifting through the system, keeping tabs on the situation. We shall join him."

"Won't you get picked up on radar?"

"Perhaps, but if we stay in the shadow of that big planet, we can get pretty close."

"How long?" Mitch asked.

"An hour, maybe two if we're extremely careful," Qwii said. "Why don't you study with Hollis while I move us into the system?"

Mitch was impatient, but he couldn't think of an excuse to stay with Qwii, or to speed him along. They obviously didn't want to alert the Space Force. And Mitch was content to let his new companions make those types of decisions. Mitch could certainly think of a number of ways he could convince them to stand down and listen, but he felt that a display of the Power would be self-serving. And while he knew that the time would come for him to help the human race move forward, that time had not yet come. He wasn't ready, and neither were his people.

An hour and a half later Mitch was surprised to find Arq and Juj waiting for him on the Observation Deck.

"How did you get here?" Mitch asked.

"The same way you did," Arq replied, as if it were a simple matter to move from one vessel to another in the cold, hard vacuum of space.

"We have heard of your progress, Mitch Murphy," Juj said. "Welcome to the Order."

"Thanks," Mitch replied. "I appreciate being chosen."

"He is anxious," Qwii said. "Your message was cryptic."

"I know, and I apologize for that," Arq said. "At the time, we didn't know how quickly you were progressing in the Power and the Knowledge."

"He is a fine student," Hollis said. "A very quick learner."

"We came from the Osterious system," Qwii explained. "We were attacked there by the Fray."

"The Fray?" Juj asked. "In the Osterious system?"

"It was a hunter and his apprentice."

"You are both here and you have all your limbs," Arq said. "Did you confront this hunter and his apprentice?"

"We did," Qwii replied. "Hannoi and his protege, a Sertilian named Flek, were given the chance to surrender peacefully."

"Hannoi doesn't know what peace is," Juj said. "He killed Ort on Kallaius Prime."

"And many others," Arq said. "I wouldn't think the council

would send someone as new to the Power and the Knowledge to confront so dangerous a threat."

"They didn't," Qwii said. "We were sent to help the Osters in their conflict with some Lomtuc Raiders. We were preparing to leave when Hannoi entered the system. They came to us and found more than they bargained for. Mitch Murphy is a skilled warrior."

"I didn't do anything by myself," Mitch said.

"Of course not," Arq said. "But the High Council should know that you faced Hannoi and his apprentice. Stopping a Fray hunter is no small feat."

"We came here as quickly as we could. I hope we are not too late," Qwii said.

"No, you are not," Arq said.

"What's happening?" Mitch asked.

"Your military forces are back on the planet," Arq said. "They are confronting the Lymie invasion force."

"As is there right," Qwii said. "Surely, you did not call for our assistance in this matter?"

"No," Arq said. "I'm sure you have sensed everything in the system, old friend."

"Four human ships, and a multitude of satellites and sonar buoys," Qwii said.

"Four?" Mitch asked.

"That is correct," Arq said. "Although I do not think your military leaders onboard the *Marathon* are aware of it. We have intercepted most of their communications. There have been none from the fourth ship. It is a different type. Stealthy, and loaded with dangerous munitions."

"I don't understand," Mitch said.

"Nuclear warheads," Qwii suddenly said. "I didn't do a full scan when we arrived. I just assumed it was more military fighters."

"As anyone would," Arq said. "The Space Force leadership from the Sol system ordered the *Marathon* to engage the enemy and use conventional bombs. Shortly afterward, the fourth ships arrived in the system."

"With nukes," Mitch said. "Why?"

"They intend to use them on New Terra," Juj said. "If your military forces fail to regain control of the planet, the fourth ship will drop nuclear arms on the surface, destroying everything and leaving the planet unfit for life for at least two hundred years."

"We do not interfere in the issues your people are struggling with, Mitch Murphy. That is not our mandate," Arq said. "But if your military is preparing to slaughter the native life on New Terra, and render the planet in hospitable for life of any kind, we must act."

"This is why we sent for you," Juj said. "Perhaps you can stay their hand."

"What makes you think they'll listen to me?" Mitch asked.

"There is a battle taking place as we speak," Arq said. "If you were to intervene, it would save many lives."

"By killing the Lymies?"

"That is probably necessary," Juj said. "Their hive ships have left the system. All that remain on the planet are their warriors. They will fight you at every turn, and with no hope of holding the planet for long. Eventually, the warriors will die and there is no one to replace them."

"Because they were left behind when the other ships left the system?" Mitch asked.

"That is the truth of the matter. If it were any different we would not interfere," Arq said. "But the Lymies are destined to die in the end. And if stopping them now saves the planet, then we should do it."

"Agreed," Qwii said. "You were right to send for us."

Mitch wanted to say they almost hadn't come. What would have Arq and Juj done then? Mitch didn't want to think about it.

"All right, get me down there," Mitch said. "I've got to do something."

"Good luck, Mitch Murphy. We shall be watching," Arq said.

"If you need us, you have only to ask," Juj said.

They gave short bows, then the pair of them walked off the open platform and drifted away in cold space.

"That's amazing," Mitch said.

"It is only possible to do so for short distances," Qwii said. "The air temperature around a person's body quickly drops in the vacuum of space."

"Why doesn't it here on your ship?" Mitch asked.

"This vessel is made of Dronium Crystal," Qwii explained. "It naturally regulates its environment."

"Oh," was all Mitch could think to say. He had never heard of Dronium Crystal, or of any substance that could maintain heat in space without expending energy to do so. But ships and exotic minerals weren't what he was focused on. He watched as the *Luska* moved quickly around the gas giant and sped toward New Terra.

CHAPTER 30

"HERE THEY COME," Jingo said.

Mara was fifty feet away, just inside the tree line of the river. Flash and Ninja had returned two hours after her makeshift surgery and finding the refugees that Lieutenant Murphy had saved. They were packed onboard the transport, twelve in total. One of the refugees named Bart was set to drive them to the final rally point.

"Wait for my signal," she ordered, as the first of the Lymies crawled out of the forest and into the clearing by the river. It looked around nervously, then went to the water and dipped its head down. More skittered out from the trees. Mara couldn't help but wish they had explosives and land mines. Her little squad of four was spread out along the trees on their side of the river. They would hit the Lymies with a heavy barrage, but it wouldn't be the same as a real ambush. That would have to come later.

"Come to papa," Flash said.

"Did somebody call an exterminator?" Jingo asked.

"For Hawk," Ninja said in an angry growl.

"Easy, wait for more to come out," Mara said.

The alien waded into the water, its companions following. There were nearly two dozen out in the open when the first alien made it across the river. It was maybe three meters from the trees. Mara was behind a tree almost directly in front of the alien. She already had her gun at her shoulder. Only her upper body was to the side of the tree. Another grew in close so that she was sort of wedged between them. It limited her ability to aim from side to side, but the trees also gave her support. Mara let the alien move directly into her sights and then pulled the trigger.

One shot, one kill. Instantly her companions opened fire. Ninja was sixteen meters to her left. Flash was spread out to her right, with Jingo beyond him. The transport was behind them, hidden in the trees.

"Don't let 'em jump," Jingo warned.

Mara was shooting fast. There were eight Lymies in her area. She had to roll out from between the two trees to target them. One jumped over the river and landed close. She fired, the bullet from the GAR ripped the lower part of its face off, and the alien went crazy. It slammed its face on the ground, then charged forward, crazed from the pain. Mara flicked her weapon to three round burst mode and fired again. The bullets managed to splinter one of the alien's legs.

Two more rushed up out of the river. They could see the muzzle flash, even if they couldn't see Mara. She fired four bursts, wounding one of the aliens, and killing the other. Those in the river were hesitating, but Mara knew it wasn't from fear. They were making themselves easy targets while the rest of the Lymie army closed in.

"Time to move!" she shouted.

"What?" Jingo replied. "You're breaking up."

She didn't really understand what he said because his voice was laced with static.

"Retreat!" she ordered. "Pull back now. To the transport."

"There's still enemy forces out there," Ninja complained. "We have to kill them."

"Move Ninja! That's an order," Mara snapped. She didn't like giving orders. That was for officers, but in the heat of battle it was sometimes necessary.

"Movement on our flank," Jingo said. "The bugs are crossing the river upstream."

"Go, go, go!" she shouted.

Waiting for the Lymies to get to the river was a risky decision. The open ground was a perfect ambush site, but they had to let the Lymies get close. The big, spidery aliens were faster than humans on foot. Mara's squad of enhanced Marines could probably outrun them on open ground, but the Lymies could jump long distances, bounce from tree to tree, and drop down on her team from above.

Mara was the first one to the transport. It was already a meter off the ground and pointed away from the approaching aliens. She didn't get inside. There was no more room. The refugees were crammed in the passenger compartment, along with the weapons and ammunition for the final show down with the aliens.

Mara jumped onto the back of the vehicle. There was a footrail there and a bar that ran from one side to the other along the back of the personnel carrier, allowing Marines to ride on the outside. She held on with her left hand, ignoring the pain in her side, and holding her GAR in her right hand. Flash burst out of the trees and joined her. A few seconds later Jingo arrived.

"Ninja, where are you?" Mara asked over her comlink.

"I ain't coming," he said.

"What?"

"This is where I make my stand, Sarge. It's been an honor."

"Ninja, don't be a fool," Flash said.

"Kinda busy right now."

"Should we go get him?" Jingo asked.

"It's too late," Ninja said. They could hear his GAR blasting away, and the screams of the aliens. "They're all over me. I can't make it."

Mara hated making the hard decisions. They could fight their way in, try to save Ninja, and themselves, but it was a hopeless situation. And they still had a mission to carry out. She wanted to curse, but instead she banged on the roof of the transport. It started to move away from the river clearing.

"For Hawk," Ninja shouted.

They heard his weapon stop firing and knew what was coming. Ninja was a skilled knife fighter. But he wasn't facing a human opponent. The Lymies were big, powerful aliens with thick hides that wouldn't be easy to kill with a knife.

"Go for the legs," Mara said, her voice cracking with grief.

They didn't get a response on the comlink, but Ninja's death cry could be heard echoing through the forest.

"Damn," Flash said.

"I can't believe he's gone," Jingo added.

Mara was crying. It had been difficult losing Hawk, but they had time to prepare for that possibility. In the stress of running for their lives, to lose Ninja felt like someone was ripping her heart from her body. As a Sergeant it was her job to keep the squad together and focused on their task. She should have seen Ninja was breaking down. She should have kept him closer.

"It's not your fault," Flash said. "Ninja knew what he was doing."

"Bought us enough time to escape," Jingo said. "And like it or not, the bugs killing him may be what drives them on to get the rest of us."

Mara didn't speak. She knew that Ninja was grieving for Hawk. They were lovers after all, and it shouldn't have been a surprise that he would sacrifice himself for the squad. Mara thought they could have all made it out alive. Maybe Ninja saw something she didn't, or maybe in her grief she wanted to remember him as a hero that laid down his life for his friends.

"This changes things," she said, her voice shaking with emotion.

"Same mission," Jingo said.

"We'll see it through," Flash added.

"No, I mean tactically," she said.

She banged on the roof of the transport and it slowed to a stop.

"What are you thinking?" Jingo asked.

"I think we slow down, stay in sight of the enemy until we're out of the forest," she said.

Flash shrugged. "As long as we stay together, don't make no difference to me."

"The two of you need to get on the roof," Mara said. "We'll power on the running lights. I'll drive."

"I'm good with that," Jingo said.

"Just watch out for low bridges," Flash said with a chuckle.

They scrambled up onto the roof of the transport and Mara went around to the cab. Bart was waiting there.

"Trouble?" he asked.

"Change of plans," she said. "Slide over. I'm driving."

The cab had room for a driver and a passenger. Some of that space was taken up with equipment. They had stowed one field communication unit in the cab of the transport. Bart slid over and Mara got in with a grunt of pain. Her wound hurt, and she could tell she had a fever. The thorn had done more than just stabbed into her side. It had left something behind that couldn't be removed with tools. She could feel it burning through her veins, turning her blood into a fiery liquid that scorched her from the inside out. But there was no time to worry about the way she felt. Pain was just a reminder that she was alive. At least that was what her old drill instructor was fond of saying.

She flicked on the transport's running lights. LEDs lit up along the sides, alternating between the top and bottom of the transport. Her helmet view screen lit up from the sudden brightness outside. She didn't bother with the headlights. They would only show her a few meters into the forest, and ruin her helmet's low light amplification. She could see better with the headlights off.

"Won't they be able to see us?" Bart asked, referring to the aliens.

"That's the plan."

"You want them to see us?"

"We want them to follow us," she said. "Space Force is launching an air raid. Our job is to get the Lymies in the right place at the right time."

"Well, that's great for you," Bart said. "How the hell do I get off this ride?"

"You can't," Mara said. She felt sorry for the man, but the facts of the situation were undeniable. "There's an army of Lymies behind us," she explained. "There's nowhere for you and your people to hide from them. They're sweeping through this entire part of the forest. You would all be killed if we let you out."

"Sounds like we've got a damn good chance of dying if we stick with you," he snapped.

"Good. Hang on to that anger. You'll need it."

"What's that supposed to mean?"

"It means, when we get to the ambush site, your people will be fighting right alongside mine."

"That's crazy," the man said. "We're not Marines."

She knew that was true. She was taller than he was, stronger, faster too, but none of that mattered. They were both humans, and the Lymies would kill them all given the chance. The refugees wouldn't be very good fighters, but all they needed to be able to do was fire a weapon. The goal would eventually be to simply hold the enemy back until the bombs started dropping. Mara could only hope that they weren't all killed in the attack right along with the enemy.

"I have a question for you," Mara said.

"What?" Bart asked, still sulking over the situation he found himself in.

"What happened to Lieutenant Murphy?"

"How should I know."

"You were down here with him, when ..."

"When you all dropped nukes right on top of us?"

"That wasn't my decision," Mara said. "Lieutenant Murphy was my CO. He's a good man. I just want to know what happened."

"Can't help you. I thought the Lymies got him, but Carter saw something."

"What did he see?"

"Some sort of ship," Bart said. "Didn't hear it, but he saw it take off from the airfield before the dust got too thick to see anything. We were in the forest when the bombs dropped. If not for the Lieutenant we'd have all been killed. He sent us south in a baggage hovercart. Carter just happened to be looking up when we passed through a small clearing. He *claims* he saw a UFO, some sort of moon-shaped ship rising into the sky. No one else saw it. None of us heard it, and it was pretty quiet. If the Lymies didn't get him, then I guess whoever was on that ship did."

It didn't answer Mara's question, which was if Mitch had gone willingly, or if he had been forced onto the alien ship. She was just thinking that she would probably never know what really happened to him when her comlink broke into her thoughts.

"We've got movement on our six," Jingo called over the comlink.

"You want us to waste 'em?" Flash added.

"Only if they get close," Mara reminded them. "We want them to continue chasing us, remember."

"I remember," Flash said. "But I got an itchy trigger finger."

"Yeah, don't seem right to see the bastards and not try to kill them," Jingo said.

"Save your ammo," Mara said. "We gotta make this thing last a few more hours."

The sun came up shortly after Leo Squad lost Ninja. There

was something about the light that gave Mara a boost of confidence. It was a new day filled with opportunities. She milked the time, keeping an eye on the power gauge. When they reached the edge of the forest four hours later, the transport was low on battery.

"All right, time to get into position," she said, checking the GPS location via her helmet's navigation app. There was too much interference from the nearby horde of aliens for her armor to be tracked by the orbital satellites, but she had downloaded the information before the battle began and started a directional program that showed her exactly where Captain Marcs had ordered her to make a stand. "Hold on back there," she added, before thrusting the control sticks forward.

The low power light was flashing, but they only needed to go a couple of kilometers to reach their destination. It was a rocky formation, some sort of geological formation from eons in the past. As she raced ahead across the open plain that stretched from the forest to the swamp lands beyond, the Lymies hesitated. Fear wasn't in their nature, but they weren't stupid. The aliens had learned a lot about fighting the humans, especially Leo Squad. And what they expected was that at every clearing there was a trap.

"They're holding back," Flash said. "Staying in the forest."

"Cowards," Jingo added.

"They'll wait until they've got their entire army gathered together," Mara said. "Then they'll come in numbers."

"How long you figure we need to hold out?" Flash asked.

"Three hours till the bombs fall," Mara said, pulling the transport around behind the big boulders sticking up out of the grassy plain.

"Let's hope the desk jockeys aren't late," Flash said.

"I'm more worried about their aim," Jingo said.

Mara powered down the transport. It had less than three percent of its battery life left. She wasn't even sure if that was enough to get it off the ground again.

"All right, last stop," she said. "Everyone out."

There was a lot to do. The rocks were simply that, a jumble of huge boulders that some tectonic force had pushed up to the surface. It would have been good cover in a firefight, but the Lymies didn't use weapons. The rocks would merely make her squad more visible to the enemy. But that's where the Space Force pukes had said to be when the bombs fell. And she could see some wisdom in that.

Mara pulled open the side door of the transport while Jingo and Flash jumped down from the roof.

"Flash," Mara said.

"On it," he replied, hurrying off to the highest of the boulders to keep tabs on the enemy.

"All right people, listen up," Mara said. "In three hours the Space Force is going to turn this place into hell on ... New Terra. We're safe here, but we've got to hold back the aliens until the cavalry arrives."

"Sounds like a suicide mission," a young woman named Adele said.

"It does, but that's the only chance we've got."

"We could keep running," a man named Carter suggested.

"The transport is out of power," Mara explained. "The forest is full of Lymies. The swamps have dangers of their own. Even if we could run, we've got nowhere to go."

"We were doing pretty good until you lot came along," another of the refugees grumbled.

Mara smiled. "The way I see it, you can help us, or you can die."

"We shouldn't have come with you," Carter responded.

"If you had stayed behind you'd already be dead," Jingo said. "Now stop complaining and help get these weapons unloaded."

There were two .50 caliber machine guns on tripods, and six shoulder mounted rocket launchers, along with the crates of ammunition. The GARs were too big and too heavy for the refugees to shoot, but they could throw grenades and help reload the various weapons. Bart and Carter set up the belt fed .50 caliber machine guns, while Adele saw to the rocket launchers. They weren't happy, but they had enough sense to realize that fighting was their only chance. Or maybe they just wanted to kill as many Lymies as they could before they died. Mara could relate.

Once the transport was unloaded, she gave the group specific instructions.

"Right now, I want you to rest," Mara said. "The Lymies are going to come at us. It might be an hour from now, it might be any minute. But once they do, I'll let you know to man your weapons. Keep in mind, the standard issue rifles won't do much against the Lymies. If you have to use them, aim for their legs. That's their weak point.

"Now, when the bombardment happens, the plan is to take cover inside the armored personnel carrier. So when I give that signal, drop what you're doing and run for the transport. When the bombs stop, my squad will check for survivors and put them down."

"If we survive," Bart grumbled.

"That's what we're all hoping for," Mara said. "Until then, we make the enemy pay in blood for every meter of ground. This is one battle they will never forget."

"Yeah, baby," Jingo said. "Time to squash some bugs."

Mara followed Jingo into the jumble of rocks and said a silent prayer that somehow, someway, they could survive the next few hours.

CHAPTER 31

IT WAS WORKING. General Mercer was sipping coffee. He no longer tasted it, but he needed the caffeine. His bladder was full, and his eyes burned from long hours spent monitoring the battle on New Terra. Of course there wasn't a lot to monitor. All they could see was the blur of the Lymie interference. But as long as it continued moving south through the forest all was well.

"They're right at the edge of the forest," the radar operator said.

"It's too soon," Admiral Darcy Wilcox said. "The drones just launched an hour ago."

"Three more hours," Lieutenant Colonel Jerome Banks pointed out.

"They'll hold," General Mercer said. "That's what they're trained for."

"Um, excuse me," the commander of the drone pilot squadron spoke up, unsure who to address with his nugget of information. He was a senior NCO, a Chief Warrant Officer with thousands of hours of drone flight experience. The pilots weren't flying the drones in real time, but had programmed their drones to fly to the drop point autonomously. Admiral Wilcox had ordered the drone

Commander to stay with them in the CIC to answer questions about the aerial bombardment.

"Go ahead Chief," Admiral Wilcox said.

General Mercer was tired. They were all on the verge of exhaustion. Mercer, Admiral Wilcox, Command Hughes, Colonel Banks, and Captain Frank Marcs had all been in the CIC since the battle began, nearly twenty four hours straight. The crew of Space Force officers had rotated out, but the senior leadership stayed to monitor the situation on the ground.

"The weather is changing," the drone commander said. "We'll have a strong northeasterly front moving through that area in a couple of hours."

"What the hell does that have to do with anything?" General Mercer said. "These Marines won't melt if starts raining."

"Aye, General, that wasn't my point. I was just thinking the drones might struggle to stay on course."

"They're on autopilot, correct?" the Admiral asked.

"Aye, Admiral, and autopilot will work to keep the drones on course, but it's the bombs that I'm in reference to. They might be blown around as they drop."

"Are you saying they might miss the targets?" General Mercer demanded, angrily.

They were tired, which led to short fuses. Anger was being fed by fear that the operation might not be a success. General Mercer needed a win, a big one, a public example of how potent and invaluable the SSO squads were. If the drones missed the Lymie army then the last twenty something hours of intense work would be for nothing.

"They'll still hit in the area, General," the drone Commander explained. "But our calculations will be off. I can't vouch for the safety of the people on the ground."

"You're saying that Leo Squad might be killed," Captain Marcs asked.

"Yes sir, that's what I'm saying."

For a moment the CIC fell silent. Everyone knew that they were talking about the lives of men and women, loyal Marines, and yet they also knew the mission couldn't be called off. It was both strategically, and logistically impossible.

"Sir," Captain Marcs said. "Give me a drop ship. I'll go get our Marines."

"No," Admiral Darcy Wilcox stated from her place by the holographic plot that showed the planet and surrounding space. "You'd be landing in the middle of a battlefield. We would lose the ship and its crew. We can't take that risk."

"A couple of SSO Squads could turn the tide," Captain Marcs argued. "Hell, we could parachute in, flank the Lymies."

"There's no need," General Mercer said. "We can't recall the drones at this stage, and you'd all get killed."

The drone Commander cleared his throat. He obviously disagreed with General Mercer's assessment. The drones were still three hours out from the battlefield. They could be recalled, but the Commander didn't want to draw any more of the General's ire and wisely kept his mouth shut.

The General continued, almost as if he were giving a speech. "The only option is to see it through. Those brave Marines are fighting for all of us. We will honor them by making their sacrifice count. We drop the bombs and end the Lymie threat once and for all."

He settled back down into his seat. His back hurt, and his tailbone was aching from the hours he had spent in the chair near one of the consoles. His focus was on the big screen beyond where Admiral Darcy Wilcox stood. He could see the blob of interference from the Lymies. Laid on top of the satellite imagery was an opaque map that showed the forest, the grassy plain, and the swamp beyond it. There was a bright red dot directly south of the alien interference. That was where his people were. He didn't know their names, or anything about them. He was a general after all. His duty was to make the hard decisions and he had made them. The die was cast, and all that remained was to see how well his plan achieved its tactical and strategic purpose. A few dead Marines were a small price to pay in comparison to the army of aliens swarming over New Terra.

"Just a few more hours then," Colonel Banks said. "Then we can begin our mop up operations."

"Once it's safe for the drop ships to land," Admiral Wilcox insisted.

"Yes," General Mercer agreed. "Soon enough it will be."

It had to be, he thought. His entire career depended on a decisive victory on New Terra utilizing the SSO squads. He had set everything up, like a chess grandmaster, always thinking several moves ahead of his opponent. The Lymies weren't even the real enemy. He was overcoming all the obstacles in his path to greatness. And everything hinged on what was happening on New Terra.

"Admiral, new contact bearing one, eight, niner!" the radar officer called out.

"What is it?" Admiral Wilcox asked.

"Can't say for certain," the radar officer replied. "I'm not getting a heat signature or exhaust. They just came cruising in. I'm not sure why we didn't pick them up sooner."

"Is it a Lymie ship?" General Mercer asked, fear making his tough persona crack.

"Negative, negative," the radar officer said. "I've never seen anything like this."

"But we have," Admiral Wilcox said, looking over the radar control officer's shoulder. She turned and looked directly at General Mercer. "The crescent-shaped spaceship is back."

"How? Where did it come from?" he asked.

"Impossible to say," Admiral Wilcox said. "It only gets picked up on visual scans or when it's close enough for a radar return."

"General," Captain Marcs spoke up. "Isn't that the same ship that took Lieutenant Murphy?"

"Maybe," General Mercer said, his mind whirling. "It could be the same ship, or one like it. Where is it going?"

"Looks like it's landing," the radar operator said. "Maybe five hundred kilometers from our ambush site."

"Excellent. It's too far away to interfere."

"For now," the Admiral pointed out. "We'll keep tabs on it."

The door to the CIC opened and Major Swift walked in. She looked no more rested or refreshed than anyone in the CIC did, although she had on a clean, wrinkle-free uniform. General Stanley Mercer rarely judged people on their personal feelings, but it was clear to him that his science officer didn't care for him. She judged him as being cold and heartless, a man who could order people to their deaths. It was all true of course, but what she failed to understand was the fact that any good military leader needed those exact traits. What made him a bad person in her mind was also what made him an excellent military commander.

"Mark their position and see what the sat feed can tell us when they land," General Mercer said. "In the meantime, everything proceeds at planned."

He could feel Major Swift staring at him, but he didn't care. All that mattered was the mission, and his ultimate success.

CHAPTER 32

THE *LUSKA* SETTLED GENTLY on New Terra. Qwii had brought the ship down on the southern side of the forest, but several hundred kilometers from the battlefield.

"Where is everyone?" Mitch asked. "Are we too late?"

"You must learn to rely on your sense of the Power and the Knowledge, rather than on what your eyes see," Qwii gently chided. "I kept us far enough away that it wouldn't terrify the Lymies."

"They fear you?"

"They fear the Order of Scion," Qwii said. "Their society is strictly regimented. They have no interest in living peacefully with another race."

"I guess no one has ever been invited to join the Order?"

"Sadly, no. But they have been removed from more than one world to save a weaker people."

"So why not land right in front of them?" Mitch asked. "I'm expanding my senses, but I can't reach anything."

"Your control and sensitivity will grow in time," Qwii said. "I did not want to stop the Lymies. That is for you to do, Mitch

Murphy. This is your re-introduction to your people, and the first chance we have to show them that the Order of Scion wants only their good."

"But how am I supposed to do that from so far away?" Mitch asked.

"You won't," Qwii said. "I will teach you a new way to travel. It is not unlike what we do with our space vessels."

"Now you're talking," Mitch said.

It only took a few minutes to learn to surround himself with a bubble of anti-gravity and direct himself where he wanted to go.

"This is fun," Mitch said.

"Your joy is contagious," Qwii said. "Let us go and meet your people, Mitch Murphy. We must hurry."

Mitch was indeed having a good time. He felt a bit like a super-hero. It wasn't the first time he cut the ties to gravity and levitated himself, but it was the first time he understood exactly how and why he was doing it. It only took a few seconds and the two of them were racing over the grassy plains. It wasn't until sometime later that it occurred to Mitch that he had missed something. Talking, while they raced along several meters above the ground, wasn't easy. Mitch had to shout for his voice to reach Qwii without the sound waves being left in their wake.

"What did you mean we *must* hurry?" Mitch asked.

"Pardon me?" Qwii asked.

"You said we need to go and meet my people, then you said, *we must hurry*. What did you mean?"

Qwii, who looked like he was standing calmly instead of racing through the air, gave a shrug. Mitch wasn't satisfied with that answer.

"What aren't you telling me?" Mitch demanded.

"Use your senses," Qwii said. "There is a battle taking place. Part of our responsibility is to learn all we can from the senses granted us by the Creator."

"Just tell me," Mitch said. "What battle? What's going on?"

"It is, I suppose, the plan of your military," Qwii shouted. "They are drawing out the enemy into the open."

"Why?"

"Why do you think, Mitch Murphy?"

The truth was Mitch knew exactly why the Lymies were being drawn out. And he knew what the CMC was capable of. He didn't need to ask Qwii, but in his panic he wanted the older alien's confirmation and maybe even his instructions as to what was the best plan of action. He let his awareness of the gravity around him extend. He could feel about as far as he could see. There were trees and grass, animals of all kinds, even insects in the soil. He could feel the constant pull of the planet, and the building pressure as a weather front moved toward them from the south. But he couldn't sense the battle yet. He couldn't reach the Lymies or the Marines fighting them. And that made Mitch nervous. If the CMC was drawing the aliens out into the open, it was because they had a way to hit them hard. Maybe another kinetic warhead from orbit. Mitch tried to reach up into space, but his awareness of the gravity waves wasn't strong enough. A panicked thought pushed its way to the front of his mind. What about the stealth ship with the nukes on board? What if the CMC was drawing the Lymies out so they could drop a nuclear weapon right on their heads? Nukes hadn't been used in centuries. They were too dirty, too dangerous a weapon for use on earth, or any of the precious colonies they fought so hard to construct on Mars or the moons around the gas giants. Of course, if the brass planned to drop a nuke, they could drop it anywhere. They didn't need to draw the Lymies out of their lairs to wipe them out with nuclear weapons. It might make sense to draw them away from the colonies before nuking the aliens, but from what Mitch could tell they weren't all that far from the colonies. Why nuke them? But if it wasn't nukes, what else could it be? He had to know, and that meant reaching out farther than he ever had before.

The flight took time, a little over two hours to cover the distance to the battlefield. What Mitch saw took his breath away. Well over a thousand Lymies were marching out of the forest. A tiny group of soldiers were working to stop them, but it was obvious that they were going to fail. They worked hard and would kill two or three hundred Lymies, but eventually the swarm would overwhelm them. Mitch and Qwii stopped in the distance, watching the battle.

"What should I do?" Mitch asked.

"That is for you to decide," Qwii said. "I cannot intervene. This is not for the Order of Scion. Only you can step forward in this moment."

"I have to do it alone?" Mitch asked.

"Yes, and you must trust your senses. Trust what you can feel in the Power of the Creator, not just what you see."

Mitch stretched out his awareness of the gravity waves once again. Rain was starting to fall, cold fat drops that found the collar of his robe. He pushed the distraction aside, focusing with all his strength on what he could feel. At first he was caught up in the desperate struggle. His power didn't give him access to what the Marines in the rock formation were thinking or feeling. He couldn't even recognize them with his sense of the gravity waves alone. But he could tell what they were doing. There were weapons being deployed, and quick, desperate movements.

Then he expanded his focus. The battle was obvious, he told himself. What lay beyond it? That's when he felt the drones. It took some time to identify them. Space Force issue autonomous vehicles, each one loaded with clusters of high explosive warheads. His stomach dropped and fear made the hair on the back of his neck stand out. There were dozens of drones, each with enough bombs to take out the Lymies. What Mitch couldn't feel were the usual radio waves that were used to control the drones. They weren't being controlled by pilots. And Mitch realized that if they bombed the battlefield they would kill hundreds of Lymies, but also the Marines fighting them.

"I have to stop it," Mitch said.

"You must do what you think is right," Qwii said. "But trust the Knowledge, it will guide you, Mitch Murphy."

"Thanks," Mitch said, rising up in a gravity bubble. "I shouldn't be too long."

"You know where to find me," Qwii said.

Mitch nodded, then turned his attention to the battle. He had a tide to turn and a squadron of bombers to stop before they killed the Marines who were in the struggle of their lives.

CHAPTER 33

"HERE THEY COME," Jingo announced.

It had taken the Lymies two hours. Mara could see the trees two klicks from her position. It looked like they were in constant movement. The aliens swarmed on the ground, up the tree trunks, in the canopies. But they hadn't come out for nearly two whole hours. It had given her people time to prepare, but there was still a solid hour before the bombs would arrive. She wanted the aliens to come out and fight, but not too soon.

"Permission to start picking them off," Flash requested.

They all had GARs, but they also had rifles with big scopes for exactly that purpose. The Lymies didn't come out in full force. They sent scouts ahead of them. Mara had expected as much, which was why they were ready with the long guns.

"Granted, fire at will," she told the two remaining members of Leo Squad.

The refugees were slumped down, either sitting or lying down. Behind them they could see rain coming up from the south. Mara guessed that the reports from the rifles would be enough to get them up and moving. If not, she would kick Bart, who was only a few feet away, snoring softly. She couldn't blame them for sleeping. It had been a long, stressful night. Some obviously couldn't release the stress and go to sleep. Others embraced the opportunity and were blissfully unaware that the Lymies were starting their attack.

She sighted in one of the Lymies and took a breath to settle her heart rate. Long distance shots required patience. She was no sniper, although she had good vision and steady hands. Hawk was the true long distance shooter. She could hit tiny targets four and five kilometers away over and over again. Mara was glad the Lymie scouts weren't that far off. Still, fifteen hundred meters was a long shot by any standard. She let her breath out slowly, held it, then feathered the trigger. The gun bucked and when the scope settled back into place, she saw a Lymie fall onto its back, the long, spindly legs curling in death. That's one, she thought to herself as she racked a new round into the chamber using the rifle's bolt action, a thousand more to go.

"What's happening?" Bart asked.

"The fun's beginning to start," Mara told him. "See to your people."

"The aliens are attacking?"

"They just sent their scouts. They're testing us. We've got about an hour to hold them off. We should be able to do it."

She fired again, hitting and wounding a Lymie, but not killing it. That required a second shot. A group of six formed a line and charged at their position. Jingo killed the lead alien, but the others leapt over the body and continued the charge.

"Switching to my GAR," Jingo said, as he set down the long rifle and swung his Garrison Assault Rifle around on the sling he wore across his massive shoulders. The GAR looked small in his beefy hands. He fired quick bursts, taking down the next four aliens in the line. Mara killed the last one. Her long-range bullet wasn't the same penetration round used in the GAR, but the bullet was as long as her middle finger and had a copper-jacketed point. It hit with more force than the standard rounds used by the

Marines, and blew a fist-sized hole out of the side of the alien's head.

It took ten minutes to put down the scouts that were close to the rocky outcropping. They let the ones exploring to either flank go, but Mara assigned Adele to watch them. She was up on the tallest rock with a pair of binoculars and a comlink stuck in her ear.

"They're just standing around near the swamps," Adele said.

"That's fine. If they move this way, say the word," Mara ordered.

"What comes next, Sarge?" Flash asked.

"They'll come in a concentrated wave," Mara said. "Bart, how's that .50 cal?"

"It's ready," he said.

"Carter is ready on this side," Jingo added.

"All right, we follow the plan. We've only got a limited amount of ammunition, but don't let anything get close to us. It won't help us if we're killed trying to save ammunition."

"Got it," Bart said.

The second wave was exactly what Mara predicted. The aliens marched out in a tight mass. They weren't like human troops. They didn't have any sort of formation, or coordination. They just moved in a bunch, which made the job of stopping them a little easier. The shoulder-mounted rockets fired first. All six rose up in unison under Flash's command. They fired medium-sized rockets. Normally, the shoulder-mounted launchers fired ground to air missiles, but Mara had only taken ground to ground missiles from the armory in Alpha Colony. They shot ahead, streaking toward the mass of aliens, and killing dozens with each explosion.

"Now," Mara ordered Bart.

He and Carter opened up with the belt-fed machine guns. The bullets didn't have the penetrating power or depleted uranium tips that the GARs had, but they spewed death. Bart was selective, moving his machine gun back and forth as he fired volley after volley into the horde. Hundreds died in the attack. And none got close enough to the rocks to be a serious threat. But some began to jump to avoid the high intensity of machine gun fire. Mara, Flash, and Jingo took the jumpers down. The wind was at their back and in the face of the aliens, making it impossible for them to spool out thread and fly toward the Marines and human refugees. It was the first real factor to break in their favor, she thought.

The attack lasted eight minutes, before the horde withdrew and Mara gave the order to save their ammunition. Killing the enemy was great, but their mission was to draw them out in order for the bombardment to wipe them out completely. The fact that it would probably wipe Leo Squad and the refugees out too was just the way it had to be.

"Damn," Flash said. "I bet we killed over two hundred of those monsters."

"And it won't stop them," Jingo added.

"It might," Bart said. "Maybe they'll decide we aren't worth it, and retreat."

Mara shook her head. "First of all, those are warriors. Fighting is all they know. They're like army ants. They're bred for fighting, and it doesn't matter what the odds are, they'll keep coming."

"But not in the same way," Jingo said. "They're too smart for that."

"Agreed," Mara said. "They'll try to flank us. Divide our resources, and maybe even get around behind us. Time is on their side, or so they think. Which brings us to point number two, which is our mission. We don't want them to retreat. We want as many of those spidery bastards as we can get right out here in the open so that the Space Force can bomb them to hell."

"And us too," Bart pointed out.

"Maybe, but you can bet the eggheads on the spaceships have done all the math," Mara said. "They've made provisions for us right here."

As she said it, the wind picked up and the rain started to fall. It took another ten minutes for the third assault. And just as Mara predicted, there were two fronts. Both were several kilometers away, one to the east, the other to the west of the rocky formation where Leo Squad was making its stand.

"Standard pincer movement," Flash said.

"Too far for rockets," Jingo said. "The .50 cals could reach 'em though."

"We'll wait," Mara said. "The bombers should be here in about twenty minutes. All we've got to do is hold them off one more time. No one fires until I give the order."

Everyone was ready. The shoulder-mounted rockets were reloaded. The .50 caliber tripod-mounted machine guns were turned to face the hordes coming from east and west. Every refugee had a rifle and access to the grenades they would need to throw when the enemy got close enough. Mara didn't like their odds, but they had fulfilled their mission. The enemy was converging on them at the perfect time. Hundreds of spidery aliens came from the east and the west. She knew even more were waiting in the trees. They would come from the north again.

Lightning crackled in the thick clouds behind her, and the thunder rolled in an ominous, booming crash. The light went from bright to a dull gray. The rain was cold, but Mara was hot. In fact, she was so hot she wanted to pull her helmet and armor off. It was madness to remove the protective gear in the middle of a battle, but the temptation was awful. Her skin felt like fragile paper, and eyes burned dry from the heat raging through her body. Worst of all, she felt tired. But it wouldn't be long, she told herself, and then she wouldn't be tired anymore. She wouldn't feel anything, or need anything, ever again.

"Rockets," she announced, as the first of the Lymies on her side of the rocky formation closed to within a thousand meters. "Hit 'em where it hurts."

Three rockets shot to the west. The Lymies didn't try to dodge or escape the deadly missiles. In fact, several brave aliens jumped toward them. The rockets exploded, ripping the aliens they hit to pieces, but it was too far ahead of the crowd and the missiles didn't have the same impact.

"Reload," she ordered. "Wait for my command."

The aliens marched on. Hundreds, more than she could hope to stop. She gripped her GAR with both hands. *Come on,* she thought. *Just a little closer. I'm here. Come and get me.*

"Bart, give 'em hell," she said, tapping him on the shoulder.

The .50 caliber spewed death and destruction, but it only sped the Lymies forward. They knew the longer they allowed the big machine gun to operate the more of their own would die. The aliens began to leap forward, moving in a zig-zag pattern to make targeting them more difficult.

"Drones!" Adele called. "I see them coming."

"Where?" Mara asked.

"East of us. Way up. Just below the clouds," the refugee said.

"I see them," Jingo said. "Right on time."

"Who would have thought it," Flash said. "I could kiss me a Space Force puke right now."

Mara turned. They all did, even Bart. The drones were their salvation. Not that they would save them from death, but it would be the end of the battle, the end of the Lymies who were converging on them. Better to die in a split second from a bomb blast than to be torn apart by the spidery aliens.

But just as Mara turned to look, the drones began to drop out of the sky.

"What are they doing?" Adele asked.

The first explosion told them everything they needed to know.

"Stupid Space Force idiots," Jingo said. "They're way off target."

"Hang on," Mara said. "They aren't bombing. They're crashing."

"What's going on?" Flash asked.

"I don't know but we're fighting for our lives now," Mara said. "Kill as many Lymies as you can."

Bart didn't hesitate. He opened fire. But there were too many aliens. The refugees with rocket launchers opened up. But with only three to a side, and the enemy sacrificing individuals to save the swarm, Mara knew the outcome was a foregone conclusion. All they could do was take as many out with them as they could. If she was going to die, and that was a certainty, then at least she would die fighting.

She lifted the GAR to her shoulder and began to shoot.

CHAPTER 34

IT TOOK ALL his mental strength to pull the drones out of the sky. They would have been a powerful weapon against the Lymies, but it was one that Mitch didn't need. And he couldn't let the Marines die from the friendly fire. Wind blew hard, ruffling his robes. There was still an army of Lymies between him and the Marines. He could feel them in the waves of gravity, some jumping, others running, a horde closing in from the east and from the west. Still more lingered in the forest, waiting for the right moment to attack.

Mitch reached out and caught the leaders. He added gravity to them until the spidery aliens were pinned down. He was close enough to hear the Marines shooting. In the ebb and flow of the gravity waves he could sense the bullets. On the far side Mitch sent the Lymies flying into the air by cutting off the gravity between them and the ground. They floated up, spinning out of control, rising higher and higher.

It didn't take Mitch long to feel like his mind was splitting into a dozen shards. He was smashing some aliens, and sending others flying. The group closest to him had turned, seen him approaching in a slow drift, several feet off the ground. They panicked. Some ran back toward the forest, others toward the swamps. Mitch let them go. He dropped the Lymies in the air. They fell hundreds of meters and slammed to the ground. A few tried to spool out enough silk to save themselves, but the drop only lasted a few seconds. They couldn't get enough webbing out to slow, much less stop their fall. They crashed on top of their comrades. With a tug of sideways gravity Mitch sent over a hundred tumbling away from the rocky outcropping. They smashed into the ground, rolling and tumbling, hitting one another, their legs snapping, their insides rupturing under the pressure of the impacts.

The tide had turned in a matter of moments. Over a thousand Lymies were either dead, wounded, or running. Mitch suddenly had a clear view of the rocky formation and saw, as well as felt, the rocket fired in his direction. He couldn't blame them. He was in strange clothing, and flying. He must have looked like an alien with great power. Better to shoot first and ask questions later, he thought approvingly.

It only took a thought to smash the rocket into the ground with a swarm of gravity. It exploded halfway between him and the rocky formation. He landed and started walking toward them. A machine gun opened fire. Mitch already had a bubble of powerful gravitational forces around him. The bullets were pulled to either side of him. It was like a river of hot lead and he was the stone separating the waters. Then the suddenly the shooting stopped. A huge man jumped out the rocks. He was in full battle armor, but his hulking muscles were obvious and familiar. The Marine had a Garrison Assault Rifle in one hand, but it was pointed at the ground.

"Far enough," his voice boomed out across the battlefield, which was strewn with dead and dying aliens. "Who the hell are you?"

"Don't recognize your own, Jingo?" Mitch called out. "I got some new threads, but it's still me."

"Lieutenant Murphy?" Jingo said. "No way."

"Fraid so," Mitch said. "I should have known they would send Leo Squad to fight an entire army of Lymies."

"Yeah, I guess so," Jingo said, clearly shocked.

They approached each other. Mitch held his hands out, and dropped the gravity bubble around him. Jingo pulled his helmet off and held it in his free hand.

"It's really you," he said. "Rumor was you left the planet."

"I did," Mitch said.

"You been gone a month, man. Where'd you go?"

"Long story," Mitch said. "Let's make sure the Lymies aren't a threat, and I'll tell you all about it."

†††

Mara had seen it all, but she didn't believe it. She thought maybe she was dead, or perhaps the fever was causing her to hallucinate. She saw the Lymies rushing toward her, too many to stop, suddenly get squashed flat. It was like an enormous, invisible hand had smacked down on top of them. She quit shooting and so did the people around her.

A glance over her shoulder showed Lymies flying up in to the air. They went straight up, and then fell. She heard the thump of the bodies hitting the ground. The impacts could be felt through the stone she was leaning against. The Lymies in front of her that could, scattered. Some ran for the forest, others toward the swamps. A part of her knew she should be mopping them up, but she suddenly had no strength left. She couldn't even give the order to the others to keep fighting.

The world tilted wildly with no warning. She thought for a moment the Lymies were coming up out of the ground. But then she crashed onto her side. Flash was by her a second later.

"Yo, Mara, you okay?" he asked.

She couldn't answer. Her mouth was too dry. Her body too weak.

"Jingo!" Flash yelled.

"What the hell is happening?" the big man cried.

"I don't know, but Mara's down," Flash said. "Adele. Get us some water."

He pulled her helmet off. The rain falling on her face felt good. Her body was on fire, and somehow she was suddenly cold. Her chin quivered and her teeth chattered.

"Damn, she's burning up," Flash said.

"There's something out there," Jingo said. "We ain't done yet, Flash."

The big man vaulted over the rocks, and Adele hurried to Flash with a canteen of water. He dribbled some into her mouth. It was tepid, but it was wonderful too. Mara's mouth worked involuntarily, her tongue and lips eager for more. She swallowed it down, felt a sense of relief, then passed out.

Flash wasn't sure if she was alive or dead. He pressed his fingers to her throat, felt a pulse, and breathed a sigh of relief. Then Jingo's voice was loud in his comlink.

"Ain't nobody gonna believe who I found," the big man proclaimed. "It's Lieutenant Murphy!"

"Awesome, glad you made it LT," Flash said. "But we gotta do something to help Mara."

"What's wrong?" Mitch asked as he and Jingo hurried to her side. "Is she wounded?"

"No, man, she's burning up. She's sick or something."

"The thorn," Jingo said. "She got one stuck in her side, just above her hip. I pulled it out, but it must have been poisoned."

"We need to contact the *Marathon*," Flash said. "Get a med ship down here ASAP."

"There's a radio in the transport," Bart said. No one had even realized he was there. The refugees were all gathered around. Some were weeping with relief that they were still alive. Others seemed broken up to see Mara so low.

"It won't get through," Jingo said. "Too much interference."

"We gotta try something," Flash said.

He ran to the transport and ripped open the cab. The communication unit was bulky, but he had no trouble lifting it and powering the device on.

"*Marathon, Marathon* this is Leo Squad, do you read me?" he asked.

There was static, but a voice was trying to get through. He pressed the speaker against his ear.

"Say again, *Marathon.* Say again!"

More static. He hurried back to where Jingo and the strangely garbed Lieutenant Murphy were hovering over Mara.

"They can't hear us," Flash said.

"Doesn't matter," Mitch said. "It would take too long."

"We can't just let her die?" Jingo said.

"We won't. I've got her. Where's the closest medical supplies?"

"The airport was overrun," Flash said. "Probably in the hospital at Alpha Colony. If it's still standing."

"That's where we'll be. She needs IV fluids. Maybe antibiotics. I'll take her, you lead the refugees there."

"What about the Lymies?" Jingo pointed out.

"They're fleeing," Lieutenant Murphy said.

"How the hell do you know what they're doing?" Jingo asked.

"Yeah, we don't know what just happened," Flash said. "And then you show up, LT. What is going on?"

"I met some friends," Mitch said. "They showed me how to do some stuff. Trust me, the forest is clear to the north. Take your time. I'm pretty sure it'll be safe all the way back. I'll get coms working in the meantime. Meet me in the hospital."

They were looking at Lieutenant Murphy like he was crazy. Then Flash shouted in alarm as Mara and the Lieutenant suddenly floated up into the air.

"What is happening!" Flash said.

"It's okay, Corporal. I've got her."

It happened right in front of him, but Flash still couldn't

believe what he saw. The Lieutenant and Mara, still unconscious, just zoomed away. They rose up over the forest and disappeared.

"What the hell, man!" Flash said. "I mean, what the hell?"

He was shouting and he knew it. Jingo didn't have his helmet on. The big man's eyes were wide open and he looked more frightened than Flash had ever seen him.

"I don't know," he said. "But we're alive, right?"

"Yeah, I think so," Flash answered. "Then I guess we follow his orders."

"Back to Alpha?"

"Yeah," Jingo said. "Live to fight another day, right?"

"Okay," was all Flash could say.

"Was that Mitch Murphy?" Adele asked.

Flash just shrugged his shoulders. He didn't know anything for certain any more. But he didn't want to stay out in the rain. He gave the orders and the group of refugees shouldered their rifles and started marching.

CHAPTER 35

"IT'S CLEARING," the radar operator announced. "We're getting a picture."

"What the hell happened down there?" Colonel Banks asked.

"I just got word from my people," the drone Commander said. "They're all down. No contact, nothing."

"They missed the target," General Mercer said, staring at the screen across the CIC that showed the video from the surveillance satellite looking down at the battlefield.

They knew the bombs went off target. They didn't see the explosions, but they saw the disruptions in the interference those explosions caused, and they were several kilometers from their intended target. Well outside the effective radius. Plus, they detonated in a cluster, minimizing their impact.

"Would you look at that?" Major Swift said.

"Movement," someone called out. "I see people moving down there."

A crackle came through the communication channel.

"Someone's trying to get through," the coms officer said. "But I can't make them out yet."

"Those are dead Lymies," Major Swift said. "Hundreds of them."

"Hell yeah," Captain Marcs said. "You don't mess with the Marine Corps."

"That's more than one squad," General Mercer said.

"Hard to say for certain how many," Colonel Banks said. "Looks to me like a dozen or so."

"What was that?" Admiral Wilcox demanded. "You saw that right? Something just moved across the battlefield. Is there some type of vehicle down there?"

"Still too much interference for coms," the communication officer said.

"They're mobilizing," Captain Marcs said. "Preparing to move out."

"It doesn't make any sense," the Admiral complained.

"The ship," Major Swift said. "The crescent-shaped vessel, is it still here?"

"Right where it landed," the radar officer said. "Hasn't moved."

"We need answers," Admiral Wilcox said.

General Mercer wanted answers too. His well-conceived plan had worked, with some modifications. His mind was turning the information over and over in his head. The result was exactly what he wanted. The Lymie army was destroyed in one decisive military action. But how it had happened was still a mystery. He had an inkling that maybe it wasn't his SSO team that deserved all the credit. And if that was the case, then his rise to the top might be slowed, or even stopped. He couldn't let that happen.

"Yes, we read, Leo Squad," the communication officer said suddenly. He stood up from his console and hit a switch. "You're on with the Admiral now."

"I don't suppose you're seeing any of this?" a voice said.

"We see you," Admiral Wilcox said. "Who am I speaking to?"

"Corporal Lee Jenkins, they call me Flash, Admiral."

"What happened down there Corporal?" Captain Marcs broke in on the conversation. "How did you defeat the Lymies?"

"We didn't sir," Flash replied. "The bomber drones failed to reach the target. We thought we were goners, but then Lieutenant Murphy showed up. It's hard to believe, but it seems like he defeated the Lymies all by himself."

General Mercer felt a cold shudder of fear.

"Seems like?" Admiral Wilcox said. "What does that mean, Corporal? What exactly happened?"

"Some just died. They dropped just like the bomber drones," Flash said. "Some went flying up into the air. It was unbelievable and I was here. I saw it all. Those that weren't killed, scattered."

"Where is Lieutenant Murphy now?" Major Swift interjected.

"He sorta left with Sergeant James," Flash said.

"What does that mean?" Captain Marcs asked.

"He flew. Call me crazy, but the man up and flew right out of here. Not like Superman or anything, just floated up away. Told us to meet him at Alpha Colony. He was taking Sergeant James for treatment."

Everyone in the CIC just stared at one another. It was hard to believe, but the proof was right in front of their eyes. Hundreds of dead aliens. The Marines still alive. It didn't make sense, but it was reality.

"Who is with you, Corporal?" Jerome Banks asked.

"Refugees. The same group that Lieutenant Murphy had been helping before we arrived. They've been hiding in the forest. We picked them up last night and they were here with us during the battle. They helped us fight."

"And you defeated the enemy?" General Mercer said.

"I wouldn't say we did it, but the enemy is defeated," Flash replied.

There were more questions, but few answers. Along the way, General Mercer realized that he could spin this entire situation in his favor. Lieutenant Murphy was under his command after all.

Once they had a reasonable explanation for what happened, he would solidify his own report, but the main thing was that his people had stopped an army of Lymies. That was what the brass needed to hear. The LE program needed every candidate it could get. General Mercer was in charge, and they were going to be a big success. In fact, he might end up being the most successful general of all time. And nothing would stop him from rising in power until he was ultimately in total command. Not just of the Colonial Marines, or even the Space Force. He had much bigger goals. And the gift of all gifts had just been dropped into his lap. Lieutenant Mitch Murphy could do things no one in the history of mankind had ever done. And like it or not, Murphy answered to General Stanley Mercer. The two of them had worlds to conquer, and the General was determined not to let anyone or anything stop them.

CHAPTER 36

MITCH SAILED OVER THE TREES. He could sense the Lymies below him. They were running in every direction except for south. They wanted no part of him, and that was good. A few minutes later they sailed over the airfield. Somehow it was even more of a wreck than when he had left it. In the distance he could see Alpha Colony. Something huge had torn a path right through it, knocking down buildings and destroying everything in its path. Fortunately, the hospital was still intact. It wasn't a big building, just a one story structure that had been added onto multiple times.

Mitch landed just outside the emergency room, but continued to levitate Mara and kept a protective bubble around himself at all times. He was learning to use the Power like the other members of the Order did. It was a constant source of both protection and information. There was one Lymie in the hospital. Mitch didn't worry about it. He would feel the creature coming if it decided to run him out. And he would change its mind about that when the time came.

The doors to the emergency room were closed, the power off, but the glass was shattered so that all that remained was the frames. Mitch went in first, and levitated Mara behind him. Some of the trauma bays had been looted. But it didn't take him long to find what he needed. Mitch was no doctor, but he had seen a battlefield trauma tutorial and practiced a few first aid skills back when he was first traveling to the Terra system on the *Wellington*. Mitch managed to start an IV drip with a bag of saline water. By the time he found a laser thermometer Mara was awake.

"Hey," Mitch said. "Good to see you responding to the IV, Sergeant."

"Mitch," she said in a drowsy, slurred voice. Her mouth was still dry and her tongue was thick.

"Yeah, it's me," he said.

"Am I ... dead?" she asked.

"Not yet," he said, scanning her forehead. "You've got a fever though, a hundred and three. You're pretty dehydrated too. I found some apple juice, hang on a second."

He stepped away. She wanted to sit up but didn't have the strength. Mitch found a small refrigerator. The power was out and the cooler was warm, but the apple juice inside was pasteurized. He opened one, took a sip, then grabbed two more. It wasn't very good warm, but he didn't think it would hurt her.

"Here you go," he said, opening one of the juices. "Have a sip of this."

She took a drink, and smiled. He felt a huge sense of relief seeing her smile.

"That's good," she said. "More."

He lifted her head and helped her sip the juice. After that he helped her get her boots and armor off. There were still pillows and blankets. He made sure she was comfortable. The IV was helping. Her temperature was down to one hundred and two point five when he scanned her again. When she nodded off, he went and found some antibiotics. He wasn't knowledgeable enough to administer the drugs, but he wanted to have them close to hand.

While she slept, he checked the wound above her hip. It was red and hot. A whitish liquid was seeping out. The foam in her wound dissolved in warm water. He washed it out, and sprayed the area with more disinfecting antiseptic spray, then used some medical tape to hold the wound closed. For a while she slept. He swapped out her IV bag for a fresh one when the first ran dry. And when she finally woke up, her temperature was down below a hundred.

"It looks like you're kicking this thing's butt," he said. "Your temp is way down."

"Thanks to you," she said, her voice sounding more normal.

"Thanks to the IVs," he said. "You were dehydrated."

"Where did you go?" she said, reaching out for his hand.

"That's a long story," he replied.

She held his hand, and he didn't pull back. Instead, he rolled over a doctor's stool and sat down by her bed, taking her hand in both of his.

"You came back," she said. "I missed you so much. I should have followed you off the drop ship."

"Your ankle was busted, remember?"

"We searched for you," she said. "Looked all over. Even in the alien ship."

"I was on another planet," he said. "Learning some new things."

"What kind of things?"

"Answers to some of our oldest questions," he said.

"How did we survive the fight?" she asked. "I think maybe I was hallucinating."

"Maybe," he told her.

"I can't believe this is real," she said. "But I don't think I would dream up that robe you're wearing. What is it?"

"It's what the Order of Scion wear," he told her.

"The Order of Scion?"

"Yeah, it's part of that long story."

"I don't want you to leave, Mitch. I know I shouldn't say that. You're a Lieutenant and I'm not. And it's selfish, but I don't care. I don't want you to leave."

"I can't tell you what the future holds, Mara. But I don't want to leave you either."

"Good," she said, squeezing his hand.

She closed her eyes and Mitch wondered if he could make her happy. He wanted to, but he had obligations that were bigger than ever before. He was a member of the Order of Scion. And he still had so much to learn. But he knew he wanted Mara in his life. Somehow, someway, he had to make that happen.

AUTHOR'S NOTE

Thank you for reading Gravity Masters. I'm just getting started with the Order of Scion stories. There's a lot to explore and I hope to write several series of books in this universe. As I write this on March 6th, 2024, I've gotten started on book three. Look for it in April. In the meantime, check out my series of books about four brothers looking to strike it rich in *Space Fever*.

SPACE FEVER

TOBY NEIGHBORS

SPACE FEVER CHAPTER 1

"Here's the receipt for your one-time payment, Chief," the General said, handing Easy his certificate of service. The senior officer seemed bored as he wrapped up the retirement ceremony. "Thank you for your service. You are officially dismissed."

Master Chief Edgar Zacchaeus "Easy" McCoy took the flimsy paper in his calloused hand. He was more used to holding weapons than receipts, and he didn't bother looking at it. He saluted the general out of respect for the Galactic Navy, not for the officer in front of him. The bored general might not think much of Easy ending a thirty-year career, but it was important, and Easy wanted to do it right. The general waved a hand in the air. It was the kind of lazy, undisciplined salute that a drill sergeant would have thrown a fit about. And much like the rest of the ceremony, if it could be called that, it was done with halfhearted disinterest. Easy turned on his heel and left the office. He was in full dress uniform with a chest full of medals earned in combat. He was used to being knee-deep in mud and blood, but he doubted the General had ever been in real danger or suffered more than a paper cut in his career.

Easy walked down a short hall, through a waiting room, then

out into the concourse of the Galactic Navy shipyard. His rucksack was packed full of his belongings, and a heavy crate on tiny wheels contained the only possessions that Easy had acquired in the three decades since graduating high school and joining the Navy. He stuck the receipt in his pocket without looking at it, picked up the rucksack and slung it over one shoulder, then took the handle of his hardcase and started walking.

There was a line at the central dispatch station. Easy waited his turn, and when he finally reached the stressed-out petty officer processing the Navy personnel passing through the shipyard, he handed his official ID to the overweight man.

"Master Chief McCoy," the officer said, finally looking up from his console directly at Easy. "Retired! Congratulations, Chief. You've got full privileges. We'll find you a spot on any transport as long as it isn't on a combat tour. Where do you want to go?"

"Home," Easy said simply. "Esbe Four."

"The Skara Brea system," the officer commented, focusing back on his terminal. "If you're ready to leave now, there's a cargo ship leaving for that system in one hour, down on Bravo deck, gate 39."

"That works," Easy said. "Thank you."

"Yeah, no problem. Enjoy your retirement, Master Chief. Don't spend that pension payment all in one place."

"Copy that," Easy said, taking his ID back and heading for the lift that would take him down to Bravo deck.

The shipyard was essentially a giant space station. Part dock, part administration facility, it serviced the massive interstellar warships of the Galactic Navy, as well as the thousands of cargo ships that helped supply humanity's military effort across hundreds of systems. Easy rode the open-air gravity lift down Bravo deck. It was essentially a tube with its own gravity generators. Easy stepped off into open space, holding his rucksack with one hand, and his rolling hardcase with the other. He gently floated down past Delta and Charlie decks until he reached Bravo, where he managed to step past the invisible barrier back into normal gravity without losing his balance.

Long docking arms formed the gate, and Easy also had a long walk to reach the ship he would be riding on. But after thirty years in the military, Easy was accustomed to tight schedules and showing up on time. He moved down the open concourse with purpose and reached his gate in plenty of time to make his flight. He slipped his ID card into an automated reader. It chimed, opening the door to the docking arm. A long, narrow hallway led to an airlock that opened onto the crew section of a Class D cargo ship.

"You McCoy?" a crewman in dirty coveralls asked.

Easy nodded.

"There's a lounge down that way. You can rest there while we finish loading and make our maneuvers."

"Thanks," Easy said. "What's the ETA for Esbe Four?"

"We're taking a load of alloy girders for the space station in the Skara Brea system. You'll have to catch a shuttle to wherever you're going from there. We're four and a half hours from the jump point. That's all I know for sure."

"Thanks," Easy said, adjusting his rucksack that was slung over his shoulder. He started for the lounge.

The ship was exactly what he expected: small, cramped, dingy, and on the verge of being worn-out. Cargo ships were working platforms where crew lived for months at a time while they ferried goods across the galaxy. Easy was a former RAKE or Reconnaissance, Acquisition, and Kinetic Engagement specialist, a Special Forces Operator who was used to spending months hidden on backwater planets when on mission. He could find a way to survive in almost any environment. Many naval vessels were a mix of pristine and practical. And he had spent most of his military career on the lower decks where function was king, and form was whatever happened to be the most practical in a given space.

The lounge was a mix of dining room and passenger type

spaces. Easy took a seat on a padded chair that was bolted against the deck and the wall. It wasn't going anywhere. Right next to the chair was a rack built into the wall itself. His hardcase slid into a slot under the rack, and his rucksack went on top. There were simple bungee cords with S hooks to batten his luggage down.

Once his gear was carefully stowed, Easy pulled out a Cherry iLink Z from the inside pocket of his dress uniform jacket. The device was new, purchased to replace his military grade Personal Computer Link, or PCL as they were called in the Navy. He powered the iLink on and let it sync with the ship's network. From there he could download private messages and access the ship's destination log that showed how long he would be in transit.

"Forty-four hours," he whistled quietly to himself, thinking he should get comfortable for the long trip to the Skara Brea system.

He pulled his one set of civilian clothes out from the top of his rucksack and stepped into the little bathroom across from the lounge. By the time he finished changing there was another passenger on board, a tall and lean man with a black pointed beard. The passenger didn't look up as Easy walked past and packed his neatly folded dress uniform into his rucksack. The man seemed obsessed with his PCL. But it was only natural to glance up when someone came into a room. To a former soldier used to assessing every situation for danger, the failure of the man with the pointed beard to look up was a red flag. But all Easy could do was wait to see how the situation played out.

SPACE FEVER CHAPTER 2

"Kitt McCoy, you old man. What the hell happened to you?"

"Did your parents have any children who lived?" Kitt asked.

"Not a one," Hutch McCoy said as Kitt stood up from the table.

They hugged. Not the brief, back-slap type hug most men made, but a genuine embrace. The two siblings hadn't seen each other in a very long time. The bar was one of several at the lavish resort, and wasn't crowded yet. It was mid-afternoon after all, and the Royal Telmus on Esbe Four was a high-end casino and resort on one of the planet's many islands. The bars and restaurants would get noisier once the sun went down and people came in from playing out in the sand and surf. Fortunately, there were only a few patrons in the establishment at two o'clock in the afternoon.

"You been waiting long?" Hutch asked.

"Not even long enough to finish my beer," Kitt said. "It's good to see you."

"It's good to be seen. When does Zacchaeus get here?"

"I don't know, he hasn't made contact yet. Probably a couple of days."

The two men sat down. A serving droid brought Hutch a beer. It was cold and frothy, if not very flavorful. Hutch took a drink, then wiped the foam from his mustache with the back of his hand.

"You seen Big Candy yet?" Hutch asked.

"He left me a message. Said he was working, if you believe that, and he'll meet us for dinner."

"Big never worked a day in his life," Hutch said.

"He always had the golden touch," Kitt agreed.

"He's not a kid anymore, none of us are. It's been twenty years since dad passed, can you believe it?

Kitt shook his head and tried not to let a gloomy sense of depression settle over him. He hated thinking about his age and the fact that perhaps his best days were behind him. But the older he got, the more difficult it became to face the reality of his life. Depression had become a regular battle he had to fight, but he didn't want his brothers to know.

"I've got some news," Hutch said.

He was grinning, his thick mustache hiding his upper lip, but his smile was wide and bright. Kitt noticed the deep lines in his brother's forehead and around his eyes, yet he still had the features and mannerisms Kitt remembered from when they were kids. They were all approaching an age when people would begin to give them senior citizen discounts. If they were wealthy men they would have already paid for age reduction therapy. Kitt was fifty-four years old by galactic standards. When he looked in the mirror he sometimes didn't recognize the older man looking back at him. He was exactly nine months and thirteen days from crossing what pilots called the MRA, mandatory retirement age. He wouldn't lose his license, but no company would hire him to pilot their ships any longer. He would have to give up flying, and he wasn't sure what he would do.

"What's your news?" Kitt asked after another sip of his beer.

"I found something," he replied, leaning forward and crossing his arms on the tabletop. "I can't verify it, but it looks legit."

"What?" Kitt asked.

"Do you remember Dad's obsession?"

"The quartzite mines? Sure."

"What if I told you I found a way through the Fanning Belt?"

Kitt leaned back in his chair, not sure if his brother was pranking him or being honest. The Fanning Belt was a massive asteroid field in the Harpazo system that orbited a young star. It was located on the edge of the galactic arm, right on the tip of the long spiral, and was completely unstable. The matter in the Fanning Belt was in the process of forming a planet. It just needed a few million more years of heat and pressure, but it was at an ideal stage for mining quartzite. The only problem was getting through the Fanning Belt. Rumor had it that someone had successfully plotted a course through the huge asteroids, but mining quartzite crystals was highly regulated by the Galactic Union's Natural Resources Bureau. Getting permits took years and millions of credits. Small independent mining operations had been squeezed out and forced to sell their ores illegally on the black market.

Eustace Melchizedek McCoy had had four sons, and he told them stories when they were children of finding a passage through the Fanning Belt and mining quartzite crystals. They were crucial to building dark matter coupling isolators, better known as perpetual motion engines that could power a starship by pulling in free isotopes from space and converting them to usable energy. The technology was in use on large government spacecraft, but quartzite was incredibly expensive. Most ships relied on fusion generators that required large amounts of hydrogen. Creating a tiny sun to power a starship was effective, but required a lot of maintenance to keep the reactor from burning up the ship, or compromising the hull, which was just as deadly. A person who could mine quartzite could make a fortune on the black market, as long as they didn't get caught.

"It's just an urban legend," Kitt said. "Dad knew that. Stop pulling my leg."

Hutch shook his head. "I found it."

"What are you saying?" Kitt asked. "You found quartzite crystals?"

"No, of course not," Hutch said. "This is even better."

"You found a way through the Fanning Belt?"

"Keep your voice down," Hutch cautioned. "You never know who's listening."

Kitt leaned forward and looked his brother in the eye. "You're not lying, are you?"

"Like I said, I can't prove it. Not yet, but..."

He let the thought hang between them. Kitt didn't need to be prompted. They both hadn't forgotten their father's stories. The old man had dreamed of finding a way through the asteroid field. He talked about getting a ship and crew together to mine for quartzite, but as Kitt got older he realized it wouldn't be so simple.

"The Fanning Belt is in the Contested Zone," Kitt said. "Even if you had a reliable course through the asteroids, how would you get past the blockade?"

"We would need a really good pilot," Hutch said, flashing his big grin. "Do you know anyone?"

"Shut up, you old fool."

"Hey, it might be possible. If we had a ship, we might make it through. Just one run would be enough to make us all rich men."

"Or dead men," Kitt argued. "And we don't have a ship. You can't be serious about this?"

"I've been thinking about it," Hutch said. "It was a long trip from the Mardux system."

"Tell me what you found," Kitt relented, tapping an icon on the table between them to order more drinks. "And don't leave anything out."

SPACE FEVER CHAPTER 3

Easy had heard the rumors. The Independent Coalition of Planets, better known as the ICP, were recruiting fighters from all over the Galactic Union. It was dangerous work, since the GU would prosecute the recruiters as spies and execute them for treason. One wrong word to the wrong person could be deadly.

Even after thirty years of service–some might even say especially after thirty years–Easy had little love for the Union. Government was a necessary evil, and what started as a good idea often fell prey to corruption and bloated into enormous bureaucracies that crushed the hopes and dreams of the little guy. The Galactic Union was no different, not inherently evil but susceptible to the same type of people who tended to favor political power. In the Navy there were climbers, usually in the officer track. They were people who just wanted rank and cared nothing for the actual mission and values of the Navy.

The cargo ship had left the dock and was cruising out to the designated launch area where it would transition to hyperspace. Easy had sent a message to his brothers using his iLink and kept the ship's progress pulled up on the handy device while he waited for the man with the beard to make a move. The only question in his mind was if the man was a spy recruiting for the ICP, or a counter-intelligence agent there to see if he was a threat to the GU.

Patience was a skill learned through long hours of standing watch and refined on the battlefield. Easy had taken part in sixteen combat operations, including wars on three planets. The time between battles was a crucible of the mind. Anticipating the horror of war drove some people crazy. Others were hardened by the waiting, like hot steel in the hands of an expert who hammered out the impurities and fashioned the raw metal into a lethal instrument. Easy was content to sit and wait for the bearded man to make his move. And eventually, he did just that.

The bearded man got up, fixing himself a coffee in a paper cup. He took his time pouring in sugar and cream, then swirling it all around with a tiny straw. Easy watched out of the corner of his eye, the way a mongoose watched a cobra as it slithered closer and closer.

"You going to Skara Brea?" the bearded man asked as he returned to his seat.

Easy nodded but didn't speak. He was comfortable with silence.

"I've got business on the station there," the bearded man went on. "I'm hoping to get down on Esbe Four at some point though. The water down there is pristine, absolutely beautiful. You ever been down there?"

"Grew up there," Easy said.

"Is that right? Well, you know then. It's a beautiful place, just stunning."

Easy didn't feel the need to explain that not every city on Esbe Four was for tourists. He had grown up the youngest of four brothers in an industrial hub that was far removed from the golden coast or the resort islands. A river ran through his hometown, but it was muddy brown and stank of chemicals. Leaving had been a simple choice and one he didn't regret. But his years in the Navy were over, and it was time to find a new life. He hoped that seeing his brothers back on Esbe Four might give him some clarity.

"You're military," the bearded man continued. "I saw your gear there. Not trying to be nosy, just thought a little conversation would be nice. What branch do you serve?"

"Navy," Easy said, going along with the man simply to see where he was headed. "Retired."

"That a fact? I had a sister in the Navy. Don't see her much anymore. My name is Connor. This is some terrible coffee. I usually take it black, but it's so bad I had to take the edge off."

"Call me Easy, everyone does."

"Interesting name," Connor said. "So what takes you back to Esbe Four? You have family?"

Easy nodded.

"That's good. How many years did you serve?"

There it was. The obvious question all the chit-chat had been leading up to. Easy was glad to finally be getting to the point.

"Thirty," he said.

"Wow, that's impressive," Connor said, setting his coffee on the flat armrest of his chair.

He reached into a bag and pulled out a strange-looking device. It reminded Easy of a computer terminal, the kind carried by techies in the Navy with heavy duty, shockproof cases and beefy encrypted communication modules. Connor opened it and typed a few key commands. Then he rotated the screen toward Easy and his friendly demeanor changed.

"Thirty years for enlisted personnel, that should be around one point eight million credits in your retirement lump sum payment," Connor said.

Easy heard the words, but his focus was on the man's right hand, which was below the armrest of his seat. It was impossible to tell if he had a gun or a knife, but there was no doubt in the former RAKE operator that he was about to be threatened. Obviously the man wasn't an agent or spy. He didn't know that Easy was an expert in hand-to-hand combat. He was just a thief trying to steal the money the Navy had paid him for his years of military service.

"Why don't you hand over the receipt they gave you and we'll transfer that money to an account so it gets distributed to whoever you want?"

"Why would I do that?" Easy asked calmly, his eyes studying the bearded man, whose name he was certain wasn't Connor.

The man smiled. "You've got to transfer the money, you know. Someone is going to get a cut of that. I used to be in banking, and this is how it works. Now, give me the receipt. I'm not going to steal your money. This is all legal. I can transfer it wherever you want before we leave the system. It will be waiting for you when we reach Skara Brea."

"And if I don't, I suppose the gun in your hand is just part of your sales pitch?"

Connor's grin faltered, and he raised his hand. He wasn't holding a gun, but a knife. He pressed a button, and the long, double-edged stiletto blade shot forward.

"Doesn't have to be like that," Connor said.

Easy saw that the man was breathing faster. His face looked a little pale. Fear was written all over him. Fear and desperation. Easy had no doubt that Connor planned to take every credit of the retirement payout and was probably going to kill him too. So he stood up. Easy was forty-eight years old. There were deep wrinkles around his eyes and across his forehead. His short hair was more gray than brown, and his joints popped when he moved, but he was strong. He could outrun most new recruits, and there was no unnecessary fat on his frame. He didn't move fast, but he was smooth and that was sometimes mistaken for speed. Connor flinched, raising the knife in a threatening gesture.

"Careful!" he said.

Easy raised his hands palms out, trying to calm down the criminal.

"Just getting the receipt out of my pocket," he said.

He could have tried to calm the thief, make up a story about how Connor was actually doing him a favor. But Easy didn't want Connor to be calm. He wanted him jumpy, on edge, tense.

"Just take it slow, okay," Connor ordered, as he got up to face Easy.

It wasn't lost on the former Special Forces Operator that Connor had to push himself up off the chair, or that his stomach pressed against the front of his shirt. Still, a desperate person was a dangerous person. Easy pulled the slip of paper from his pocket and held it out with two fingers. Connor reached for it as if the receipt were food and he was a starving man. Easy let the paper drop just as it brushed Connor's fingers.

"Sorry, sorry," Easy said, holding his hands up again.

"Damn it!" Connor cursed. "Don't you move. I don't want to hurt you but—"

He never finished his sentence. Connor was bending down to pick up the paper Easy had dropped when a lightning-fast kick knocked the knife from his hand. Shock registered on the thief's face as he glanced up. Connor had just enough time to see the glint of danger in Easy's eyes before a fist connected with the tip of his chin. His head snapped backward, his eyes rolled in their sockets, and his body dropped to the floor.

Easy walked calmly across the lounge and picked up the knife. It was a cheap, spring-loaded switchblade. Easy tossed it into the trash chute that went down into the bowels of the ship. Then he returned to the unconscious thief. He picked up Connor by one arm and slung him back into the seat he had been sitting in. The grifter was out cold, his head lolling toward his left shoulder. Easy picked up the computer. The screen was a blank field with two boxes in the center. One said routing number, the other account number. He closed the computer and took it to his rucksack. There was just enough room to hide the device among his clothes.

Finally, Easy picked up the paper he had dropped. It wasn't his pension payout receipt, just the reservation confirmation his brother Big Candy had sent him a month prior. He was going home to see his brothers, and not to the dirty industrial slum they had grown up in, but to a fancy resort where the wealthy played and the lucky could win big. Easy had no intentions of gambling his pension away or buying into whatever scheme his older brother had running, but he wouldn't mind a little vacation. After all, he thought to himself, he had earned it.

SPACE FEVER CHAPTER 4

Big Candy loved the feel of cards in his hand. He was a big man, nearly three hundred pounds, and always had a drink nearby. On the table in front of him there was a cocktail with fruit juice, soda, and just a splash of alcohol. There was also a bowl of chocolate-covered almonds. It was all part of his persona, his personal brand. Born Derick Bartholomew McCoy, he had been nicknamed Big Candy by the kids in his neighborhood before the age of ten. He had always had candy and made a tidy profit peddling it to his classmates at recess or in the bathroom.

After school, Big Candy had ventured into a variety of business ventures, but eventually he settled on gambling as a profession. He knew how to win, and more importantly, the type of people to play against. Wealthy tourists were his bread and butter. Losing to a pro like Big Candy was an experience that many vacationing businessmen would brag about for the rest of their lives. They were sloppy with their money and easy to read. Big had no qualms about taking their money.

He was in the middle of a game with two very wealthy businessmen and one young aristocrat who thought he was better than he was. The kid had more tells than he did ideas in his head, but he was from an incredibly rich family and was down nearly two hundred thousand credits. It was the type of game that rarely came around. A typical week at one of the resorts might net Big twenty or thirty thousand credits, enough to keep him comfortable. But occasionally he landed a whale, and Big had the kid on the line. Beating him at cards was the easy part. Knowing if he should or not was more difficult.

"You gonna play old man, or did your heart stop?" the kid said with a smirk.

He was barely old enough to go into the casinos, yet he had more money than all the other patrons of the resort combined. And because he hadn't earned a single credit of his vast fortune, he didn't respect it.

"Just making up my mind," Big Candy replied, popping a chocolate almond into his mouth and crunching it. "You scare me."

"This?" the kid said, waving at the mound of casino chips on the table. "I spend more than that on a haircut."

Big looked at the kid. His hair looked as if he had just rolled out of bed, and yet there was no doubt that he'd paid someone thousands of credits to make it look as if he didn't care. His clothes were designer brands and fit his thin frame well. There were two women in tight dresses sipping soda water and watching him play poker. Big didn't mind the women; it was the man in the dark suit with dead eyes that made him hesitate. The trio were part of the kid's entourage, and Big wasn't sure if they were his handlers or his servants.

"You're out of your mind," Big said, not bothering to look at his hand of cards. He knew exactly what he had and was almost certain that his opponent was bluffing.

The two businessmen at the table were watching with rapt fascination. There was another pro at the table too, but he was losing interest in the game. Big had already won plenty, around twenty thousand credits. He could fold his hand, take his chips, and leave while he was ahead. Or he could go all in, force the kid to show his hand, and maybe take close to two hundred thousand.

"So make up your mind," the kid said. "I'm throwing a party in my suite, and you're starting to bore me."

The businessmen chuckled. Big grinned. He knew his brothers were waiting for him. Their baby brother was on his way home after putting his neck on the line for thirty years in the GU Navy. That had been a real risk. Big felt a stab of guilt about the fact that his brothers had all gone into legitimate professions. Candy was the black sheep, the hustler, the guy no one took seriously until he took their money.

"I guess I'll chance it," Big said with mock humility as he slid his chips into the large pile at the center of the table.

The kid's smirk shifted from arrogance to annoyance. As Big laid down his cards he watched the man across the room. Dead Eyes didn't move, didn't shift his weight or even blink.

"Damn it!" the kid shouted, throwing his cards at the dealer, as if it were her fault. "This is stupid. You're all a bunch of cheaters."

"There's one card left," the dealer said calmly, arranging the kid's hand on the table in front of him.

"I think you're all in this together," the kid said. "Do you know who I am? Desmond Rosenshield, as in Rosenshield Shipping."

"We're aware," one of the businessmen said, his mouth turning up in a gleeful smile.

While their wives were being pampered in the spa and their children frolicked on the beach, the businessmen were playing cards at the poker tables. And it wasn't about the money they lost, but about the stories they would tell. Watching the young scion of a well-known family lose more money in one hand than they earned in a year was exactly what they were hoping for. It would be a story they told their peers, friends, and business associates for the rest of their lives. And the more the kid acted like a fool, the better their story would be.

"I don't care about the money," Desmond snarled. "But I won't be cheated."

He slammed his hand down on the table. It was a solid piece of furniture, thick and heavy, covered with the finest felt. Big watched as a vein began to throb on the side of the kid's neck.

"The game isn't over, sir," the dealer said.

"Why don't we just call it a push and go our separate ways?" Big suggested, even though he knew they couldn't do that. It was all part of the game.

"Screw you, old man," the kid snapped, before turning to the dealer. "Finish it."

The dealer flipped the last card. The odds had been against the kid winning, and it was no surprise to Big when the game played out just as he expected. What was surprising was the kid's reaction. He didn't throw a fit, yell, or scream. He didn't pound the table or accuse him of cheating. Instead, he leaned across the table toward Big and spoke in a quiet, even tone.

"This isn't over," he said. "We'll meet again."

"It's just a game," Big said, raking in the chips. "It isn't personal."

The kid turned to the dealer and pointed at the chips he hadn't lost. The kid had come to the table with nearly a million credits in large denomination poker chips. He still had most of them. But he had yet to win a hand outright, or any real money. Pointing to his chips he said, "See that this is put back on my account." Then he spun around and stormed from the room.

The two women both stood up together and followed him, their tight dresses and tall, spiky heels making them take quick, short steps. Big normally would have admired their figures, even if they were completely artificial, but his focus was still on the man in the suit. Dead Eyes. The man didn't move to follow his young companion immediately. Instead he looked at Big for a moment, no emotion on his face. Big didn't look away. If the kid wanted to come after him there was nothing Big could do about it. And he refused to show any fear. In his mind he hadn't done anything wrong. No one pushed the kid to throw his money away gambling, but the Rosenshield family might not see things that way. It wouldn't be the first time Big found himself in a jam because he beat someone playing poker.

"Well, that kind of spoils the mood," Big said, pushing his bowl of almonds toward the businessmen. "Would either of you care for a chocolate almond?"

"I'm good," said the first man.

"Why not?" said the other enthusiastically.

"Let's play poker, eh?" Big said. "Dealer, we need more drinks. I'm buying."

He flipped her a thousand credit chip, which she tucked away inside her shirt and then began shuffling the cards.

ALSO BY TOBY NEIGHBORS

Lorik the Protector

Lorik the Defender

We Are The Wolf

Welcome To The Wolfpack

Embracing Oblivion

Joined In Battle

The Abyss Of Savagery

The Vault Of Mysteries

Lords Of Ascension

The Elusive Executioner

Gryphon Warriors

Regulators Revealed

Avondale

Draggah

Balestone

Arcanius

Avondale V

Third Prince

Royal Destiny

The Other Side

The New World

Luck Holds

Zompocalypse

Spartan Company

Spartan Valor

Spartan Guile

Dragon Team Seven

Resistance

Conquest

Occupation

Extraction

The Signal

Battle Orders

Base Of Fire

Hard Site

Recall

Evade

Assault

Action Zone

Covert Infil

Armor Brigade

Havoc Squad

Thunderbird

Ghost Tactics

Quantum Combat

Infinite Threat

Shadow Threat

Evolving Threat

Lingering Threat

Latent Prowess

With Pete Garcia

Apocalypse One Percenters

www.ingramcontent.com/pod-product-compliance
Lightning Source LLC
Chambersburg PA
CBHW020933260626
47169CB00006B/1699